THE WICKER MAN PRESERVATION SOCIETY

DAVID F PORTEOUS

1

The island of Ensay is home to four-hundred-and-seven people, and I know all of them. I know their faces and their names. I know them by the way they speak. I even know how they like their tea.

My mum says that the island is like a family. That there is no place on the mainland where everyone knows everyone else. And sometimes I wonder what it would be like to make it through a day without being asked—

"Eleanor, my flower, how are you?"

"I'm very well, thank you, Missus Macleod," I reply, hoping that this will be enough, knowing that it never is.

"And how," Mrs. Macleod asks, "is your condition?" Her eyes are watery. Her hand touches my elbow as I lean down to put the tray on the table. The cups rattle.

"The same as always, Missus Macleod" I say – because it's true. "It's very kind of you to enquire."

She pats me, like you might pat an old dog, and I move the teapot, the strainer, the cups, the matching milk jug, and the sugar bowl from the tray to the table.

"You're a good hand to your mother," says Mrs. Arbuthnot. This is high praise from a mother of five daughters who all grew up and left the island to live in foreign places – Glasgow and Birmingham, and one as far as London. Nevertheless, it is praise that could also be won by a spaniel that's learned to fetch its own lead.

The two old women have been coming for tea at the hotel every Wednesday for as long as I can remember. The same seats: the table in the bay window that gives a view of the cobbled High Street down to the curved stone wall of the harbour. The same order: a single pot of tea – English breakfast – which they split. Mrs. Macleod takes milk and one sugar; Mrs.

1

Arbuthnot just takes milk.

They inspect the cakes when they come in, fancying themselves great connoisseurs of cake. They have opinions about icing, and will debate at length whether an almond has been blended or nibbed, and whether jam is homemade or bought. Only once in a dozen Wednesdays will one of them take a slice home. They never have cake with their tea.

If they were having our full experience, then they'd have a choice of teas, sandwiches with the crusts cut off, scones, and a slice of cake. Any jam in the cakes is always homemade, despite rumours to the contrary. For a special occasion, a glass of Prosecco per person is available for a very reasonable surcharge.

The Ensay House High Tea is quite famous – as far as I can tell. Though, as I've lived in the hotel all my life and worked in the tearoom since I was six, I may have a skewed perspective.

It has nearly five stars on all the review sites. People say nice things about me specifically, and hotel guests often try to get a photo with me before they leave. There are a lot of photos of me on the internet holding teapots. I might be in more teapot-holding photos than anyone else in the world.

"Can I get you ladies anything else?"

My mum says that any group of women should always be referred to as *ladies*. A group of women are never *girls* unless they are drunk. Presumably a similar rule applies to men, but there are so few groups of men who visit the Western Isles for high tea that it's never come up.

"How is your mother?" Mrs. Macleod asks.

"She's well, thank you for asking."

"That's good," she says, and she smiles at me and gives me another pat.

Mrs. Arbuthnot coughs. "Thank you, Eleanor."

I leave them to pour the tea for themselves. This is how they've always done it and I've three other tables and a hundred other jobs besides. I am especially busy for the same reason they are more inquisitive than usual: we are expecting visitors.

Not visitors to the island – those are already here. It's the first of June – three weeks from the solstice – and we are in the midst of tourist season.

All the islands are welcoming during the long, light summer, but Ensay more than most. There are still crofters and weavers and fishermen; people living from the land and sea in much the same way their great grandparents would have. But there are more of us doing new jobs.

The islands all do well for walkers. The bigger islands are preferred by cyclists, but because Ensay is in the sound between North Uist and Lewis and Harris, we pick up more kayakers and canoeists. There's usually at least one twitcher at the hotel all summer. And every one of these people is in the market for local charm. Seventy years ago, no one would have recognised *local charm* as a valuable commodity; they'd have mislabelled it as grim poverty and polio.

Mr. Murdoch retired as a history teacher to take guided tours. He wears the full highland dress every day – which must be some kind a fetish, but it keeps the tips rolling in. And to be fair to him, he knows the land better than anyone else, at least between Hacklet and Talbert.

His wife, Mrs. Murdoch – English Breakfast, soy milk – paints semi-nude portraits of people wearing nothing but a bolt of their clan tartan. Or another tartan that they like better. But she's very strict about the nudity; they must be genuinely nude, even if they are only fraudulently draped in tartan.

My mum isn't the only woman on the island who makes her own jam. The boat brings in a hundred glass jars a month. Empty, they're worth twenty-three pence each. Filled with jam and wrapped in a penny of tartan ribbon, they're six pounds fifty.

Jewellery's popular; like jam, nobody really knows how much jewellery should cost. There's more up-selling with the jewellery though.

People assume jam is local and authentic – though there's never been a single apricot grown on Ensay. With silver brooches and earrings, the maker has to do a little talk about how the island's history is as much Norse as Celtic. How the artistic traditions have similarities, but the piece they're looking at is a true blend; in many ways unique (with the exception of the six other identical items sold last month).

This song and dance is what keeps the wolf from our door. The Gaelic name for the chain of islands that hedges the mainland from the Atlantic is Innse Gall – islands of the strangers. If ever there was a place designed for tourists, this is it.

None of this is to say we don't take our business seriously. On Ensay, we take everything seriously. The jam is good. And the last person to bed is often Mrs. Mackenzie – green, lemon. I've seen her workroom lit-up when the whole village is in darkness; so, there's nothing Made in China about her silversmithing, even if she is copying all of her designs out of a book of tattoos.

I check in with two of the three other tables and I'm on the way to the third when the service bell summons me. I check my watch: it's three o'clock; she should have been back by now. I mean it's not as if there's anywhere to go.

Ensay House used to be a grand private home a hundred years ago, so it has a proper entrance hall. The floor is a black and white checkerboard of heavy tiles. They're an original feature and would be cleaner than they are if we used wet-weather matting all the time instead of just an hour after it started raining and immediately when it stopped.

The walls are dark green and are dotted all around and up the stairs with watercolours and small oils of various highland images. It is an eclectic art collection acquired from house sales, gifts, eBay, and to the right buyer it might be worth as much as nothing.

A piper stands at the foot of the staircase, his cheeks reddened, the scene captured mid-puff. He wears a strongly coloured Royal Stewart – the red tartan; the particularly Scottish one seen on coasters, shopping bags, and sometimes even semi-nudes. He is surrounded by a white expanse where faint pencil lines suggest a landscape that was never finished.

On the landing, just as the staircase takes a left turn, a woman in a threadbare shawl looks out on a stormy sea, under a sky of impossible scale. The grey clouds press down all the way to the horizon – heavier than air, denser than wool, and dark as smoke. There's no name on the painting and no signature, but it feels like an island, if not this island.

There is a saying about weather in the Western Isles – *if you don't like it, wait ten minutes.* And though the weather might be changeable one day, a storm front can roll up the coast of Britain for a week, making everyone smell like whatever plant or animal their clothes came from. The artist who made this painting had been to the ragged north-east of Scotland and had seen that kind of storm.

The girl is different. She feels, in a sense, too authentic to be real. She is considered and posed. Her clothing is what a poor crofter's daughter would wear if she'd been plucked from obscurity for a crofting-themed catwalk at London Fashion Week. Her hair is long and red – she's *that* Scottish – and while it's been given a good tousle, it's not alive in the same way the waves are.

She's facing away from the artist, and I imagine she's crying as she channels her inner shepherdess-who's-lost-her-shoes. The model posing for the painting had definitely studied acting. She'd owned several stereotypical wigs.

As she stands on the artist's studio floor imagining a grassy dune, it's not the sea that frightens, but the character of the shelter the storm drives her towards. When she gets home, she'll have to explain herself to a tyrannical Calvinist father – wild eyes, great big bushy beard, little bible in his shirt pocket. He's furious – his beard vibrates. Out all day long losing shoes when there's sheep to be sheared and God to be worshipped. She's in for a skelp, and possibly some incestuous sexual abuse.

My least favourite picture in the hall is under the staircase, between the entrances for the single-occupancy male and female toilets. A bad hedgehog. Googly eyes on acrylic on paper. Early twenty-first century. The artist aged three. Winner of an annual art contest with one eligible participant. The other contest winners have been taken down and hidden by the artist, but the hedgehog's frame is screwed to the wall as if it held a fire evacuation notice.

Reception has been organised against one wall, with a carved wooden desk in front of a grid of pigeonholes. In the room behind reception is the restaurant, opposite are the tearoom and the lounge. Towards the rear of the building are the kitchen, laundry, and the private dining room (which is always locked). Like most old houses there are two sets of stairs: the main stairs for use by guests and the back stairs for use by us.

There is a couple at the reception desk. They're in their early sixties and American. The man is wearing dark-blue, knee-length shorts – which is fine, it's fifteen degrees today and I'm also finding it uncomfortably warm. He leans against the desk and has one hand pressed to his side.

The woman is wearing a puffer jacket and a woolly hat with a pom-pom, managing to look like one of those children with that disease that make you age faster than you should. She pauses with her hand over the service bell when she sees me.

"Mister and Missus Wolanski," I say, my best smile on and turning my accent down to Edinburgh. "Lovely to have you staying with us. My name is Eleanor."

"My husband has hurt his back," says Mrs. Wolanski, not in the least impressed that I knew her name. Of course, she knew her name too, and I hadn't drawn her attention to the magic trick of knowing the name of the only guests checking in today.

"Oh dear. Would you like a chair? Or a doctor? The chair I can get you right away, the doctor might take about eighteen hours. Tell you what, I'll get you a chair and you can have a seat while you think about it. There's no rush."

I push a chair under Mr. Wolanski, and he slouches onto it like a sack of potatoes that can say *ow* and *Margaret, my pills*.

"They're in the suitcase," says Mrs. Wolanski. She looks at me and asks, "Can you bring it in? He dropped it at the door."

I peer around, espying the edge of a suitcase poking around the door frame. It's Samsonite and large enough to hold a dead body and/or cripple an old man. It is luggage designed for airports and cars, not boats and cobbles; wheels like a dream on a flat surface, pulls your arm off going down stairs.

"Health and safety," I say with a shake of my head. I knead Mr. Wolanski's shoulders sympathetically, which seems to cause more tension than it eases.

"What's health and safety?" Mrs. Wolanski asks.

With a conspiratorial whisper I tell her, "Nobody knows. But unfortunately, I can't touch it unless it's actually in the hotel. If you pull it forward about three feet, just past the threshold, then I'm happy to take it from there."

"You're not serious."

"Won't take you a minute, a big strong woman like yourself." I push Mr. Wolanski forward in the chair and work my hands down his spine, checking for any obvious herniations. He groans again, as much in shock as pain, though certainly also in pain.

5

"I beg your pardon," Mrs. Wolanski says.

"Someone will be by in a minute if you don't want to," I tell her. This is true. Nothing is ever stolen on Ensay. If things occasionally go missing, it's only because someone believes they have *found* something which was lost, and are having difficulty returning it to its rightful owner.

To her husband I say, "I don't think it's a slipped disc, Mister Wolanski, probably just a muscle spasm. Worst-case scenario is a trapped nerve. Tell me if this feels like the best thing that's ever happened to you."

Between the spine and the lowest rib there's a nexus of muscles that interact with all the other muscles in the back. I find the spot on either side of the spine and knead into him with my thumbs. In response to this, Mr. Wolanski makes an extraordinary sound that begins high and sharp – a yelp of pain from a dog – transitions to a lower sound – a cry of indignation – rumbles towards the lowest edge of his vocal range, and becomes barely audible low frequency – the purring of a cat.

Mr. Wolanski is in paradise. His head dangles between his knees, a picture of pink contentment, as I swirl my thumbs in the fleshy folds of his back. Given his wife's reaction, I have no doubt that I am the only human being ever to have touched him in this way.

"It's just a muscle spasm," I say. "He'll be fine in the morning."

Mrs. Wolanski is paralysed. But while she struggles to come to terms with what she is seeing, I hear the sound of alarms from her. It isn't clearly coming from her mouth or her nose; rather it is as if her whole head were vibrating in incredulous outrage. Unlike her husband, she begins low and ascends; alerting dogs, raising insurance premiums on antique crystal.

And then she stops, as a Samsonite suitcase is rolled onto the black and white tiles.

"Mister and Missus Wolanski, is it?" asks the woman wheeling the suitcase. "Let's get you checked in."

* * *

There is a lot of activity left in the day after three o'clock. Once the afternoon teas are dealt with, there's prep for dinner. As there's no other restaurant on Ensay, if a visitor to the island hasn't made friends with a local, they're eating with us. It's around twenty covers a night when all the rooms are booked.

Mrs. Alexander does two hours in the evening during the season, and gets her own meal and cash-in-hand for making everyone else's. She's broad and no-nonsense; an archetypal housekeeper who probably came with the house. At seventy-three, as her responsibilities have reduced, mine have increased, and she asserts with increasing frequency that this year will be her last.

I assume she means her last year in catering, though she says it as if she were talking about a final end to her graveward trudge. She's adopted the phrase *I'll be dead soon* as a mantra, like a Buddhist who regards the transition from being to nothingness as the ideal way to avoid making another chicken Balmoral. Other than specific instructions and general complaints, she says very little to anyone, and nothing conversational.

We keep her away from the guests as much as possible, which is easy. Her shift finishes exactly at eight; anyone who hasn't had their dinner by eight is going hungry, or making-do with a block of frozen broth returned to a liquid state in the microwave.

The hotel is closed to non-residents after dinner. Those looking to experience the nightlife on Ensay can visit the Wee Man. The island's sole public house is open until ten o'clock, except on Saturday, when it closes at ten-thirty. There is no rule which says the Wee Man must close earlier than pubs in the rest of Scotland, and in practice all opening times are variable and can be extended if people keep buying drinks for the landlord, Mr. Urquhart – coffee, whose mood is usually black and temporarily lightened by the influence of a few drams of Speyside. Those who aren't going for an early bed and an early rise opt to shuffle five doors down the High Street, press themselves together in the smallest pub in the Isles, and fail to befriend its proprietor. They leave the hotel with the reminder that however late Mr. Urquhart stays up, *the hotel doors are locked at eleven.*

It's almost nine o'clock before she sits down and bids me sit down with her at the small table in the kitchen. There used to be a wood-burning, cast-iron range under the brick arch of the kitchen fireplace, and behind it was a boiler that once provided hot water to – at best – nine of the fourteen bathrooms. It was one of the first things my mum removed, replacing everything with oil-burners. She has put one of the ovens on to a slow cook setting and opened the door. It is a practical fire, marrying necessity and convenience.

My mum – Earl Grey, one sugar – has made the tea. She has a steady pour, and doesn't seem tired. She runs her hand back through her dark, wavy hair to push it out of her face. Her eyes, like mine, are hazel.

"So," she says.

"I did exactly what a doctor would have done in the same circumstances. What was I supposed to do, leave him in agony for the better part of a day? Would that have made his wife feel better? And if I had asked permission first, would he have said yes? I don't think he would. Then he's left in pain anyway because he's too stupid to accept help when it's offered to him, and everyone else is too small-minded to insist he take it. And what exactly is the point of learning anything at all if you're never allowed to use it? There's no sense or reason to any of it and I won't apologise. Do what you want. I think if we asked him, he'd say he doesn't even want an apology. Imagine

7

demanding an apology on someone else's behalf, as if they can't ask for an apology themselves. It's rotten. The whole thing is rotten."

I breathe.

She says, "Drink your tea."

I drink.

There are sounds that bodies make just filling space with blood and bone, and watching. I suppose I am used to being watched, though I know it's different than being looked at. Strangers might look at me; as if I were a picture of a girl instead of a real person; as if I were a substitute for middle-distance: a stand-in for absence. But people who know who I am only watch me.

Even her.

"Better?"

I nod.

"I explained to him—"

I interrupt, "You shouldn't have to explain. It was a good thing. And you don't mean explain, you mean excuse. You excused—"

"*I explained* to him . . . that you had completed an online course in therapeutic massage, and one in biology, and human physiology. I explained that you sometimes act without thinking."

"I did think—"

"*And I told them* that if they were offended, I would be happy to refund everything they'd paid and arrange for them to move to another hotel in the morning."

"What other hotel?"

"Oh, it doesn't matter; they aren't going."

I fold my arms and look smug.

My mum says, "I also told them you would apologise—"

"Never!"

"*—for not asking* what Mister Wolanski's pills were for before you treated him."

She takes the fine-mesh tea strainer from its holder and rests it on the rim of my cup. Habit makes us formal; there are no tea bags in the building, unless guests have brought their own.

She tops-up my cup and says, "That is what you're supposed to do, isn't it? I assume. You took the course, so you would know what the first thing you're supposed to do is."

"Yes."

"What is the first thing you're supposed to do?"

"Ask if the patient has any pre-existing medical conditions or is currently taking any prescription medications or is currently receiving treatment from any other practitioner."

"But you didn't do that?"

"No."

"So, what do you think the right thing to do is?"

"Apologise."

"Good girl. Drink your tea. They'll be here soon."

I am still furious. She watches me seethe. I must seem ridiculous to her, and this only makes me angrier.

She reaches out to touch my cheek. When I flinch, she pauses with her hand an inch from my face, then continues. Her fingertips come to rest in the contour between my jaw and my neck, her thumb runs gently along my cheekbone.

"You're doing so well," she says, and she takes her hand away, rests it on her lap, next to the other.

"Will I meet them tonight?"

"Them?"

"The sisters. Will I meet them tonight?"

"You know all the sisters. And they know you. They've known you your whole life."

"Yes, but will I *meet* them?"

She considers this. Her mouth purses, but I know she's not thinking about the answer to my question, only how to phrase it so that it doesn't upset me. Or upsets me the least possible. Of course, she isn't stupid, and she's my mum, so she knows that I know her patter and her tells just as well as she knows mine.

"You're fifteen," she says. I throw up my arms. "Don't be in such a hurry to grow up."

"It's three weeks!"

"And I expect they'll want to meet you soon after that."

"How soon?"

"Eleanor, you're being absurd. If a time had been set, you'd have been told. It's not up to me. You know it's not up to me and you know this is how it's done. You've always been told this is how it would happen, and we are not going to revisit this tonight."

"But—"

There is a knock on the door between the hall and the kitchen, we both turn to see it's being knocked on even as it's being opened. The figure at the door wears a hooded, black cape which is slightly too long; its hem is muddy. With the hand that isn't knocking the drum beat of *Sunday Bloody Sunday*, it pushes back the hood to reveal the smiling round face of woman in late middle age.

Mrs. Olafsson – Lady Grey, Irish – says, "Hello my darlings, that's us here." My mum checks her watch as she stands up. Anticipating the reaction, Mrs. Olafsson shakes her head dismissively and adds, "Anyone can wait two minutes."

"I'll open the door," says my mum, who fishes the old, iron key out of her pocket and goes through the open door with the key held out in front of her, like a torch or a talisman against evil.

I stand up as she leaves, eliciting a cooing noise from Mrs. Olafsson who crosses the room and, without any invitation, places her hands on either side of my face. She squeezes me. I remain absolutely still until she stops, but I manage to avoid making a noise.

"Oh, you're a heartbreaker, Eleanor," she says. Mrs. Olafsson is prone to exaggeration. And touching. My mum says she is a *tactile person* and I should try not to mind. "Not long now." She says this with a conspiratorial wink, as if we are two giggling girls with a common secret.

"I asked my mum if I might—"

"No," she says – still smiling, but the *no* is firm. My mum also says that Mrs. Olafsson is *intuitive*. She obviously knew what would be on my mind tonight before I did. After all, she went through it forty years ago, and every year since. One of her hands is on my shoulder and she pulls me down level with her face, her eyes twinkling.

"But I am still out here, so we haven't started yet, and there is nothing to say that you can't stand outside and wish the sisters a good night before you go to bed."

"I won't get in trouble?" This is a question in two parts, because there are two kinds of trouble. There is the serious sort of trouble for infractions against rules which, though never written down, are nevertheless well-understood, policed and punished. And then there is mum trouble, which comes from not-breaking-but-obviously-thinking-about-breaking rules that are neither written down nor comprehensively communicated.

Mum law is like other sorts of law in that ignorance is no defence, but unlike the rules that govern nations, wars, private contracts, and public behaviour, mum law can be retrospective. She has never told me not to *look* in the private dining room when the sisters are there, only that I'm not to *go* in. She's said this to me hundreds of times; she's never wavered, she's never changed her instruction.

However, I feel like this might be one of those things where – even though she could not have been clearer – what she actually meant was not to go in or to look inside, or listen at the door with a glass to my ear (which doesn't work anyway), or to plant a tape recorder in the room. There are any number of prohibitions which she would say were implied and that I should have known. And even though I've done nothing I was told not to do; I still end up in it.

Trouble.

I rub the palm of my hand against the side of my head in a clockwise circle.

She takes my hand down and presses it between hers.

"We'll go together," she says. "I will make sure that nothing happens. Do you trust me?"

She is touching me just about as much as it's possible to touch someone. Her left hand is on top of mine, her right hand is underneath. From my wrist to my fingertips, I can feel her feeling me. There is no part of my hand which is not being touched and if it were anyone but Mrs. Olafsson I wouldn't have been prepared.

It takes me several seconds to nod my response to her question.

I do believe that Mrs. Olafsson is trustworthy, but she'll be home by midnight and my mum will still be here tomorrow. She'll sit me down and tell me that somehow, I was the one who co-opted Mrs. Olafsson into a scheme of my making. It will be ridiculous, but she'll say it, and I'll realise she's right.

However, Mrs. Olafsson can't read my mind and has already received all the permission she needs. She puts my hand on top of her arm; it's an affected gesture, from an age much older than her, when women wore cortices and bustles and hoops, and could no more slip a hand into the crook of a gentleman's arm than ride a horse.

Her cloak is cotton on the outside with a polyester lining. It is machine washable – probably useful given the mess it gets in – and smooth to the touch. It forms a barrier between us and I can feel myself relaxing for all of a second, until I realise we're moving as a two-person procession, and we're going to the private dining room.

Through the kitchen door and into the entrance hall – which is empty. It's seven steps from the kitchen door to the private dining room. Each one feels like I'm falling and I'm surprised when my foot hits the tile in front of me instead of passing straight through the floor, plummeting, dropping into some black space deeper than the earth goes.

It is only our hall floor. The checkerboard is the same and I've never fallen through it before. I keep my eyes on it just in case.

The double door is closed. It is a dark-stained, oak-panelled door, not like the other doors in the house. On the ground floor there are fire doors to the kitchen and glass doors to the public rooms. On the first floor all the bedroom doors are painted white to match the skirting boards. There is a plain, wooden door to the attic, but it's not like this door.

Though I know it can't be true, I feel like this door was put down first, then the frame built around, and finally the house was erected over the top and filled in underneath. The door is somehow older than the room it opens onto: the door is permanent, while the house is a passing convenience.

It isn't otherwise interesting or even very impressive. The best-made door in the house, yes, but it's still domestic; in some ways no different than a wooden spoon. It isn't intimidating. I walk by it a hundred times a day and this door does not, in the least, frighten me.

Yet, I've always had this feeling that it should.

Mrs. Olafsson raps smartly on a panel – two bars of *I Fought the Law* by the Clash.

The sound of the key turning in the lock jerks my vision upwards from the floor, and I must have tensed because in the corner of my eye I see Mrs. Olafsson turn to watch me.

The doors open inwards, a sliver turning into a scene. There is a formal dining table set around with twelve chairs, though there's easily room for sixteen. All but two of the chairs are occupied by women wearing similar but not identical black capes. There is, of course, no supply company for secret societies which can provide a uniform, so everyone has done their best to make or buy something appropriate. Some of the capes are recent, while others have decades of wear.

At the head of the table, she sits. She is the first one I see when the doors open. Mrs. Douglas has just turned sixty (she celebrated her birthday in the hotel last week), and though she was appointed at only forty, by tradition all high priestesses serve until sixty-five or death. Her cloak is an inheritance; made of black wolf fur and passed down as a symbol of office since a time when there were wild wolves in Scotland.

By comparison, all of the other ladies look like they are pretending; that tonight is a game of dress-up. Mrs. Douglas is serious. Her grey eyes are piercing and she is somehow staring straight into my eyes from the instant the door opens.

"I thought it would be nice if Eleanor came to say goodnight," says Mrs. Olafsson.

Mrs. Douglas is not a horror movie villain. When she smiles at me, it is genuine.

"I remember that Missus Olafsson was granted the same privilege," she says.

"Now it's a tradition," Mrs. Olafsson says.

"So it would seem," Mrs. Douglas replies. There is the most fleeting tone of warning in her voice. She is not happy that I've been brought here, but she is unhappy at Mrs. Olafsson. I think it's possible Mrs. Olafsson knew she would get this reaction and did it deliberately. I catch a change in her expression, from breezy to feigned unconcern.

Mrs. Olafsson takes my hand and puts it down at my side, in the process giving it a small squeeze which she almost certainly means to be comforting, then she walks into the room, rounds the table, and takes the vacant seat to the left of Mrs. Douglas.

"Is there anything you'd like to say to us, Eleanor?" Mrs. Douglas asks. All the hoods turn toward me.

I have not prepared. When I asked my mum if I could go, I had not imagined she would say yes. She'd never said yes before. *Yes*, was a ridiculous answer.

I stand quietly for a moment and try not to sweat.

Talking is something people do all the time. They talk to each other; they talk to themselves. If a person is left for long enough, talk will just start coming out of them. Knowing that talking is supposed to come automatically doesn't help when it doesn't.

I realise it has been a full six seconds since anyone has spoken. It's just under two-thirds of the time needed for a verbal countdown before shooting a man into space. This is only one-thirtieth of the time needed to boil the perfect egg. It's one three-hundred-and-sixtieth of the running time of the television show Countdown, excluding adverts. Six seconds is nothing . . . unless it's six seconds of silence.

"I won't let you down," I say, and as soon as I have said it, this feels like a very stupid thing to have said.

"I'm sure you won't," says Mrs. Douglas, whose expectations of how much I would screw up this exchange were clearly lower than mine. "Goodnight, Eleanor."

"Goodnight ladies," I say and am horrified to find that my knees are bending into a curtsey.

They all chime in with their *goodnights,* and the door on the left begins to close. The twelfth cloaked figure reaches for the door on the right and draws it in.

"Goodnight, Eleanor," my mum says. Under the hood, her face is not smiling. When the doors close, the click of the lock is a dismissal.

I sigh.

Trouble.

DAVID F PORTEOUS

2

My room is the highest point in any building on Ensay, and besides that, is the largest and best room on the island. The main stairs of the house don't reach here; it's at the top of the servants' stairs and on the other side of the plain, wooden door.

When the house was built, the attic was divided into six rooms. There are still marks on the sloping roof where the divisions used to be and six pretty haunted-looking fireplaces – one at each end and the rest built into two brick chimney stacks.

My mum had planned to convert the attic into guest rooms too, until she found out about me, then it just made sense to tear everything out except the once-shared servants' bathroom and give me the space.

I'm glad she did. I can't imagine what it would be like living in a normal-sized room, with one view, filled up with a wardrobe and a bed; basically, being smothered with furniture. I know it's unusual, but it's only one more unusual thing.

The windows at the front of the building look north-east-ish and back to land. Because the island rises up to the east and south, there's no sea visible on that side, just a transition from the green sweep of nearby grassland to the coast of Harris to the haze of green-brown mountains.

Immediately below these windows is the High Street, which starts on the stone wall of the harbour and ends at the house of the other Mrs. Mackenzie – no relation. The street itself diminishes before it reaches her front door, becoming narrower and patchy so that sections of what should be stone are turf, and the street transitions entirely into open grazing without any fence at its end or any well-defined end at all. As a street, it is slightly shorter than it needs to be, poorly disciplined besides, and sets the tone for all its neighbours; they ramble on unevenly then vanish into a terrain feature – a hill, a copse of trees, the sea.

It is difficult to tell if there were perhaps more houses once, then the village contracted; absorbed the building materials back into itself, cobbles and all. Or if the village is instead a living thing, like the moss that grows in the guttering, and is spreading slowly across the island at a rate of one cobble per year.

There is nothing resembling a road on Ensay. We have two cars that I know about – only one of which is actually usable. The other is in the garage of a glass-and-timber-built house sitting on the coast directly north of the hotel. Two summers ago, that car was brought over the sea on a specially hired ferry. Mr. Maxwell drove the car up into the garage, closed the door and hasn't opened it again since. People talked about it for a month.

They called it *Maxwell's Folly*.

Most of the people on the island are quite old and have a pleasant, book-learned sense of humour. There wasn't even television reception until ninety-six, so my mum says. Ensay was probably the last place in Scotland to hear of Billy Connolly (when they did, they thought he was *okay*). The island still relies on an undersea cable for telephone and internet – the cable was laid in seventy-five and some of the older ladies still regard the pre-telephone era as being a better, simpler time – though I cannot imagine much has changed since.

Around half of all the houses on the island are on the High Street, with the rest clustered nearby. Nearly all of these are two-storey cottages built of irregular local stone and heavily mortared. Their roofs are a grey-green slate, some of which bear mossy patches. They sag in places and bulge in others; time has rendered them organic, seeming to be a colony of misshapen seals sheltering in a fold in the island's geology.

The side of the hotel nearest the harbour has only one window in the attic, but it is unquestionably the best view. The stone curve of the harbour wall stands fifteen feet above sea at low tide, and a mouldering boat ramp runs down an arc of sand which, at high tide, is entirely under water.

Beyond the harbour is the North Atlantic Ocean. I think that I know what it is like to live at the edge of the wild. I've read about other wildernesses, but the story of uncivilization is always the reverse of the writer's home town. People who grew up in the shelter of rules describe a world of mystery. Children of cities find desolation. Everyone sees beauty, though for some it's terrifying.

The ocean is as bleak as a desert, and trackless as deep woods. It is weather: not a thing to be described once; given its character for the ages. It can be photographed, it can be painted, but all these descriptions are just bottled water.

The other windows in the room look back onto the island. There are steep slopes to the southeast, the houses giving way to grass, which gives way to gorse. The highest point on Ensay looks lilac, as the purple of our scattering of heather blends into the blue of the sky. On the winter solstice, the sun rises directly behind that hill, and then it looks black against the pale gold light. At least that's how it looks from my room.

I usually wake up early – earlier still in the summer. Mum insists that I do three hours of study every day, but isn't all that fussed about when. This morning it is Geography – redistribution of energy by atmospheric and oceanic currents – and English Literature – *The Glass Menagerie* by Tennessee Williams.

The book is from the syllabus; everyone else in the class will be reading it in October. If it had been selected specifically for me, it might be a little on-the-nose. In the play, a girl – Laura – has a childhood illness that makes her a shut-in. Her mother wants the best for her, and in her mind that means marrying her off. *Haven't you ever liked some boy?* But the mother – Amanda – is also resentful; in part because of the loss of her youth and freedom, in part because her kids are both duds.

This isn't my life. That isn't my mum. But it's not a story about life on Mars in the far future.

I email the five hundred words I've written about the Gulf Stream and the two-hundred words on my first impressions of the play. I am not, strictly speaking, home-schooled. In America it's reasonably common – home-school is, I'm sure, an American phrase. There, someone is actually given lessons by a parent acting as a teacher. My mum takes an interest, but she's not my teacher.

I am registered at Sir Edward Scott Secondary in Tarbert and I have never missed a day of school – despite having never actually gone there.

If anything, not being physically in school has been a huge advantage. Although I started a year late, I was skipped forward a year when I was eight, and again when I was thirteen. Last month I sat my first batch of Highers – results patiently awaited. One of the reasons I'm ahead is because I don't take holidays. I don't get distracted. I don't have to get on a boat in the dark, in the middle of winter. At seven-thirty weekday mornings Mr. Jones's boat makes its first trip of the day across the narrow stretch of water that separates Ensay and Harris. And because I don't get on that boat in the freezing night, I don't catch colds.

But it also means I won't get any feedback on my work until the beginning of September, when the school reopens after the summer holidays.

So, I could be totally wrong about Amanda Wingfield – maybe she's not a half-price Blanche Dubois cut with a fifth of Norma Desmond. I mean of course she isn't – since *The Glass Menagerie* was staged in forty-four, before *Streetcar* and *Sunset Boulevard*. But she also so obviously is.

I read *A Streetcar Named Desire* last year and *Sweet Bird of Youth* the year before. To have written so many neurotics and hysterics, Tennessee Williams' group of friends must have included the worst women in the world. I expect he could never keep a drop of gin in his house. Though I didn't say this in my short report – that sort of thing does not earn extra marks, especially when it's true.

It's eight o'clock. I click the power button on my iPad and go for a shower.

The fittings in the bathroom are original, as is the bath. It's enamelled, worn around the plughole so that the dark-brown iron is visible, but its clean. And it was built before people worried about conserving water – or drowning – so it's dramatically huge. Two people could fit in this bath and never inconvenience each other in the least.

I pull the shower curtain into a horseshoe shape around the bath, wait the thirty seconds it takes for the water to hit the right temperature, then slip in and perform Lola – *elle oh elle ay: Lola* – to an audience of haircare products, body lotions and a loofa. It's probably the most famous song ever about a man falling in love with a man dressed as a woman. When I sing it, it's a song about a girl pretending to be a man who falls in love with a man dressed as a woman. I can't decide which set of circumstances is the more scandalous.

It takes twenty minutes to dry my hair, which is longer than it takes to wash it. I have relied on my mum to cut my hair all my life, and she's not very good at it. When I was nine, I had her best attempt at a celebrity-inspired haircut, and spent two weeks refusing to come out of my room. Now I let it grow for as long as I can and wear it up when it becomes a problem – falling in soup, that kind of thing.

Wet, my hair goes to the small of my back. Dry, it has a heavy wave and finishes at my shoulder blades. I plait it, then roll the plait up and secure it with half-a-dozen butterfly clips. I probably won't think about my hair again until tonight when I take the clips out, unplait it, and look in the mirror, being exactly as unsatisfied with it as I am now.

Individually each of my hairs is good. I don't get split ends. I don't get broken hairs. I'm pretty low on frizz. But I don't have good hair, collectively. The total is less than the sum of its parts. Possibly I could wear it across my face to seem mysterious. Or I could shave it all off to make people think I had cancer – which would be a change, if nothing else.

I'm fussing with my hair because I don't want to go down for breakfast.

While I only work afternoon into evening, my mum's been up since six. I haven't seen her since she closed the doors on me last night. Between my room and the kitchen there is a single storey of bedrooms, and a void of uncertainty.

I get dressed, opting for dark jeans and a grey top; the closest I can get to urban camouflage. No makeup yet, as the back stairs go straight to the kitchen and I won't meet people there or on the way. Lacking proper eyebrows and cheekbones, I look and feel like my own ghost.

My stomach growls and I know this can't be put off any longer. I unlock my bedroom door – because it's a hotel and I'm far enough removed from the rest of the house that I'd be raped and murdered twice before anyone got here. And I lock it again after I leave – because it's a hotel and I've left my iPad propped-up and charging on my bed. The key is as old as the house; grey iron and five inches long, it operates a heavy mechanism that turns with a reverberating clunk.

The stairwell is nearly dark. A tiny window in the roof lets through a spotlight that illuminates the step immediately before the attic door. There's a dim light on the first-floor landing, but as the staircase is a narrow spiral, there is only a differentiation of shadows before me. That light socket is temperamental, and I've often had to find my way through the dark just by feel, with each handhold where uncut surfaces meet being familiar.

Much of the house is built of stone, but this stairwell is the only place that has been left unplastered. The rough texture and occasional colourings – barely visible even on the brightest days – hint at an attempt to whitewash or paint the stones in the obscure past; a job half-done by someone long forgotten. My mum has never bothered with them in the all the time she has owned the hotel.

I'm not half-way down before I can smell bacon and black pudding. The stairwell door opens directly into the kitchen – which is probably a fire hazard. Light pressure makes the door swing open, revealing the door to the restaurant, the service area, the door to the hall, the table by the cookers, the cookers, and finally the door to the laundry room.

She isn't here. My mind fills with the heady dream of making it to the oven where the bain-marie sits, filling a plate, then escaping back up the stairs unnoticed. A breakfast ninja.

The restaurant door opens and my mum comes through. She holds two plates marked with greasy smears, used cutlery balanced on top.

"Good morning," she says. She doesn't break her stride on the way to the dishwasher.

"Good morning."

"That's the last of the breakfasts." By this statement she means two things – that the restaurant is now empty, and that anything remaining is available for me. "Do you want me to make you an egg?"

"Yes, please." This egg talk seems a good sign. Eggs are the only component of the traditional Scottish breakfast which are made to order. The sausage, bacon, black pudding, haggis, potato scone, and baked beans are all cooked before the first guest is served, and kept warm until the last is finished. It's possible to do scrambled eggs the same way, but fried and poached eggs turn solid with continuous heat. There's also toast, of course, but asking for brown bread toast isn't the same thing as asking for *two eggs, over easy*.

There are a range of reactions to the full Scottish breakfast. If the person eating it is from Britain, they'll note the regional variations. An Irish breakfast would have white pudding instead of haggis, and might add soda bread. Some places in Scotland – mostly the Highlands – will have fruit pudding. An English breakfast will invariably have fried bread, fried mushrooms, no haggis, and often no black pudding – the English are being pretty substantially short-changed on their breakfast – and a tomato of some kind. The tomato is random; it can show up anywhere, but is never welcome. We only do baked beans.

I haven't had any of these other breakfasts personally, but I once read a hotelier's guidebook that was mad keen on localisation of menus.

I think there's even a Welsh breakfast that includes seaweed, though that doesn't feel like something that would be true. It's like one of those early explorer stories. Pioneering international thieves found that everywhere in the world was much the same as where they were from, just hotter or colder, so they made up tales of sea monsters and people with two heads to convince women to sleep with them.

However, if someone isn't from Britain, then their reaction to the full Scottish is to be appalled. Americans expect more bread – waffles, pancakes, biscuits – and more syrups. Asians are terrified by the whole idea of a meat-blood-potato medley at eight o'clock – and they'll only pick at their porridge.

Europeans aren't in favour of any cooked food in the morning – they prefer a deconstructed ham and cheese sandwich first thing, which is boak. The Germans are different; they think our sausages are *not sausages,* but the rest they love.

"Have you finished your assignments?" she asks as she cracks an egg into a pan and discards the shell into the bin. This happens with robotic precision. We go through around forty eggs a day and there's always a few days' worth piled in cardboard packing. My mum can make eggs in her sleep.

"Were you aware that the average speed of the Gulf Stream is four miles-per-hour, moving one-hundred-and-ten billion litres of water per minute, more than all the world's rivers combined, and that the interaction of the Gulf Stream with cold water off the coast of Newfoundland creates super-dense fog that's hazardous to shipping?"

"That must be very dense."

"You know what I mean."

"Good."

With a clean plate in hand, I open the oven and use tongs to pull a sausage, a slice of bacon and the last piece of black pudding out. I leave the plate by my mum for her to add the egg, and I pop a slice of bread in the toaster.

English breakfast tea for Scottish breakfast. I should have started the tea brewing first, but the problem about being a ninja is that you never know how much time you have. I sacrificed tea for speed.

The egg is transferred to the plate. The toast drops out of the conveyer belt toaster. I butter the slice and cut it in half, then add it to the plate. I squeeze a gloop of ketchup and a gloop of brown sauce onto the edge of the plate. I retrieve milk from the fridge and line this up with the cup, strainer, and the sugar. Then I wait a further forty seconds.

Only then do I pour.

"Would you like a cup?"

"No thank you," she replies.

I return the milk to the fridge and turn around to find that she is sitting at the table, opposite cutlery, my breakfast, and my tea. There will be no escape. She is the true breakfast ninja.

"What are you going to do this morning?" she asks.

I sit down. "I don't know. Nothing."

"Nothing?"

I pick up the knife and fork and saw the end off the sausage. "Mm-hmm."

"Today, almost aged sixteen, for the first time ever, you're going to do nothing for three hours?"

I dip the sausage into the brown sauce, then the ketchup. "Yup."

"Eleanor."

"What? You don't even want to know what I'm doing; you're just asking me what I'm doing so you can use it like a wedge to open me up and make me feel bad about last night. Why does it even matter? I was going to paint – *oh, you painted quite the picture of yourself last night.* Or if I say I'm going to do yoga, you'd say – *you certainly twisted Missus Olafsson around your little finger.* Just be mad at me; stop looking for a segue."

I can't eat the sausage now. It sits on the end of my fork and I lower it down to the plate and stare at it.

She says, "I didn't know I did that."

"Well . . . sometimes you do." There is an unreasonable pause while I give far more scrutiny to the sausage than any sausage could endure and still be appealing. "Are you upset?"

She breathes before she speaks. "I am upset, Eleanor, but I'm not upset with you. I just can't believe how quickly it's gone. You know how important this is."

"I know."

"I know you do. But at the same time, though you have to do it, I also don't want you to. Because then you won't be my little girl anymore."

"Mum—"

"You will, of course you will. Always." She lifts my chin with her fingertips. There are tears in her eyes. I feel a knot in my stomach. "Always. But . . . I've kept you away from it because I know what it means. We all know. It's not fair, you understand that, don't you? We all know it isn't fair."

21

"I don't mind." She strokes my face and, despite myself, I shudder.

"It used to be there would always be a choice. There would be several girls and it was an honour. Three other girls turned sixteen the same year I did. All beautiful girls; it could have been any of them instead of me."

There was another girl my age, but she died of an infection when she was three. The Robertson twins will turn sixteen in February – much too late. Three years ago, they made an exception for Charlotte King, whose birthday wasn't until two days after the autumnal equinox. My mum was not happy about that, but it had to be done.

"But life isn't fair," she says, summarising her thoughts and drawing a line under the issue. "This year it's only you. It all falls on you."

"I know." I say this mostly because I want her to stop looking at me.

Mothers tell their children at different times. I was six when she told me about the Purpose and my role in it. I suppose I must have been curious about babies and sex. I learned what I needed to at the time, and more as the years went on.

"Of course," she says, then dabs at her eyes, as if it were possible to push tears back in.

The service bell rings at the desk; one of the guests is checking out.

She stands and smiles and says, "Eat your breakfast." Then she leaves through the hall door.

I think other girls my age must feel more pressured than I do. They must grow up wondering what they'll do, and whether they'll fall in love. Whether – in fact – their lives will matter at all.

Girls and boys are the same now. They are all expected to become something – which by implication means they are nothing. A boy is not a worthwhile thing. A girl has no value.

I have read that teenagers did not exist until the nineteen-fifties; that there was only childhood – dependence, which is its own kind of servitude – and adulthood – a state of being responsible for others. Adolescence, brought into being by affluence and idleness, provides a decade-long uncertainty, ending in a test which can be failed, and is failed more often than passed.

I have known for nearly ten years that I was special.

I am the acolyte. Once I turn sixteen, I must choose a man and give him my virginity.

Not necessarily *on* my birthday; any time before the fifteenth of September is acceptable; in fact, it's considered bad form to rush into it, and it's never to be done before the end of May, regardless of when the acolyte turns sixteen.

Then on the eve of the autumnal equinox, we seize the chosen man and bind him with rowan branches. On the afternoon of the day itself, he will be carried to the western-most point of the island, to the edge of a basalt cliff, and placed into the belly of the god.

As the sun sets, the high priestess lights the fire, and the man I have chosen will be burned alive.

I'm not nervous. From what my mum says, once I pick the man I want, everything will just happen. The hardest part is done, because I've already made my choice.

3

She was right, though, about me doing nothing. I can't do nothing; if I did, I'd go stir crazy. People complain about not having enough hours in the day, but I wish there were fewer. Twenty hours instead of twenty-four would leave me with no time to fill; a seamless run of activity from sleep to sleep. How to fill those four hours – three after breakfast and one before bed – that's my constant worry.

This morning I tinker with an oil painting I've been working on. It's a still life of a can of Gillette shaving foam that I used on my legs. It's empty and has the lightest crusting around the nozzle. Conceptually, what I'm going for is somewhere between Warhol and Emin, asking whether there is a place where design, art, and rubbish meet. What is a functional thing when its function is complete? What does it mean to exist without function? Now that the object does not serve me, is it more itself or less?

Holbein was doing much the same thing five hundred years ago, with his *The Body of the Dead Christ in the Tomb* – though obviously with a different colour palette and without any pop art influences.

After an hour I feel like I'm only circling without getting any closer; adding and removing without revealing.

There are perhaps thirty of my paintings on the walls of my room, all fairly recent; I can't tolerate looking at anything more than two years old. The only emotional resonance I have with the work is a non-specific feeling of shame; but even this is more like the embarrassment of someone who's stepped through an unmarked door and found themselves in a gallery of shitty art made by the children of co-workers and friends. Offended, but unable to express any critique for fear of offending. As if *The Twilight Zone* had been made in Britain, and was therefore fundamentally about manners and social norms instead of science fiction.

The current exhibition is heavily themed around the role of the viewer in giving art meaning. Last winter I went through a phase of painting views of things, so now it seems like the sloped ceiling walls of my room are punctuated by windows on other places.

A partially opened doorway reveals the dust sheets that cover a guest room in the off-season; bored furniture ghosts glimpsed in passing; the cover of an IKEA catalogue guest edited by H. P. Lovecraft. If the viewer had been there a day before, the same place would have appeared differently. If the door was slightly more open, what might they see through the window that is the only source of light? Is this art? What about six inches to the left?

A two-part series hangs side-by-side. The first is the view from my bedroom window on December seventh – I remember because I titled it *From My Bedroom Window, December Seventh*. The landscape is grey and lit by the faintest, cold sunlight which conspires with the pale sky to be pure white instead of yellow and steals every colour from the scene. The houses are black fronted, with the stones picked out in a sawdust mixed in with the paint.

The second in the series is a painting of the first, next to the window that inspired it. I remember feeling very proud of myself at the time, but now I can't think why.

I pull a sheet over the easel to conceal the work-in-progress. Not that it matters; nobody comes up here. Covering isn't authorial vanity; it's about consciously excluding the work from my mind while I do something else.

My room is otherwise spartan. A radio stands on the dresser, more than four years silent. Before the house was wired for WiFi and I got the iPad for school work, I used to play the radio all day. As either a quirk of the broadcast signal or the radio itself, it only reliably received BBC Radio Two. Not even Radio Scotland, which should have had at least as good a signal, but never did. I have listened to tens of thousands of hours of Radio Two – perhaps more than anyone else? More than anyone else I know. And the sponge I have for a brain seems to have absorbed it all; from the exact middle of the road that was the breakfast slot – I remember every song from Terry Wogan's last breakfast show: The Bluebells, *Young at Heart*; The Who, *Pinball Wizard*; Katie Melua, *The Closest Thing To Crazy*; Elvis Presley, *Always On My Mind*; all things beloved of mums and inoffensive to grannies – to the tumbledown weirdness of late night with whoever picked up the death mask of John Peel and spoke through its frozen mouth.

I hit shuffle on the iPad and start my treadmill. I don't run every day, but I try to walk for an hour, usually while listening to music or watching videos. The front of the treadmill is pointed at the windows to the rear of the house and that is about as close as I get to being in the great outdoors.

Mum says that I'm getting better; that eventually I'll be able to go for a walk somewhere other than a scrolling rubber surface that's almost within arm's reach of my bed. I think she believes that, but every year I'm less sure.

My heartrate rises. I push the speed up to match.

* * *

"I suppose you've heard." This is her typical opening, though she is certain that her companion has not.

Mrs. Brown – peppermint, of course – is the postmistress for the island. Unlike the post service in other places, on Ensay everyone goes to the post office to enquire if there are any letters. There is no home delivery. As there aren't enough letters going in either direction to justify having a post office at all, she is also the newsagent, the general store, and the bank.

Mrs. Brown knows everyone's business, and doesn't mind that everyone knows it.

"No. I've not heard a thing. Heard what?" Mrs. MacArthur – English breakfast, milk, two sugars – is a credulous crony. She is not especially interested in anything, as far as I can tell, but she enjoys being told things, and being outraged by them.

"They're going to celebrate the solstice in Leverburgh." Mrs. Brown folds her arms and sits back in her chair.

"No!" Mrs. MacArthur's exclamation rouses the attention of all the others in the tearoom. In a lower voice she whispers, "Well, isn't that just like them." Her criticism isn't levelled solely at the residents of Leverburgh and equal opprobrium might have been directed at any of the towns and villages in the Western Isles. *We* are the last island that holds to the true faith. Everything wicked is just like *them*.

"It can't come soon enough," says Mrs. Brown, with a shake of the head that is joyfully exasperated.

"I agree with that," says Mrs. MacArthur, delighting in her fury. "They'll be sorry when they're burning in the fire."

She means the generic fires of hell, not our specific fire. Doctrinally speaking, we don't believe in a hell where people are tortured forever, but my mum says there are Jews and Muslims who eat bacon, Christians who work on Sundays, and Sikhs who cut their hair. So, nobody really minds if Mrs. MacArthur talks about hell – as long as Mrs. Douglas doesn't hear about it.

"Good afternoon, ladies," I say, notepad and pencil in hand – I use them for effect; nobody likes a waitress who thinks they remember everything even if they do, and it's sometimes useful to have a place to look that isn't someone's face.

"Good afternoon, Eleanor," says Mrs. Brown. "How are you feeling today?"

"I'm very well, thank you Missus Brown, it's very kind of you to enquire."

"And how is your mother keeping?"

"She's very well too; I'll let her know you were asking."

"That's good," she says. She flattens down her skirt across her knees, and adds, "It was nice to see you last night."

"I hope no one thought it was too forward."

"Oh, I expect it was a little bit, but respectfully done. I was gone five minutes ago saying to Missus MacArthur that I thought it was very respectful."

"Indeed, she was," says Mrs. MacArthur, as if I am to believe Mrs. MacArthur would ever contradict Mrs. Brown.

Mrs. Brown is one of the twelve senior sisters (*the* sisters), and when Mrs. Douglas steps down, the power struggle is expected to be between her and Mrs. Olafsson. Five years away and already they are positioning themselves as her successor.

"Yes," says Mrs. Brown with arch consideration. "I believe I might have done the same. Though, of course, you've always been especially close with Missus Olafsson."

"I don't think especially so," I say. "I've always felt great kindness from all of you."

Mrs. Brown is satisfied by this and smiles smugly. It is an artless dissemble, one intended to flatter. Mrs. Brown is not necessarily susceptible to flattery itself, but she does appreciate obvious attempts at ingratiation. Mrs. MacArthur has also noticed, and gives a knowing nod to her tea mate.

The position of high priestess is elective. Any living former high priestesses receive five votes – and typically, they will vote last, symbolically anointing their successor but almost never changing the final outcome. Any currently serving senior sisters receive three votes and, by tradition, must vote first. Officially, a candidate declares they are willing to accept the responsibility by voting for themselves, though the real campaigning lasts years. The other sisters – which is every woman over the age of sixteen, not otherwise entitled by office – can cast one vote. The politics is complicated and the memories are long.

"What can I get for you?" I ask.

They order their usual teas.

"Was that a lemon drizzle I saw earlier?" Mrs. Brown asks.

"It was. Fresh made today."

"I'll have a slice of that."

"Two, please, Eleanor," says Mrs. MacArthur.

They continue their conversation about the people of Leverburgh. The small village is a couple of miles east, arranged on a cross section of streets near the ferry road on Harris. Some few places in Scotland celebrate the summer solstice, though there's no ritual around it. Where it is marked, it is as separate from spiritual meaning as Christmas, Easter, and all the other heathen bacchanals. Still, I can't help wondering whether their festival will be a glow in the darkening sky, or if they will launch fireworks – which I could certainly see from my window – or if there will be no visible signs at all.

I am slicing into lemon drizzle when the Wolanskis enter the tearoom. Mr. Wolanski, a bounce in his step, comes first. He peers around with the flexibility of a friendly owl. Mrs. Wolanski follows him, her pride still injured, her guard up.

"Take a seat anywhere and I'll be with you in a moment," I say.

I bring Mrs. Brown and Mrs. MacArthur their order, then Mrs. O'Leary wants to pay, and it's five minutes before I get to the Wolanskis.

"I just want to say thank you." Mr. Wolanski speaks first, while I'm still on approach. "I've had that ache for years, but this morning I woke up – and I tell you this – I could touch my toes." He laughs and looks at Mrs. Wolanski to share the joke. She does not. "My toes!" I touch my toes all the time – I think it must be something you only get excited about if it happens infrequently.

"I'm glad I could help."

"You really should have asked," Mrs. Wolanski says. He shushes her, but she is not for shushing. "No, Henry, we talked about this. We talked about this." Turning back to me, she raises her voice. "It's not that I'm unsympathetic. Your mother explained that you're not all there, but that's all the more reason that you behave yourself. Do you understand?"

I notice only when it's gone. I am fuelled by this manic energy that makes it impossible to sit still; I'm never at rest, and if I am, it's not happily or for long. Activity is my background radiation; the hissing noise my universe makes. This sound diminishes, like the setting of a star on the black edge of the sky, and the quiet in me is louder than the sea.

It occurs to me that I could push my pencil into her eye and slit her husband's throat, and the other people in the room would help bury the bodies. I don't do this, of course, because it would be gross. And we don't randomly murder people, because it's uncivilised and bad for business. It's just that *if* people did get randomly murdered, the last things we'd want on the island would be search parties and sniffer dogs.

"You're right," I say. "I should have asked. I apologise for being disrespectful and I hope it hasn't given you a bad impression of us."

"Well," says Mrs. Wolanski. She did not actually want an apology. She wants to stay angry. It bubbles in her; it makes her feel. I can see this, and in the moment, I know her better than she knows herself. Just as Mrs. MacArthur bathes in her own indignation, Mrs. Wolanski needs something from this experience.

Perhaps this trip was Mr. Wolanski's idea. He has some ancient ancestor that called Scotland home. His wife feels no connection and wants his consent to call this vacation a fiasco; his implicit agreement to be blamed for his decision. What she wants is an apology from *him*, and in this way to make him again dependent on her. She cannot ask for any of this; she will never find the words to say how she is broken, and what evil thing is required to mend her.

He says, "Water under the bridge."

She squirms.

I smile and ask, "Are you here for afternoon tea?"

* * *

It's three o'clock when the Wolanskis rise to leave, having outlasted everyone else. Mr. Henry "Hank" Wolanski has told me several stories about being a marine in his youth, and about his dog – Scruffles, in a kennel that is costing almost as much as their holiday. With the exception of their daughter – Justine, in Alberta studying lichen for her PhD – there seems to be nothing to say about his thirty-one-year marriage to Margaret Wolanski. Excepting the time spent speaking to me, they were silent as they consumed several rounds of sandwiches, scones, and cake – he, gratefully; she, grudgingly.

He leaves the tip and behind his wife's back gives me a mute shrug. This is not the first time he has had to make apologies for her. I offer a slight smile in response.

They're booked into the hotel for another two days, leaving Saturday, so this will not be the last I see of them.

Mr. Wolanski is, in my opinion, far too old to seduce – and in this matter my opinion is the only one that matters. Though my mum says other acolytes have done it.

If I were to guess, the girls who choose older men probably wanted to feel nothing. It would be easy to convince themselves that an old man having sex with a young girl was disgusting, and that an old man being burned alive was no great loss. Easier still to imagine compartmentalising the actions, keeping them separate from everything else they did before or after. I see the argument.

We've already shared some physical intimacy. I could make an innocent invitation to provide him with a proper massage, and make some remarks about the breadth and strength of his shoulders. He's long in decline, but was clearly an impressive soldier, marine, whatever, thirty years before. Forty years ago, he may even have been handsome.

Yet even if he were staying here after I turn sixteen, this would still feel dishonest. The sacrifice is supposed to be a sacrifice; having met Mrs. Wolanski, Mr. Wolanski's death by fire would be a mercy.

"Good afternoon."

"Good afternoon."

The voices carry into the tearoom from the hallway. One is my mother's, the other I also recognise. I suspend any actual tidying up and begin pretend tidying up to allow me to move closer to the doorway, while I dust picture frames with a moistened sponge not intended for that purpose.

"Good afternoon," he repeats, pauses, and continues. "I need a room."

"You need a room?" my mum asks.

"Yes," he says.

"I'm afraid we're all booked tonight."

"No, not for tonight, sorry."

"Are you feeling all right?"

We keep bottled water and soft drinks in a small fridge in the tearoom. I grab one of the bottles and try not to run into the hall. He has his back to me, facing the counter.

"I'm sorry," he says, absently, not really thinking about the words as he says them.

It's the rasping sound of the chair's two rear feet being dragged across the tiled floor that makes him turn. He has tawny brown hair in waves and large blue eyes, which are reddened, though I think more from sleeplessness than crying.

I ask, "Would you like a seat, Mister Maxwell? Or a drink of water?"

"I—" he seems ready to refuse out of something like politeness, something like pride, but I see him begin to fold. The simile is perhaps too specific to ever be usefully employed again, but he folds almost exactly like an old man called Hank, who's overexerted himself with luggage weighed down with his wife's impractical holiday shoes. I push the chair behind him and he sits automatically. His movement brings us into brief physical contact; skin through fabric, my fingers brush against the back of his arm.

I unscrew the top from the bottle – fumbling slightly; the top skitters across the floor – and hand it to him. He places his lips on the plastic rim of the bottle and sips.

I think I would like him to kiss me. I have thought about this a lot, but reached no firm conclusion. He is thirty-five, twenty years older than I am. Old enough, as they say, to be my father. There is something about the gap in our ages and experience that frightens me. It is more than a question of relative physical strength – he makes me feel small and ungainly: foalish; like a piece of furniture that wobbles on a level floor. And though he scares me, I believe that if I were against him, all my feelings of inadequacy would evaporate.

I have imagined him kissing me – and imagined him refusing to kiss me; raking my neck with his permanent three-day stubble, but never pressing his lips to mine. The expectation of being kissed is a firecracker: it fizzes between my teeth; it tastes of fire and gunpowder. It is terrifying.

There is a moment where I am staring at his hair and I imagine my fingers burrowing through those loose curls. I can see the top of his head and he shows no signs of balding, not that it would matter. I'm aware that he is speaking again, and it takes effort to translate the sounds he makes into words.

"—suddenly. She'd been having treatment, but the last I heard she was . . . Obviously she wasn't, though. Obviously."

"You can't predict how these things will go," my mum says. Her hand is pressed over her heart. "She was your younger sister?"

"Older."

"Are you from a large family?"

"No, it was just the two of us."

I put my hand on his shoulder. It's easy for me to touch other people, touching people is like touching objects. Being touched by people is like being touched by objects that are sometimes surprisingly moist.

He doesn't seem to notice the gesture. To my mum he says, "I'm going back tomorrow to arrange the funeral."

"What do you need the room for?" I ask.

"Oh," he looks up at me. Am I pushing my chest out too much? I probably am, but now I have to wait for him to look somewhere else before I can stop. "I never got around to putting a bed in the spare room. Or anything else. I just need something short term while we decide what he's bringing with him from Ireland and what I need to order new." He looks at my mum, I deflate. "My sister's son – my nephew – will be staying with me before he goes to university."

"I see," she says. "You'll be back?"

"By Wednesday at the latest."

"That's fine. There's nothing to worry about. We'll keep a room for him as long as he needs."

"It's so good of you to take him in," I say. I give the shoulder a squeeze and he looks up at me again. "Grief is a terrible thing. If there's anything you need. If there's anything I can do. Please tell me." Am I pouting? My mum is rolling her eyes.

He says his *thank you*s and leaves. Mr. Jones will take him to Harris, then he'll go north to Stornoway and fly to Dublin from there. Benbecula Airport is closer, but there's no way to get there from Ensay today.

We watch him go down the street from the doorway of the house.

She says, "Try to be—"

"I know. Don't spook the horses."

"No, I'm saying be careful."

"He's gone for nearly a week."

"And back for two before your birthday. Slowly."

"I know."

"You were almost drooling over him."

"I was not!"

I was.

"You were. Remember you're not an experienced woman and there's no sense pretending you are. You can't seem too eager with an older man. You have to give him explicit permission to pursue you – then you have to let him pursue you. If he thinks of you as a good, sweet girl first, then everything else will feel right. He needs to feel powerful, but not irresponsible."

"Was my dad older than you?"

"A little," she says it while her mind is elsewhere. Two seconds later she realises what she's done and frowns. I don't struggle when she takes me by the wrists and stares at me. "Do not ask about him again."

I nod, and she lets me go.

.

4

By nine o'clock I am exhausted. There is a weight on me as heavy as I am. Each arm lifts twice itself before it lifts anything else. The soles of my feet hurt and the walk upstairs to my room is a kind of masochism.

For every action there is an equal and opposite reaction – so I stand in opposition to the whole weight of the world; it pushes against me only slightly, while I push against it with everything I am. In Australia, a kangaroo bounds and returns to earth, and my calves are the balancing mechanism that keeps the planet on its axis. Or that's what it feels like. Damn kangaroos.

Before Newton, gravity governed the tides and guided the movement of stars. There are other rules like this. They are not written down – writing them down does not give them force – but they are well understood.

The fire obliterates. When we make a sacrifice, it means sacrificing everything. The body is burned and the bones, if any are left, are thrown into the sea. Any personal belongings are destroyed – nothing as innocuous as a toothbrush or a photograph remains. We do not speak their name again. We expunge them from our memories. The fire obliterates.

My father was a sacrifice.

My mother can't answer any questions; she isn't supposed to think about him at all. But though I daren't ask anyone else, I have always been curious. As I am the same height as my mother, does that mean he was taller or shorter? She and I have the same colour of eyes, but maybe he did as well. Is my hair different than my mum's because I take after him, or is it a legacy from some older ancestor on her side of the family tree?

I can deduce that he and my mum had sex very soon before the autumnal equinox, because my birthday was on the solstice the following summer. Nine months later, give or take a couple of days. But human fertility isn't clockwork, and as my mum's birthday is in March, it's impossible to tell if they had a long romance or a single night of passion.

I know exactly one thing about my father for sure: his surname was Carlyle. I am Eleanor Carlyle. My mother is Mrs. Carlyle. My parents were never married; acolytes take the name of their sacrifice and pass it on to their children, if they have any.

At any given time, there are around fifty former acolytes on Ensay. Most stay on the island – especially if they become pregnant – but those who leave do so immediately afterwards. Mrs. Arbuthnot never held the honour herself, but of her five daughters, two were acolytes. Sophie, her youngest – left the day after the equinox, wearing what she had on the night before, and she has not come back to visit since.

I knew Sophie a little. She's four years older than me, so we weren't friends. But knowing that I would one day also be the acolyte, I had hoped she'd be able to tell me things in confidence. Things the sisters would not tell me, and will not tell me. All I know about the Purpose has come through my mother. This, she says, is how it has always been done.

I don't need to turn on the light to cross my bedroom. The sky is still rose coloured, almost bright enough to read by, though I've no interest in reading tonight. I sit on the edge of my bed, kick off my shoes, and look out of the window, focusing on nothing. I know that to undress I'll have to stand up again, so I put it off for a minute.

To the southeast, the first stars are punching through the day. In an hour there will be thousands of them, but now there are only three. It's been dry, and warm, and the air inside is stale. I reach over and – because I'm not entirely committed to the movement – budge the sash window up about an inch before the effort becomes overwhelming.

The breeze is brief, verdant, and carries notes; something that might be a flute is playing something that might be music. With tremendous effort I prop myself up on my elbows and shuffle forward so that I can see over the window ledge.

The house five down has a well-kept garden. This is not to say the garden is neat – creepers and vines run rampant, hedges are untrimmed, and colossal ferns loll over a seldom-cut lawn. But these plants are barriers that preserve the privacy of the house's owner. From any side the garden is entirely concealed, but not from above.

Before I was born – at least before I can remember – work was already well advanced on the garden. The house is much the same as the others, though it has been fitted with patio doors that are currently open. Strings of fairy lights wind their way through the foliage, illuminating flowers in rainbow colours, and marking a path to a large painted wood summer house, where candles are burning and a portable speaker plays.

In the garden, Mrs. Olafsson dances naked. Her huge breasts swing in an arc of their own making, disrupting the leaps of distant marsupials, and baring no resemblance to what the rest of her body is doing. In a sense, she is communing with nature in much the same way her ancestors did thousands of years ago; celebrating the power of woman as a primal force ranked equal with air, earth, water, and fire. Though her dance of choice is the hustle, popularised by the nineteen seventy-five song of the same name.

I can't actually tell for sure that it is Mrs. Olafsson at this distance. I couldn't testify to it in court. It could be any fifty-something overweight lady Mrs. Olafsson's height dancing naked in Mrs. Olafsson's garden at nine o'clock on a Thursday evening. If this were a detective story, it's at this point where a callow and naïve youth would be deceived – *she had a twin sister?!* This would take the reader on a misleading path and enable a brilliant late twist. *Mrs. Olafsson was the ghost all along?* Or less a less *Scooby Doo* ending.

Anyway, it's her.

As she dances, a second figure emerges from the house. They're turned slightly away from me, heading from the patio doors to the summer house, so I can't see their face, and much of their body is obscured by hedge. In each hand they carry a martini glass and when Mrs. Olafsson urges them to dance, they make a reasonable attempt – though the hustle is a full-body endeavour and there's no way to do it justice and also preserve the integrity of a brace of cocktails.

Then he half turns and he is obviously a man. Obviously. I've never seen a penis in real life, even at a distance. It's altogether a messier thing than the ones I've seen online, and as overgrown as Mrs. Olafsson's garden. But it's weirdly transfixing, and all I register about the man before he turns away again is that he has a beard. And a lot of back hair.

As *The Hustle* ends, Mrs. Olafsson follows him into the summer house to the sounds of Maria Muldaur's *Midnight at The Oasis*, which is muted when she pulls the doors closed behind her. There aren't any curtains on the glass doors, but even if I were inclined to watch what happens next, the angle is wrong.

Is it unusual for a former acolyte to take a lover? I have never thought to ask this question. Mum has never had boyfriends, but if I'd thought about that at all, I'd kind of assumed that was because of me. But the idea that all the ladies of the island are having secret affairs is impractical – for a start, there are ten women on the island for every man.

Some of this is for the obvious reasons: women live longer than men; the sacrifice is always a man. Most of it is because the women of Ensay do not raise sons. My mum says that hundreds of years ago baby boys were thrown into the sea. Now they are adopted. Any woman would know that her son would eventually be selected by an acolyte.

But we are still here: there is a continuing supply of daughters. Logically, there must be ongoing access to men – at least by the younger residents. I imagine Mr. Jones piloting his boat to the mainland with a cargo of painted women, running it aground in the Glasgow docklands and letting nature take its course.

This idea is so shocking that I find the energy to take off all my clothes. I judge that insulation, music, and distance are covering all the sounds Mrs. Olafsson and her rugged gentleman friend might be making, so I decide to sleep with the window open.

* * *

Tonight's special is fish. Though fish is what we have every Friday, so it's not *that* special. To be fair to Mrs. Alexander, she does vary the specific fish based on whatever the cheapest local catch is. This morning Mr. MacGregor landed an unreasonable number of halibut, so this evening it will be served in a cream sauce, tomorrow it will be available fried in breadcrumbs, and anything that remains will be back as a special on Sunday in the fish curry.

Mrs. Alexander's doughty right arm whisks in a bowl held under her left. The sauce is threatening to split and she is red faced and furious. I am boiling potatoes in one pot and peas in another; this masterful multitasking I manage to make seem simple by not involving myself in the process at all.

"Potatoes?" Mrs. Alexander asks.

I plunge a fork into the boiling water and judge the potato's readiness by its give. "Two minutes."

"Plates."

I put two plates in our arranged position. The specific two-square feet of work surface serves as both the area where the food is assembled, and the pass – where it waits to be taken out to diners. Mrs. Alexander does not acknowledge that the plates have been put into position, or that I have done anything at all. Her focus is on whisking.

"Mrs. Alexander," I say, "have you ever taken a lover?"

"No, Eleanor, I've never taken a lover," she replies automatically. She is used to these kinds of questions and, to be honest, has very little time for me. Only after she processes what she's been asked does her beating slow and she asks, "Have I what?"

"A lover. Have you ever taken a lover?"

"What kind of a question is that?" One she has no interest in answering it seems. I press on.

"I mean after you were an acolyte you lived on the mainland for years, didn't you?" I know this is true. "You must have had admirers."

She puffs in annoyance. "Well, when I was young, I had boyfriends, and there was even a man I thought I might marry, but – no – I wouldn't say I'd ever *taken a lover.*"

"Is that semantics or is there a real difference? You've had other sexual partners?"

"I don't think this is an appropriate conversation. These are the sort of things a girl discusses with her friends."

"Yes, but I don't actually have any friends, Mrs. Alexander. I know you don't like me very much. Still, I would appreciate some simple answers to simple questions, since at school we're taught to respect the experiences of our elders and be open about our questions about sex, and acknowledge our sexual identity. And if it makes you slightly uncomfortable, then maybe that's a good thing because sometimes discomfort is a sign of personal growth."

She slows, then stops whisking entirely. Her eyes are wide, but her expression is not her normal dismissive superiority. She is surprised.

She asks, "Eleanor, wherever did you get the idea that I don't like you?"

"Oh. Well." There is an abundance of evidence, but if I provide all of it, she likely will not provide any answers at all. "You always leave right after you finish work. You're very strict about starting and finishing on time. You never have any small talk before, during, or after. We barely speak in sentences. And you never come in for tea in the afternoon."

"I see." She seems taken aback by this list, then puts down the bowl and turns to face me, all business. The sauce, which had consumed her for the previous five minutes, is now doing whatever it likes. "Ask me anything you want."

"Tell me something."

"That's your question?"

"I don't know where to start. Tell me something. Anything. Tell me about the first man you met after you left the island."

"Hmm. The first one. Well, he wasn't a man. He was a boy. I was eighteen and so was he. I'd left to study catering at a college. This was all very new back then. This was sixty-two, or thereabouts. Colleges hadn't been taking girls for long and women didn't work in restaurant kitchens. Domestic cooks were women, professional chefs were men. But I was a feminist, and I'd decided that there was nothing I couldn't do."

"Was the boy in your class?"

"No. One had to maintain a professional distance. If we were going to work together every day, I couldn't have them knowing what my knickers were like. And if one found out, they'd all know. No, my boy was a grocer – or, rather, he was the son of a grocer, and his dad had the contract to supply all the fruit and veg for the college."

"Did he ask you out?"

"He did not." She clasps her hands under her bosom and lengthens her neck slightly. She is still red-faced, but some memory shines through from fifty years before. "I asked *him* out. Showed him who was boss. We went to see *Lawrence of Arabia* in the Odeon, Leicester Square, then I took him back to my room and let him have his way with me."

"Missus Alexander!"

"Although if I'm honest it was more the other way around."

I've already done a *Missus Alexander* and have no other exclamation at hand.

"Plate up those two and let's get them out," she says, a head nod to the fish in the stainless-steel skillet. We execute this with military precision; I scoop the potatoes into place, she adds a sprinkle of parsley and a scraping of butter. I move the fish over; she applies the sauce – which she has successfully reconstituted. I put the peas on the plate – and that's it, there's nothing that happens to the peas.

I shuttle the plates out and bring back a few empties and a dessert order.

"What happened to him?" I ask, keen to take advantage of Mrs. Alexander's unexpected glasnost after so many years of taciturnity.

"I think if we had been born a hundred years before then, we would still be together. He was a simple boy who wanted simple things. He asked me to marry him and I said no. That was that."

"You didn't want to marry him?"

"I didn't want to marry anyone. It's a ridiculous thing. Virginia Woolf said a woman should have her own room and her own money—" It's a misquote, but I let it pass. "—and that's what I wanted. Financial and social independence. The ability – not just the right – to choose who I associated with, where I went, whether I had children and when."

"You couldn't do that and get married? We need a sticky toffee pudding with cream, and a cranachan."

"Marriage is a compromise," she says, taking one of the pre-made puddings in plastic pots out of the fridge and popping it in the microwave. "I was eighteen years old, full of piss and vinegar, and in no mood to compromise with anyone. I hadn't gone all the way from Ensay to London just to become a grocer's wife."

"Did you want to be a chef?"

"I was a chef – later. I was the first woman to be sous chef at the Savoy Grill in nineteen-seventy."

"I didn't know that."

"Not many people do," she says and she puffs air up to her rosy forehead to cool herself. "Probably nobody at all, now."

"Did you like it?"

"Did I like it? To be an artisan of high skill, to cook at one of the finest restaurants in the world, and to be regularly manhandled by a skilled labourer – that was the twentieth-century feminist ideal. I think the two years I worked there were the happiest in my life."

The microwave pings, she takes the pot out and upturns it onto a plate. It is a steamed pudding with a thick layer of dark brown syrup on top that begins to roll down the sides, a tiny, toffee volcano. My mum makes a few every day; cake is not something she ever delegates to Mrs. Alexander, or me.

I prepare the cranachan while Mrs. Alexander puts the finishing touches to the pudding, then I take those out and come back with more plates and an order for two starters, another halibut, and a chicken Balmoral. Mrs. Alexander checks the time and states *they're very late to be starting dinner*, but begins work automatically.

"Why did you stop working there?"

"Well, I fell in love." This simple phrase seems to convey a hundred emotions. I had not thought Mrs. Alexander was built for love – or even like.

I ask, "With the skilled labourer?"

"Billy – William. He was a kind man. He loved me for a long time before I loved him back. I put him off the idea of marrying me from the very beginning. *I am not the marrying kind* – I told him that. He didn't mind. And *I am certainly not having children.* He didn't mind that either, so he said. But then of course things happen, and when I became pregnant it felt like the most normal thing in the world.

"Four months in, I got the sack and that was that. I never worked in a proper restaurant again. To start with, the times never made sense for looking after William – that's my boy's name, William. Then later, well, I suppose they thought I was too old for it. They never said that, of course, but that was why."

"You weren't happy with Billy?"

"Oh, sweetheart, I can't believe I never even said. Isn't that the strangest thing? Billy died. He was hit by a car coming home from work one night. We never found out who did it. William was only three months old when it happened, and he doesn't remember anything about his dad.

"My mother had died the year the before. And when she died my sister went to live in Canada, so I had no family left on Ensay. I had to raise him by myself. And as Billy and I weren't married there was nothing due me from his pension."

I want to hug Mrs. Alexander. I want to be able to hug her.

"Still, he grew up to be a good man – and if a mother can say that then she can hold her head up anywhere. He lives in Australia now. He has three children and the oldest one is getting married in November."

"Are you going over for the wedding?"

"I am," she says, and she leans in slightly as if to confide a secret. "They're flying me over *business class.*" She nods knowingly and I make an appropriately impressed face.

We finish the starters, then I bring back more plates and another order for dessert – just one, a sticky toffee pudding; Mrs. Wolanski is not hungry.

"Did you ever have a boyfriend after you came back?"

"To Ensay? Ha! There's hardly much to choose from. No, I only came back because I was finished with all that. That's why all the old women come back here, if they ever leave. There needs to be a phrase for being broken-hearted past mending, and tired of it too."

"Heartsick?" I suggest.

"That's what brings them all back in the end. The ache of it. Pain makes you long for home, whatever your home was. Even to a tiny island in the least accessible part of nowhere."

Mrs. Alexander is wonderfully quick with a knife. She cuts a pocket into a chicken breast faster than I could butter toast. In a small pan she cooks off a tablespoon of haggis and stuffs it into the cavity, then fries the whole thing. It's a whisky sauce for the chicken, with potatoes and carrots.

Then we repeat the process with the fish, the potatoes, the peas, and the cream sauce – which is splitting again and sorely testing Mrs. Alexander's patience.

"But there must be some women on the island who still…."

"Take a lover?" she suggests. "Oh, this is what all your questioning was aiming at?"

"How does it happen?"

"How does what happen?"

"Well. There aren't many men here. At least there aren't *enough* men here. They can't all fancy Mister Murdoch."

"I don't think even Missus Murdoch fancies Mister Murdoch."

"Missus Alexander!"

"Oh, come on. You don't think she's painting all those people with their clothes off because of artistic integrity? The woman's rabid. Foaming. She needs a rugby team or an old washing machine, and she won't be happy until she gets one or the other. But she's buttoned it all up and called it something else and she won't be told."

She puts another sticky toffee pudding in the microwave.

I ask, "But how does everyone else do it? I mean . . . where do babies come from when there are no men?"

She nods: the question which had seemed socially awkward is actually technical simple.

"It's easy enough to plan a week in Spain, and a single woman attracts attention everywhere she goes. You've that to look forward to. There are romances, of course, and some women move away and come back when it all falls apart, bringing a child or three with her. But I understand that the internet makes it easy to have your itches scratched. Two people exchange photographs then meet up at a hotel somewhere. Usually Glasgow—" I knew it! "—because bed and breakfasts in the islands are nearly always run by terrible gossips."

"Does everyone know?"

"I can't say what everyone knows, but I know everyone does it."

"Not everyone. I mean you didn't."

"I was a special case."

"And I know my mum hasn't had a boyfriend."

"Oh, do you now?" Mrs. Alexander scoffs. "Well, *maybe* she hasn't, but your mother keeps secrets much better than Missus Brown does, and more of them too, I wouldn't be surprised."

"What does that mean?"

"I made my peace with that a long time ago," she says, and pushes plates towards me. "Chicken Balmoral and halibut in cream sauce – let's get them out."

I do as I am told. In the restaurant only three tables are still occupied. One couple is spinning out their desserts with the second half of their bottle of wine. Mr. Wolanski smiles at me while he waits patiently for his pudding. My mum steps in to clear the third table of its finished starters as I bring in the mains. We've rushed this a bit, but Mrs. Alexander will be gone in three minutes, so the other American couple were only barely served at all.

My mum hostesses. She seats people, makes small talk, gives sight-seeing advice, takes orders, and judges the exact right time to offer people more alcohol. She watches me place the plates on the table and I am sure she can read this evening's conversation from my face. Even if she can't, the fact that I suspect she might be able to, must make me seem suspicious. I try not to dawdle, but she's catching me for a conversation.

"This is my daughter, Eleanor," she says, introducing me to the unnamed Americans.

"Good evening, Eleanor," says the man. He has an extraordinarily deep voice which, in only those few words, manages to become monotonous.

"How are you today?" asks the woman. I assume from her question that my mum has already indicated I'm some kind of social spastic.

"I'm very well, thank you for asking. Are you enjoying your stay?"

"Very much so," says the man. "You have a very beautiful country."

"Oh, it's gorgeous," she says.

"Thank you," my mum replies, as if the appearance of Scotland has anything to do with us. It's pure coincidence that either of us should be here, and it all looked this way before we arrived. *I love your mountains – oh, thanks, I put them up myself just last week; they came flat pack and all the instructions were in Swedish.*

People think it's good to have a sense of pride in their country, but I've only ever seen pictures of Holyrood Palace and I didn't think it was all that great. If the border had been drawn three hundred miles to the south, I'd be expected to be proud of Cardiff, and I've never been there either. At least Americans can claim their ancestors murdered their aboriginal peoples and stole their country – or bought it.

You have a magnificent Louisiana – it's so nice of you to say; I traded Napoleon for it: he got six live chickens and a painting of a woman with her boobs out, I got half-a-

million square miles of swamp and infinite crawdads.

He continues, "It reminds me of the coast of Maine. Have you ever been to Maine?"

My mum replies, "We've never had the pleasure."

"This is very much like the coast of Maine," he assures us.

"It was nice to meet you both," I say, and excuse myself with a smile, taking the plates back to the kitchen.

"She's a good worker," he says to my mum. The door swings closed and if she replies anything to this slave-owner praise, I do not hear her.

The kitchen is empty, save for a sticky toffee pudding which has been plated and sits next to a ceramic pot of single cream. It is one minute past eight. If the Americans want anything for dessert, I'll have to cope with it myself.

The dishwasher is already full and chugging through whatever black box process goes on in there to clean things. Is it full of water? Like, all the way full? I go to the sink to add to the small stack of plates I've already piled there.

She is on the floor.

I hear the sound of cutlery bouncing away and plates breaking. I do not see them smash. I do not feel them leave my hands, though I know this has happened.

Her legs are folded underneath her, as if she fell straight down and slumped backwards. Her mouth hangs open and her eyes stare straight upwards. Her face had been red all evening, now it is pale. A sheen of sweat is still visible on her forehead. There is no blood.

It seems that, at any moment, she might clear her throat with a cough and stand up again. This is only a still image of a woman alive, and in any single picture anyone might appear to have died.

I feel as if there is someone else in the room with us – with me and the body of Mrs. Alexander. A presence draws close for a moment, and then departs, taking all warmth with it.

Her expression is difficult to describe. Is it pained? Is it confused? It's possible that I have never experienced what Mrs. Alexander was feeling at that moment, and I have no reference. It's possible that the muscles of her face have relaxed into an expression that means nothing; conveys no information at all.

A hand touches my arm. I scream and the hand withdraws instantly.

"It's okay," my mum says. She touches me more tentatively – and this is worse. Anything uncertain is worse. The tickling sensation of fingers is a cutting edge. I shove her away, but she persists, and – remembering me – grabs me and holds me tightly against her.

She turns me so that I'm not looking directly at Mrs. Alexander, and she whispers vague cooing noises.

There is a body in the room. A woman I have known all my life is dead.

I am being *held*. Yet what makes my skin crawl — what fills me with weird alarms in my stomach and on every inch of exposed skin, is the bare two-square feet of countertop.

Mr. Wolanski's sticky toffee pudding is gone.

5

Mrs. Olafsson tuts as she drapes a tea towel over Mrs. Alexander's face. I think the towel is probably not clean, and I am unsure whether this is the most- or least-important thing in the world at this moment. I say nothing.

"Very unfortunate," she says to my mum.

"Right in the middle of the season," my mum replies.

"Of course," says Mrs. Olafsson. "Did you find her?"

"No, Eleanor found her."

"And how are you, Eleanor?"

I can't make eye contact with her, but I believe she attributes this to shock rather than the memory of her naked tribute to disco. I probably am in shock. Does realising you're in shock make you not in shock? Or does that only work with dreams?

I can't frame anything coherent or useful to say, so I stare at the tiles immediately in front of me. Mrs. Olafsson strokes my head.

"It's a terrible thing," says Mrs. Olafsson, then to my mum asks, "You've sent for Missus Douglas?"

My mum nods.

There is a protocol that ensures a controlled spread of information. Mrs. Douglas is telephoned first. Then Mrs. Crevinge — at sixty-four the oldest serving senior sister and therefore the second-most senior. Then Mrs. Olafsson — who is formally allowed to deputise for Mrs. Douglas, though I cannot recall a single occasion on which she actually has. And finally Mrs. Brown. Of course, Mrs. Brown will already know the news by the time she receives the call, because Mrs. Crevinge is a gossip, but it is Mrs. Brown's job to put a notice on the community message board at the post office.

"There will be nothing for it until tomorrow night," says Mrs. Olafsson.

"I can't keep her in the kitchen," my mum says. "I've got to do the breakfasts, and until tomorrow afternoon the hotel is fully booked."

"Does anyone at the hotel know?"

"No – and that is hardly the point."

"You could put her in your laundry room."

"Missus Olafsson, I am not keeping a corpse in or near my kitchen."

"Well, Missus Carlyle, you can't put her out in the street in a black bin liner."

"But if she had died at the back door." My mum leaves this suggestion to hang in the air.

If one of us dies, the body cannot leave the house it is in until it is going to its final resting place. Normally, this means the person stays in their own home, rather than going to a funeral parlour or a morgue somewhere else – the island doesn't have either of these. Occasionally, someone dies in someone else's house, and can become an unwelcome guest for several days.

Strictly speaking, we believe in leaving the dead where they fall. Rearranging Mrs. Alexander's legs and arms to a *more comfortable* pose would be highly taboo. People die on the toilet, and that's where they stay until arrangements can be made. An understanding neighbour – or a bucket – is always useful on Ensay.

But our custom has been somewhat moderated by tourism. Now it is accepted that if someone dies outside, then they can be taken home or to some other convenient location. This was already normal practice by the time I was born. Covering the face is less acceptable, but it happens, and is pretty normal if there are children present.

To my mum's statement on the location of Mrs. Alexander's death, Mrs. Olafsson replies, "She died where she died." In saying this she has not said anything. My mum straightens, having been leaning on the counter by the body.

My mum says, "I know my views are traditional . . . but I am not unsympathetic to reinterpretation."

"Missus Carlyle," Mrs. Olafsson replies, arching an eyebrow wryly, "if you aren't a traditionalist, who is? I don't believe anyone is more committed than you to our ideals, or more conservative in their application. But I assume that you are not about to try and trade me your vote – *in five years* – for anything at all, least of all the convenience of cooked breakfasts tomorrow."

The silence is charged and gives Mrs. Olafsson all the answer she needs.

But it is Mrs. Olafsson who speaks, saying, "Take her feet. Eleanor and I will take her under the arms."

"What?" I ask. I both heard her and understood; the sound was reflexive – I might as well have said *durr*.

"If it's to be done, we'll have no witnesses – only conspirators. If there are witnesses, then the thing cannot happen at all."

My mum nods and says, "Eleanor, come on, quickly."

"What will Missus Douglas—"

Mrs. Olafsson cuts me off, saying, "Nothing if we act now. Hurry."

There is something alive about Mrs. Alexander's dead body. She is still warm to the touch, though not where she has been in contact with the floor. An end to circulation means she is graduating to room temperature – though this is not really one thing and does not happen at one rate. The air is warm and still, while the tiles are cold and sit directly on the old foundations of the house; they leech the heat out of her faster and pass this into the ground.

I grab her right arm. Mrs. Olafsson takes the left. My mum adjusts the legs and hooks one hand around the back of each of her knees. Mrs. Alexander's weight is significant. She is easily the largest of us by any measure, and we move in short, urgent steps while negotiating turns as if we were relocating a not-necessarily-valuable piano.

The laundry room is nearly filled by the two large metal boxes – a washing machine and a tumble dryer, both industrial in scale. A plastic hose, perhaps eight inches wide and kept open by internal metal hoops, leads from the dryer to a hole cut in the wall above head height. The dryer will often belch steam into the garden behind the house all day in summer. In winter, when there aren't any tourists staying with us, it only goes on once a week, and the steam cools quickly, falling over the garden as a localised fog.

My mum lowers Mrs. Alexander's legs and for a moment her body is almost standing, then Mrs. Olafsson and I droop her over the washing machine. My mum turns the Chubb lock on the back door and pulls it open, then braces it with her foot.

A rectangle of evening peers into the house. Half purple sky, its amber notes in long decline. Half grey grass, its colours stripped by the approach of night.

This is as close as I ever come to outside. I could extend my arm and my fingertips would cross the threshold of the house. I could take one step forward and though my feet would still be on the laundry room floor, my hand would move from the protection of the black guttering to under the naked sky. Fourteen billion lightyears of space would weigh down on me. Ever so much heavier than a leaping marsupial.

At any moment the door might swing closed, somehow catch my arm, and drag me. Then I'd be outside completely. This is the worst of it by far: I am certain, in every way it is possible to be certain, that once I cross that threshold, I will never be able to come back inside. The thought fills my head and overflows into my body like ice water. My shoulder twitches, my hands shake, I am losing my sense of time as I am overwhelmed by panic. Why isn't anyone doing something?

"Mum," I manage to say.

"I know," she says and I feel her hand bunch the clothes in the small of my back, and she pulls me.

I step away from the door and she takes my place. Together she and Mrs. Olafsson negotiate the last few steps. Mrs. Alexander's feet cross the threshold onto the back step.

"We have to drop her," Mrs. Olafsson says.

"Why?"

"On three," she says, not explaining. My mum follows Mrs. Olafsson's example: they hoist Mrs. Alexander's body to a close-to-standing position. The *one two* is followed by the outline of the woman descending, and a *three*, and an unpleasant wet thud as she hits the garden path face first. "All right. Now, walk around her. Do what you would do if you found her here and you were checking if she were alive."

My mum obliges, having understood the plan.

"She still has the tea towel on her face," I say.

Mrs. Olafsson lifts Mrs. Alexander's head by the hair and slips the towel out. I can see it's been marked by dirt and blood. She comes back into the house and puts it into the bin, taking time to ensure that it is buried in with other items rather than left on top.

My mum closes the back door and we are all in the kitchen again. Mrs. Olafsson scans the floor for any sign that Mrs. Alexander died there, but finds none. A look of satisfaction crosses Mrs. Olafsson's face and I finally feel relief, but also exhilaration. And a disgust that twists in my stomach and climbs up my spine with creeping claws. Each emotion passes over me in waves until I can't distinguish one from the other.

I have broken a taboo.

A woman is dead.

I am not *safe*.

A clock somewhere in the house chimes one bright note, and at the same moment we all turn to watch as the door to the hallway opens.

It is nine o'clock and Mrs. Douglas has removed her makeup for the night. Her facial features are less distinct than they usually are, her cheeks flatter against her face, her mouth only a line of peach-coloured skin. She saves her only smile for me, and even this is tight-lipped; an unfortunate-circumstances smile, acknowledging me and my lesser status in the group.

She wears a plain grey dress that comes to her knees and a pair of even darker grey court shoes. They *clack* against the tiles as she crosses the room. No coat. No purse. She has come here expeditiously, if from somewhat farther than Mrs. Olafsson.

She used to be headteacher at a secondary school – somewhere, I don't know where – and even though she's been back on Ensay for thirty years, she still carries an air of unimpeachable authority; the power of an adult amongst children. Mrs. Douglas is not only our spiritual leader in the sense of advising and leading by example; she is the one who will be told if we misbehave, and the one who will punish us.

"How are you, Eleanor?"

I realise this is not the generic question I have become so used to. She is not making conversation. "I spoke to her five minutes before she died." The statement comes out of me suddenly and I put my hand to my face to cover the reaction that follows it. I feel hot tears against my fingers. Until now, I had not cried.

"I understand," she says, though she makes no gesture to physically comfort me. To my mum and Mrs. Olafsson she asks, "Where is the body?"

"This way," my mum says and takes her through to the laundry room. Mrs. Olafsson follows her and pulls the door to the laundry room closed behind her. Because the laundry room is so small, the door swings into the kitchen, and to stop it interfering with anything going on in the kitchen, it opens towards the back of the house.

Hanging on the back of the door, where it always is, is a beige-coloured knitted cardigan. Mrs. Alexander knitted it herself. She took it off to work, but if she had left the kitchen to go home at the end of her shift, she would have put it on again.

My tears stop and I feel my whole body break out in sweat.

Maybe she was so unwell that she forgot – is that believable? Or is that the kind of inconsistency that would make Mrs. Douglas suspicious? If I move the cardigan, would the absence be noticed later? If the cardigan is found – having been moved – then that must expose the lie.

I cross the room quickly, snatch the cardigan from the hook and shove it into the cupboard under the sink.

I am committed. If the cardigan is never found, what difference does it make? Who would even look for it?

I go back to where I was standing and wait and resist the temptation to move the cardigan again – somewhere more discrete, to the bin, to my room, or back to the hook on the door of the laundry room. It's only the number of options that prevent me from doing anything at all.

"She's let herself become a dreadful size," says Mrs. Douglas, returning to the kitchen.

"She was the best cook on the island," my mum says. "She'll be impossible to replace."

Mrs. Douglas only replies, "I'll have Missus Gough bring her wheelbarrow around."

"There must be someone else," says Mrs. Olafsson, it is a reference to the irreplaceability of Mrs. Alexander and not a slight to the wheelbarrow of Mrs. Gough.

"If there were anyone other than Missus Alexander, don't you think I wouldn't have hired them instead?" my mum says.

"I don't think that's an appropriate topic for discussion," says Mrs. Douglas, "given the circumstances."

"Yes, well," says Mrs. Olafsson. "Couldn't you bring someone in from the mainland?"

"For fourteen hours a week spread over seven nights?" The question is rhetorical. We all know the answer – anyone who could take the job would need to live on the island.

"Perhaps we can talk about this in the morning," says Mrs. Douglas. "Obviously there will be a short-term interruption anyway. It will have our full attention once we've dealt with our sister."

"Yes," says my mum. "Of course."

"Who found the body?" Mrs. Douglas asks. The person who finds the body has responsibility for it – she was always going to ask.

"I found her," I said.

"You did?"

"Yes, Missus Douglas."

"You found her at the back door?"

"Yes, Missus Douglas," I say and swallow. This is the first time I have ever lied to Mrs. Douglas. In fact, it's the first time I've ever known anyone to lie to Mrs. Douglas. My mum and Mrs. Olafsson are standing slightly behind her, so she cannot see their faces. Mrs. Olafsson seems unconcerned, while my mum's lips are held tightly shut.

Mrs. Douglas tilts her head to the side, perhaps by only one degree. It is the most subtle sign. She doesn't blink. I can feel her watching me for every reaction. Then she says, "You found her body *outside*?"

"I didn't go outside," I blurt, as if going outside were prohibited. "I was inside when I saw her."

Mrs. Douglas turns and walks to the back door of the house. *Clack, clack, clack.* She unlocks the door and pulls it open all the way. The soles of Mrs. Alexander's shoes are visible on the step, her ankles just in sight, her tights are tan coloured.

The door sits entirely still at the full extent of its hinges, then Mrs. Douglas releases it. I can't breathe. I daren't. And I see it start – the door, which is as old as the house and hangs fractionally askew on its ancient hinges, begins to fall slowly closed. It hits the jam smoothly, but with enough weight that the lock clicks back.

The door closes itself.

She touches the locking mechanism idly as if thinking about something else. She faces me again; the question is in her eyes.

I say, "I saw her from the kitchen window. I was about to do the last few dishes." My mum has already removed the broken plates from the floor; all that remain are a few unwashed items that still sit by the sink. The dishwasher still hums through its cycle.

I have no idea whether Mrs. Alexander's body is visible from the kitchen window or not. Mrs. Douglas and I are around the same height – she could expose the lie in an instant by taking three steps to the side. My face must be the colour of blood.

"She's still only fifteen," says my mum.

"There's no question of her lighting Missus Alexander's funeral pyre," says Mrs. Olafsson. "Even if she could leave the house."

On the western edge of the island there is the rocky cliff that looks uninterrupted on the sea. There we make the sacrifice. There we burn all our dead. I have never seen it with my own eyes. I have no memories of being outside of this house, and I have not crossed any of its thresholds since I was three years old.

"You think not?" says Mrs. Douglas. The question is addressed to Mrs. Olafsson, but she is looking directly at me. "You don't think since Eleanor is the person she regarded most highly that an exception should be made? It has been done before."

"At the request of the child."

"And would Eleanor not request? Why would we not ask the child what she wants?"

This is also a rhetorical question. Mrs. Douglas is making a point about Mrs. Olafsson bringing me to the meeting. She is making it clear to Mrs. Olafsson that she can always subject her to embarrassment if she chooses. And by asking for the impossible, she is telling all of us that she knows exactly what we've done.

My hands are clasped, but in the periphery of my vision I see them start to shake. I fight the urge to look away from Mrs. Douglas.

The response that comes out of my mouth is, "Missus Alexander spoke highly of me?"

Something changes in her face. Her focus has turned inward. What was it? What unexpected power did that question have?

"Of course she did," my mum says. "Everyone on the island loves you."

Ignoring the fact that this statement can't possibly be true, I say, "Missus Douglas said *the person she regarded most highly*. Why would she think better of me than any of you?"

"People are people," says Mrs. Olafsson. "We all recognise different qualities in each other."

I say, "With Missus Alexander dead and Mister Maxwell in Ireland, there are four-hundred-and-five people on this island. Until tonight, I don't think Missus Alexander and I had ever had a proper conversation. Why would she think better of me than any of her sisters?"

"What did you have a conversation about?" my mum asks.

"Missus Alexander was a very practical woman who took pride everything she did," says Mrs. Douglas, cutting across the previous question. She doesn't necessarily mean her remark as a compliment; we regard pride as wicked. "Perhaps Missus Olafsson is correct and she recognised a similar trait in you. Both hard working. Both strong willed. And both given to too much pride." She delivers this reproof with the same tone she had previously reserved for Mrs. Olafsson. I have gone too far. But her response to my question was an *attack* intended to put me back in my place and the fact that it makes me afraid also makes me angry.

"Respectfully, Missus Douglas," I say, careful to ensure my own tone is unchanged. "She didn't just like *me*. She must also have held opinions about all of *you*. And you must have known what those opinions were, and they must have bothered you, otherwise you would never have mentioned them."

My mum freezes completely. I even register surprise on Mrs. Olafsson's face, though this is an out-of-focus shape somewhere behind Mrs. Douglas. Is she angry as she takes a step towards me? She surely wouldn't hit me, though if she did nobody would stop her. But her expression never wavers. She is not a monster: she is the administrator of rules.

"Yes, Eleanor. She did have opinions. She did not always regard any of us as highly as she should have. But there are some things which are our private business. Do you expect the high priestess to explain such things to you? Do you expect me to explain these to anyone?"

"No, Missus Douglas."

"Then you will not ask those questions again."

"No, Missus Douglas."

Turning to my mum, she says, "Govern the child."

My mum looks at her feet.

Mrs. Olafsson asks, "Would you like me to handle the arrangements for Missus Alexander?"

"No. Missus Carlyle will make all the arrangements. And she'll do it without any help from you, Missus Olafsson. Without any help from anyone else. It's a long way to push a wheelbarrow and it will give her time to reflect on the evils of the world."

"Missus Douglas," Mrs. Olafsson's tone is an incredulous protest, "under the circumstances—"

"I'll do it," my mum says.

"You—" Mrs. Olafsson begins and is silenced.

"She'll do it," says Mrs. Douglas, and there is no room for objection.

Mrs. Olafsson lets that sit for a moment and asks, in a telephone voice, "May I at least assist with gathering wood?"

Mrs. Douglas replies, "Yes, I was about to suggest you do. If that's all? I'll bid you goodnight."

We harmoniously respond with our *goodnight Missus Douglas*es and she takes her leave of us – as unassuming an exit as it was an entrance. When they are confident she is gone, my mum exhales, and Mrs. Olafsson pats her shoulder in sympathy.

They look at each other and then at me. Their expressions are completely different and both are unreadable. We are bound together now by the secret of Mrs. Alexander's death, but I'll learn nothing else tonight about the secrets she kept in life.

"Is there anything I can do for the burning?" I ask. I think I say this mostly because I need to fill the silence.

"You heard Missus Douglas," is all my mum says.

"You are not very good at telling lies, Eleanor," says Mrs. Olafsson, her cheeky grin reasserting itself. "I think it would be best if you stayed honest from now on."

* * *

You made us feel at home – this is a lie – *from the moment we arrived. We very much enjoyed our stay* – this is also a lie – *and we only wish we had more time to see your beautiful country. Mr. & Mrs. Wolanski.* The message is from Mr. Wolanski; had his wife written it she would probably have used a special ink mixed from her blood, sweat, and tears. And her message would also have been less friendly.

Our hotel guest book is a large leather-bound register that sits open at reception. A pen rests in the place where it falls open, as an invitation to contribute. The edges of its pages are watermarked with swirls of coloured ink – a security measure intended for financial accounts; looking at the edges would immediately reveal if and where any pages had been removed.

The first entry is from the autumn of fifteen years ago, then there is a gap until the spring of the following year. The way my mum tells the story, a guest at the hotel purchased the book from an amateur bookbinder and, after deciding their airline would charge them a fortune in overweight fees, they gifted it to us.

The cottage bookbinding industry on Ensay folded almost immediately. Though the book itself is beautiful, it's for a niche market that's entirely different than the one we attract.

Mr. Wolanski's message is the most recent entry, and while the guest book isn't a complete record of everyone who's stayed here over the years, the pages are bowed by thousands of entries. With just over three sides of paper left, the book will be finished in the coming weeks.

I am alone. The knowledge of this is difficult to define, but I am so accustomed to the sounds of creaking floorboards, doors opening and closing, and muted conversations, that when these things are absent the silence is thick. It is not unusual for my mum to leave me – as she has today, to take care of Mrs. Alexander. But I cannot recall the last time the hotel was empty in summer.

It is a bright, warm Saturday morning and the air smells more of grass than sea as it breezes through the open front door.

Of course, the hotel is never really empty. I am always here.

Agoraphobia. This is the catchall term for what I have. My condition is *acute and unusual*. It is not a fear of open spaces or the sky – people believe that. When they ask how I am, they ask as if I'm scared of clouds or allergic to sunlight. *Are you still frightened that clouds will eat you today, Eleanor? Do you still think the sun will make your head catch fire, Eleanor?* Nobody actually says that, but I know it's what they're thinking. As if what I have is so completely different from their experience of the world that I must be broken. Simple. Special. Touched. Unlike.

Weird.

Agoraphobia is the first fear inside the oldest and most primitive part of the brain: a genetic gift from some small, burrowing antecedent that lived a short, terrified existence. But that fear is why the rest of the brain is still here. It is the fear that there is no escape.

I am afraid that I will step outside of the house and that door will slam closed and will never open again. I am afraid that someone will grab me and never let me go. I am afraid of the same unnamed expectation that we are all afraid of – when we watch horror films, when we are aware that we are alone.

"You look—" I start so suddenly that my feet leave the ground "—a million miles away."

Mr. Jones has come through the open front door. He is a broad, round man of around sixty with a grey-brown beard that descends to the middle of his chest. He wears degrees of oilskin depending on the weather – in summer it is only trousers with elasticated ankles; by January there are layers on every part of him.

"I'm sorry," he says. "I didn't mean to startle you."

"Nothing to apologise for, Mister Jones, I was only daydreaming."

"Pleasant daydreams, I hope." He has a lilting Welsh voice which is very pleasant to listen to, but does make him sound a little stupid, as if at the beginning of every sentence he's just rediscovered the same forgotten pound coin in his pocket.

"I was just thinking we'll need to replace our guest book." I thumb the pages to draw his attention away from my face. I've always found Mr. Jones's pale blue eyes to be very disconcerting; completely different from those of anyone else I've ever met. Though he has always been unfailingly kind to me.

"Oh yes, so I see. That looks like Missus Winthrop's work. You'll never get another one like that – seeing as she's been dead for ten years, maybe fifteen."

"I don't remember Missus Winthrop."

"Well, you wouldn't. She would have been a very old lady and you would have been only a little girl when she died. Pneumonia. Went in the winter. I'll keep an eye out for a replacement, if you like?"

"A replacement old lady with pneumonia?"

"Ha – very good." This is a lie: it's only casual, over-the-counter banter. "Where do you want these?"

He gestures to the cardboard tray under his arm. Two dozen glass jam jars are pressed tight together by a layer of tough, transparent plastic. I take them – they aren't that heavy.

"I was sorry to hear about Mrs. Alexander," he says with the formality of remorse. "I understand you found the body."

"I did."

"I've seen a couple of dead people. The thing I never get over is how strange someone's face looks once they've died. I mean, they look normal, but they also look a little confused."

"Yes, that was how she looked."

"Oh?"

"Exactly like that."

"But—" his bushy brows crouch around his pale blue eyes "—how would you know that?"

I tense. I was supposed to have seen her from the window. She was face down. They took her away by the back garden gate, which is closer to her house anyway. I would never have seen her expression after she was dead. The details of Mrs. Alexander's death would be the only thing discussed today, and would be discussed by everyone on the island.

"You're right, of course," I say. "I must have imagined it."

He moves his eyebrows again, like roiling storm clouds or the marshalling of armies on the field. One goes up, the other doesn't. He leans over the counter.

"I understand," he says.

Does he understand? How could he understand? I say nothing while I consider the implications of this. Mr. Jones is – of course – a man. Men are always outsiders on Ensay; even those who have lived here for most of their lives. They live by our laws. Though they are forbidden from participating, they must *know* about the sacrifices. Despite these things, they aren't like us. Perhaps Mr. Jones thinks we are ridiculous, or insane.

He leans back and says, "She was very fond of you, you know."

"People keep saying that," I tell him automatically, my frustration cutting through my reticence. "I feel like I barely knew her."

"That was her way. Not everyone is lovey-dovey all the time. I spoke to Missus Alexander three weeks ago – no, tell a lie, it was two weeks ago – and the only thing she talked about was you and how your cooking was coming on. She was very proud of you. I'd wager she thought of you as her apprentice. Missus Alexander took that kind of thing very seriously."

"But . . . She never said *anything*."

"Well, some people are sayers and some are doers. She did things. Do you know how to gut, bone, and fillet a whole salmon?"

"Everyone knows how to do that."

He laughs. "Oh, no they don't. I reckon you know how to butcher every part of a cow too? And a lamb? You can spatchcock a chicken? Am I right?"

The word *spatchcock* is absurd, but nevertheless, I nod.

"She's given you a hundred different skills, I've no doubt. She did that instead of telling you. I reckon—" he's in a reckoning mood "—that she's been like your fairy godmother all these years."

I have seen many interpretations of a fairy godmother and Mrs. Alexander corresponded with none of them. Half the time we were together we worked in silence.

"But why?"

"Well, isn't it enough just to do a kindness to someone?" Mr. Jones replies expansively, becoming temporarily huge, like a dog shaking itself dry. "Does there have to be a reason?"

But there is a reason. There *was* a reason. Mrs. Douglas knew what it was – they all knew what it was. I stop myself from asking Mr. Jones. Perhaps I don't believe he would know, if it were a secret Mrs. Douglas wouldn't broach. More than this, it feels wrong to talk about it with an outsider.

I say, "I suppose," though I doubt Mr. Jones is persuaded that I am persuaded. "Do you want the money for the jars now?"

"I'll settle up with your mum tomorrow. I've got a load of wood coming in this afternoon with four bottles of paraffin, two musicians, and a tray of macaroni pies."

"It's very good of Mr. Urquhart to have the live music on such short notice."

"Oh, he's happy to do it. Well, I don't know that he's *happy* to do anything, but him and your mum split this kind of thing. Need to keep the tourists distracted for a couple of hours, nothing better than a bit of clapping and fiddling."

"They'll be sharing a double bed tonight; you can tell them that. It's all we have free."

"Oh, they might not even bother you if the drink keeps flowing. In any case, if they need it, they'll be too drunk to care."

"And one of the guests is a vegan."

"Your mum already told me. That's why I ordered the macaroni pies instead of the meat ones." He taps the side of his nose in acknowledgement of his own genius.

I say, "The pie crust might be made with lard and the macaroni will certainly be made with cheese."

"I should hope so," he replies, looking shocked. "Otherwise, we'll be sending them back."

"Vegans can't eat either of those."

"No?"

"I'm afraid not. No animal products at all. I think their shoes are made from bananas."

"Well," he says, this being the most extraordinary thing he's ever had to deal with. "I'll phone the baker and see if they can do something vegan then."

"Let me know if they're stumped. I can make a salad sandwich."

"Salad and what?"

"Just that: salad and sandwich."

"That hardly seems like a meal. Macaroni pies, ham salad sandwiches without ham, and ready salted peanuts aren't going to keep them fed for longer than a night. Any word on who's replacing Mrs. Alexander?"

6

I am replacing Mrs. Alexander. At least on a temporary basis. My mum has not agreed to this – yet – but there's no one else and she'll have to.

By seven thirty all the tourists still on the island have been funnelled into the Wee Man and the folk music duo of Angus and Duncan have started a fiddle and accordion extravaganza that will carry on long after everyone has lost enthusiasm for it.

A slow parade begins soon after, weaving its way along the dirt path from the other Mrs. Mackenzie's house, around the island and out of sight. From my vantage point in my room, I cannot see any faces – everyone has their back to me and does not turn around – but I know the earlier black cloaks belong to the older sisters. They are, though one would not say this, mostly dark grey. It's difficult to keep a black cloak truly black, even if it only needs cleaning once a year.

Those joining later, closer to eight o'clock, are younger and walk faster. Because of the staggered departure, all the sisters will get there at around the same time. But the ceremony begins when Mrs. Douglas arrives, and she is the last to leave, taking a stately pace to ensure she is both anticipated and uninterrupted by latecomers. If it were a moonless midnight on the winter solstice, Mrs. Douglas's cape would be visible – as dark as a lighthouse is bright.

As I watch her, I can't help but feel as if I am the one being observed. That she knows. And if she were to turn around just as she crests the final rise, she would look straight into my eyes. I withdraw a pace from the window so that I am entirely in darkness, though this does not make me feel less exposed.

But she does not turn, and while she may know she is being watched, it is only because she is our high priestess, and she is always being looked to as an example of proper conduct.

There is nothing to do in the hotel tonight. Even though my mum has been gone all day, with no dinner to prepare, I was able to change and wash sheets and run the tearoom by myself. I don't feel tired so much as sick – an undiagnosable expectation sets all my nerves on edge. I don't know when this began, or what will make it stop, so I have been busy with a dozen little tasks which I needed to do more than they needed doing.

Ironing tablecloths. Inventory of dry goods. Topping up the salt in the dishwasher. Refresh strategic positions of rat poison – we don't have rats and I intend to keep it that way. Check that I haven't accidentally topped up the dishwasher with rat poison.

All that's left to do is wait. I know the ceremony is short – we're not sentimental about our dead. My mum has been vague when describing it, but there have been dozens of burnings that I can remember. In winter they are defined by the red glow that creeps into the sky, reflecting on dust and fog. In summer, no light is visible from the village – by eleven, when the sky gets really dark, the pyre has died down. What I'm watching for is the smoke.

It starts as a thin wisp, something easy to miss if it's not being looked for; a dark grey curl like a few strands of hair, twirling in space and rising and dispersing. In a minute it becomes a solid pillar and is no longer spiralling; it flows upwards: an inversion of water pouring out of a bottle.

I wonder if it is possible to smell the smoke, but for exactly that reason I've closed all the windows, and in any case, I can see the wind is taking it out over the grey-blue sea – a happy accident and the opposite of what normally happens.

We are all made of stars. This is true, in a sense. Everything that isn't pure hydrogen is in the same sense made of stars. Dirt is made of stars. I'm not sure about water – oxygen is formed in stars, but I'm not sure if it's the only way. Is all oxygen *made* by plants actually just *released* from molecules containing oxygen? This is a question that would have come up in an ordinary science class. I know for a fact that all calcium is made in stars and that – unlike hydrogen and oxygen – calcium is very difficult to burn.

Mrs. Alexander's bones will not burn in an outdoor pyre. Crematoriums have special furnaces which reach heats well above what we can achieve on Ensay with a wood pile and accelerant. And they can't burn bones either. When people on the mainland get the ashes of their relatives, it's only because their bones have been smashed in a machine like a tumble dryer full of metal balls. The reason it's still possible to dig up the bones of people who died thousands of years ago is because bones are nearly indestructible.

We have our own way of dealing with them.

When the fire has died down – probably tomorrow, but sometimes not until the day after – my mum will pick through the ashes and recover everything that's left of Mrs. Alexander. Her bones are thrown into the sea, and time does the rest. Sand grinds them. Rocks smash them. It's possible some residue of the person is still on them, and the crabs eat that.

My mum tells me that on calm days she's seen the bottom of the sea by the cliff, and the sand there was white as snow.

What I feel is anxiety. This isn't unusual. I am often separate from events on the island and waiting for something to happen – or for something to stop happening so people can come back and tell me about it. What I imagine is spectacular, though I know the reality will be mundane.

I go back down stairs to reception and dust things that aren't really in need of dusting, but the routine helps the minutes slip by and it's nine o'clock when I check the time again, then nine thirty-five.

A shape catches my eye – a figure in a black cloak, walking down the street. I glance at them for only a second and can't tell who it is. Though it is a sign that the formal ceremony has concluded. Most people don't stay for longer than is required of them, though there's an interval of decency where no one wants to be noticed as leaving first. A second and a third hooded figure follow on the heels of the first – again, I have no sense of who these women are.

By ten o'clock I've stopped counting and have run out of things to dust. My mum still isn't back and the first of the tourists could return from the Wee Man at any minute. I am fidgeting uncontrollably; it has turned into pacing from one end of the house to the other.

I don't know why I feel responsible for any of this. So strangers see a procession of black-cloaked women. So we are found to be burning the body of an old woman who died of natural causes. This isn't news. We work so hard to keep what we do private from the rest of the world when they should be grateful for us. They should admire us.

I walk back into the hall to find my mum leaning heavily on Mrs. Olafsson. My mum looks shattered. Her hair is matted with sweat and her hands are filthy from fingertip to wrist. Her eyes are distant and she doesn't register me even though I'm standing six feet in front of her.

"What happened?" I ask.

"What was supposed to," says Mrs. Olafsson. "Let's take her into the kitchen." I move to my mum's left side and we make slow progress, with dragging steps, from the hall to the kitchen table, where we sit her down.

She looks up at me, and for a second, I think she still doesn't recognise me at all. She says, "Water" and I bring her a glass. She lifts it to her lips with both hands, the way a child would.

"What happened to your hands?" I ask.

"A full day of hard labour," says Mrs. Olafsson.

I kneel beside my mum, and when she has sipped as much as she can, I take the glass from her and hold her hands in mine. They are ragged and filthy. The palms are bloody. I can see where a layer of skin has worn through and she hasn't stopped working. Every line is caked with dirt and dried blood.

"The bones will need to be moved, but that doesn't need to be tomorrow," says Mrs. Olafsson. "Perhaps Missus Douglas will have relented in a couple of days and someone else will be allowed to help."

"All because she moved a body?"

I look up at Mrs. Olafsson. She nods. And I realise that she looks tired too. She does not believe that Mrs. Douglas will soften in two days; though whether this lie is for my benefit or hers I can't tell. It has no effect on my mum, whose eyes are heavy; she is not listening to either of us.

"Get her to finish that," I say, and I fill a basin with warm soapy water and bring that and the first aid kit to the table. The sting of the water on her hands seems to bring her back almost immediately.

"Eleanor," my mum says, sounding sleepy and embarrassed, "I can wash my own hands." There is the vaguest and smallest of efforts at defiance, a sort of shrug of dignity, but in that moment, she lacks the strength to lift her hands out of the water.

"Sssh. When was the last time you did the online first aid course for cuts, grazes, and burns? Have you ever? I'll finish this, then you'll go to bed, and I'll handle the breakfasts in the morning."

She does not object again, and though I can feel her discomfort as I massage her wounds clean, she is nodding towards sleep. I pat dry her hands on a clean towel and dot them with antiseptic ointment before bandaging the palms. Her fingers are red raw, but there are only small cuts and burst blisters there – difficult to bandage and for no real benefit.

"I'll get her to bed," I say to Mrs. Olafsson. "Thank you for bringing her home."

"You'll let me know if there's anything I can do."

"She needs rest – and so do you."

Mrs. Olafsson embraces me and it is my turn to give up resistance. I feel like all my nervous energy has washed out into the bowl with the dirt and the blood. She kisses the top of my head, then without another word she takes her leave.

My mum's bedroom is on the first floor, next to the back stairs – directly underneath my bathroom. We manage the stairs together and she undresses to her underwear, then slips under the covers. I fill a glass of water from her ensuite sink and put it on the side table next to her bed, by which point she is already asleep.

I turn off her electric alarm clock at the wall. She has a second, mechanical alarm clock, but she has not wound this today, and it has stopped at five thirty-seven.

I have never seen her so frail, and I don't linger in the room stroking her hair or singing her lullabies. She would not want me to remember her weakness, and when she is well again, she will not thank me for looking after her. I turn out the light, close the door, and put her out of my mind. In a few days this will never have happened, and none of us – me, my mum, anyone – will ever speak about it again.

I am back at reception in time for the first of the trickle of returning guests. They are merry and slightly deaf. We exchange warm regards. I answer questions about breakfast and ferries and airport transfers. I do not have any CDs of the music they heard tonight and I do my best to feel sad about that.

I do not have any CDs of any music at all, because it is the present day and people don't have CDs anymore. They feel sad about this. I remind them that the hotel has WiFi and they can probably find Angus and Duncan online, but it is not the same thing as having a CD.

These conversations take half an hour in total. By the end I tell people we've sold out the CDs, because it's quicker and less depressing for them. They are not surprised we have sold out. Their opinion of the music is very high. Their opinion of the salad sandwich is also high. It is late though, and they are tired. I agree that it has been a long day.

It is eleven o'clock. I hear silence. I can't say whether some oppressive noise has just stopped, or if I have only now started listening after the barrage of drunken small talk. There is no music from the Wee Man. I have made a mental tally of our guests and all have gone upstairs to bed. The occasional creaking floorboard notwithstanding, the hotel is still and for the first time today I think it is getting cold.

My mum would already have locked the front door. Tonight, it is still open, and a pair of moths dance around the porch light, threatening to fly inside and become a temporary nuisance. Once inside they would quickly fly towards the blue light of the bug zapper by the front door. It's there in case of midges, but it takes out its fair share of moths too.

I kick out the doorstop, but unlike the back door, the front remains in the same place until I push against it.

The door closing is interrupted by a shoe inserted into the gap.

"Easy," says a voice. "That's my best left foot."

I pull the door open again and step back.

Their hair is a little too long and sweat has formed it into long points that stick to their faces and necks. Each wears a plaid shirt open over a band t-shirt. They are also physically similar, being tall and lean, with shoulders disproportionately broader than the rest of their bodies. At twenty, maybe twenty-one, they are not quite fully grown. It is unlikely that Angus and Duncan have performed tonight in fancy dress – each pretending to be the other – though both would have been convincing.

It's been a year since they were last performing at the hotel. It takes me a moment to remember which is which – though, of course, Duncan carries a violin case and an overnight bag, while Angus is wearing his accordion across his back like a rucksack.

"All right," says Duncan, not moving his shoe. "Can we come in?"

"That's not little Eleanor, is it?" Angus asks.

"Yes, and yes," I say, and wave them in. With the instruments there's no room for me, so I leave the door open and walk back into the hall.

"Jesus, but you've grown, haven't you?" Angus says. It is not really a question and even if it were, I wouldn't know how to respond to it. He breaks eye contact with me to stare at my chest, then rolls his gaze farther down me and back up again. He grins at me – a stupid, drunk and lop-sided smile. He has very white teeth. And his breath smells of whisky.

Duncan rolls his eyes, as if to say something and nothing, and sways a little on his feet.

"They all enjoyed themselves," I say, attempting to change the subject. "There was an old lady with a ten-pound note burning a hole in her purse – she would have loved a CD."

"We've sold out," Duncan says, a little apologetic, a little smug. "We're getting more printed. It's cheaper if we do the new album and the last one at the same time. If you get her address, we'll send her a signed one – no charge for the postage."

"Oh," I say, actually impressed. "You've sold crap to old women before."

"She's not a fan, Angus." As Duncan says this he turns idly around, peering at the art on the walls.

"I think she likes me fine," says Angus, who is still smirking.

"I'll let her know to catch you at breakfast tomorrow," I say to Angus.

Angus has taken hold of my arms. It is not a grab. If I think about it, I suppose it happened quite slowly. Did he run his fingers over my forearms before he closed them, lightly, just above my elbows? I can't remember. He's taken a step towards me and I feel the edge of the reception desk against my back.

He tilts his head and closes his eyes the instant before his lips connect with mine. I discover in that moment that he also smokes. He is sweaty, and smoky, and . . . whisky.

Kissing is curious. A sensation of touch, pressure, heat – a part of me I never think about being cold is suddenly hot. And there is a counterpoint I can't easily define as external sensation; it comes from within me; it is directionless and shapeless, without quantity or unit of measurement. The part of him that reached out to me has a partner, and it reaches out for him – crudely, entirely without my consent.

His lips are moving against mine, not aggressively, not eating my face. He is not trying to pry my mouth open with his tongue. There is something chaste and innocent about his mouth and I feel like I could indefinitely endure the touch and the smell and, creeping in now, the first taste of him. And he would give me hours and years of his attention in just this way, letting me become warm and soft, and melt into the shape of him.

His mouth is an expert communicator, and is giving me an entirely different message than the erection that is poking my hip.

The palms of my hands are flat against his stomach, as if I were trying to separate us, though I'm not sure that I am. At least I'm not doing it successfully.

What Angus is doing is kissing *me* – I am certain. Angus has gears, and he has picked one. He has decided that I am innocent and he is kissing me the way he has decided innocent girls should be kissed. Expect to be kissed. Want to be kissed.

For my part I am sure that I have remained statue still. When he stops kissing me – and I have no idea how long the age of kissing lasted – I make a very small sound. A rush of air because I hadn't been breathing. Nothing else. It was *not* a moan.

He puts his hand on my cheek. The change makes me aware that my mouth is very slightly open – so I close it, my teeth making the loudest clicking noise ever recorded: an expletive in Dolphinese.

Angus whispers to me, "You're a real girl, you know?"

I do not know what he means, but I don't like it. And I also do. This was basically assault. I should slap him. I'm pretty sure Hollywood and feminism would expect me to slap him. But just like being kissed in the first place, the slapping issue is taken out of my control.

Duncan has Angus by the arm and has pulled him back.

"Easy, mate," says Angus. "I was only giving her a little kiss."

"Are you fucking mad?" Duncan says, and shakes his friend fiercely. "Have you forgotten where we are? We're on *Ensay*. And she's their fucking queen."

Angus is too drunk to sober up, but he turns suddenly pale. The last thing I need tonight is for him to throw up on hall floor.

"I didn't mean anything by it," Angus says.

"It's fine," I say.

"I was just saying you were a pretty girl and—"

"It's *fine*."

"—I've had too much to drink, and I'm stupid, and I didn't mean anything by it."

"Angus, shut up," I say. I retrieve the last room key from behind the counter and push it into Duncan's hand. "You did mean something by it and you know you did, and if you're going to mean something then mean it. But whatever. Go to bed. Everything is fine. It's a small double, so you can leave the instruments down here if you'd prefer."

Duncan says, "I'd rather—"

I say, "Then go to bed. Quickly. Quietly."

Duncan more or less drags Angus away. His previous overconfidence has been replaced by a kind of childish shock and the more his face turns imploringly apologetic, the more I am repulsed by him.

Today has been too long, and tomorrow will be here any minute. I'm thankful that I'm tired, otherwise anxiety would never let me sleep.

When I go to close the front door, something stops me.

There are no streetlights on the island. By tradition, people who live on the High Street leave their lights on if there is an event planned for the evening, but every one is out now. A parallelogram of yellow light spills out of our doorway, the only illumination in a night finally turned dark and a sky rendered starless by a rolling bank of cloud.

The wind has shifted. There's going to be a summer storm – a big one.

And at the edge of the light, on the opposite side of the cobbled street, I see a colour darker than black.

Fatigue overrides any emotion; I respond to the stimulus automatically, saying, "Goodnight, Missus Douglas."

I do not see her face under the hood, though her voice is clear. She says, "Goodnight, Eleanor," but does not move away.

When the door is closed, I watch an unfamiliar hand tremble as it turns the key in the lock, as if it were not my own hand, as if it belonged to someone who had reason to be afraid.

7

The first sound I hear is the rain on the slates. Persistent yet somehow variable, the character of an individual raindrop is briefly audible amongst a million others as it splatters out of existence, becoming part of the flow that runs along the gutters and gurgles down the drainpipes.

Grey light coming through every window tells the future of this Sunday. It is going to rain heavily and it is not going to stop. Neither is this a coquettish day; it will not temporarily lighten, bat its eyes, suggest that it might be persuaded to turn sunny and resume the downpour. No. Not today. This is a rainy day with conviction. In it for the long haul. It's planning to be here tomorrow morning, knocking on my window, and doing the weather equivalent of a *here's Johnny*.

I listen to the rain until the alarm on my iPad goes off. The part of the day that belongs to me is over. Even my showering belongs to someone else.

I have to cover breakfast. We have three check outs today and those rooms need to be turned around for the three check ins tomorrow. I have to do dinner tonight – fish curry special, obviously.

And it's raining. The guests who aren't leaving are going to need lunch and a constant supply of drinks and charming banter. I am not in the mood for charming banter. I'm possibly not even in the mood for tea.

I stand with my hands in my hair as a crash helmet of strawberry-scented foam dissolves and runs down my face.

Mrs. Douglas *saw* Angus kiss me.

I know she saw.

What I don't know is what she'll do.

Sausages.

And bacon. Black pudding. Haggis. Potato scones. I already smell like black pudding and nobody's come down for breakfast yet.

I push the bain-marie back into the oven, check there's hot water and cold milk and sliced bread, and *come on*, it was only a kiss.

Are kisses forbidden? I ask myself this as if the answer can be logically determined. Either they are or they aren't – and I don't know which it is.

The guests are subdued by headaches and unsettled stomachs. The first couple both opt for porridge, then I have to make porridge, but I find my rhythm somewhere around table three. He's already got oilskins on and a bag of photographic equipment sits on the chair opposite him. A twitcher. They're not put off by the weather, and he eats a full breakfast, knowing he'll be out all day and won't get anything else.

Angus and Duncan descend last and sit quietest. They mumble their thanks for the food. Angus keeps his eyes on the tablecloth; on a blank patch between the toast rack and the bottle of HP Sauce. Does he think I'm going to do something? Does he think we're in the same position? Or that the ground is going to open underneath him alone?

I feel both repulsed by his cowardice and slighted by his silence. I make a point of not saying goodbye when they leave the restaurant. They drop their room key at reception immediately afterward, choosing to huddle near the harbour in whatever cover they can find for half an hour before the ferry leaves.

That was the boy who gave me my first kiss.

If I end up getting punished for *him*, I will be furious.

On completing the checkouts of the three couples, I glance at the guestbook. I am hoping more than expecting its few remaining inches will contain some personal message for me – a repudiation of recent actions, its tone optimistic; inappropriate, bordering on evidentiary. That kind of ardent foolishness is something I feel I could easily forgive – but its absence cements my opinion of Angus. I stomp upstairs to strip bedding from the recently vacated rooms; the smell of their previous occupants and the humidity of morning showers make each one its own jungle, so when I have finished cleaning and stuffing the washing machine with sheets, I am scarlet, heart racing and doused in other people's sweat.

I allow myself two minutes in the laundry room to cry, and I make excellent use of this time.

In the kitchen I splash cold water onto my face and adjust my hair using my reflection in the rain-streaked window. I could not possibly face a real mirror.

It's gone ten o'clock and – experience being any guide – I would guess the first requests for fluids will come soon. The television is on in the lounge and someone is going through the contents of our bookshelves with great distaste. If I can hear books two rooms away then they're being treated too roughly.

The door to the back stair opens. My mum is pushing it with her elbow.

THE WICKER MAN PRESERVATION SOCIETY

I move to help her but she is already through.

There are grey circles around her eyes. She smiles at me, close-lipped but warm, an expression which is an effort.

"You should go back to bed," I say.

"I can't sleep. I haven't been in bed that long in months." She moves without her usual grace to the table and sits down, a fleeting expression disclosing some internal discomfort. "Did you turn off my alarm?"

"Yes. Can I get you a tea?"

"Sit down."

I do as I am bid. My hands fall naturally into my lap. With only a few feet between us, can she tell I've been crying?

"I haven't seen Missus Olafsson," I say. "I thought she might have called on you this morning."

"There's no need."

"Was she helpful to you yesterday?"

"She was. As much as she was allowed to be."

"How do your hands feel?"

"They are painful. But it is useful pain."

"Useful?" She nods. "What do you mean?"

"Pain removes everything that isn't pain; it makes things clear. If you stub your toe, it's because you weren't thinking about where you were going or what you were doing. The pain reminds you." She is watching me. I can feel her. My eyes search across the tabletop for a point of focus.

I say, "She shouldn't have punished you."

"What?" She sounds surprised. "No; that's entirely wrong. I broke our rules. It can't have been easy for Missus Douglas to have given me such harsh treatment."

"It can't have been easy for *her*?"

"If she were to let me go without punishment, I wouldn't respect her. I wouldn't respect the sisters. In fact, if my respect hadn't wavered in the first place, I would never have considered moving Missus Alexander. She saw straight through to my wickedness and she knew what to do about it."

She does not often speak this way. I can tell that her faith has been refuelled. She is burning with it.

"I cooked the breakfasts," I say, trying to change the subject. "Three, five, six, and ten are ready. I was about to start on something for lunch."

"No, I can do that."

"You should go back to bed; I can do it for a day."

"No, Eleanor. You've done these things because you love me, and because you believed they needed to be done. Just like I believed Missus Alexander needed to be moved. That was vanity. Faith is the only necessity. Caring for me was also a wicked kindness. It was weakness that made me accept it and you only offered it in ignorance."

"I'm sorry."

"I know you are. I know you love me. And I know that you can be a good girl. You can find your way to faith and duty."

"I have—"

"But I have to punish you."

"Mum—"

"Missus Douglas has made it clear to me—"

"Mum, please—"

"You will accept it." She grabs me by my right arm – so suddenly that I can't move, so fiercely that I am frozen – and she stands up, pulling me from my chair.

I am screaming. I can feel the air leaving my lungs. My mouth is open and wordless. But I can't hear the sound I make, or what my mother is saying. I try to pry her fingers off me and push one of her hands away, but she strikes me with the back of her hand across my face. I had not won; she latches back on again, drags me to the stair door, and pushes her way through.

I fight her on every step and she beats me. At the first floor landing she hits me three times, four – five – as hard as she can, I think. And she is stronger than I am. The impact spins my head, she hits the back, I lose my footing, she drags me up again, if only to give my body resistance: to make the blows have impact.

I am present. I have heard that some people leave their bodies during trauma, but this is my face, and my mother's hand, and our blood. She bleeds too, as she strikes me, those wounds on her hands opening like stigmata that shine red through the loosening bandages, and by a flicker of the first-floor light I see the pain on her face – and the fury. She looks like an angel.

And I hit her back. My free arm flailing and spinning; punching her in the stomach and the side. I do nothing to shield my face – I'll point the wounds at her; they'll be my weapons to punish her long after my punishment is over.

She seizes a fist of my hair and kicks out my leg. This time when I fall, I move forward, and she drags me by the hair. I bounce on the stone steps. I put my fingers in the cracks in the walls, but they are not enough; they have never been enough to hold me in place; they have never been enough to stop me from falling.

On the top step she forces me down to the stone so that I feel tiny traces of dirt embed in my cheek. I will leave a blood smear on this stone again. She puts her knee in my back while her hands search my pockets, easily discovering the long key. She drags me into my room and backs suddenly away – she knows me – as I leap to my feet and smash my fists against the closed door.

The lock clicks.

I can hear again. I am no longer screaming. The sound I make is unnameable; it is the anguish of a dead dog: the self-pity of spite: anger's unwinding: the sawing of offal in a living thing: grief at the death of grief: all nonewhich words from neverplaces: guttural crying that sputum strewen, wrecks a ruin of dignity: soft crying: nothing at all.

I lie down next to the door; an animal waiting for its owner to return.

* * *

How is your condition?

This is the question they ask me every day. They are not asking if that morning I woke up to discover that I was a different person; in the night having sloughed off my mind like a snake sheds skin. They are asking if today I feel the madness more strongly than usual.

They have heard the screams before, of course. Everyone on Ensay has heard me screaming at one time. They are accustomed. An unruly child that has to be beaten to be kept in line – surely this is the least surprising thing about our village.

And the guests? Well, the guests are all informed on check in that I am prone to outbursts. That I cannot be controlled. That they may hear sounds in the night. But that I am not dangerous to any of them. Most of them leave having seen or heard none of this, the rest pretending that they have not.

It will be longer this time.

When I was six years old my mum locked me in my room from six in the evening until six in the morning. I have never asked her whether she thought six, six, and six seemed like natural justice; whether there was a harmony – or an onomatopoeia – to my punishment. At six I did not have the language to describe the idea, and by seven there had been other punishments; so many that asking about any one would be ridiculous.

Twelve hours is a long time for a six-year-old to be confined, and though it was symbolic (I slept through it), the symbolism was powerful. When she opened the door, I was repentant, though I don't now recall what I did to earn the punishment, which perhaps means I never knew.

My mum's gift, along with cakes and jam, has been to perfectly judge how much willpower I have, and to go beyond it. By the time I had turned ten my confinement periods ran to two days. I never know how long I will be kept, though at twelve I assumed I could easily amuse myself for any amount of time. I had the internet. I had exercise. I had painting. I had a guitar I was certainly going to learn to play eventually.

She had food.

I would not encourage anyone to go three days without food. A person in a safe environment with access to water can live for two months, provided all they're expected to do is lie down or sit. Gandhi – at the age of seventy-four – went on hunger strike for three weeks. I have never been at any risk of dying. But three days alone, with no food, is tough.

Eating is a habit, I think, like smoking. After a couple of hours, the chemicals in the human body start going haywire. Anyone who has skipped two meals in a day has been lightheaded and unable to concentrate. The second day is awful. The stomach and bowels are completely empty – the average Scottish person will never know what this feels like unless they are very sick; because surely even poor people can afford to eat every other day. But despite the pangs and pains, a person is still a person. Society is not three-square meals away from anarchy – perhaps it's eight. Whatever the number is, it happens on the third day. I will not be myself anymore, and the vows I make now, lying on the wooden boards, will be forgotten.

Knowing everything that awaits me, I am full of anger rather than fear. She will not open the door until she has broken me, and so I resolve, as I have resolved before, to die in this room. I will not be broken again.

But this time it will be longer.

On the other side of the door, I hear her move away, treading slowly down the stairs.

Overhead the rain still gurgles through the guttering.

8

In the morning I run a bath. I will lose enthusiasm for bathing before I am released, so I can reduce my overall discomfort by getting it done now. Prisons, concentration camps, army barracks – films set anywhere with limitations on where people can go always include tips and tricks from an old hand, a trustee, or someone who was shipped in six weeks prior. I am a veteran and have learned my own tricks. Should I find myself confined with a fresh-faced, cock-sure young ragamuffin I would tell share my hard-won wisdom with them like cigarettes – one at a time and infrequently.

Do not eat toothpaste. Even if the warnings about swallowing fluoride aren't true, there's no nutritional benefit. But have a supply of toothpaste, because sometimes a clean mouth feels nice, especially once the ketosis breath starts. My liver will break down my fat into an acid that can be used like glucose – I will, not to be too dramatic, begin to eat myself.

Do have a deep and broad collection of music.

It's not enough to simply have lots of music, one must possess variation. Every song released in the last year will sound a lot like every other song released in the last year. The song writers, musicians, and producers grew up with the same influences, experienced the same present political realities, and understood words in much the same way. When Bob Dylan said that the times were *a-changing* it was because everyone believed they were; Zimmy wasn't doing prophecy, he was doing reportage. When the Rolling Stones said that a man couldn't be a man because he *doesn't smoke the same cigarettes as me*, it reflected a mainstream growth in awareness of a Madison Avenue powerhouse that was already in every aspect of life, and by nineteen sixty-five had transformed Madison Avenue from a street name to a geographically non-specific concept.

Music is a chronicle of thought and language. Nobody said *daddio* in ninety-eight. There is a rise and fall of *yeah, yeah, yeah*s which peaks somewhere before disco, and a definite long-term decline of *doo-wops* culled by an unknown extinction-level event that took place in the late fifties. There is precisely one *goo goo g'joob* in the whole of music – in the Beatles nineteen sixty-seven song *I Am the Walrus*. Lionel Richie's *All Night Long* in nineteen eighty-three includes the line *tom bo li de se de moi ya – yeah, jumbo jumbo*, a stream of nonsense words that conveyed the idea of an African heritage without being encumbered by meaning.

It was only when Paul Simon released *Graceland* in nineteen eighty-six that a real African language entered European and American pop charts. *Diamonds on the Soles of her Shoes* opens with *o kodwa you zo-nge li-sa namhlange*. I have no idea what that means. I don't think Paul Simon knows what that means. But a music collection without *Walrus*, *Long* and *Diamonds* doesn't have *goo goo tom bo li de se de moi ya o kodwa you zo-nge*. On a long enough playlist, the absence of those words is like a diet deficient in vitamin k.

The size of a music collection is also necessary to avoid too much of a good thing. It's possible to overdose on early Elton John – back to backing *Your Song, Mona Lisas and Mad Hatters*, and *Tiny Dancer* is a cry for help. The recommended daily amount of Frank Sinatra is one song per day, with no repeats in a month. And Van Morrison's *Moondance* should be sampled no more frequently than once every six months for maximum effect. I'm not as sure about the dose frequency of Manfred Mann's cover of Bruce Springsteen's *Blinded by the Light* – once a year at least and at most.

I think Paul Gambaccini must have been imprisoned by his mother, with nothing to do but read the publication details of the records he listened to. How else would anyone acquire such an encyclopaedic knowledge of music?

As I walk by a window, I see the other Mrs. Mackenzie in the street. She wears a raincoat with an oversized hood, but her face is tilted upwards; a little oval of cream-coloured skin stands out in the otherwise grey scene. She has been looking into my room. Our eyes meet. It lasts longer than a second; more than the time it takes to realise someone is looking back. I wonder if she actually sees me, or if it is only a shadow she can see behind the glass. Her face has no expression, then her head tilts down again. She moves along the cobbled street and is quickly out of sight.

Do take a bath.

Most calories are used endothermically. Breakfast – used to stop the brain from freezing. Lunch – used to keep blood piping and hot. Dinner – if any meal is staving off gangrene caused by temperature-related reduced circulation, then it's dinner. Those after dinner crisps – they're fuelling the run for the bus, the stair climbing at work, dialling in to the conference call with marketing, thirty minutes of cross-training, the run for the bus, and the sweet lovemaking with any and all significant others. Crisps are important.

Lacking food, it is possible to substitute heat. Or so I say.

The water is around chest high, so I turn off the taps and slide in. From the other room I can hear Fats Domino. *Though we're apart, you're part of me still.* I wet a face cloth and drape this over my face. *For you were my thrill.* My lips sting, my right eye pulses. *On Blueberry Hill.*

Do clean wounds. This is one of those do as I say, not as I do things. Last night I should have washed my face with water, applied TCP to any cuts like my mum showed me, and rubbed *Arnica montana* and *Aloe vera* into any swollen areas. Ice would also be helpful. I am grateful that she doesn't wear rings; there won't be anything that might require stitches.

But I haven't even looked at my face in the mirror, and I don't know what's waiting for me.

I imagine that when I take this facecloth off, my skin will come with it in one contiguous layer, and underneath I will be perfect again.

The song has changed to *Brand New Friend* (nineteen eighty-five, Lloyd Cole and the Commotions' second biggest hit, which peaked at nineteen in the UK singles chart). Their song *Perfect Skin* was the bullseye of meaning the universe was aiming at, but I'll take it; it's close enough.

The facecloth comes away with rust-coloured patches and if I squint there is – with help from the part of my brain that evolved to spot tigers in the forest – the outline of my face. My own Shroud of Turin. I destroy the relic with a dunk into the water, and dab at the parts of me that hurt most until each contact is clean.

My knees are also bloody from the stairs; one has turned purple and will turn black. Strangely it does not hurt to move, only to touch. I shuffle to a sitting position so that my knees are under the water and I shake them from side to side. This hurts, but it's the kind of pain that feels therapeutic.

A red spot. I'm bleeding into the water. My period is early.

I stare at it, wondering if it's nothing more worrying than stress making it happen, or if something inside me has been damaged.

There was already blood in the water. This feels different. I stand, step out of the bath and grab a tampon from the box under the sink. Plugged, I feel able to dry myself, though I am nostalgic for the barely pink bath I have just left. I have been exiled from the house for my behaviour, and cast out of the bath for being a woman.

Bathe and the world bathes with you, menstruate, and you menstruate alone. Possibly.

I'm clean now. And dry. I must face myself.

* * *

I know what the house sounds like. I know it better than she does – better than anyone else ever could. I know the sound of each door as it opens and closes. I know the stairs like a sequence of musical notes. I can hear the difference between an empty space in the house and one which is occupied by someone standing silently, listening.

I bang my fist on the door.

"I know you're out there! Let me out you fucking bitch!"

She does not speak. The things I shout become less coherent. After a minute of abuse, I fall silent and I hear her move away.

Do not give her the satisfaction. I forgot that one.

* * *

Of course, I could be mad.

It's ten in the evening on Tuesday and I'm not really listening to *Night Fever.*

Do try to sleep as much as possible. I can't say for sure that sleep uses fewer calories than being awake, but it speeds up the experience. I try sleeping in different positions for the novelty of it. Like diving, I award each attempt a difficulty rating. Anything on the bed is never going to have a multiplier higher than three-point one; it's a straight dive from five metres and there's only so much twisting and somersaulting possible in that height. Time is distance divided by gravity. Well, not *divided by*, but certainly reduced by.

On the floor or on the treadmill are slightly more difficult, but they are just other flat surfaces. In the bath, again, slightly trickier. The bath is metal, it has not the least bit of yield, and when the water is out that's very noticeable. Bodyweight rests on bones, and even three hours in the bath leaves me aching.

The highest difficulty I have successfully accomplished is forming a tripod with one of the brick chimneys at my back. I spread my legs and lock my knees so that my weight is pushing down. Despite this, I've found that I'm more likely to be jerked awake by the sensation of falling, rather than tipping over to one side. I once managed twenty minutes sleeping against the chimney, which is gold-medal standard sleeping in Europe. It wouldn't warrant a podium finish in the world championships; not since the Chinese cracked sleeping standing-up, unsupported. *They have robot knees. Their spines have been fused. Every competitor has a cochlea replaced with a spirit level.* We've all heard the stories. Maybe they're true. Personally, Jim, until the urine tests come back positive, I don't think there's anything Team GB can do about it.

Standing-unsupported sleeping is the holy grail. It's an arm stand reverse four somersaults from the ten-metre platform. Maybe unmodified human beings aren't physically able to do it; maybe we have to admit that at the edge of human strength and speed and skill, there is a new frontier of what is possible chemically, mechanically – perhaps even psychically. All I know for sure is that the first person to achieve it in a European competition is going to get a pretty big sponsorship deal from somebody, and a little slice of immortality.

Do come to terms with the inevitability of talking to yourself. Or, if not to yourself, to Jim Moir, the BBC's commentator on all competitive sleeping. *And it's snore, snore, snore!* Classic Jim. Some say he stole that line from Murray Walker, but until the urine tests come back positive, I don't think there's anything Team GB can do about it.

"I'm sitting on my painting stool this time, Jim. Hands resting on my knees. Somewhat slouched. It's a three-point six difficulty and a good showing will put me ahead of the Spaniard, Isabella Siesta. Is it racist, Jim? The word siesta is Spanish, and anyone who thinks sleeping at this level is lazy hasn't seen Isabella's downward dog on incline gravel. That's what's made her one of the top sleepers in the game and I'm taking the challenge seriously. Do I consider her decision to eat a starchy paella twenty minutes before competition to be cheating? No, Jim, it's a time-honoured tradition. The Italians use pasta. The Americans binge on turkey. Britain, as you know, favours mashed potato, and under optimal circumstances, I'd have tatties coming out of my nose by now, but I can't Jim. I can't because I've been locked in the attic by my own mother and I haven't eaten since breakfast on Sunday, and that was only a bit of toast and didn't even have any jam on it. Always a pleasure, Jim. I'll see you on the other side."

* * *

It is still raining. There are cups clinking in the tearoom – and if I can hear the cups over the guttering then someone is being too rough with them. They're proper cups, Jim. Bone china. They won't put up with clinking.

I feel like I have been listening harder than usual, all morning, as if expecting that my mum will come early. It isn't expectation though; it's hope. This is how my resolve collapses. When the iron wall of my anger has weathered, hope grows in the cracks. A most pernicious weed, Jim. Its roots get everywhere.

I am lying on my bed, facing the door, with my iPad in between. It has been playing through my curated playlist for seventy-four hours. I have prepared two-hundred hours of music, and I am confident that I will be free before the end, one way or another. It moves from a crackly old recording of *Anything Goes* (with the original lyrics referencing Anna Sten, Lady Mendl and others whose significance is lost to history) to Imagine Dragons' *Thunder* (a song about becoming famous and being very pleased with oneself, written by someone who hasn't heard the original lyrics to any Cole Porter song).

I hear a noise on the stairs. Footsteps. Heavy footsteps. Then trying to seem quiet. But definitely ascending.

I press pause on the music to listen more carefully.

Having heard music for three days straight, it feels like I have been plunged into water. There is no sound at all. Then the rain sounds like a monsoon, though it is now only a drizzle – like me, the rain has reduced from fury to sullenness.

My finger hovers over the play button. I have imagined the footsteps. I have heard a drum sequence differently.

The door handle turns and the wood bulges in place.

I sit up and stare. The handle turns back.

Nothing.

Did I imagine the handle turning? It wouldn't be the first time I've seen a trick of the light, or a shadow that shifted in place, becoming something from my imagination.

If it happened, it was not my mum. She has the key and would not try to open a door she had locked.

I ease myself off my bed and cross the room, avoiding those floorboards which I know are emotional and prone to outbursts. I kneel down in front of the door.

The keyhole has covers – what might be called escutcheons if they were made of brass, but which are probably just called covers when made of wood and painted to match the door. They keep dust and insects out of the mechanism. As each side moves independently, they also prevent me from seeing out into the stair.

I can hear someone. The sound of their breathing is amplified by the stone staircase, but I think I could hear it anyway – fast and deep, fight-or-flight breathing. It is a man. I am certain it is a man. The sound has bass. There is *a man* sitting on the top step of the stair, probably facing away from the door.

There is only a certain amount of time one can listen to another human being breathe without the act of listening becoming an intrusion. In his shoes, I would find it very embarrassing if someone heard me breathing. If they made judgements about me based on my breathing – like phrenology of the throat; *someone who breathes that way likes goat cheese and is of Slavic descent and wears turquoise.* What if they heard me talking to myself like some kind of maniac, Jim? I agree – just like the twenty-sixteen Rio Olympics all over again. And if manners are for anything, they are for helping other people to avoid embarrassment.

I clear my throat.

"Hello?"

9

He makes a short but nevertheless grotesque sniffing noise and says, "Hello?"

"You can't sit there," I say, confident in my authority even as a prisoner. "This area is off limits to guests."

"Oh," he says. I hear him shuffle in place, probably to face the door.

"There is a guest lounge on the ground floor."

"Do you work here?"

"Yes. Now, off you go."

"What's your name?"

"What's my name?"

"Yes."

"Eleanor . . . Is there anything else I can help you with?"

"I can't really go down to the guest lounge, Eleanor."

"Then you need to go back to your room."

"I definitely can't go back to my room. Have you stayed in one of those rooms? It's all walls everywhere you look."

I am about to tell him that this is how indoors works, and in a thoroughly unsympathetic tone given both my current and long-term circumstances, but a series of facts wave at me urgently. The man is actually a boy. The boy's accent is Irish – not the ridiculous *top of the morning* Irish accent they have in Cork, but a *the Irish are the blacks of Europe, and Dubliners are the blacks of Ireland, and Northside Dubliners are the blacks of Dublin* Irish accent. And the boy sounds like he's trying very hard to conceal that he's been crying.

I ask, "Are you Mister Maxwell's nephew?"

"I suppose," he says, surly, with a teenager's dislike of other people's labels. "How do you know that?"

"I work here."

"As a talking door?"

"What's your name?"

"Connor."

"Connor Maxwell?"

"That's right." His mother's name, not his father's. I've spent enough time around old women to judge that.

"Well, Connor Maxwell, you can't sit on my landing; you're not allowed to be here."

"Can I come in, then?"

"Into my room?" Even if I had the key to open the door, I would only open it to give him a telling off for his impertinence. If this were the fifties – when casual violence between men and women came part-and-parcel with tipping hats, wearing a petticoat, and being permanently office drunk – then I'd slap him. "You may not!"

"So, I can't come in?"

"No."

"Can I sit out here then?"

He has an unflappable and unmovable resistance to being told *no*. On Ensay this is both charming for being rare and dangerous for being stupid.

"Why can't you go downstairs?"

"I can. I'm not a cow; anyone who says otherwise is a liar."

"Why won't—"

"Moo."

"—you . . . Did you just say *moo*?"

"Definitely not."

"You use jokes to avoid answering questions."

"You use doors."

"I use *one* door – and I've answered every question you asked expecting one."

"Sure. Fair play."

"You—"

"He's looking for me."

"Your uncle?"

I think I hear him nod. I get a sense of something ruffling, and his voice sounds slightly different when he says, "He wants to talk. I've had five days of it. He came over and just looked at me, waiting for me to talk. Actually, I've had months of it. When I didn't just pour my heart out, he asked me questions. *How are you? How do you feel? Do you want to talk?* When you're the closest person to someone who's died you become a drain for everyone else's sadness. You need to be unhappy for them, you need to accept their old stories and their loss. You need to stand at the church door and shake hands with strangers. With people you've never so much as heard mentioned before in your whole life. Strangers are always pushing their way into your head when how you feel is none of their business."

"Your mum died."

"You heard too?"

"Sorry. I mean, there's not anything I could do about knowing. I just overheard Mister Maxwell talking to my mum. She owns the hotel. He was booking you a room."

"Yeah. See, I don't want to talk about it anymore."

"That's fine. I understand."

"Do you?"

"I think so. We don't need to talk about anything if you don't want to."

"Thanks, door."

"Do you like Sam Cooke?"

"Can't say I've met him."

"He's up next on this playlist I made. Nineteen sixty-four, *A Change is Gonna Come*. The year after Dylan's *The Times They Are A-Changing*, but—" I stand up, wobble, and retrieve my iPad from the bed.

"But?"

I sit back down, legs crossed, my knees touching the door. "—somehow more honest. Living with discrimination and looking forward. Cooke was talking about an experience of society and civil rights to which Dylan – yes, a Jew, but still – was essentially an observer. And while Dylan was always clever and arrogant – with a kind of spit-in-your-eye cynicism that came from a self-classified outsider privilege – Cooke was mournful and earnest – but then he was ten years older than Dylan when he recorded it, and he'd already buried his first wife and an infant son. It's all the more poignant because he was dead before it was released. Shot and killed in a motel, while naked, some say it was a robbery, some say it was in self-defence."

Connor says, "You're a weird girl, aren't you?"

I always thought it was aliens – Jim's a conspiracy theorist; he thinks the French tried to fake their own moon landing in fifty-nine, and would have gotten away with it too, if it hadn't been for all the smoking and visible lingerie.

I skip the rest of *Thunder* and press play.

* * *

Mr. Maxwell moved to Ensay for business. He might be the only man to have done so in a hundred years.

I can't actually see it from my window – the other building he put up. It's just beyond the curve of the coast, in a cove gouged out by a trickle of water from a natural spring high on the far side of the island. The spring was converted into the village's mains supply in the late forties.

There's a footpath from the town – better laid than the High Street – which goes to his distillery, and only there. I think that everyone who visits

Ensay walks out to look at it – even Mrs. Wolanski. It is our sole attraction and, I am told, there are actual tours of the building which end in the tasting of samples of excellent whisky. None of that whisky comes from the distillery on Ensay, however.

Whisky is made with time. There are hundreds of barrels of crystal-clear grain alcohol from our island ageing in a warehouse on the Clyde. Mr. Maxwell owns shares in two other distilleries, and they have joint storage and bottling facilities in an industrial estate. But the one on our island is his alone; his special project. The first palatable whisky from here is still six years away.

If one were to believe the pamphlet that sits on the desk in our reception, then the island was home to a small distillery a century and a half before. A trio of brothers – McArdle – made whisky and shipped it along the coast in small boats. They travelled by the light of the moon and slipped under the noses of the customs agents.

It's a swashbuckling and highly romanticised version of events. The McArdles were cutthroats who made what might charitably be described as moonshine, in a career lasting perhaps six months. One was shot by a customs agent. One was captured and hanged in Ayr. The last made his way back to Ensay – where we burned him alive and tore down the little shack they had built.

Lately I have wondered whether there was a reason for the brothers McArdle being on Ensay – one different than either version of events suggests. The guided tour of the distillery tells the not uncommon tale of smugglers making fast money. We say they were nothing more than petty thieves and murderers whose three-day-old whisky was just a sideline to take the edge off a nightmare lifestyle. Both concur that they were not welcome on the island.

But there weren't any package holidays to Spain in the nineteenth century. Did the sisters bring the men to Ensay under a white flag? Was that flag actually a petticoat thrown to the winds? Mrs. Alexander's answers relied on modern convenience, but the reality of previous centuries must have been more rugged, more improvised and opportunistic. How much choice did the acolyte have then? More than now? Less?

The more I think about it, the more the island of Ensay seems impossible under its own laws. We should not exist. My thoughts are hazy, but there is something I know I can't see; there is a secret behind the secrets we keep; there is a deep untruth which is concealed by my mum, by Mrs. Douglas, perhaps by everyone.

But what is there that would frighten an island of women whose Purpose is to bring about the end of the world?

It's five in the morning and a curious half-light clothes the town in whiter shades. The slates are greying. The rain has stopped. The grass and the ground are turning to dryer hues. Where I can see the water's outline of sand, it pales, becoming yellow where it had been beige. Even the sea has changed colour – a translucent blue where there had been steel.

I started painting at – I don't remember what time; it was dark. There is a bruise on my jaw, at the corner of my mouth, which has blossomed into a bouquet of yellows and purples. I study it in a hand mirror and attempt to replicate it on canvas.

Skin is not one colour. It isn't a question of where light falls and doesn't. In places the skin is plump pink with blood, in others it is grey blue. So, the colour of skin is not something that can come out of a tube; it has to be mixed from other colours. Raw umber, a dab of flesh tint, vermillion, ultramarine, Sorrento yellow, a spot of titanium white because I'm an indoor girl, then moving outwards with more of each and adding in tints of other colours as necessary. Cadmium red for the swell of the cheeks. Viridian green for the shadows around my hair.

Physical injury makes me look distinguished. The swelling has mostly subsided – swelling looks bad on everyone. What remains is as close as I am likely to get to a war wound. It feels better to think of myself as a warrior who has been defeated, than as child who has been beaten. It is not true, but the self-deception will get me to tomorrow.

Traditionally, portraits are lies. People spread maps and finger globes to demonstrate their mastery of the world. Everyone exists in Vaseline focus; appearing younger and more diffuse; a memory of themselves. Even as I paint the damages, I am claiming them as assets. My own fierce eyes stare at me. What challenge have I put there? Who is it for?

A pang of hunger stabs at me.

I have no advice for day five.

I wake up, noticing first that my paintbrush is on the floor, having slipped from my fingers. That fault will count against me. The Canadian judge is a grizzly bear. Long-distance sleepers think they know everything; they've no respect for style sleeping. He really shouldn't be allowed to judge this event without having any experience in the competition. Also, he's a bear.

There is a knock on my door. This may be the second knock, the first having woke me.

"Eleanor?" It's Connor.

I leave the brush – it's oil-based, not acrylic: it won't stick to the floor – and move over to the door by combining forty-five-degree angles. I press my hands against it to stop myself from falling all the way down.

I think about the formality of *hello* and *good morning*, the oddball *how do you do* or *bonjour*, and settle finally on "Hi." It comes out croaky.

"Are you going to open the door today?"

"Uh – why?"

"Because that's normal. It's the kind of thing people do without having to explain it. They explain other things that are less normal than that." He has me there.

You have chickenpox. The inspiration is like the imaginary voice of sleeping commentator Jim Moir whispered into my ear.

"I have chickenpox." Great work, Jim.

"Is that all? I was beginning to think you had two heads." He has been thinking about what I look like. "I had chickenpox when I was a kid; I'm fine."

You've screwed me, Jim. This is Helsinki all over again. I say, "I look terrible."

"I'm sure you don't."

Are you? Because I really do. I can feel the oil on my skin, the dead cells; I need to be scrubbed, but my fatigue has overpowered my self-respect. I am rotting from the outside in, and from the inside out. In another couple of days, I'll be a thin layer of viscera, fit only for being examined under a microscope. The coroner will conclude that I died from starvation and blackheads.

"Look, I'm sick; I'm covered from head to toe in gross red blotches, and I'm not going to let anyone see me until I'm better. Right?" Vanity: that was something he would believe. Girls were all body conscious; from Dublin to Dubai – both ways.

"Oh," he says. "I understand. So, you don't want to come for a walk around the island with me today?"

He hasn't talked to anyone – at least not about me. Yesterday I played music to a door for hours. Mostly we listened; if anyone was talking much it was me. I talked about pianists and why I think people write better songs on pianos than on guitars, though I also argued that *better* was subjective. He didn't express an opinion, which I think was wise.

"Not today," I say. I push my fist into my mouth. Why did I say that? I could have just said *no thank you and bonjour.* Instead, I've raised his expectation that tomorrow or the day after I'll emerge from a cocoon of scabs and go skipping through meadows with him.

"Maybe tomorrow?"

"Maybe." I bite my knuckles again. "I'll see how I feel." And now, day five, is the first day I actually want to die. Not through isolation, starvation, aexfoliation, but by imbrogliation – death caused by the social awkwardness of being unable to correct misconceptions about oneself.

"You're not catfishing me are you, Eleanor? You're not going to open this door and I find out you're a fifty-year-old man named Bernard?"

"My name's not Bernard."

"Phew."

"And you should never ask a lady her age."

"Sure, that's not what the Gardaí say."

"But I'll be sixteen in two weeks."

"So, you're fifteen now?"

"I'm fifteen and twenty-five twenty-sixths." Being sixteen feels important.

"All right," he says. His voice becomes fainter as he moves away from the door. "I'm going out. I'll hear you later."

* * *

I put the shower on and sit underneath it, crowding my bones onto the spot where the spray hits. The sensation is uncomfortable. Water that had been soothing a few days ago is a hundred pinpricks of heat. I am exhausted. Exhausted by the pain of hunger. Exhausted by every sensation: it hurts to see, so I have closed my eyes; it hurts to hear, I turned off my playlist hours ago.

I can't remember the anger. I know that I was angry, because I remember screaming and fighting. I remember the oaths. If I hadn't been angry, I wouldn't have behaved that way. But anger is a sinew, and all my sinews are slack. A memory of strength is not strength, any more than a picture of a potato is chips.

"You've chosen to go for a seated, under shower with five-day fast. It's your toughest bathroom sleep yet. How do you keep going?" Jim leans through the shower curtain, his shirt sleeve rolled up, and puts the waterproof microphone under my head.

"I'm doing it for the fans, Jim. It's all for the fans."

"And this has nothing to do with your sponsorship from Mister Muscle Kitchen and Bathroom?"

"I'm obviously grateful for the support of Mister Muscle and all my sponsors – Silent Night, Virgin Atlantic Business Class, and Pepsi Max – maximum taste, no sugar."

"Other brands of Pepsi are available," says Jim, because he works for the BBC and he has to say stuff like that.

"My strategy has always been to finish in the bathroom. I've put in a good performance in the earlier rounds and I've always thought of the bathroom sleep as my strongest style."

"You've come into this with a points advantage, you must be confident of a medal – the question must be whether you can hold on and top that podium."

"I've been sleeping for nearly sixteen years and what I've learned is not to get cocky. I'm going to close my eyes and try not to drown and we'll see what the judges say. Of course, if I do drown, at least the suffering of being alive will be over. In many ways, Jim, this contest offers me two shots at the gold."

"Good luck, Eleanor. Possibly we'll speak to you later. And now it's over to a packed-out velodrome where Sir Chris Hoy is still retired from competitive cycling and is dunking biscuits into milky tea."

* * *

There is some knocking that turns into *knock-knock-Eleanor*-ing and a bit of *one second, I'm in the shower*-ing, then drying and even though I know he can't see me I wrap myself in a towel.

"I've got you a present," Connor says.

"Oh?"

"Will you open the door so I can give it you?"

"No."

"I thought you'd say that."

I hear movement on the other side of the door and my eyes follow the sound down. From the gap between the bottom of the door and the floorboards – a gap which is about the same thickness as a Jacob's Cream Cracker – emerges a small flower. Five purple leaves in a star formation around a yellow centre, the whole thing smaller than a dandelion.

Connor says, "It's a cuckoo flower."

I pick it up. There is an instant of tension as he senses me and releases his grip. I turn it around to look at every angle. I have never seen a flower like it before. For all I know, Ensay is covered with them and they're weeds on a Japanese Hogweed scale of virulence and loathsomeness. It could be poisonous. Or it could be the last of its kind, plucked from some perilous edge overlooking the sea. I say, "It's very pretty."

"I would have picked you a bunch, but I don't know how I would have got them under the door."

"One at a time?"

"Now you're making me look a proper fool."

"Nobody ever brought me flower before."

"You're only fifteen and twenty-five twenty-sixths. I should hope you're not getting flower from every wandering rogue."

No, just the one. "Do you know a lot about flowers?"

"I did Spartans. It's like scouts. You try to live in the wild, off the land."

"In Dublin?"

"There was a minibus. We'd go down to Wicklow. There's mountains, bits of forest; it's like Scotland, I think. There were twelve of us, and we'd all be told to find something – a leaf or a flower or something – and if we found something that nobody knew the name of then we won a Toblerone."

"A big one?"

"Yeah. Mister Laragh has family in Portugal so he was always at the airport. Course, you couldn't eat a whole big Toblerone to yourself. But there's also not enough to share amongst eleven other people. And living off the land in County Wicklow usually meant heating up tins of supermarket baked beans on the edge of a fire. So, it was a thing, to win it, then you'd share it with the lads in your tent. And we'd eat it as loud as we could, so everybody in the other tents could hear. And we'd be rubbing our bellies and saying *mmmm* and refusing more because we were so full, but then changing our minds and taking more."

"That sounds like fun."

"It was. It was a good laugh."

"Did people bear grudges?"

"Course. But everybody got a turn, so I suppose that was fine."

"What else did you do?"

"Hillwalking. Craic. We made fishing poles out of sticks and thread and safety pins. Nobody ever caught anything big enough to eat. But we had hope, Eleanor. We lived on hope and we waited for fish."

"That's really nice."

"Yeah. Sometimes. You know?"

"Yes," I say, but I don't. People do that; they present a vague outline of an idea and ask you to colour it in according to your preferences, then agree with them that you both see the same thing. I assume he means that people are sometimes nice and sometimes not, or that hope can be both the thing that sustains you and the pain that gnaws at your insides, but he might just as easily have been talking about fish.

"Jesus, but I'm starving," he says, but the irony is too obvious to make me laugh. "I'm going to get some dinner." It is dinner time, apparently; I have lost track. "Do you want me to get you anything?"

Yes! I want you to get me anything at all. Anything the thickness of a Jacob's Cream Cracker or less. A pretend-cheese slice. A napkin soaked in soup. A Hobnob reduced to crumbs and blown under the door with a hairdryer.

"No, I'm fine thanks."

"Okay, so – when do you think you're coming out?"

"Soon," I say. "Maybe tomorrow." He's still keen to see me. This is a big deal for him. Girls are to boys what albino deer are to medieval knights – we're questable; they will endure *dangers untold and hardships unnumbered to reach the castle beyond the goblin city,* which, in this awkward extended metaphor, is to use their eyes to capture photons that have most recently reflected from the body of a girl.

I'm sure if I had any strength at all to feel anything, I would feel flattered and disgusted.

I hope it is tomorrow. Being locked away inside the same building is mysterious, but he'll move into his uncle's house soon and then I'll be someone who's locked away inside a nearby building he likely won't visit again. I'll be less like a princess in a tower, and more like conventional attic contents – old furniture; toys that used to belong to children long since grown, aged, dead and buried elsewhere; mousetraps which have been baited, sprung, and forgotten; Beano annuals from nineteen eighty-eight through ninety-six; the rumour of the ghost of a girl who starved to death; photographs; amateurish taxidermy; a pretend-cheese slice, still wrapped, delivered too late; copper pipes that don't seem to go anywhere but are inexplicably hot; an electric sewing machine with foot pedal; an additional electric sewing machine foot pedal with no accompanying sewing machine; a framed map of Tripoli; some grandfather's gun from some grandfather's war; a wedding dress stored in foxed tissue paper; a thousand Christmas lights tied into a festive Gordian knot; something that might be part of a bigger thing that might also be in the attic; luggage like Russian dolls, packed one inside the other, and in the smallest zip pocket of the smallest case is that thing that was urgently desired, precious beyond rubies, and the cause of vitriolic denouncement and disavowal three years ago – or was it four?; sometimes a bigger thing, broken; more photographs, this time of total strangers; a wooden chess set; a painting that isn't by Monet – though it's fun to dream; Beatles records, which will be worth a lot of money one day, unless they're not; a Polynesian idol of arcane construction intended to either attract or repel the Elder God Cthulhu; and a light dusting of bat shit.

"Okay, well, hear you later."

"Hear you later."

As I rest my head against the back of the door, I can feel the vibration of his footsteps descending the stairs.

It's easier to sleep now, and harder to be awake.

* * *

She has asked me a question. I want to answer it – I want, *more than anything*, to answer it – but I can't remember what it was.

Her hands are in my hair. She is holding me up from the floor; if she let go, I would flop backwards and crack my skull.

"Are you sorry for what you did?"

"Yes." I am.

"And what did you do?"

I can't remember. I start to cry.

"You broke our laws."

"Yes," I nod.

"You showed kindness to someone who deserved punishment."

"Yes."

"You forgot your duty."

"Yes, mum."

"You were wicked."

"I was."

"You needed to be punished."

"I did. Thank you. Thank you. Thank you. Thank you."

She embraces me and rocks me in place.

"Thank you. Thank you." I can't control the sound of my voice; everything is sobs and wails. I try to go on. "Thank you. Thank you. Thank you. Thank you. Thank you."

The smell of soup is strange and overwhelming. I feel like I will be sick. She shuffles my body around so that my back is leaning against the wall, then she lifts the bowl she's carried from the kitchen and brings a spoon the remaining inches to my mouth.

Texture is difficult to account for. My tongue has forgotten edges, so a cube of carrot has the novelty of a sea urchin. I swallow the first spoonful without chewing and feel the warmth of it in a way I've never experienced before. Each inch of my throat drinks it, as if my whole body were a sponge, I do not feel that any reached my stomach. She continues to feed me until these strange sensations fade, until the bowl is empty. I feel as full as I ever have – and I'm ravenous.

"You can eat again in the morning. A little at a time." As she says this, she strokes my hair.

I only nod.

"Do you need help to stand up?"

I stand on my own to demonstrate that my strength is returning, though it is not; all my limbs shake as I rise. It is as uncertain and unconfident a motion as I could make and still become vertical.

"You'll make us all very proud," she says. She kisses me on the forehead and produces the key to my door from a pocket, pushing aside the cover and slipping it into my side of the mechanism. "Remember to lock your door."

I sniff heavily to clear myself of the mucus of tears and digestion. "I will."

She leaves without another word and closes the door behind her. I wait for the sound of her steps to vanish and on the second attempt I manage to turn the key.

When I sit on my bed, I feel tired, but not heavy. *As if a weight has been lifted* – that is literally it. Guilt weighed on me more than hunger or pain. The guilt is gone, and I am light as air.

I make sure my iPad is on the lowest volume setting, and I press play. The queued song begins. Had I saved this? Or is it coincidence? It is Yazz and the Plastic Population – which, really, was just Yazz. I lie down, and with my left hand clenched around a small purple flower, I feel myself drift into sleep.

The Only Way Is Up.

DAVID F PORTEOUS

10

There's a lot of advice out there, and that's a big problem for anyone looking for advice. If I had been trying to find out whether a smaller blender would blend inside a larger blender, that would have been simple, there's one video on the internet, and – spoiler – it does. That's the answer and the answer is definitive.

Other people might argue that there are unexplored possibilities in the blender question. But these are *angels dancing on the head of a pin* and *bears shitting in the woods* questions. I mean, how many trees constitutes *woods*? To what density? Do you consider the distance between trunks, or the distance between leaves? If so, woods made of different species of trees will feel more or less dense. If a bear is in a clearing entirely encircled by trees, is it still in *the woods*? St John's Wood in London isn't a forest; it's an urban metropolitan district that yes, has some trees – presumably – but does the question extend to encompass formerly wooded areas which bear the name *wood* as an anachronism? Does diarrhoea count? Ultimately the question is religious, and many answers are acceptable.

In my view, the blender question is sufficiently resolved.

The pope is a Catholic.

But how I should cut my hair – that is an area of lesser consensus.

At this point there is enough of my hair to do anything. If I were a normal girl who went to a normal school and had friends, then peer pressure would already have solved this. I would have mostly done what other girls were doing, layered in with advice from them, and modified to a small degree by my own instincts and preferences. I would have dutifully conformed to what was expected of me, and I would have been happy to be relieved of the burden of making any choice about my hair at all.

I am a hair conformist, without anything to conform to.

I make my decision at around five in the morning – the ideal time to make head-altering choices; the sun is clearing the horizon and I'm in a world of half-light and half consciousness where everything seems a little less than real, including me. I pick up the scissors, and with the first snip I am committed.

* * *

The kitchen is both familiar and not. Nothing in the room has changed in the time I was gone, but I see its colours differently. My memory of the place has been a sculpture in wax which has been distorted by heat and time and its own weight.

In my mind's eye I can still see the body of Mrs. Alexander, her legs folded under herself. The hall door opens to reveal Mrs. Douglas as the clock strikes. Mrs. Olafsson touches my face.

These things, these events, are not in the room. Their shadows have dispersed like smoke and even though the facts of them are vivid, the detail is shifting. With each blink the distance between memory and reality closes, until there is only reality.

Breakfast is already being served. I can hear the occasional note of my mum's voice in the dining room, breaking through the familiar *rhubarb* of unfamiliar voices. I fix a plate and try to eat slowly, failing, and realising only when I'm half done that I have no tea or toast. My hunger mostly satisfied; I attend to these elements.

My mum does not appear in the kitchen in the seven minutes it takes me to finish everything. I slip my plate and cutlery into the half-full dishwasher and exit by the back stairs door. I feel a sense of relief as it closes behind me, as if I have escaped, or avoided a confrontation – about what I don't know.

My hair? Would she be upset that I've cut my hair? I don't think so. Even if she were, she's always more forgiving after she's just punished me.

I wind back up the stairs. The light on the first floor has gone again – in the last few minutes. The ancient electrics in this part of the house and the modern energy-saving bulbs do not get on. My eyes adjust and I think I can see a faint glow in the heart of the bulb. One percent of one candle power – an amount of light that is of no actual use to see by, but reminds me that when I change this bulb later, there's still the chance I'll be electrocuted.

On a normal morning I might have retrieved a spare bulb from the cupboard on the first floor, a mere six feet from where I am standing, and replaced the bulb now to save me a task later. Today I feel sluggish from breakfast and still tired.

And weird. I am conscious of feeling weird; unsettled in a way that has nothing to do with food or lack thereof. I am not myself and I don't know if that's a good or a bad thing.

Back in my room I make my bed, then kick off my shoes and lie on top of it. The sheets feel cool below me and my eyes trace familiar patterns in wooden beams above.

I don't know what the cakes are. Having been away from the tearoom for so long, my mum will have made an entirely new selection. And since it's the season, there's a strong possibility of overtly Scottish ingredients. Heather. Whisky. If she's found a way to make a cake with a bolt of tartan I'll be impressed, but not surprised. I might not even know any of the guests – I can't remember if we had any planning to stay beyond today. The anchors that gave me purpose and station in the house are gone – for a while I will be a guest in a place where others have become at home. This thought is frightening, or at least it is entirely new.

When I hear the knock, I realise that I've been waiting for it. I am on my feet before I decide to be and I've crossed the room before I think this might be strange.

"It's Connor," he says.

I pause with my fingers above the handle. I know that Jim isn't real, never felt real, doesn't feel real. But now that it comes time to open the door, I wonder how real Connor might be. Is there a boy on the other side? I think there's a high probability that there is; that I have not hallucinated everything in the last several days. If I have, I feel like I've also unnecessarily spent a lot of money on buying music over the years when I could have imagined it for free.

There might be degrees of real. Or versions of real. And when I open the door, I'll be left with the one and only Connor, which could be nothing like the boy in my head.

And there's the tiny chance that he doesn't exist; that opening the door obliterates him. I wonder whether it is better to live with a pleasing illusion than suffer a painful reality – then I decide.

His eyes are deep blue. Not the colour of the sea or the sky. Prussian blue; at their centre almost black, then lightening as the disc of the iris touches the whites. I know this colour. It is the colour of medicine for removing caesium from the intestine, and of Prussian military uniforms, and of Van Gogh's *Starry Night*. An invented colour, made in a laboratory. Before the eighteenth century it would not have been possible to paint him faithfully, and there is still no film development process or TV screen that can perfectly reproduce that hue.

He looks at me in silence, and I feel a sense of panic; that he will find some quality lacking in me, that I will have the wrong nose, and the tiniest piece of the sky will fall down and crush an entire village which had hitherto never suspected its fate was tied to the judgement of a nose. But then the corners of his mouth twitch. Upwards. His lips part into a smile.

"I thought you were never going to open that door," he says.

His hair is black. Short on the sides, longer and messy on top. It is not a *good* haircut, but it is possible to imagine the good haircut that was being attempted.

"Yeah," I say. *Yeah*? I can't open with *yeah*; I don't even say *yeah*. I'm pretty sure I'm a *yes* girl. Maybe an *okay* girl. He says *yeah*, and it's been rubbing off on me. I throw myself blindly into a follow-up. "I need to open it sometimes to keep the hinges working." Saved?

"So?"

"So?"

He makes a bodily gesture which, objectively, means nothing whatsoever, but subjectively expresses a state of *outness* and how awkward that is. It's like a frustrated penguin walking on the spot. "Can I come in?"

I hold open the door and he takes a few steps through and stops with his back to me, looking around.

If I had an expectation of his height – and I must have – then he is what I expected. I don't have a measuring tape in my room and even if I did it would be difficult to check his exact size without violating several social norms. He's five-foot-eight, nine, ten, eleven, six feet-ish. Taller than I am, but not outstandingly tall. The NBA haven't scouted him. Women he's known have retrieved items from shelves themselves, rather than enlisted his help. Five feet, ten inches – I have decided.

And those black jeans were a tight squeeze.

He turns. "Did you paint these?"

"Did I paint what?" I ask, looking very deliberately at his eyes.

"All the paintings?"

"Oh. Yeah. *Yes*. I did."

"Cool." He moves closer and I can see his eyes flit from picture to picture. I hadn't intended to make any kind of gallery space, that just happened because the only way to store paintings efficiently is to hang them. Nobody misses the two inches of space nearest to the wall, but a pile of canvases in the corner feels like clutter.

It occurs to me that nobody has looked at these paintings before except me and my mum. And my paintings have arrived one at a time – as I painted them – and disappeared at the same rate. Even I've never seen a collection of things I've done.

I expect to be paralysed by the scrutiny; I've always expected that I would be. But I am not. I'm not anxious or unsettled; any reserve I felt about his views on my face, or my hair – or my bum for that matter – don't matter here. Maybe I even like them being looked at. Maybe what I like is him looking at them.

I ask, "Do you paint?"

"Me? Naw. I like these though. Is this one my bedroom?"

"I don't know what room you're in. It could be."

"I think it is. It feels right."

"I've always thought that was a very sad painting."

"Yeah," he says and moves down to the easel, his fingers touch on the sheet covering my work in progress.

"That one's not finished yet!"

He backs off, hands up, fingers spread. "Sorry." His contrition is short-lived though and the scolded look breaks into a grin. "I've seen your hedgehog."

"What?"

"You heard me. I've seen your hedgehog."

It takes me three seconds. "Oh. The one screwed to the wall downstairs?"

"The very same. Now *that* is a work of art."

"Because of the eyes?"

"They follow you 'round the room."

"One follows you 'round the room, the other is following a spider around the ceiling."

"Ha, yeah right. Why don't you hang these around the hotel?"

"I—" do not have an answer to that question. Maybe it's because they all feel a bit like googly-eyed hedgehogs to me. I don't know how good your paintings are supposed to be before you're allowed the hang them. I know the hedgehog is screwed to the wall because I took it down twice and hid it the second time. "—suppose I could."

"I think these are much better than all that twee stuff."

"Like what?" I feel a sensation of being exposed, of becoming vulnerable. The question gives away more than any answer could receive in return. After all, his statement is only something people say; a noise to crowd out the silence. I am ridiculous to care at all.

He flaps, then says, "I dunno. All of it? I mean, the ones downstairs in the hall – they're what I expected. I bet there are fifty b-n-bs that have the same things. Maybe the exact same pictures in the same frames. I feel like if I could paint, I could have painted them without knowing anything about what it's like to live here. I could have guessed there would be a woman looking out to sea and I could have guessed the colour of her hair. This all feels . . . unexpected."

He points to *The Gull* – my only wildlife painting – where a common gull stares out impertinently with one orange eye, and much of the rest of the world is only suggested. The bird has no legs; it is not standing on the roof below it; indeed, that roof barely exists. It has wings, but it isn't flying, and the sky above is unpainted canvas. *The Gull* is suspended between worlds which it defines. Is it happy about this? I don't know; I think if I knew the answer to that question, I would never have painted it.

He says, "Look at this mad bastard. Nobody would have expected him to be on the wall downstairs. If you came looking for a piper in a kilt, this would blow your mind."

I ask, "What makes you think it's a him?"

He shrugs.

"Maybe that's why it's not downstairs," I say. "People don't want to be challenged by the walls of every b-n-b in Scotland. Maybe people like being challenged on their terms in their own time."

"Yeah, I suppose," he says. "You've gotta give people what they're paying for." I think he imagines he's said something wrong. He becomes softer; more circumspect, as if he has heard a different tune and changed his dance to match. "Do you like—?"

"Don't do that," I say.

"What?"

"Don't change what you think just because I don't agree with you."

"I wasn't."

"You were."

"I had barely thought about it."

"And neither had I," I say. "I don't know what I think about it at all, I was just talking. I don't want people changing their mind to please me when I don't even know what I think, and I certainly don't want people changing their mind to agree with me because they don't know what *they* think. So, stop it."

He looks at me shrewdly, his blue eyes become dark slits, his mouth tight-lipped. He makes me conscious of my own expression until I slap my hand up over my face to cover most of it.

"Sorry," I mumble.

"No, you're right. I was just . . . You know?"

He takes my hand off my face. His fingers around my wrist. He moves it down in front of me. He smiles, awkwardly, then releases me.

I do, in fact, know.

"I was going to go for a walk," he says.

"Oh."

He looks at me for a long time, then says, "Do you want to come?"

"Oh! Right! Uh – I'm working this afternoon. I work afternoons in the tearoom then evenings in the restaurant."

"What about tomorrow?"

"I work every day during the season, so does mum. We're usually close to full from June to August, but we're basically closed from October to March. I mean we still have guests, but they're in-person bookings, emergencies, one-night stays."

"This place must get pretty spooky in winter."

I say, "I'm mostly free in the morning."

"What?"

"I can't go for a walk with you, but in the morning, I'm mostly free. If you wanted to—" the words stick in my throat and come out higher than I'd intended, as if they were a question "—hang out."

"Okay," he says, and smiles. "Cool."

"Cool."

* * *

"I expect you've heard," says Mrs. Brown.

"No," says Mrs. MacArthur. It occurs to me that Mrs. MacArthur often says she hasn't heard something before she can possibly know. There are no unknown unknowns in her world, only the certainty of ignorance.

I place the pot of peppermint tea next to Mrs. Brown and the English breakfast next to Mrs. MacArthur. There is a tiny miracle of sunlight dancing on the table, reflected from a window of the house across the street, onto the mirror-polish surface of the urn which must be bubbling with hot water, then onto the cloth. It is a brilliant day; so bright that it hurts my eyes to look outside.

I put two slices of cake into the sun – lavender and honey sponge. Mrs. MacArthur doesn't like lavender, but she hates ordering differently from Mrs. Brown. When ordering tea, it's *the usual* to avoid having to say it. I can't imagine living in a world where I'd be afraid to choose what I wanted.

"Can I get you two ladies anything else?" I ask.

Mrs. MacArthur indicates the sugar bowl on the table, which is empty. I take it away for a refill while Mrs. Brown *well the thing is*es and her confederate *oh I never*s. I come back to what is evidently a most sensitive piece of intelligence; Mrs. Brown's face is a visual shoosh.

"Ah, uh," Mrs. MacArthur says, and I know what's coming. "How are you today, Eleanor?"

Oh, you know me, always high on paint thinner. I'm a huffing fiend. And still a little weak from the starvation, truth to be told. Did you hear the screaming on Sunday? I imagine you did, and I'm sure we all have our own manners that need to be respected, but neither of you bitches has said a thing about my haircut, and I think anyone would feel aggrieved about that. And there's a *boy*, Mrs. MacArthur. There's a *boy*, Mrs. Brown. And I think he likes me and I've never been liked before and I don't know if I like him or if it's just the incandescent novelty – the unprecedented uniqueness – of someone seeing *me* instead of a fucking condition.

I say, "I'm very well, thank you for asking."

"It's not long until you turn sixteen," says Mrs. MacArthur.

"On the solstice," I say.

Mrs. Brown says, "Yes. I remember."

"Mrs. Brown was a beautiful acolyte," says Mrs. MacArthur. Her compliment feels semi-ritualistic; she says it sincerely but is focused on adding a second spoonful of sugar into her cup.

Mrs. Brown dismisses the comment, as she has a hundred times before, while at the same time becoming ten percent larger and more splendid. Her right hand drifts to her earlobe where she wears an impressive, if old-fashioned diamond earring. The set is not just old, though, they are antique, and I imagine they were a gift marking the event, handed-down from someone else – perhaps her mother.

Now past fifty, it's difficult to see the girl she used to be. Her face is strong and round, and her forehead is high. If I were feeling unkind, I would say she reminded me of George Foreman – the boxer and electric grill salesman. Though she is, at least, pre- rather than post-fight Foreman. She might once have been a beautiful acolyte, but it could also have been a bad year for the island.

"Not that I had much to choose from," Mrs. Brown replies with a dramatic arch of her eyebrows. "Do you remember *Mister* Brown?"

"Not very well," I say.

"You're better for that."

"It's always been difficult to find someone," says Mrs. MacArthur. "Mister Jones has nearly had to do it twice." Mrs. Brown laughs at this – a deep and indiscreet belly laugh which catches her by surprise and rattles her teacup.

"What do you mean?" I ask.

"Oh, it's just a joke," says Mrs. MacArthur while Mrs. Brown covers her mouth with a napkin and continues to chuckle. "So, is there a young man who's taken your fancy?" Mrs. MacArthur's eyes twinkle at her question, like cut glass in a gargoyle. "Your mother has told you it's up to you to choose someone hasn't she?"

"I don't know that I'm supposed to say."

"I hear that she was quite taken with one of those musicians," says Mrs. Brown, confiding this to Mrs. MacArthur as if I were not standing two feet away.

"Ooh!" says Mrs. MacArthur – a long, excited sound.

My heart sinks as her voice rises. As I had suspected, Mrs. Douglas saw Angus kiss me. If she told anyone, the news was bound to get back to Mrs. Brown eventually. And I was gone for five days; that must have raised eyebrows. If I'd been here, I suspect it wouldn't have come up, but they probably think that's what I was punished for.

I feel foolish for not expecting everyone to know. We have a saying on the island – *two women can keep a secret, provided one of them is dead, and the other one isn't Mrs. Crevinge.* Who would ever be inclined to keep my secrets?

"As it happens—" I say, feeling myself pulled up, as if I were being lifted by the head, "—I was kissed quite unawares, and if Missus Alexander hadn't just passed and I had been in full possession of my wits, I should most certainly, or at least most very likely, have protested the act on my person."

"I see," says Mrs. Brown.

"Youth," says Mrs. MacArthur, rolling her eyes at Mrs. Brown. "You wait until you're my age, then see how much you'd protest a young man having a rummage."

"He did *not*—"

"I'm only saying," she says.

Mrs. Brown pats Mrs. MacArthur's hand and smiles. "You'll forgive us a little joke, won't you, Eleanor? A little curiosity and nostalgia from your sisters who won't walk that way again."

"Of course," I say. I'm unnerved by being asked for forgiveness when, surely, I am the one in the wrong. I remember the order of a cheese toastie which is probably ready, and I say, "If you'll excuse me."

They nod their acknowledgement, all the time their close-mouthed grins feel lecherous, and I turn away from them to head to the kitchen.

"It'll be the new boy, then," Mrs. MacArthur whispers.

"Yes," replies Mrs. Brown with the same hush. "Yes, I think so too."

11

The kitchen is hot. Steam rises in an unbroken plume, sucked up by the huge extractor, but it can only do so much. I breathe, and stir six things.

Pork – or *short human*, as the cannibals call it – is a much-maligned meat in Britain. According to a *Guardian* article from four years ago (which was the first item on Google and good enough for me), we eat less pork by weight than ham and bacon. And both of those combined are less than the amount of chicken we eat. We are chicken eaters. The (slightly out-of-date) statistics are unequivocal. The Department for Food and Rural Affairs and the data team at a major newspaper have got my back on this. I should *not* have run out of slow-cooked pork loin with apples, celeriac mash, and Savoy cabbage. Yet here I am.

And if I were to criticise slow cooking, and I were – am – then the first and most important of my criticisms would be that it is slow. After the eight portions go in the first ten covers, I obviously can't make any more, and rather than the special allowing me to spread work more evenly over the whole service, by seven thirty I'm making every course from scratch.

My mum enters the kitchen, says, "Risotto and chicken Balmoral," puts the order slip down on the counter in the wrong place, then breezes out again as if she hasn't just dropped a live grenade. There is another risotto already going and I do not have enough cooker space to start a second, which means table eight is going to wait half an hour for food. Risotto in less than twenty minutes is just a bowl of fat rice.

I breathe. And stir six things. And a bead of sweat drips from my nose into the soup of the day – which nobody is eating – drinking. I don't know how Mrs. Alexander didn't have a heart attack years ago – stroke, whatever.

For the time being the kitchen is mine. Mrs. Douglas and my mum are looking for a replacement, though part-time seasonal work when the season is so far advanced makes this very unlikely. They have not said this; they are optimistic. This – me being here – is a temporary measure. How this is supposed to be temporary I don't know – and it's not as if I am going anywhere.

My mum knows about Angus, and she has said nothing.

I don't know whether she knows Connor and I have already spent hours together, with the door between us, or that he has been in my room. She hasn't baited me to disclose these events, and she normally would – for any indiscretion at all. She did have to run the hotel by herself for the best part of a week while recovering – her hands are still red, but no longer raw. And it's not as if my room is bugged and surveilled. Still, I find it difficult to believe there is anything that goes on in this house which she does not know.

The first risotto goes out and in come the first orders for desserts and, finally, one soup. Mrs. Alexander was a professional chef and if there were any lesson I was conscious of her teaching me, it was that a kitchen must make money. Or precisely, I think she said, *the purpose of a kitchen is to make food, but the reason for a restaurant is to make money*. The seafood special which became the fish curry was the most obvious example of her careful management of costs, but she had an itemised cost for everything she cooked. Following her example, I know that the ingredients in the pot of soup cost one pound and ninety-two pence and will serve ten. We charge three fifty for the soup, which includes a small bread roll and a pat of butter, together costing thirty-one pence – which is insane, but includes the extra cost of Mr. Jones bringing all our bread from another island in somewhat better conditions than required by carrots and cabbage and nails.

Although one bowl of soup sold covers the ingredient cost for the whole batch, it doesn't push us into profit. Soup needs time for someone to chop veg and cook, cooking requires oil for the burner – we burn fuel oil rather than gas on Ensay – dishes need to be washed, one in a five hundred servings results in a plate broken or a spoon lost or stolen – that all needs to be covered, plus a hundred other overheads, plus tax. If we sell only one bowl of soup from a pot of soup, then we actually lose – I don't know what the figure is, but it's about ten pence, give or take twenty pence, depending on what the soup is. And it gets worse – if we *hadn't* served soup, that person would probably have ordered something else that would have made a profit.

Right now, I'm standing in this sweltering kitchen looking a proper fool. A naïve optimist who risked everything on hot vegetable water futures. They'll crucify me in the *Journal*. *The Financial Times* will call for the board to remove me. And even if I make it to the AGM, I'll be out with a golden parachute that wouldn't safely land a hamster.

Ah – but if we sell a second bowl, well, who's laughing then? Me. All the way to the bank. That second bowl puts this whole caper on Easy Street. I'll be dripping with diamonds, signing copies of an autobiography I didn't even write, and whispering my wisdom into the ears of emperors and presidents. *Psst! – economics is the science of gambling on soup: bet everything on broth; minestrone is the next Viagra; mulligatawny is going to open huge.*

I feel lightheaded. I have a glass of water. I sit down for a minute. I stir six things.

Whenever my mum comes into the kitchen, I am busy. I am also busy when she is not here, but then I'm only *being* busy and not trying to *look* busy. I feel like any eye contact would reveal – what? That I have the smallest secret in the world? The secret every girl has – and which, it would seem, is already common knowledge to the island's gossips.

Today she isn't watching me. If anything, this lack of scrutiny makes me more nervous. Between this anxiety of being unwatched, and the apoplexy of being asked to make a vegetarian chicken Balmoral, and the rush of selling that second soup, it is unexpectedly nine o'clock. The clock chimes it. The last of the cranachans departs. The kitchen is closed.

I've made it.

I *did* it.

At this point I feel that it would be possible to wring out my t-shirt and refill that glass of water I drank. It is a magnificent feeling, which I also hate, and it lasts maybe fifteen seconds. It is replaced by a yawning hunger; in my stomach there is a fold in space which could comfortably accommodate an entire roast chicken. Not even roast. If I could swallow a live chicken, it could live in that pocket dimension inside me and I would not feel the least bit fuller.

"Missus Alexander's dinner!"

I slap the countertop and realise I've said it out loud to the empty kitchen. Mrs. Alexander got paid, and she got a meal each night – that was her arrangement with my mum and had been for all the time I've been alive, as far as I can remember. On the night she died, she didn't have time to make her own dinner yet because she was talking to me.

Every night, without fail, she would make her dinner, plate it up, cover it with tinfoil and take the plate home. She always went home with it. She took it home because she didn't want to be in the same place as my mum for any longer than she had to be. Not Mrs. Douglas. Nor Mrs. Olafsson. Mrs. Alexander was avoiding my mum.

And Mrs. Douglas and Mrs. Olafsson both know why.

So when Mrs. Douglas turns up and sees Mrs. Alexander's body in the back garden – fine, she died in the back garden. I hid the cardigan, because the cardigan was the evidence *that was there*. What Mrs. Douglas noticed was the evidence that *wasn't* there: she *Curious-Case-of-the-Dog-in-the-Night-Time*d me. When she saw there wasn't a dinner plate thrown across the grass like a frisbee or smashed to bits on the steps or smothered by Mrs. Alexander's double-f bosom, she knew that Mrs. Alexander had died before her shift

105

finished. Simply put, that meant she had died in the kitchen and that we had moved her.

Did she know that I had moved her? Or Mrs. Olafsson? Could my mum have moved her alone? Not easily, but she could have. She must have at least suspected all three of us moved the body from the tone she used with us. Mrs. Douglas talked about making me go outside, but there was no suggestion of Mrs. Olafsson being punished. Why would she punish me and my mum, but not Mrs. Olafsson?

Mrs. Olafsson *volunteered* to help my mum build the pyre, but there's nothing my mum could do, or would do, for her in return. *Under the circumstances* was the phrase Mrs. Olafsson used to intercede on my mum's behalf. What circumstances? My mum cut her off, didn't she? There were circumstances which Mrs. Douglas was aware of, which Mrs. Olafsson believed should result in no punishment, and which my mum thinks I don't know – and I don't know, as far as I know.

It occurs to me that Mrs. Douglas might not have punished my mum for moving Mrs. Alexander's body.

She might have punished her for killing Mrs. Alexander.

The idea seems ludicrous, and yet it feels right. I know my mum didn't do it, but Mrs. Olafsson never asked, and since Mrs. Douglas knows that I lied anyway she wouldn't believe me. Perhaps she even thinks I helped. *Under the circumstances* the death of an old woman who hated us means very little. *Under the circumstances* perhaps Mrs. Carlyle should get a medal.

Under the circumstances . . . it was the only way to stop Eleanor from finding out the truth.

A noise from the hall interrupts my circular cleaning of a small patch of counter which I would otherwise have rubbed a hole right through. I leave the cloth and open the door just as a second *hellooo* sounds.

Executing the final steps of their three-legged race are Connor and the twitcher – a man of fifty something with a beard like a bird's nest, and whose name I don't know. He is not the same twitcher staying with us a week ago, but he is a like-for-like substitute. Connor has his arm around the older man's shoulder, while the twitcher grips Connor at the waist. The reason for their closeness is obvious – Connor's right leg is being held off the ground and his face tells the rest of the story.

"What's happened?" I ask, and I pull a chair across the floor for Connor to sit on. The same one I used for his uncle, and for Mr. Wolanski. It's seeing much more drama than any of the other furniture in the house.

"It's not broken," says the twitcher. His accent is one of those middle-to-north England regional accents; he'll be from somewhere I've never heard of, which will also be somewhere exactly like Dudley or Bromley. "The leg that came through the roof is just a bit scraped, but he's twisted the other one."

"The roof of what?" I ask.

"My hide," he says. "It's a cut-in to the hill overlooking the nesting grounds with a wooden ceiling covered over with turf. There's three of them that were built by the RSPB in two-thousand-and-four. I used to work for them; we'd planned to build a network of hides on seabird nesting sites across the Western Isles, but we only got enough funding to cover, I think, six."

Connor yelps after trying to adjust his own leg. He says, "Maybe if you'd built them better, I wouldn't have fallen through one."

The twitcher shrugs that off – a little defensive, a little derisive – and says, "There's been a lot of rain recently, and I think the hide's probably forming a runoff from the hill. If it had been allowed to dry out a bit more it could have lasted another thirteen years."

"I'm sure it was a very nice hide," I say.

"It was," he says. "Still. It was funny. I'm watching these couple of red-necked phalaropes start to get very agitated, and I think they're looking at me. I'm checking that I haven't got the sun reflecting on anything, and I haven't, and even though I've got my headphones in, I turn off the music – then boom! Dirt and splinters everywhere and one human leg dangling right in front of me. Let me tell you – it wasn't what I'd been planning to spot this morning." He laughs at what must have been a joke. "Ah, well. After that I had to walk back with him from the other side of the island. Took us nearly two hours on three legs."

"He was on the other side of the island two hours ago?" I ask. I know that Connor didn't come back for lunch, because I would have seen him. He's been out since we spoke this morning – which is pretty much the whole day.

"Could you not talk about me like I'm not here?" says Connor. He's filthy and his face is caked in a way that indicates he's spent a fair part of those two hours crying. The twitcher doesn't acknowledge any of this.

"You've been through the wars," I say to Connor. "And you've lost. You're basically Belgium."

"In which World War?"

"Either." I kneel down in front of the chair. "I'm going to touch your leg, okay."

"Sex*eee!*" His paper-thin veneer of invulnerability is pierced by the shriek. It doesn't put me off. I get a sense of being watched through the glass door of the dining room – my mum, guests, I'm not sure. Whoever it is, they don't come out to intervene. It takes me another ten seconds to get a sense of his range of motion.

"You fell sideways through the roof?" I ask.

He nods.

"How did you know that?" the twitcher asks.

"He can hold his leg up with some discomfort, but the sideways motions are very painful. That tells me it's the adductor and not the quadriceps or the hamstring. I'll want to get a better look, but if it's just a pull, you'll be on your feet in a couple of days. If it's a tear then it'll be a bit longer. But if you were going to have an injury of a muscle in your thigh, this is probably the best one. Good job."

Connor says, "Thanks."

"Do you want some help getting him up to his room?" the twitcher asks.

"It's only one flight of stairs," I say. "I can manage him from here."

"I'll just go in for dinner, then."

"The kitchen's closed."

"Oh, but I only missed it because I was——"

"Give me a minute and I'll bring you some soup."

"I was thinking——"

"And a sandwich."

"Right."

"And a bit of cake."

"Okay."

"All on the house." My largesse with the soup is imperial, my offer of free cake is grudging. The cake always sells.

"Oh," he says, brightening. "Well, thanks very much."

"All right, soldier, let's have you on your feet," I say this, out loud, to Connor. *Soldier.* Is he five?

He struggles upwards and I put myself in the twitcher's place. Connor's arm goes over my shoulders and mine goes around his back, my hand pressing just below his ribs. He feels cold against me; he's been out all day wearing just a t-shirt. I think we both realise at the same moment that this is the most physical contact we've had, and pause at the foot of the stairs.

"My name's Alan, by the way," says the twitcher.

"Thanks Alan," Connor says and we begin to awkwardly ascend – he's had a couple of hours more practice than I have.

"I'm Eleanor," I say, remembering my manners and finding my rhythm on the third step.

"Sorry?" Alan says.

"I'm Eleanor," I repeat, a little louder.

"Eleanor?"

"Yes," I say, and at the small landing where the staircase turns, I turn, and smile at him. He has his hand on the dining room door. He is wearing the strangest expression. Connor moves again, and I follow, and Alan and I lose sight of each other.

* * *

Connor's room is not the room from my painting – that one is two doors further along the corridor, but it is very similar. This room has been visibly occupied by him, in the same way I imagine the armies of Napoleon occupied Spain – discarded clothes everywhere and sort of sweaty, cheesy smell in the air. His large suitcase, which might hold every season of clothing: every item he owns, lies open on the floor by the window, its contents heaped and overflowing in a way that seems both badly packed and rummaged through.

I have seen any number of different ways of packing a suitcase, but I feel like there are two broad philosophies. One – transfer clothing in the way it is stored at home, with only a few additional folds or rolls for items larger than the suitcase itself. Two – innovate a new storage solution which attempts to make optimal use of the volume of the suitcase, usually this involves many different types of folds and rolls, forming a range of shapes that are combined like a drystone wall.

I don't know if it makes all that much difference, but I imagine there's a psychological payoff; a feeling of a job well done which reinforces the behaviour.

Unpacking is also interesting. Some people don't. They live out of the case and form subdivisions of dirty and clean; with the divisions being more difficult to understand as more and more clothes become dirty. Then, with a jarring suddenness, the distinctions of class between socks collapse, and all foot coverings become equal in a new Sockulist utopia where everyone calls each other *comrade* or *argyle*.

But I've also seen those who unpack all the clean stuff, and only dirty or unused items go back into the case.

I have never packed a suitcase myself: I've never gone anywhere: I've never arrived anywhere: I've never unpacked my own things in a different place.

The door closes behind us and we execute something like a three-point turn, and something like the Gay Gordons, so that we are standing with the bed behind us. We sit down together and try and loose ourselves from each other without that seeming too awkward.

"It's nice to sit down," says Connor. "I feel like I've been on my foot all day."

"Right," I say: the word is decisive and all business. "Let's get your shoes off."

I scoot off the bed and kneel down. He's wearing red Converse high tops which he's laced up tight. I pick apart the knot on the right shoe and begin loosening the laces.

"Sure, I've never had a girl take off my shoes before. Will you be after my jeans next?" Connor becomes more friendly and more Irish when he is nervous. His accent revs, his mouth and eyes become wider; his whole personality inflates to double the size. It is a defensive act: a pre-emptive attack to control the tone and content of the exchange that follows.

I reply, "Yes," as I drop the first shoe on the floor.

"Oh," he says – it is an involuntary sound, and from this point on it will always be the sound I imagine a blowfish making when it deflates unexpectedly. "Do you need to do that?"

"Yes."

"But—"

"Connor, there are basically two types of injuries." Knot. "There are injuries which will get better if you don't do anything – rest, drink lots of water, eat, don't pick at it, pray if you like, moisturise – all that sort of stuff." Laces. "Then there are injuries that need intervention – surgery, physiotherapy, intravenous fluids, drugs, voodoo black magic, adamantium fused to your skeleton, eye patches – actual medicine." Shoe off. "And if you use the wrong one then you only make things worse." The second shoe hits the floor.

"But you're not a doctor."

"I know the names of all the muscles in your body. Do you?"

"No."

"This," I say, drawing my finger down the outside of his shin, through his jeans, "is your fibularis longus. Whereas this," I move my finger an inch to the right and trace the line of that muscle, "is your tibialis anterior. Did you know that?"

"No."

"Then I'm more of a doctor than you are."

"Yeah, but you're less of a doctor than a doctor."

"I mean, it's me or nothing."

"Can't we call for a doctor?"

"You can call for whatever you want, but because this is an island, the first time a doctor will arrive is at eight thirty tomorrow morning and the doctor will do exactly what I'm about to do now. Unbuckle your belt."

He doesn't move, I think this is to establish that he has the right to not remove his trousers on command. It is a power move, in its way. And I think he is probably very surprised when I do it for him, but once the belt and the button are unfastened, he couldn't stop me pulling the jeans down even if he tried.

He smells. It's not an unpleasant smell; he's showered this morning, so it's the smell of a human body unwashed for only the better part of a day – thirteen hours, maybe fourteen. I suppose there must be an extent to which everyone is the same and everyone is different. I've been in the tearoom during the afternoon and in the sweltering kitchen all evening – I must smell the same as he does if not worse. But there is also something completely different about how he smells. I struggle to think of a word other than *male*. That can't be the right way of describing it – I do, after all, have very little experience in this area.

But there it is. Male, by Calvin Klein. And the faintest possible residue of a common deodorant, not by Calvin Klein, applied hours ago.

I am absolutely scrupulous in not looking at his underpants – which are plain black. I have kept my eyes in the most prudish places possible while still being useful in removing the jeans of an eighteen-year-old boy.

His legs are bare between the bottom of his underwear and the tops of his socks. He has dark hair everywhere, not actually curly, but not straight either. It is thicker than the hair on his arms, and slightly longer. I have been shaving my legs since I was twelve – not because they really needed it, but because it seemed like the thing to do – and until being presented with a radical alternative, I don't believe I'd ever considered not doing it.

He is fascinating. I'm sure I've never found my own body fascinating. At best my body is inconvenient; in constant need of some kind of maintenance, frequently bloated, usually so sensitive that everything feels like a wire brush. Which is not to say that I neglect my body, or that I don't appreciate it. But I think about my body the way a Corgi-registered plumber thinks about pipes.

He is still very surprised.

"Can you lie flat on your back?" I ask. He had gone from sitting to propped up on his elbows when I jostled him, and now he reclines slowly and rigidly, the reverse of Dracula getting out of his coffin.

"What are you going to do?"

"I'm going to move you around until I can work out exactly where you're hurt and how you're hurt."

"It's my leg."

"I don't think it is."

"But it's *my* leg."

I pick up his heel and lift it directly into the air so that his leg, straight, is at the height of my chest.

"How much does that hurt? Scale of zero to ten, where ten is the worst pain you've ever experienced."

"I dunno. Two?"

"And how about—" I lift his leg an inch higher so it begins to pull at the muscles in his groin.

"Eight!" I lower his leg immediately.

"Okay, well, with earlier, that's pretty conclusive. When you experience pain, is it—" I point to the spot on his uninjured leg "—there?"

I am not touching his skin. I am touching the fabric of his underwear, on the inside of his upper thigh. I had not considered before pinpointing the position that it would put me as close to a penis as I have ever been.

Connor nods.

"Okay," I say.

"Is it?" he asks.

"No, I mean, I acknowledge that this is a thing you've said and I have

111

understood it. Okay. I'm going to put my hands on your knees and hold them apart, then I want you to push in and try to bring them together. It's going to hurt. I just want you to push as hard as you can for a few seconds when I say."

I brace myself and push hard against him. When I tell him to go, he easily overpowers me – though not without pain.

"Okay. Good. It's definitely a groin strain, but I think that's no worse than a grade two. We'll know for sure in the morning if there's swelling or bruising. But I think you'll be fine if you have a few days of bed rest. Maybe a week."

"Okay," he says.

There is a change. Not of position – I don't think either of us move at all, even to breathe. It is like a picture which is two things at once, though you can only see one at a time, as your perspective shifts between them. My hands are on Connor's legs. The instant before they had been there because it was necessary; a strength test is how you determine the severity of the damage to a muscle. Then the way I saw the world flipped. My hands did not need to be there, and I can feel the firm muscle, the soft, tight skin and the bristle of hair against my fingers.

I like the way it feels. The way *he* feels. I can hear the blood in my ears and feel the empty tingle in my stomach. I am motivated by a directionless urge – I want to do something, though I don't know what that is.

I spread my fingers. It is a movement of millimetres, and its significance is epoch defining.

Connor is still flat on his back, looking up at the ceiling, but I feel his attention shift. He made himself concentrate on remaining relaxed, and as that message cascaded down his body from his brain, I felt the ripple of it. A decision: his decision to comply with whatever I wanted to do.

Or perhaps it was just a willingness to see what happened next? That would be like him, I think; to be in the moment and see what the moment offered him.

I am not ready to take control: to set the speed of this – whatever this is. And I *can't*. And I *want to*.

I touch him and there is irrefutable biology in play; a force as powerful as gravity, but coiled up and buried inside me in a place that I cannot name, could perhaps point to, but which I understand with same familiarity as those parts of me I was born with. My hands know touch, my tongue knows taste, my skin knows ice and fire. This awakening part of me knows want and it rings wordless and clear as a bell. I do not believe it existed even six months ago; it is as if I have grown a second stomach which has different appetites that I don't know how to feed.

And above the biology there is the knowledge that to go further would have consequences I could not control. My choices are life or death. The acolyte's choice is death.

I do not love him – this is ridiculous – I do not know him. But I did not consider how much I would otherwise feel, when it came to it; when the choice was before me. Love is the part they talk about, but love is only part of it. If I were an animal, if we had never learned to speak, I could lay down beside him and feel him against me, and feel the same as I do now.

It is not *love*.

But it is *next*. And it divides my soul in two equal, unalike pieces.

And I am ready.

And I must not.

Connor begins to stir. A twitch in the black fabric. It is involuntary. (I have read all the sex education materials and I know it is involuntary). A natural, biological reaction – happening more or less at eye level, about a foot away from my face.

There is a knock on the bedroom door.

Two seconds of chaos follow, and I have no idea what I'm doing or why. My hand is resting on a small dresser, next to a boxy plasticky television that has never, and shall never, pick up Channel Five. I have managed to inspect all four corners of the room and found them free of cobwebs.

He is standing on the other side of the room, and the bed between us might as well be a wall. He holds his jeans balled-up in front of him. I want to say that it's fine; that I know; that even more than fine, I like it. But I can't close the distance any more than he can. The order of events has been upset and there is the briefest sensation of falling without moving.

I remember the shamed guilt and the fear of Angus; it is a feeling in my fists as much as my heart. There is a voice in my head screaming at him – *don't you dare you look away from me.* This is not an awkward moment to be avoided. My life is not someone else's mistake.

But he is looking at me.

His face is a mirror. Something has passed between us and we are tied together by a rope whose length is shortening even now.

A second knock.

I pantomime whisper, "Get on the bed!"

Remembering that he is hurt, Connor sort of falls onto it and does his best to align his head with the pillows.

I place myself in front of the bed and open the door, wearing my best *who-may-I-say-is-calling?* face. It is Mr. Maxwell. His eyes are large, with his brows turned upwards in the middle, and though he is looking straight at me, I feel that he doesn't see anything at all.

If I think about maintaining a calm appearance, I'm sure my face will curl up my forehead like the false shirt front of a waiter in an old cartoon – so I don't think about it.

"Is Connor here?" Mr. Maxwell asks.

Those shirt fronts were called dickeys – shut up brain. I definitely don't think about dickeys.

"I was just helping him into bed," I say, because I apparently have all the self-control of a master criminal desperate to be caught.

Would you like one of my scones, Mr. Holmes? Some say they're the Crown Jewels of my afternoon tea. Or perhaps you'd like a slice of my, Professor Moriarty's, stollen? Whichever you prefer. Professor Moriarty's stollen? The Crown Jewels? Do make up your mind, Mr. Holmes, I have an urgent appointment at Pentonville.

I stand aside and he enters the room.

"I heard you were hurt," Mr. Maxwell says.

"I'm fine," says Connor.

"He has a moderate strain and should have two or three days of bed rest," I say. There is that word again. *Bed.* It is literally and figuratively the biggest thing in the room. Before anyone can respond I add, "I'll leave you to it. Connor, I'll check back in on you in the morning."

I step backwards through the door and pull it closed as I go. In the corridor I put my head on the door frame. I am seized by the anxiety of a thought – had he not injured himself, he would likely have gone home tomorrow. The glass house on the promontory is his home, though he has never lived there, perhaps has never been inside. Now he shouldn't be moved. He must not be moved. For a few more days he has to stay at the hotel. For a few more days he is mine.

"Excuse me."

An elderly couple shuffle past me on the way to their room. I look up, smile – we exchange closed-mouth smiles of the sort strangers share – and I head downstairs only to run into my mum on the half landing by the picture of the girl with the ginger wig. She stops at the top of the lower stairs with her hand on the bannister.

"I've dealt with Mister Melville," she says.

"Who's Mister Melville?" I ask.

"The gentleman who helped Connor back to the house." *Alan* Melville.

"I promised him a piece of cake."

"And the soup and the sandwich. It's fine, I've dealt with it."

"Was that okay? It seemed like the least we could do under the circumstances."

"It's fine. You did really well tonight managing the kitchen by yourself."

"Thank you. I was spinning a few plates – not literally; that wouldn't have been helpful. The pork loin took me by surprise." I hear myself say it and feel myself turn red. The jig is up. I might be able to bluff past Mr. Maxwell, but my mum will see it written across my face like a prison tattoo. I tense from head to toe, knowing something will happen, not knowing what.

She says, "There were a lot of compliments."

"Good," I say and nod. "Good."

"Are you off to bed?" She is casual and conversational.

I make a long *umm*. I can't have gotten away with it. I can't have slipped this under my mum's otherwise perfect radar. But she lets me *umm* – I think she'd let me *umm* until three other members of an awkward barbershop quartet joined me on the landing and together we were *umm*ing a full c-chord.

I say, "I was going to fill the dishwasher, then go to bed."

"Don't worry about it. I'll do it. You've had a long day."

Until this moment, I have never had a day that was long enough to be excused from a task. I might be prevented from doing it because I was locked in my room as a punishment. When I was eight, I got chickenpox and was made to stay in bed for two days – mostly to avoid disturbing the guests. But being *excused* while I'm fit and healthy and asking to do it?

She knows. But she isn't concerned. If anything, she's put on a thin, happy smile – which I wouldn't be suspicious of at all if it didn't seem so forced. My mum is not an idle smiler. She smiles the way people use torches – with purpose, infrequently, and with a hint of concern that the batteries will go flat at the worst time.

How could she possibly know? I left him two minutes ago and almost nothing happened. It's not as if she heard the sound of passionate lovemaking through the restaurant ceiling. Even if she had the hotel full of microphones and concealed cameras like the Moscow Hilton – or whatever fancy hotels they have in Moscow – and she doesn't – it's not as if she has the feed wired into her brain. She was pouring a bowl of soup, making a sandwich, slicing a piece of cake, and talking to a twitcher. Show me the FSB agent who can multitask espionage and catering – they don't exist.

She doesn't know. She can't read it from my face. It's a *secret*.

"Okay!" I say it a little too enthusiastically and force myself into a tremendously exaggerated yawn. "See you in the morning!"

I bounce halfway to the first-floor landing before she says, "Eleanor."

I stop, turn on the spot.

"Have you forgotten something?" she asks.

"No?"

"I think you have," she says.

I wrack my brains. The back door is locked. The oven is off. I've cleaned the floor and wiped down all the surfaces with disinfectant. I put the soup into containers with labels and dates. I've done everything I should have, except loading the dishwasher and that was because she told me not to. If there's anything else it's not in my head.

She points to her cheek.

I step down to her, lean in and kiss her on the cheek.

"Good girl," she says, and she smiles at me again. A close-mouthed smile, which is just friendly enough, just kind enough. A smile that the batteries could run out on at any moment. The kind of smile someone would give to a stranger.

12

The dream – I'm sure it's a dream – slips away from me. I remember that a second or a minute or some non-linear, dream-based time unit ago it was vivid. The colours were deeper than in real life; high saturation, high contrast, but as I emerge from the dream all the definition vanishes and I am in darkness. Lying still, in an unbroken dark that clings to me like heavy black velvet.

I know that I am not awake. It is almost the solstice, and it is never entirely dark in my bedroom at this time of year. Somehow, I know I am also in my bedroom, in my own bed. Is it the smell? Can I hear a familiar sound? As I try to find what makes me sure, even the black hole dream fades.

One potato. Two potato.

My eyes are closed, though I am awake. I can hear the room is empty, that it is early. And I am wet. This last sensation comes to me first as a feeling of cold. My sheets are stuck to my chest and back. My pillow is soaked. I peel the sheets away from me and sit on the edge of my bed. Rather than drowsy after a long sleep, I feel hyperalert and uneasy. I am a rabbit and every angular shadow is a hawk.

In the bathroom I turn the water as hot as I can stand and get in, scrubbing myself until my skin glows pink, then I switch everything to pure cold water and endure it for as long as I am able.

Twenty-six potato.

I don't check the time until I'm dry; it's coming up on five. Low as a spoken-word poem, I play *Summertime* sung by Ella Fitzgerald. Since I can't go back to bed, I strip off all the sheets and remake it with fresh linens from the chest of a drawers. Smoothing out the wrinkles in the material, I am sure that this is the first time I have thought about him today.

One of these mornings you're gonna rise up singing. There are some, I'm sure, who would say Miss Billie Holiday sang it better. Some might even say the best was Loulie Jean Norman – she did it in the film version of *Porgy and Bess*; this was back when Hollywood overdubbed singers in films and thought nothing of substituting the voice of (black) Diahann Carroll (who could sing) with the (white) voice of Norman. *And you'll spread your wings and take to the sky.* And though I would certainly listen to these opinions respectfully, they would be wrong.

But till that morning, there ain't nothing can harm you.

I open all the windows – it's freezing, so I close half of them again. Summertime on Ensay isn't the same as summertime in South Carolina. Then, because the thought is in my head, I find *Substitute* by The Who and switch to that.

By six, I have read my biology textbook chapters, made notes, and can confidently explain the difference between a transect study, a point count, and remote detection, and make informed judgements about which of these to employ when studying different kinds of plants and animals under different circumstances. Now, some might say, that as I can't leave the building, I am unlikely to need to know how to conduct a transect study and use it to estimate the coverage of St John's Wort over a wide area. Some might say that a point study where the location of my point is inside, is unlikely to result in detection of a wide variation of fauna, regardless of season. And though I would dismiss these opinions as nonsense, they would be correct.

At the end there will be an examination. An invigilator from the Scottish Qualifications Authority will travel to Ensay and we'll sit together in this room. They will quietly read a book for two hours while I write my answers *by hand* on *paper* – like a *savage*. And they'll take these scribbles away, try not to fall into the sea and drown, there's probably some kind of marking involved, and three months later I'll get a plasticky sheet of paper in the post telling me whether or not I'm stupid.

It does also come out as an email now. I am waiting for just such an email from the exams I finished in May. I know it's going to arrive on Tuesday, the eighth of August. Other than that, I don't know, and I don't like to speculate. Mrs. Olafsson tells me I'm *bright as a button*, but I only get feedback on my work from my teachers – many and various, and whom I have never met. It's difficult to take praise from strangers – and from people who love me. The best praise, I think, is the kind that comes from people who know me in passing, and it should only be delivered third hand. If someone else says someone I know said something nice, then that's saying something.

It has been easy not to think about the exam results for the last couple of weeks. I am, after all, only days away from my birthday. Becoming the acolyte is more exciting than becoming the girl who got three Bs and two Cs at her Highers.

Do I still mean exciting? The thought isn't in the middle of my brain the way it was a week ago. In itself that feels punishable. That is where my attention should be.

So, can I knock on someone's door at six o'clock in the morning, or what?

This feels like a slippery slope. I start by taking off his trousers against his will, then I'm showing up at his door nine hours later – stand back Mae West, I've got this sexually liberated woman thing covered – and before either of us knows it, he's going to be holding my hand. This slope appears to slip uphill.

I could really go for a hand-holding right now. Entwined fingers. A little sweat. Yeah. Hold that hand. Hold it – hold it real good.

I stand up, because that is what people do when it is time for ridiculous things to stop and sensible things to come back in, straighten the furniture, and hose everyone down.

Connor didn't have any dinner last night. I know this for a fact – because I didn't make him any, and my mum would never have thought to. As it happens, I never thought to either – whatevs, shut up. He's probably woken up in the night and eaten a tiny bar of soap – he's never been starved before; he wouldn't know not to do that. It is my responsibility as a host and as a trained first-aider and, yes, even as a human being, to bring him something to eat at a time when there's a real possibility he won't have a top on.

* * *

Malcolm Gladwell popularised the idea that to be great at something, a person needs ten thousand hours of practice. I am great at carrying trays. From an early age I have trained in the mystic art of balancing things all the way up one arm and still having two things on the other arm. Table of six people wants soup? One trip.

Is Ringo Starr the best bus boy in the world? He's not even the best bus boy in The Beatles – John Lennon, trademark, copyright, etc. probably.

I ascend the flight of stairs from the kitchen to the first floor in the much the same way a duchess would, if she were any good at soundlessly bearing two full Scottish breakfasts, a pot of tea, and two cups without so much as a rattle or a clink. (All the cutlery is in my pocket – that's the secret).

I back through the landing door and parade along the corridor with great dignity and ease. Then, when I reach his bedroom door, I have to kick it because I've no free hands and I'm not actually a magician. A real duchess would have a footman to kick doors for her, of course. I kick it again, to remove any doubt that this was an accidental kicking or an encounter between the door and the luggage of another guest. This was a foot knock.

I hear movement followed by an *ow-fuck* then more movement and the loud mechanical sound of the lock opening like a bank vault.

Connor appears in the gap in the door. He is still wearing the same t-shirt he had on last night. I can tell by how it's crumpled that he's slept in it, and I can tell by the foggy expression that he's been sleeping until a few seconds ago.

"I've brought you breakfast," I say.

"What time is it?"

I hold the tray up slightly. "Breakfast time."

"Okay," he says because to resist something, a person has to be awake.

He flicks on the bedroom light, though it adds very little illumination; the closed curtains are infused with morning, and he sits down on the bed with a suppressed groan of pain. I put the tray on the bed beside him, then drag the bedside table out from the wall. Some of the rooms are big enough that they have a separate table or desk, but not this one. It has a bed, two bedside tables, a dresser, and a wooden chair. Built into the space behind the door is the world's smallest wardrobe not intended for a dollhouse – it can hold three items, or no items if one of the three items is a coat. It's all in good condition; solid wood furniture lasts forever. I lift the chair over to sit opposite him and put the tray onto the bedside table between us.

The two plates are each covered by their own cloche – a cylindrical lid of polished metal with two holes in the top intended to function as handle and steam outlet. I pull off the cloches with panache, leave them on the dresser, and hand Connor a knife and fork from my pocket.

He is absent for several seconds. Events are happening near him rather than to him. When the world connects with his senses, there is full-body whiplash, a judder, a shake of the head, and he settles into his body the way a ghost might possess a psychic medium.

He says, "I am starving," and shows breakfast no mercy. He is a sausage in before he remembers I'm there, pouring tea, while he is still just in his t-shirt and pants. I wouldn't permit it in the tearoom. I can pinpoint the moment he realises, then shrugs it off. We've been here already. No sense being prudish now.

He uses his fork like a spoon. He's been allowed to grow up feral.

"Thanks," he says – in relation to the tea, the breakfast, just in general; I'm not sure, and it doesn't matter.

"How are you feeling?"

"Worse than last night," he says with his mouth full. After swallowing he adds, "It's bruised and swollen. Everything except being still is sore."

"That's fine." I have been reading up on this. "I'll get you some ibuprofen and paracetamol."

"Careful, don't want me getting addicted."

"We might have codeine, but the chemist section of the shop only does ibuprofen, paracetamol, toothpaste, and tampons. And tan-coloured tights.

Did you want any tights?"

"I'm good. For tampons too. I'll take any codeine you can find though. And opioids. Do you have any opioids?"

"Not since that narco tanker beached itself on Berneray. Two-thousand-and-fifteen – it was heroin galore 'round here. Missus Torrence ran out of veins in her arms and had to start using the ones in her feet. And she is – and she'll tell you this – a martyr to the arthritis in her feet."

"If you see any though."

"Oh, sure – you've got dibs."

I'm hungry too, now that my nervous energy has been dispersed. We eat to the sound of knives and forks clacking through cooked meat. He finishes first and holds his cup of tea close, with both his hands, hugging it as if to warm himself, though by this point it can't be any warmer than he is.

"You were out a long time yesterday," I say. I had tried for a conversational observation but his focus on the cup tells me I've missed something.

"I'm out a long time every day."

"Oh."

"Yeah."

"Most people are out all day," I say. It was a throwaway remark; noise filling up the gaps; little stones between bigger rocks and of no more importance than that. He is quiet, but I feel him thinking. Rather than sand and shale passively filling space, my remark was a wedge and it is pushing him open.

I say, "I imagine your uncle was upset."

"Yeah," he says. "Maybe relieved. I think he was scared I'd been badly hurt. He's looking after me for my mum; I think he feels responsible."

"He feels sad too."

"I know. But why is that my problem? We don't really know each other. Nobody died and made me the boss of him."

I'm not eating now – and it would speak better of my character if it were because of subject matter rather than because I have cleaned my plate.

"You're the only part of her he has left."

"I'm not part of anyone," he ruffles at the implication. "I'm not a bit of my dead mum. I'm a person that he doesn't know. Maybe he wouldn't even like me if he did."

But that's not it. It's true, of course it's true; it's impossible to guarantee families will get along. Brothers and sisters are strangers to each other's children. I read books, lacking personal experience. But there are two things happening with Connor. He's not socially awkward; he's not wandering the moors like Cathy's ghost because he can't talk about the weather or pass five minutes in chat about last night's football.

"Why aren't you living with your dad?" I ask, though I fancy I know the answer already.

He shrugs. "I never knew him. Don't think mum did much either. It was just one of those things, but she decided to keep me. Well – she was properly Catholic, I'm not sure she *decided*; it was who she was."

This is probably the most intimate detail of Connor's life he's ever discussed, and I am nervous to move or to breathe for fear that he will close up again and retreat the way a snail sucks in its eyestalks when they touch something. I consider reaching out to put my hand on his, which sits idle on his knee. What a strange thought that is; I hate it when people suddenly touch me, why would that be how I try to console him?

Connor says, "I got a sense, and this was maybe five years ago, that she had heard something. Or maybe read something in the local paper. Because she asked me if I wanted to know who my dad was and when I said no, she seemed relieved. Or, not relieved, but that she felt the whole thing was settled. I reckon that means he's either dead or in prison."

"You didn't want to know?"

"I was thirteen. It's not like he hadn't had enough time to get involved. You don't get to be somebody's dad just by being a sperm donor. There were a couple of million minutes where I needed a dad and had to do without, then I didn't need one anymore. Anyway, I think if he'd been alive my mum would have told me when she got sick. She would have wanted me to have the choice later."

I bob my head in a silent sign that I never knew the woman and have no reason to suspect he's wrong. It's the polite thing to do, even though she might have been a mad bitch and his father could have lived next door all that time. One feels a certain obligation to the truth, but nobody wants to have their recently deceased mother j'accused of not being a saint.

"Do you want to know now?" I ask.

"No." He says it easily – it's the answer he's been ready to give for a long time. It's not defiant. Maybe it was once an answer full of conflict and hurt. A persuasion: a trick intended to convince an audience of his independence and bravery; the bravura of an amateur Olympian who wins the hundred-yard dash then lights up a cigarette for the cameras. Or maybe it was a simple kitchen knife that he'd sharpened beyond sharp – until its edge altogether disappeared.

Finding his dad now might be like asking him to change who he is, and I can't blame him for refusing.

Would I make the same choice? If it were possible to meet my own dad, would I? Like Connor, I know that I am missing something other people have, but this is not the gap a missing jigsaw piece would leave – I am not the remainder of anyone else; I am the whole and complete me. It is not a fresh wound or an old scar. I am unmarked by injury. Nothing has been taken from me which was precious. Nothing has been substituted. But if a bucket full of water is whole and complete, and can still be added to though it overflows, then I wonder what parts of me would be washed out by this new experience and what this new complete person would be.

In the centre of my chest there is a question – and one feels a certain obligation to the truth.

"I'm going to have a shower and go out," says Connor. "Do you want to come with me?"

"You can't go out; you need to rest."

"I'm not goin' roamin'. Down to the harbour. I can nearly see it from here."

"You can see the sun from here too, and you can't go there either."

"Out into your back garden then. It's got a wall 'round it – that's practically indoors."

"You need to stay off your leg for at least a couple of days."

"Sure, and once I'm outside I'll stay off it. Bum on the grass, Doctor, just you watch."

He stands up as he speaks and the sudden slice of pain makes him steady himself against the wall. He doesn't sit down though. He's gotten used to it in the last few hours and though it likely feels worse rather than better, he won't be restricted by it.

"You'll only make it worse," I say. There is a pause, he shrugs – and *that's* it. He doesn't care if it hurts. Connor looks around at the walls, as if each had advanced on him an inch and when he looks back at me it seems like he is ready for a fight, or has just lost one. He knows in that moment that he has revealed more of himself than he intended.

I ask him, "How long was your mum in hospital for?"

I have never seen him angry before; the intrusion on this memory is as real as if I had pressed my face to the window of that room. My presence is unwelcome. But it passes and is replaced by emotions I can't as easily name.

He says, "You could walk me out to your garden."

I say nothing – what can I say?

"For the last two weeks she didn't wake up." He begins at the end, telling me where this is going. Spoiler – she dies. There's no happy ending, and I shouldn't dare try to add one. "She was in hospital for three weeks. I thought she was going to get better, but she hadn't told me everything. She'd been taking chemotherapy, radiotherapy, for fourteen months – but not to get better. She wasn't going to get better. She was holding the cancer back for as long as she could. The doctors knew – they didn't tell me until she was gone. Then one day I went in – I went in every day – and she wouldn't wake up. There was a tumour burrowing through her brain and there was nothing anyone could do. So I just waited. Not waiting for her to wake up; I didn't think she'd wake up. I just waited.

"She had been sick for such a long time and nobody came to see her.

That was my fault – nobody wanted to deal with me. I get it, you know? I get how tough it is to deal with someone else's grief. But that was when I felt it – when it was happening to me. I know it's selfish, but it was happening to me as well as her. That was when I needed somebody to be there – just to wait.

"Afterwards, when everybody comes in, it's safe. They pay respects – it's orderly – it's no different than paying for your shopping. They have happy memories – that's how they'll remember her when they think about her at all, which is never, or nearly never. And they know how it feels because didn't they lose someone too? Some stranger. Someone they thought of as a part of themselves. And everyone is a liar, because you couldn't stand up and shake someone's hand and remind them of how good a person she was if you really knew what it was like. How cruel is that? For a hundred nobodies to remind you what you've lost. To tell you that from here on you're alone. And keep your fucking chin up."

I try, "It was good of you to stay with her. Maybe she knew."

He says, "I wasn't waiting for anything except for her to let me go."

I don't know that I understand, but I think I do. Fourteen months of dying must be like ten years of living, but only the bad parts.

I stand up and sidestep the makeshift breakfast table to put my arms around him. He pushes me away, his face registers disgust or shame. I halt, then try again, and now he doesn't resist. He does nothing for a long time; stands like a statue. Then he puts his head down to the side of mine and we stay there – me embracing him, him being embraced – for as long as I can remember touching anyone. It must be a full minute before I realise.

And I guess I'm fine with it.

Connor says, "I need to sit down again."

"I told you."

"Will you help me out to the garden?" We are sitting together on the bed as we were the night before. At some point *he* has taken *my* hand in his. I don't remember it happening and I don't look down in case he lets me go. I guess I'm fine with that too. But I wish he hadn't done it right at the same moment I have to tell him I'm a liar by omission.

"I can't."

He asks the question with his stupid face. We had a good run.

"Well," I say, "here's the thing."

* * *

She can't go outside. He can't stay inside. A new comedy coming this fall to ABC. *Did you leave the window open?* Canned laughter as we see he's dressed like a chicken. Her sister is the woman who played Janice in *Friends*. His best friend looks like the Mexican Chris Farley – *now that's a fun time for all la familia.*

Nine eastern, eight central. Either it will run for nine years or it won't make it out of pilot season.

I have opened the window of his room as far as it will go. It is far enough that a child could climb out, but we're only one storey up and neither of us has a child – I'm not worried.

"And this doesn't bother you?" Connor asks, gesturing to the window. He is propped up against the headboard while I sit cross-legged on the bed next to him, my shoes discarded by the breakfast plates.

"It's not about being outside, it's about not being able to get back inside. I'm not afraid of fresh air and sunshine."

"You are a bit ginger."

"I am *not.*"

"A little bit. You've got freckles on your nose. You're like six percent ginger. I think that's it; it's your ginger gene protecting itself from the sun." I find that I am rubbing my hand on the bridge of my nose. I have freckles?

"Just because I have freckles doesn't mean I'm ginger."

"Everyone Scottish is ginger."

"Freckles appear at all levels of the Fitzpatrick phototyping scale."

"What?"

"Black people get freckles."

"Yeah, but you didn't say *black people get freckles* – you said *freckles appear at all levels of the Fitzpatrick something scale.*"

"The Fitzpatrick phototyping scale gives a rating for all skin types to determine how sensitive they are to ultraviolet light. Freckles are caused by exposure to ultraviolet light. Specifically, it's UV-B."

He laughs, as if I'd just told him a joke rather than stated a fact. "How do you know all this . . . stuff?"

"What do you mean?"

"*Stuff,*" he repeats with added emphasis. *Stuff, Manuel. Don't mention the war.* "Like who Charlie Parker is and when and where he died—" Twelfth of March, nineteen fifty-five, the Stanhope Apartment Hotel, Fifth Avenue, New York City. He died of half-a-dozen things: pneumonia, cirrhosis, an ulcer, heroin addiction, being a black man, and jazz. "—or what colour Prussian army uniforms used to be, or that there was a place called Prussia." I mean, look at an eighteenth-century map, buddy. "I bet you know the first name of the Fitzpatrick feller with the prototyping scale."

"Thomas."

"I knew it!"

"His middle name was Bernard."

"Stuff," he says. "How can you possibly know so much *stuff?*"

I say, "I read it."

"In books?"

"And the internet. Really anywhere things are written down."

125

"You don't think that's weird, weird girl?"

"That I learned about things by reading? That's how most of the knowledge created by human beings exists; that's how it's stored and how it's passed on."

"No, it's not." He shuffles in bed and sits up straighter. "That's just what people put in books. The stuff people put in books is in books and passed on to other people through books. There are things you can know that you can't put into words."

"Like what?"

"Well, I can't tell you, can I?"

"Ah – because of words!" I slap him on the arm in an expression of false astonishment.

"Like playing football. You can't learn to play football by reading a book about football."

"There are loads of books about how to play football written for people of all skill levels; for players and for coaches."

"Well, I've never seen any."

"Maybe that's why you're shit at football," I say, even though I have no idea if he's any good, and I affect a nonchalant shrug. He frowns at this – I've challenged him and he doesn't quite like it – then I see the subtle change in the shape of his eyes. That comes first. In the second before he'll speak – having arrived at what he believes is a plan of incontrovertible cunning – his brow will soften and he'll think himself so clever that he won't be able to resist a sly smile. I fold my arms and watch my prediction come to pass. His eyebrows arrive at their destinations with the precision of Japanese public transport and the corners of his mouth turn up like the doors of a DeLorean that recently – from the car's perspective – hit eighty-eight miles per hour.

He says, "Like a kiss, then."

Oh.

"A kiss?" I ask.

"Exactly. Sure, you might think that you can write down how it feels to be kissed. But there's everything in a kiss. There's touch, there's taste – those are obvious."

"I know."

"There's pressure and smell – you have to breathe through your nose. You can hear a kiss; the sounds people make, the way they move against you. And even though you can't see them, it's because you're choosing to close your eyes; you're looking into a little bit of mutually agreed darkness that only exists for the two of you."

"I have been kissed before."

"You have, have you?"

"In fact, I have."

"Was it a burglar?" In a manner of speaking. "Did you have to throw down knotted bedsheets so he could climb up to you?" He doesn't believe me. "And do you think you could write down everything about how it felt to be kissed by your Prince Charming?" And why would it have been a charming prince? A kiss is a promise of nothing.

I grab a handful of his t-shirt from around his neck and pull him towards me as I push forward. His body recognises what is happening once I've made contact. My intrepid Venusian spaceship lands on his Martian mouth. And I show him everything I've ever learned from Jennifer Grey and Clare Danes and Audrey Hepburn, from Sylvia Plath and Giacomo Puccini and Gabriel García Márquez. With a little bit of Angus mixed in – because the text is fine work, but the play's the thing.

All of this is over in seconds, though I am comfortable, even smug; confident that I have beaten his argument.

I move to pull away, but he follows an inch. His lips feel much larger in our darkness than they looked in the light, and they are round and soft and even broken in places. I can feel weather on them. It must be imagination: I cannot taste the sea on him. After all, he has not left this room, and I have never tasted the sea. He could only taste of baked beans, but then so must I – and the algebra of these sensations cancel out until there are only the unique elements. Him. Me. A dissolving memory of ocean.

I wish I could lick his mouth the way a dog would, or how a child would consume an ice cream. I wish I could eat a small part of him – so small that he would never notice; that only I would know, but that part would be mine forever. The sudden and ridiculous notion makes me feel foolish. I must be blushing. I must be red from head to toe.

Oh.

Did I make that sound or was it only in my head? His hand has come to rest on my arm, somewhere between a hold, a caress, and an attempt to steady me. I think about his hands, the dusting of dark hair on his forearms and their natural tan. I want him to take off his shirt so I can run my hands over his skin. I want to cover myself in the smell of him – which is daft because what he mostly smells of is yesterday and Lynx Africa. And I am getting carried away, and enjoying how it feels to be carried away, and being frightened by it, and not caring, and doing all these things at once.

His hand slips from my arm to my waist. Though there is a cotton t-shirt that separates our skin, the gesture is as intimate as the tip of his tongue against mine. He pulls me closer – though it is really only a request, I do all the work of moving. There is a space between us the width of a hand, and we can get no closer in this position while keeping our lips together. If I had started with my legs uncrossed, I would be on top of him by now.

But all this has happened too slowly. I am beyond pure instinct. And I know I can't go any further than this. I put my hand into the gap between us and push myself away. I register the ache of it on his face. I leave my hand on his chest and we look at each other.

"It's okay," he says. "I understand."

He definitely doesn't understand. If he knew, he'd hop from this hotel screaming and never look back. But I understand. I had always thought it would be a sense of duty that would make me choose. One morning I would wake up and the job would need to be done and I would do it; it would be like going to war. But that's not how it will happen; I doubt that's how it ever was for anyone. It's going to overwhelm me and I won't choose – I'll submit.

I can feel his heart beating under my palm. The rhythm of it is a knock on my door.

"We don't have to—"

I interrupt whatever his suggestion was with a shake of my head and a complete withdrawal. I am on fire and what I need isn't a controlled burn, it's a cargo helicopter with a swimming-pool-sized bucket to douse me. And the temptation is too much: if I let him speak then I'll listen; if I imagine the contact of his fingers and his lips, I'll never say no to them.

I say, "Tell me about your first time."

"Now?"

I nod. "Or tell me about the last girl you were with."

"I don't think you want me to do that." Of course I don't want him to do that, but I need him to. I need the kind of distance that can't be measured with a ruler.

"Can you just – you know – do it?"

"Uh," he says, one of those involuntary escapes of angst, but no sooner has it left him his face changes like a baby that's been winded. "Right, you'll like this." He puts himself into a position which has no name I know, but would have immediately given the game away in Gorky Park. He is about to disclose secrets.

"My mate Jimmy started seeing this girl. Proper Catholic girl, convent school, dad was some big noise in the laity. She's seventeen and she's never even seen a boy, so she's—"

He stops. I supply, "Mad for it?"

He grins, shrugs, and continues. "They've been going together for a few weeks, but she's got a sister, just a year younger, and she says that unless she's got a boyfriend as well, she's going to tell their dad. She – the older sister – tells him – Jimmy – and Jimmy puts the word 'round. Now, and I can't say whether this is true, or whether I had anything to do with it, but a rumour begins to circulate at the same time that the father of these girls isn't just well connected in the next world, he's got dangerous friends in this one too. He's former IRA – well, former in the sense that they're all former – they decommissioned enough guns to make Good Friday legitimate, but everybody's got an AK in the attic."

"I thought the IRA was in Northern Ireland."

"You think there aren't republican paramilitaries in the Republic? That's like saying there are no Jews in Israel."

"Huh. So, you started the rumour?"

"I absolutely, positively did not say that."

"Right."

"Now maybe Verona was full of risk-takers, or your fella Romeo was the exception, but in Dublin, a man thinks twice about upsetting his priest and the IRA over a girl that's two years from legal and sight unseen. I'm not going to say which of those is the biggest concern – I think you'd be right to believe that it varies – but Jimmy is getting no nibbles. Eventually he comes to me and I'm on for the long con. I say it's not a good time; my mum's not well, he says I need to let off some steam, I say maybe this is sound advice you're giving me James, but we are, as the Madonna herself once said, *living in a material world* and I am without funds.

"He says ten. I remind him if I'm expected to wine and dine someone from a good family, that two meals from McDonalds could go more than ten euros, and that a young lady might reasonably want a McFlurry, to say nothing of the fact that I'm going to need bus fare. He says fifteen and we settle on twenty, because he works weekends at PC World and I don't.

"It's a Saturday and we're in town. Jimmy and I have done our hair and the girls have probably made an effort too. It's nice, you know? There's something about having a promenade with a girl on your arm; it makes you walk taller; somebody's given you a seal of approval and you're smiling from ear to ear – but only on the inside, because you can't seem desperate for a ride or you'll never get one."

I say, "Thanks for the tip."

"It doesn't apply to girls. Girls have different rules and I don't know what they are. Anyway, it starts to rain. We've done a bit of lunch, we've had a walk, Jimmy's bought his girl a top that has *vagina* written in sequins. Or it could have been something else. *Happy*, maybe? What I remember is *vagina*. It was all sparkles and italics. The day out is more or less finished when it starts to pour down – sheets of rain with no signs of it stopping, and it rains all day and into the following morning in the end.

"Jimmy gets a sudden bright idea – goes off over his head like a lightbulb. Why don't we all go back to his house. His mum and dad are out for the day and his big brother Sean is in Magaluf with the lads from the Bank of Ireland. That's two free bedrooms and no witnesses except Himself – which everyone is fine with.

"So, Jimmy's in the next room with his girl, and I'm with her sister, and we can hear them at it. And this is his house, remember, and he knows we can hear them. His brother's had a couple of girlfriends that his mum's allowed to stay over; he's been on the other side. He's moaning and groaning – it's only him; his girlfriend isn't making a sound. And her sister's getting very friendly with me.

"But I don't fancy duelling banjos with Jimmy. So, I shout – *I don't care what Jimmy likes, you're not shoving your thumb up my arse*!

"All the noise from next door stops, then the door bursts open and she runs in, completely naked. She realises immediately that she's been tricked, turns around, and runs straight into the edge of the door she just opened. Knocked herself out cold, then her sister panics, runs over to check on her. Who comes charging 'round the corner? It's your man James Mahoney. Now Jimmy's no reason to be shy in the old locker room, and he's got a rod on, so that willy's got angular momentum. Emily looks up – Emily, I think that was her name – and Jimmy's cock slaps her right across the face!"

"That's awful."

"Sure, that was just about the funniest thing that's ever happened. And I was still five euros up on the day."

"She must have been so embarrassed."

"Oh, it all came out after that. Turned out that Jimmy had been up them both for weeks. Getting me hooked up with his girlfriend's sister was just cover. I think both the girls knew as well – that was the strange thing. I think his girlfriend knew that her sister and her boyfriend were having sex, and she knew that I was there to make it okay for them all to be together without it being obvious. But everyone knew what was happening all the time."

He changes with that disclosure. His massive, stupid smile turns down a bit and his brow furrows.

I ask, "Is that story true?"

Connor holds up one hand and places the other over his heart. "I swear to Jesus, Mary, and Saint Patrick." I can't tell if this is a simple irony or self-deception, but even the pope isn't as Catholic as Connor seems when doing his Scout's Honour to God.

"Did you like her?"

"Who?"

"Did you like her?"

"Not really. Maybe. Not after that though. I saw her different, you know? And Jimmy as well – he did actually enjoy a bit of finger in the bum."

"When did you know?"

"About what?"

I don't say anything to that. He understood my question.

Connor says, "Before he asked me to go out with her. I think. I couldn't have said it; I couldn't have put it into words. But after – when it was out – it was the same shape. What I'd felt was the same as what I learned."

"How did you feel?"

He shrugs; it is more like a squirm. "I don't know."

"But when you shouted, it wasn't just a joke. You didn't know what you were doing, but you knew you were doing something."

"Yeah. I suppose."

"I think that's a sad story."

"Yeah," he says.

I kiss him again. Just a little. And as much as I dare.

13

Connor agrees to two more days of bed rest. In those two days I bring him meals, we talk, and I spend maybe an hour a day kissing him. Or he kisses me. I have discovered *things*. A consensual kiss is not always an equal partnership. Perhaps it's not even usually equal. Like a conversation, sometimes one person has something to say, sometimes one person wants to listen. The exchange can be whispered or yelled, as if trying to be heard over background noise. I like kissing him, mostly. I like to start things. But then I like it when he takes over. We are getting better at judging this; he waits for me, his eyes give me permission, but he never moves first.

This is our nearest equivalent to an arm-in-arm promenade – in the morning and the evening, a sort of near-heavy petting where I feel him swell against me and I try not to think about all the implications of his affection.

At the end of his imprisonment, in the morning of the third day, we say goodbye with a tender sincerity that I'm sure we both know is ridiculous. We have seen it before and are fulfilling roles that we believe are expected of us. I am pulling everything I do from *Casablanca*, while he is channelling *The Fast and The Furious*, *Transformers*, or something equally poignant.

I don't watch him leave, dragging the single suitcase that contains everything he owns. I don't think about him through the afternoon teas or the evening meals. When he shows up at the back door of the kitchen at nine o'clock that night, I have nothing for him, I am hollow.

He holds up a small bunch of pale purple flowers. The fragrance hits me first, and I see it – the light in his eyes, the plan he had – and I understand how he has spent half a day away from me.

"Will ye go, lassie, go," he sings – badly and with a Scottish accent – in a fractured baritone. "And we'll both go the gither, to pull wild mountain thyme from around the bloomin' heather."

I fall into his arms and he holds me up. I press my forehead against his collarbone and I cry for around two straight minutes – I race past all boundaries I might have chosen to set for myself, I am impervious to his consolation and his soothing. Being without him feels like nothing at all, and his return is the rediscovery of myself. I am joyful and absurd, and in that moment, I promise myself that I will never let him go – and immediately I know that I will not keep that promise.

He will go; he must; and I want him to, though I had not realised that is a dagger that hangs over my heart.

"It was just a joke," he says.

And I kiss him.

One day passes, and another. Time no longer orders my life. I am divided into the part of myself which is numb and dead, and the part which is with him. There must be a limit to this. Plants starved of water can be revived if they are restored in time, and this can happen more than once. But each withdrawal carries a cost. I do not know how many times I can say goodbye to him and still be rejuvenated by his return.

I have a sacred duty. I am the acolyte of the end of the world. My mum has prepared me for this all my life. But Connor has taught me a deeper truth – one which my mum certainly knows, but which she is forbidden to speak; could not speak even if she were permitted.

The acolyte is also the sacrifice. I am to send my own heart into the fire, and afterwards I must live without it.

* * *

As with many things, the principle of cake making is easy to understand, while the practice is partially alchemical. If baking were as simple as chemistry, there would be one recipe for Victoria sponge: one list of ingredients and one method. All cakes would be fascist exercises in subduing flour and caster sugar. Brownies for the brown shirts. Strudel for the SS. Actually, they probably did have strudel – they probably had infinite strudel made for them by obedient Aryan women with broad child-bearing hips.

The principle of cake making is this – based on the ingredients used, a cake needs to be baked at the right temperature for the right amount of time. But what ingredients? What temperature? What time? Should one invoke the gods of Hindustan or those of far Nippon? And what if the moon is full and Venus is in your second house? These are the questions which bakers have asked since ancient times.

When London was burned down by its great fire, it was a baker who was to blame – a novice who had not completed the pentagram, smudged his sigils, rubbed his runes the wrong way, and cast his bones on an unfloured surface. When the unsinkable *Titanic* struck ice, who can doubt that some

134

miserable pastry chef was at that very instant layering mille-feuille with crème anglaise instead of crème patisserie? Woe and horror to all those who trifle unawares.

At least according to my mum.

"I'm sure I could help," I say.

"No," says my mum.

"How about the icing? You don't even like making the icing."

"I always make your birthday cake and I always will." She says this matter-of-factly, as if describing the colour of the kitchen walls.

The kitchen has a professional mixer. It is made of steel. It has an engine big enough to operate a washing machine. I am not allowed to touch it. Like a swan, there is the unacknowledged suggestion that our mixer can somehow break a human arm.

My mum has poured diligent portions of all ingredients into the bowl and is watching them with an intensity a hawk would never use, because a rabbit would feel it from half a mile away as prickling sensation on the back of its terrified little neck.

In her view *three eggs, large* is a stupid measurement. Egg sizes differ even amongst the same chicken, much less different breeds of chickens. The volume of yoke to albumin changes based on age, diet, health, and season. Even if one were to assume that the diameter of the yoke has a constant relationship to the diameter of the thickest part of the egg, that would still mean the proportion of yoke varied based on the egg's overall size. That's just maths.

For all those reasons, three large eggs might be too much yoke one week, too little albumin the next, and a different overall volume both times. And if someone didn't have three large eggs, how many eggs of other sizes should they substitute? An egg is the least precise legally permissible unit of measurement. Every other food item is sold in supermarkets by weight and nobody would ever make a cake using *some* flour and *a bit* of butter and *as much* sugar *as a medium-sized hen can pass through its cloaca in one go*. Even the alchemical recipes for cakes call for two hundred grams of flour, not between one hundred and eighty-five and two hundred and fifteen grams.

In our house, eggs are separated into two measuring jugs, whisked, and only then is a specific millilitre amount of white and yellow added to a recipe.

Picking up my argument after a minute of silence I say, "The icing isn't the cake."

She does not look up from her task, but replies, "You'll have some clever reason why one obvious part of a cake isn't part of a cake. And you'll expect that to win the argument. And you'll expect to persuade me and I'll relent and let you make the icing."

"That was the idea."

"No."

"Can I tell you it anyway?"

"So long as you don't expect being right to change anything."

"Madeira."

"And?"

"Madeira is a cake. It's right there in the name – Madeira cake. It's a cake and it doesn't have any icing at all. Not even a dusting of icing sugar. Nothing. It's a plain cake, but it's still a cake. If you added icing to Madeira, it would still be a cake, and if you took the icing away from the cake it would be the same, and if you never put icing on in the first place, it would still be a cake. So, a cake must be a different thing to its icing."

"That seems right," she admits.

"So, I can make the icing?"

"No." She stops the mixer and tilts its mechanical arm backwards so the batter drips slowly down the whisk and back into the bowl. She has prepared three circular, fourteen-inch tins with butter and greaseproof paper. Into each she ladles the mixture in equal portions, and places them with care into the hot ovens. She'll move them all in about ten minutes – enough time that they won't collapse, not so long that they'll bake unevenly. Maybe a little longer, since these are the fourteen-inch tins – this cake will be a monster.

"You don't need to make such a fuss," I say.

"Oh – you'll be turning sixteen again next week? And the week after?"

"Not as I understand it," I reply, my tone aloof. "But it's not as if I need a cake to serve twenty-four when there's only two of us."

"Two of us?" she asks this as she checks the time on her watch.

"Me," I say, pointing at me. "And you," I add, pointing at her. "Two of us. It's always the two of us."

"This year is special. You can invite anyone you want to your sixteenth birthday."

This is awkward for a couple of reasons. She's never mentioned this to me before. All my other birthdays have been private affairs and I imagine – though I have no idea – that one should give more than a day's notice to guests. Guests to what? A party? Am I having a party?

In any case, I don't actually have any friends. Who would I invite? Mrs. Olafsson? Connor? How would I begin to explain him to my mum?

"I don't think I want to invite anyone else," I say.

She misinterprets this statement to her satisfaction and smiles. "I think you should. If nothing else you can invite Mister Maxwell." A name that sounds like a plate falling and shattering. "Don't you think so?"

"Yes." I try to push all my facial muscles upwards to disguise the fact that my heart has dropped through the floor. "Of course." Am I supposed to invite him?

"Good," she says, and she looks at me with uncomfortable intensity. It is the same way of looking at me which she has used with increasing

136

frequency in the last few weeks. I noticed it for the first time on the stairs the night Connor hurt himself, but I noticed it because it was already a familiar recurrence. It was a pop song I'd learned the lyrics to by hearing it a dozen times without realising.

When she spoke to me about touching the American tourist, it was there. When she spoke to me after Mrs. Alexander's death, it was the same expression. It is not that I have suddenly become less attentive to my duties, but I can see that she has become more anxious.

I think about asking the question, but I cannot frame it. Perhaps I am recognising the same distance between us. As my birthday approaches, I have become more conscious of everything unsaid. As I realise the strength of my feelings for Connor, I understand that she must surely have felt the same way about my own father – yet she was instrumental in his death. We cannot speak of it.

She is retreating from me each day, becoming less solid and more of a spectre. Is her skin whiter than it was before? Is it translucent? In two weeks will she be altogether invisible to me?

She says no more on the subject of the party, or gathering – whatever we're calling it, and leaves to strip a bedroom which has just been vacated.

There is a light tap, tap at the kitchen window and I see half of Connor's face peeking in, his nose a pink strip where the sun has caught him. I open the back door and he steps over the threshold into the laundry room. He smells like rain – which is actually the smell of earth rather than water, or so he has told me.

He has been wandering.

I ask, "How long have you been hiding out there?"

He says, "I wasn't hiding, I was just in a place where some people couldn't see me."

"That's hiding."

"How long have you been hiding in here?"

"Oh, touché."

"I hear you're having a party. Celebrating an event? An anniversary? An historic happening on this date but during a previous year?"

"Something like that," I reply – aiming for coquettish.

"Is it—" he swaps to his bad Scottish accent "—the Battle of Bannockburn?"

"It is not."

"How many guesses will ye gie me?"

"My mum will be back in no more than seven minutes – you can have two."

"*Twa?* Lassie, I'd be happy just to gie ye *one*."

I laugh because he's funny, but there is also a point of tension here. I think he expects that when I turn sixteen there will be a change in our circumstances – that the only hurdle he needs to clear is the technical, legal age of consent. At the stroke of midnight tonight I'll become a pumpkin he can have sex with.

Without speaking, every day he has asked, and every day I have told him no. Each refusal is a brick that builds a wall between us. It is still only a very low wall; not the kind of thing that could be used as a defensive position in the event of war, but it's high enough to trip over.

He takes my hands in his and I notice the scrape on his wrist where the top-most layer of his skin has rolled up, leaving the layer below exposed – fresh and pink as cooked ham.

"Have you been falling in holes again?"

"I tripped," he says. The word rings like a bell, because it had been in my head a moment earlier. "Over a monastery."

"You need to be more careful. Or pray. Sit down and I'll clean that."

"It's fine."

"Shut your face and sit down." He obeys and I get the first aid box. There is no point at all in having a first aid box if one is not going to use it. I have already made him wince with a sterilising wipe before it occurs to me that the nearest thing worthy of being called a monastery is on Iona, which is about a hundred miles southeast of Ensay. "Where were you?"

"On the other side of the island."

"What did you mean by *a monastery*?"

"It's one of those hip young phrases the cool people use to describe a monastery." That feels like the kind of thing I would say. I recognise the turn of phrase; my own voice coming back to me is at once familiar and strange. The exact line between us is blurring and he is now a little of me, and I am now a little of him.

I say, "I don't understand," because I don't, and facts are easier to focus on. It would have made equal sense if he'd told me he'd skewered himself on the local pyramid.

"There's the foundation of a monastery. Only a couple of stones are left, it's been taken down to ground level in a lot of places, but there's still some floor tiles and you can see the outline."

"There's never been a monastery on Ensay."

"An abbey then – a nunnery, a priory, whatever anyone wants to call it."

"No. It must be something else." I say this with conviction, but even as I press a brand name Elastoplast over the abrasion, I can't think what building it would be.

"If it's not a nunnery then it's doing a good impression of one. It had two long rooms: one of those would have been the chapel; the other one the dining hall – the, uh, refectory. They were both built on the same east-west line, so I don't know which is which, but it's an old stone building with two spaces that could both be chapels – so both of them are not, not a chapel."

"Just because you're Irish doesn't mean you can detect a chapel."

"It fucking does. If you were brought up Catholic in Ireland you can find Jesus the way sad guys with metal detectors can find bottle caps. Ping! – Jesus. Ping! – another Jesus. You can find Jesus in the dark. If the Romans had crucified him in County Kerry, they'd have known about the resurrection three hours earlier, and when he met Thomas, Thomas would have said *ping! – sure that's Jesus right there and I've no doubt in my mind whatsoever.*"

"It's probably just some old house and somebody's walled garden."

"I suppose it could be – if they were growing elephants. They'd have no reason to build walls that thick otherwise. Unless—" he snaps his fingers "— they were supporting the weight of a big, vaulted ceiling such as might be found in, say, a chapel."

I am angry with him. It is a tight knot in my chest and a prickling sensation down my arms; it is the sensation of being touched and I want to punch him for making me feel this. I pack away the first aid box as if it had injured me by being open.

I have lived here all my life and he has been here less than a month, but he knows the place better. It was a stranger to him, so he committed to exploration. I had assumed the secrets I knew were all the secrets there were. And why had I assumed that – when I already knew it was not true?

And why am I now so sure that this ruined building was a secret that was kept from me? That can only be paranoia. Why would the existence of a monastery have anything to do with me?

"How long ago was it knocked down?"

He puffs. "Dunno. There was a tree growing through some of it. So at least twenty years, but maybe a hundred and twenty."

"Okay," I say. Taking Connor's guess as in any way accurate, that would mean at some point in the twentieth century, Ensay had a monastery – or an abbey, a priory, a nunnery; all words whose subtle distinctions are lost on me – and then that monastic community was torn down to its foundations. A deliberate dismantling. Scotland is covered in remote ruins, ravaged by fire, wind, and rain, slowly collapsing as the decades erode their mortar. But this rogue abbey on the Atlantic coast was unbuilt. "Could you take some pictures the next time you're out there?"

"Yeah. What for?"

"Curiosity."

"Sure."

"And could you bugger off and do it now, maybe?"

"You're very bossy."

"I'm assertive – I'm very *leadery*. Bossy is what people say about women they don't like get *leadered* by."

"Bossed."

"Are you coming to my birthday party tomorrow?"

"A birthday party? I still had two guesses!"

I womanhandle him outside. "You took too long," I tell the closed door.

"Oh, that's the way it is," says the door.

"Send me photos."

"Stop flirting with me through doors."

* * *

On the far side of the island, beyond the highest point and likely not visible from here even when it existed, was *something*. A large, stone-built something big enough to be *most things*. Too big to be crofters' cottages. It might have been a grand house, but anyone rich enough to build a manor on Ensay would not have done so unless they were also mad. Ensay House is an anomaly, it's inconceivable that we would have two. The island is eminently suitable for a religious refuge – as evidenced by the fact that we exist.

I flick through the photographs he has sent to my iPad. This old building – series of buildings, really – can only be what Connor suggests.

"You're frowning at that screen very hard," Connor says. He is lying on my bed, shoes off, and has become bored with everything on his phone.

"I think you're right."

"Yuss!" He punches the air, but does not otherwise move.

"There's nothing like this on the islands. Scotland built tower castles, back when we built castles at all. Small bases, squarish and four- to six-storeys high. But those were border castles – not much more than fortified watch towers designed to keep a dozen people from being raped by the English."

"Racist."

"And then there were a couple of hundred years when the English were very nervous about the Scottish building any castles at all. Initially this was on account of Scotland's continuing affection for the Stuart dynasty and latterly it was just about our outrageous opposition to oppression and cultural genocide."

"Tell me more about how the English oppressed your Celtic ancestors," he says, turning onto his side and leaning on his arm.

"So," I continue without acknowledging him, "there is a significant break in Scottish castle building during which the entire world changed. In eighteen forty-four, James Nicolas Sutherland Matheson bought the island of Lewis – he was a Victorian millionaire, back when being a millionaire really meant something – and he built Lews Castle – which is a Victorian castle, back when being a castle didn't mean anything at all. It's nice enough to look at, but if the English showed up and tried to rape you, you'd be in trouble. If someone was rich enough to build a big house, like this one would have been, they'd also have been rich enough to buy a bigger island and build it somewhere else.

"After he bought Lewis, he had hundreds of families sent to the new world – mostly Canada, I think. Now, whether they wanted to go and were extremely grateful for his assistance on account of how there were no more potatoes, or were forcibly evicted and carried out of their ramshackle huts by paid thugs, is one of those things we'll never really know. Maybe it was even a bit of both. In any case Queen Victoria made him a baronet in recognition of a job well done.

"But Lews Castle is still there and families trace their origins back to Sir James Matheson's clearances. If a wealthy man ever owned Ensay, then I'd know – because there are thousands of tourists who come here every year and never once have any of them mentioned family connections here. There was no clearance from Ensay—" at least not of anyone who lacked the sense to never come back "—and to me that means there was never an owner who built any such house.

"It's not an old castle, it's not a new castle, and that only leaves an abbey. You've found evidence of the only abbey in the Western Isles."

He smiles and says, "Me trip good."

I am left with the real reason for my frown. Ensay is less than a square mile in size. While most of the residents are older women, there are children and they roam across the island. Our tourists have covered every inch of the place on foot. Mr. Murdoch would know about it; it is, after all, his business to know about the history of the island. He would also know enough to know that the abbey was not listed in any architectural record (which I could find).

I am left not with a mystery, but with certainty. It is not possible for the people on Ensay to be ignorant of the ruin. It is a secret in plain sight; known and unspoken. And this can mean only one thing – it is a secret Mrs. Douglas has asked us to keep. Or at least, it is a secret she has asked everyone else to keep. She has never asked *me*. And she has certainly never asked Connor.

"Connor?"

"Yeah?"

"There's a retired history teacher who does walking tours of the islands. His name is Mister Murdoch."

"Jim," he says, with his casual off-island informality. "I've met him a couple of times in the village and out with some Americans. His wife offered to paint my portrait."

"Sure, Jim. Will you ask him about the abbey? Specifically, tell him you've found it, and that you think you should report it to Historic Environment Scotland."

"I've never thought that kind of thing before."

"Yes, you have," I correct him. "When you were out doing Spartans in County Wicklow you took an interest in old buildings."

"Did I?"

"You did, and you've been to Black Castle and Wicklow Abbey, and to all the other places mentioned on the Visit Wicklow tourist site—"

"I didn't even know there was a Visit Wicklow website."

"—and you were *amazed* to discover that this site was here on Ensay, but there was no record of it as a listed historic site—"

"Have you been on the Visit Wicklow website?"

"—and you think it would really impress your university lecturers when you go to Trinity College, Dublin to study archaeology—"

"Eh, I'm going to Maynooth to do biomedical science."

"—if you could say you'd found a unique historic site."

"I've never been all that fussed about buildings. What made you think— Oh!" He realises. "You want me to *lie* to him to see what he says. I can do that."

"Can you, double-oh-seven? Can you? I think we're going to give you a watch with a garrotte in it and you'll cut off your own head trying to tell the time."

"I tell the time with my phone, jusht like everyone elsh."

* * *

Connor does not come around on the morning of my birthday. We had discussed this in advance. I would be getting ready, I would be doing my hair, I would be gussying up.

Of course, now it's nine-fifteen and I'm sitting alone in the attic, wearing a party dress I got online months ago from H&M, like a discount Miss Haversham. I curled my hair – which was an idea that put chocolate teapots into perspective – then straightened it again. And now I have nothing to do.

The tea room is closed for the day – that is where I am having my party.

I had worried for half the day that it was too late to invite people – and who would I invite – and how would I invite anyone who didn't wander close enough to the hotel to hear me shout *ay up petal, d'ya want to come to me party?* I'm not sure why, in my imagination, I shout socially embarrassing things in a Northern accent. It's probably Victoria Wood's fault.

I needn't have worried though, because my mum had invited everyone for me. It was still *my* party. It's just that I didn't decide that it was happening, where it was happening, when it was happening, or who was invited. She also didn't like my choice of dress: *too girlish; too summery;* not at all *sophisticated.* But my birthday this year is the summer solstice – if it's not appropriate to wear a summer dress on the solstice then they should have called it something else. (An everything but the exact middle of summer dress – even thinking about it makes me appreciate the keen instincts of the marketing man who *nope*d that suggestion). My mum seems to have expected that I would burst out of my room fully formed at sixteen, half-way through a Liza Minnelli song, throwing Fossy moves and wearing only an elaborate construct of tassels and cocktail olives.

I did not relent on the dress. It is sky blue and has a trim of unidentifiable pink flowers around the neckline – which I am, perhaps, just about able to fill out. I had picked it at the time because it was the one I liked most. And I am wearing it today because it is the one I like most, and the one I think he will like most. He has already seen everything else I own, so this will be a surprise. He will look at me from across the room. And that is about as far as my fantasy has gone. Everything beyond being looked at across a room might as well be the Profumo affair.

I cross over to my easel, where the same work-in-progress has sat covered and untouched for two weeks. I lift the sheet and stare back at myself. The mottled purple bruising on my face now feels overdone; I do not recall the cuts as vividly red in blood as I have made them in oil. I see the defiance in my eyes and I think it looks foolish. Girlish, even. It is a child's defiance which flares in the moment and burns itself out.

I pick up the palette and the brush – which is both rough from long use and stiff from unuse; it will need to be replaced. I mix my flesh tone and pick at the details. The shine reduces on the injuries. The mouth flattens to a line that is neither happy nor sad. The edge comes off the anger. It is not the wounds that grab the attention with this woman, it is the expression – which is not open, but closed. The face conceals, and the cuts and bruises are only visible to those who really look. *Look at me*, she says.

When I next check the time, two hours have passed.

I pick up the sheet, but I hear her voice as loud as any noise inside my head ever was. *Look at me*. She is much older than I am now. I have put a line by her eye and the faint contour of a wrinkle at her neck. I see different colours in her eyes, though I have not touched them today; it is the same paint that was there weeks ago. And as quickly as a blink, she is not me anymore, she is a person I do not know, though I know that this is exactly how she looks.

I drop the sheet on the floor and leave her uncovered when I go down to welcome my guests.

* * *

"Let me look at you," says Mrs. Olafsson, who is, as usual, looking with her hands. She places her palms on my cheeks and peers all around my face and into my eyes. She is, I think for the first time, looking slightly up. I have grown a fraction since last she did this. I see a tear form at the corner of her eye and she embraces me as much to conceal this emotion as because of it. "You've grown up so fast."

"I wasn't trying to," I say and she laughs, then swallows it. She releases me and looks at me again – this time with only her eyes, though her hands are still on my arms.

"Yes, you were," she says and she squeezes me just above the elbow. "You've raced us all to today."

Mr. Jones coughs. He is standing behind Mrs. Olafsson in the main door of the hotel, and is holding three boxes arranged as an uneven step pyramid. Mrs. Olafsson remembers he is there and takes charge of the situation again. "This is from me," explains Mrs. Olafsson, pointing to the top-most and smallest box, which can only be jewellery and could only have been wrapped by Mrs. Olafsson. It is surmounted by an explosion of gold and red ribbons pulled into curls which are twice the size of the box they adorn. "This is from Mister Jones," she says, pointing to the middle box.

"I could have told her that," says Mr. Jones.

"Well go on then," says Mrs. Olafsson.

". . . The middle one is from me."

"Happy now?" She asks, but it is an obviously rhetorical question and Mr. Jones only frowns at her. The present from Mr. Jones is as distinctively his as Mrs. Olafsson's is hers. It is Christmas wrapping paper, though not so obviously Christmas themed as to make him notice, and has been sealed at either end with black electrical tape. It has all the flat, oblong characteristics of a book; even wrapped it conveys the gravitas of a blunt weapon in repose.

"Thank you both," I say. "You're very kind."

"The bottom is from Missus Alexander," says Mr. Jones.

The final and largest of the gifts is wrapped in brown paper of the sort used in a different age, when meat from the local butcher and deliveries from Harrods were all packed in the same way. It is around fourteen inches long, eight wide, and four high. It was very obviously tied up by Mrs. Alexander herself; the plain string used as an additional layer of security has been knotted intensely and cut so that it would not be possible for anyone to open it and reuse the cords. I am confident that this box has not been opened since Mrs. Alexander sealed it, and I am sure she wanted me to know this.

"When did she give this to you?"

"About a year ago," says Mr. Jones. "Maybe exactly a year ago, now I come to think about it. She was beginning to feel her age and she wanted to make sure that all her promises were kept."

"What promises?"

"That was what she told me. Promises she made you, I would imagine. I told her I would look after it and give it to you if anything happened to her."

"I don't understand. Missus Alexander never made me any promises."

"Maybe it'll be obvious what she meant when you open it."

"Or maybe," says Mrs. Olafsson, "her mysterious present can be put with the others until later and when it turns out to be a jumper from Marks, we'll be no wiser than now." There is an exchange between them that is obvious, but the meaning of which is subtle. Neither of them believes Mrs. Alexander got me a jumper, but neither knows the actual contents of her gift. Both have agreed to honour Mrs. Alexander's request, though Mrs. Olafsson is in no ways happy about this.

A skein of threads untangles, becomes taut, and sings true like the strings of a perfectly tuned harp.

Mr. Jones was the naked man I saw dancing in Mrs. Olafsson's garden weeks ago.

"Are you alright, Eleanor?" he asks.

"I told you we shouldn't have given it to her," she says. "I knew it would just upset her."

I laugh, then shake it off.

"Oh no," I say. "I'm fine. It just made me think of something else that was . . . well, not amusing, not funny at all really. Good. It was good. Because people should be happy. Don't you think people should be happy? Whatever it is that makes them happy? And if people are happy and they're not harming anyone, then good. It's actually – you know what? – it's actually great. And I think you know that I'm not one to throw around the hyperboles Missus Olafsson. *Call a thingy, a thingy* – that's what I'm sure I must have said at one point. But I am really happy about it. Both of you – I want you to know I think it's great. And thank you for looking after the gift for her, and for me."

Mrs. Olafsson takes a beat to process this, then she pats me gently on the arm and says, "Try not to get too worked up about today." She smiles. "We'll put these with the others."

Mr. Jones smiles and nods. They both move through to the tea room where there is already a small crowd. I have met them all at the door, as I was instructed. They all have gifts, which is not what I was expecting. What does one get a sixteen-year-old for her birthday? I have no idea. Nobody's gone with a gift card – unless they've over wrapped it with packing peanuts and a shoebox. If everything has been sourced from Mrs. Brown's shop, there's a good chance I've got a massive haul of jam, possibly a transparent rain poncho with the Loch Ness Monster on, and maybe some paracetamol.

Sixteen. When I woke up this morning, I was sixteen and had acquired all the legal powers necessary to join the army, drive a moped, and buy a pet – on the same day, should I so choose, and providing I could get the army to station me in the hotel, mum didn't mind me getting tire tracks on the carpets, and I was visited by a door-to-door dog salesman.

But despite this I am not an adult. I cannot have my own credit card or fly a commercial airliner. I can't get a mortgage or stand for election as president of the United States. There are degrees of adulthood stretching out in front of me for another two decades. Those are just the age-related hurdles; there are experiences which build incrementally that have nothing to do with the length of time between birth and the present.

Sex – says the voice in my head like a foghorn. That's nontrivial for people who *aren't* charged with the religious, semi-mystical task of ending all life on earth. Going on holiday without parents – that's challenging even if someone isn't fixed by phobia in a Hebridean hotel, like a skewered butterfly in a museum drawer. Burying a relative – if dead, sad; if alive, criminal, but in either case significant.

And though all of those experiences shape what being adult means, it is also a state which cannot be qualified by any one thing, or any group of things. An adult – like a nation or a king or a cat – does not need to assert its identity, that identity is obvious. A child claiming to be an adult is as likely to be taken seriously as a child who wears a paper crown and says they are a king.

Without that personal sense of unquestioned authority, a driving licence and a trade treaty have all the force of a mother's note. *Please excuse the Democratic Republic of Congo from gym, it is having civil unrest.* France still thinks of Belgium as Antwerp, Ghent and Bruges standing on each other's shoulders and wearing a long coat.

"Good afternoon, Eleanor," says Mrs. Douglas, who sees me before she crosses the threshold. Tucked under her arm is a box – about the same size as the one from Mrs. Olafsson – wrapped in dark blue paper otherwise without adornment; defined by the understatement. "And happy birthday." She leans in and kisses me on the cheek. We exchange pleasantries. She indicates the box she is carrying is my gift. I thank her, explain that there is a table next door for gifts, and she enters the tea room.

On balance, it is the least stressful conversation I have had with Mrs. Douglas – perhaps ever. I wonder if there is some of the magical status of adulthood which has already passed into me. Joining the army, driving a moped, and not wetting myself in the presence of Mrs. Douglas – it's beginning to sound like a list of the more obscure abilities of Superman. By twenty-one I'll probably be melting steel with my eye lasers and using my hair to suspend weights of precisely one imperial ton for no reason.

She has not been gone for a breath before I hear the voices of Mr. Maxwell and Connor in conversation. Before they are close enough so I can hear the words, I recognise them by their tone. Their brogue is stronger when they speak to each other than when either has spoken to me. It feels as if they are trying to out-Irish one another, or at least demonstrate their heritage beyond all doubt.

Connor says, "He'll eat that ball before he'll score with it."

Mr. Maxwell replies, "Maybe, but it'll be at his feet when he gets hungry."

These appear to be excellent bons mots about a footballer, or possibly a handballer, of whom both are aware. When they get to the hotel door, they are grinning, and a certain family resemblance is clearer in that display of emotion than when they are at rest.

Where Connor's muscles move, in Mr. Maxwell's face I see the lines made by that same expression repeated a hundred thousand times. The procerus, which lifts the ridge of Connor's nose and eyebrows, has formed furrows in Mr. Maxwell's forehead. The zygomaticus major – the smile muscle – has made glacial marks on the sides of Mr. Maxwell's mouth where the cheeks have been hoisted and the upper lip raised in warm greeting, in laughter, in anxiety, and in the verisimilitude of all these things. It is Connor's stupid smile I see there, amplified.

"Gentlemen," I say, and it breaks their attention. They look at me – a shift in their focus, eyes moving millimetres in fractions of a second, and their faces pause in motion for no more time than this as their highly social visual cortexes process me and blast this information through their limbic systems. Am I an enemy? No. Am I food? No. Then, if not either of those things, am I a mate?

Mr. Maxwell moves first.

He leans in, one hand on my arm and kisses me lightly on the cheek. "Happy Birthday."

"Thank you for coming."

"I wasn't sure what to get you," he says, holding up a small tightly-bound parcel. "Connor said you enjoyed reading anything, and I thought you might like this." He passes it to me. "It's a first edition of Seamus Heaney's translation of *Beowulf*. Have you read it?"

"No," I lie safely – neither of them will know.

"It's signed to me, which I think is fine since it's not like he'll be signing any more."

"Oh," and because it is too kind, "you're too kind."

"It wasn't doing anything useful," he says of the book. "And the aim of poetry and the poet is finally to be of service." That is a Heaney quote, which he knows – not from the book he has given me – and he has paid me the compliment of thinking I would know it, which I do, though I don't acknowledge it.

Anyone with gumption and a sharp mind will take the measure of two things: what's said and what's done. But how many will notice the corollary: what's unsaid and not done? I could sparkle for him, but I choose to be matte. I could respond with something equally contrived, but I realised in the moment he made this smallest gesture of reaching out, this shadow of the act, that I would now always recoil from him. I have taken my stance.

Connor said you enjoyed reading anything.

I cannot be with Connor while he is here. He cannot stay. I cannot bear any substitute. I cannot leave. The crossroads is impossible. And he must read an expression on my face as I realise how completely damned I am. So, I smile and I pass the book back to him and ask him if he would *be so kind as to place this on the table in the next room* and tell him *cake is coming*.

Like Jesus, the coming of this cake has been foretold. Truly, this assemblage is here to celebrate Mrs. Carlyle's daughter's birthday cake and they have brought frankincense and myrrh and gold in tribute to its iced magnificence.

When Mr. Maxwell is gone, Connor says, "I don't have any spare first edition books of Old English epic poems translated by dead Irish Nobel laureates." He's practiced that – gone over it a dozen times while he's waited to speak – but it's a good line, and easily forgiven.

"I also accept surplus second edition books of current English prose translated into modern German by third-rate poets who are still alive."

"I was looking at those in the little shop and I thought that wouldn't be your thing at all."

"I'm also getting into Manga."

"They had that in the shop too. Next to the paracetamol and the tights."

"Ah, but only Russian Manga."

"Is that translated into Russian from Japanese or originally written in Russian?"

"Easy mistake – it's all *written* in Japanese, but everyone involved in the process is drunk and sad about politics."

"I'm glad I didn't get you any."

"You would have looked a fool."

"You're probably wondering what I've got you for a birthday present."

"Am I?" His hands are in his pockets. He has not got me a book, unless it is one of those very small books about how to survive a plane crash or live in the wisdom of the Buddha; the impulse purchase books that bookshops leave near cashpoints as if they were chewing gum or mints. To cleanse after a Dostoyevsky, so people don't smell the despair on your thoughts.

That is a very good bit of observational comedy for someone who has never been to a book shop. *Did you ever notice how the closer you get to paying for something, the smaller the items around you are? Way at the back of the store they sell seventy-inch televisions, then in the middle of the store is canned fish, then right at the check-out they have batteries and gum. If they moved the check-out back six feet the only things they'd sell there would be microchips and individually wrapped atoms.* There's definitely more one could do with that. *What's the deal with individually wrapped atoms?* – that's not it, obviously.

I need to take my internal-monologue-of-a-shut-in comedy on the road. I say, "Is it a little book about the Battle of Bannockburn?"

"It is not," he replies in Scottish.

"Is it a miniature bottle of Scottish whisky?"

"It most certainly is not. And I should skelp your bum fur askin'."

"Is it a tiny, wee Loch Ness Monster?"

"Not even close."

"Then I cannot imagine."

He reaches behind him – the present was in his back pocket, which is definitely cheating, even though I wasn't trying hard to guess. He brings around a slim, flat package which a fictional supermarket would sell somewhere between televisions and tinned tuna. It is wrapped in the same paper as Mr. Maxwell's *Beowulf*, but Connor has done it himself (it is much worse; practically a disaster; if the wrapping were a dress, the woman wearing it would be constantly asked *what happened? Are you all right? Do you want me to call an ambulance?*).

"Should I put it with the others?" he asks, back in his usual voice.

"Absolutely not." In the etiquette of gifts there are many rules. Official gifts from heads of state or government are typically not gift-wrapped, though they may be boxed; they should be appreciated immediately. Personal gifts from all others *are* typically gift-wrapped and should be opened individually only if given in private. Gifts presented in public should be opened later, in private. All gifts opened in private should be acknowledged in writing, as should any official gifts. There are exceptions – a gift from one's beau should always be opened in their presence if presented personally, and may therefore be opened publicly or privately, and *should* be presented and opened publicly if the gift is an item of fabulous jewellery or title to a new world colony wrested from the control of Spain. Gifts from rogue nations and ill-mannered suitors should always be returned unopened. Not being the Queen of England simplifies the etiquette a bit, though one must still be cautious not to be thought an ingénue.

"Are you going to take it then?" He shakes the package like a dog toy.

As soon as I touch it, I know it. The exact weight, the familiar shape and feel – it is as if there were no paper, and this were not a gift at all, but him simply handing me one of my own possessions. I pull off the tape where it secures a large flap of wrapping paper and almost like a magic trick involving metal rings or lengths of rope, the whole thing unfolds under its own weight.

Brushes. A pack of five. Long-handled. A pickily-chosen brand; not expensive, but *just so*.

"I noticed that the brush you were using was . . . And I thought you hadn't done anything on that painting for ages." He trails off. It is not a romantic gift; something that a girl might adore as a proxy for him: a stuffed toy: a framed picture of us together. And he worries in the moment that he has done something wrong. Because he knows what *girls* like, and he understands the forms of courtship, but he has no more experience of what is between us than I do.

How does he see everything and nothing? How can he live here and be oblivious of what I am – and still notice me?

And I wonder if I could. If I could be with another man to save him. If I could leave this house which I have never left. If I could go to Ireland and forget how people take their tea while they wait for the world to end. If I could do it for him, when I cannot do it for myself.

"Oh shit, I'm really sorry," he says, panic-struck. "I thought you'd like them. I didn't think you'd want— I didn't want you to think— I thought it was, good, but you know – safe? Christ, it's like something your gran would get you."

I am crying – of course I am. These eyes do not work for me: these eyes are traitors! I put my hand up to stop him talking. Two of my fingers go straight into his mouth.

We notice that this has happened.

It must be the release of tension that makes us laugh so loud. So loud, in fact, that I smother him again and pull him back from the door of the tea room, along the corridor, so that we are in front of the old, dark wood doors that bar entry to the private dining room.

"I haven't even got a gran," I tell him, and he holds me so that I can feel him relax. This was also a good decision.

"You like them?"

"I do," I tell his chest. "Thank you."

"Good," he says.

"I mean, if you couldn't get a Harold Pinter version of *Tristan and Iseult,* I suppose they're fine."

"I did not understand what you said at all."

"Good," I say. Then I push him away, because whatever I can and might do will vanish the instant I'm seen in an embrace with him. My own infinite quantum future will collapse into one definite reality with a single observation. "Did you get a chance to speak to Mister Murdoch?"

"About? Oh, right. I haven't seen him."

"I think he's taking a tour. Mum made up six packed lunches this morning for people leaving on the first boat – that usually means Mister Murdoch is leading people up a mountain. They'll be back tonight or we'll never see any of them again."

"Island life is harsh."

"He never does two days in a row. You'll catch him tomorrow."

"Or I could just ask people in the next room right now?"

"No," I say, then fumble for a reason why this isn't the obvious idea. "He's a proper historian."

"He's a retired history teacher – he's not Fergal Keane."

"Did you just make up an Irishman because you've never heard of Harold Pinter?"

"What harm could it do to ask?"

I have no idea. Death by a hundred cake forks? It could be the murder of Caesar on the senate floor. He might be expelled from Ensay. They might lock him up until the autumnal equinox and burn him anyway. It could do any harm that can be imagined; Mr. Murdoch is the only way to find out more that's even close to being safe.

I see her before she sees me. Mrs. Brown walks like a small bird; a series of hops followed by stillnesses where she peers intently in all directions. If one did not know Mrs. Brown, one might find it endearing.

I push Connor back toward the tea room.

"Thank you very much for the gift," I say and *put-it-with-the-others-cake-is-coming* him in a neutral and official tone. He is baffled, but accustomed to bafflement and does exactly as he is told. As he moves through the door, I turn my corporate expression to her.

"Happy Birthday Eleanor," she says, and, like a shooting star that falls to earth and kills a unicorn, immediately adds, "how is your condition?"

Truth be told, Mrs. Brown I'm a little anxious about today for several reasons, not all of which I could articulate. This does, as you'll appreciate, make me somewhat more skittish than I would normally be. The world is heightened and angular and full of sharp objects. But I feel strong, Mrs. Brown. I feel strong enough to deal with all of it. Though my strength is, I would admit, not any easier to explain than my fear.

"I'm very well, Missus Brown. It's very kind of you to enquire."

"I brought you a little something." I'm sure it's a multipack of tights. "Things that a young lady needs—" Or it could be about fifty condoms. "—which I found very useful when I was your age." It must be the polio vaccine.

"I'm intrigued. Thank you very much."

"Let's walk in together."

"I have to wait for any more guests."

"Oh," she shoos away that idea. "They're all here. I'm the last one." And if anyone would know my guest list it would be her. She'll have watched from the shop as people walked up the street, and with her bookkeeper's attention to the comings and goings of the community will have made a mental tally. She'd wanted to be last to arrive – so everyone would be there to see her arrive. She's *baby-kissing* me. I am a sixteen-year-old baby and she's kissing me – hopefully metaphorically – right in front of everyone. And just like an actual baby, I am powerless to stop it.

She takes me by the arm with a big smile and hops me towards the tea room. This is my big entrance, whether I like it or not. It's how I imagine it must feel to open for the Rolling Stones. The crowd at Glastonbury might be mad for me, but they will always have more enthusiasm for the main act. In fact, the better I do, the more rapturous the welcome for the next act. There's no way to win. I won't even have the honour of opening for the Stones – I'm warming up the crowd for a three-layer white chocolate and lemon sponge. Nobody wants to open for cake.

The tea room is as busy as it's ever been. I have not counted the arrivals as diligently as Mrs. Brown has. It only takes me a moment to note that all the sisters of any consequence are here, but the crowd – and it is actually a crowd – must be sixty strong. My birthday just out-sold the best concert the

Wee Man ever held. Mr. Urquhart is not here to see it – he is probably sleeping off some fraction of a dozen yesterdays. The season has never been kind to Mr. Urquhart's liver.

Someone makes a cheer and they all turn to look at me with their at least one-hundred-and-eleven eyes. (Mrs. Kingston lost an eye on a Norwegian cruise and wears glasses with one lens painted black – for which, she has complained to me on several occasions, she still pays full price).

A ripple of applause with a beat that seems to match my own heart. I feel a hand snake its way around my arm and find Mrs. Olafsson has positioned herself opposite Mrs. Brown. There is a subdued but meaningful tug-of-war between them where I am the rope. We all smile through this, understanding that anything else would be unbecoming.

"For she's a jolly good fellow," begins Mrs. Olafsson, and the rest of the room, including Mrs. Brown have to join in. Dante believed that flatterers were destined for worse treatment in hell than murderers – most likely because Dante himself had been flattered but had no personal experience of being murdered. Or perhaps since so many people in thirteenth-century Italy made a living out ensuring other people did *not* live in thirteenth-century Italy, he just knew which side his ciabatta was oiled. In any case, there is no circle of hell reserved for *flatterees* – being flattered is its own punishment.

The traditional three *hip-hip-hoorays* are completed. This room full of adults who know from long experience that I am not an experienced raconteur, but they watch me with expectation. Will I juggle? Will I, in contravention of food health and safety rules, spit a plume of fire across the tea room? Perhaps somewhere in this sleeveless dress I have concealed a pigeon or a knotted string of colourful tissues. I thought about putting them in my bra, audience, but I'm rolling the dice.

"Thank you all for coming." I say it, and it's happening. I am giving a speech. I am offering unprepared remarks to a group as if I'm Aristotle Onassis, or Joan Collins in one of those TV shows where women wore an inch of shoulder pads and two inches of lipstick. "My mum says that an island is like a family. It's very gratifying to have so many of my family with me today." And apparently my remarks are going to be saccharine bullshit. Who says *gratifying* to their family? *I see you've finally gotten out of your wanking chariot at two in the afternoon, son – that's very gratifying. Ah, granny, you've pissed yourself at the dinner table on Christmas – I am not gratified that you have ruined that festive chair cover made to resemble Santa's hat.* "The only thing that could make today better is cake – and cake is on its way." A rumble of approval. "And the only thing better than that would be being two years older, so we could all celebrate with whisky." Polite laughter, all very well judged, a smattering of applause and it's over.

Brevity.

"Very nice," says Mrs. Brown. "Come with me and say hello to the other

Missus Mackenzie." As she says this, she pulls me off to the right, or tries to. Mrs. Olafsson has planted her feet firmly; following the tug-of-war she has been in constant anticipation of Mrs. Brown stealing me away.

"Of course, you must speak to the other Missus Mackenzie. But Mrs. Macleod has only just been remarking about how much she admires your *dress*." The word dress is emphasised by a grunt of effort as Mrs. Olafsson pulls me to my left. The attempt is barely more effective than Mrs. Brown's was. Both opponents are prepared for battle and I, like the fields of Flanders, will be site of their dispute – not an area of any consequence, merely an agreed-upon location. I am where war goes when it doesn't want to damage anything important.

They fix each other with glares of open hostility. The successor to Mrs. Douglas, whoever that ends up being, will necessarily be unflinchingly ruthless, and for the moment these two women seem perfectly matched. I am concerned that this tussle will end in cartoon fashion with me being pulled into two neat pieces, and both parts of me being compelled to make polite conversation with the Brown and Olafsson factions.

"Perhaps, ladies—" I am at my sweetest. The sound of my voice is pure honey. "—I might have a cup of tea first, over there with Mrs. Arbuthnot." Because Mrs. Arbuthnot, mother of two previous acolytes, is well known to be undecided. She will never be high priestess, but might she be enough to decide a tight contest? "Would you both care to join me?"

Oh Eleanor, my-my-my, but you've a shrewd head on your shoulders and both of your shoulders are still attached to your spine. The ladies assent and frog-march me through the crowd, which has already lost interest in me. As we cross, I see Connor and Mrs. Douglas talking. If I had been moving under my own power I would have stopped. If my hands were free, I would have thrown a teacup at him. But I can do nothing. I am put into a seat opposite Mrs. Arbuthnot while the two remaining seats are occupied by my abductors.

"But you must know about it," says Connor.

Mrs. Douglas puts her teacup down in her saucer. I cannot see her face without appearing inattentive. She is out of focus on the edge of my peripheral vision as she replies.

"In a place like Dublin you'll have become used to nobody knowing your business, or caring whether you had any business at all. You would know the names of your immediate neighbours, perhaps, but those people three doors down would be strangers, and those in the next street might as well be living in another country.

"Life in an island community is not like that. Every island is a village and everyone who lives in a village is a gossip. There have always been rumours about Ensay, and about our *strange practices*. That's as true today as it ever was. We have learned to keep to ourselves."

Mrs. Arbuthnot has finished saying something. I laugh. This appears to have been the correct reaction.

"Is the abbey a secret?" Connor asks. Does Mrs. Douglas smile at him? What kind of smile is it? I must look absurd trying to see her and not look at her at the same time.

She says, "Ensay Abbey was a Carmelite community of nuns living in isolation. I have some records which go back to the fifteenth century, though it's possible the community and the settlement are much older.

"Being in Scotland and somewhat remote even then, the abbey avoided any involvement in the religious schisms and the wars and purges that came with them. The nuns corresponded with others in their order and paid duties directly to Rome, but the island has always been, as far as I can tell, outside of any local hierarchy. Their numbers were kept constant with the third or fourth daughters of lairds who could not afford their dowry, or with young women who were with child and out of marriage. A perfectly normal convent and it might have remained that way until today.

"But between eighteen-sixty and eighteen sixty-five a young girl came to Ensay who was said to possess the gift of prophecy. Like John of Patmos, she produced a vivid and metaphorical account of the end of the world, though her prophecy was different. She believed that Ensay had been home for thousands of years to a cult that performed human sacrifice by burning, and that this was the place where the last innocent man would be tempted to sin by the last innocent women. After this final sacrifice was burned, the fire would swallow the whole world."

Connor says, "So the nuns locked her up and threw away the key?"

"They did not," says Mrs. Douglas. "Victorian mysticism was as powerful in Scotland as in England and they were, even in their relative isolation, ready and willing to accept new prophets and new miracles. By eighteen seventy-one they named her Abbess. And it appears they she shaped their religious views for the rest of her life. At some point during her tenure, they ceased to be Carmelites. They stopped communication with the rest of their order and there were no duties paid to Rome after eighteen seventy-six."

"I feel like you're building me up for the twist," says Connor – and Mrs. Douglas laughs. I have never, once, heard her laugh. It's not even a strange sound, like she's been holding in a fart all day, or a sinister cackle signalling the end of normal events and the unleashing of dark forces – it's a normal, amused, woman's laugh.

"You were raised as a Catholic?" Mrs. Douglas asks Connor.

"I was born in Ireland," Connor shrugs.

"The Carmelites are a Catholic order and what their new Abbess brought them wasn't just prophecy, it was Presbyterianism, and perhaps even something like Hinduism. She declared that their great temple and its riches would be torn down and scattered for their god was too proud."

"Their *god* was too proud?"

"Oh yes. She had seen beyond the need for any intermediaries between the truly divine forces of creation and destruction. Gods were all false idols, whether it was the martyred Christ or the Father worshipped by Moses and Abraham. She connected with an inherent spiritualism which, today, is widely acknowledged as true, even as all the trappings of other religions fade and appear ridiculous. There are only the fundamentals – woman creates and fire destroys. Every living thing was born, and that creative force is the female energy. Everything dies. As science has since discovered, the sun will one day swell up and burn everything on Earth, and all life will end, all history will be obliterated, and we will vanish into dust.

"As her records recall, Ensay Abbey was struck by lightning and burned to the ground. The sisters survived the fire, but their last ties with their cloistered lives were severed."

"So, you're the descendants of those nuns?"

"Yes and no. Some of our community are direct descendants of those sisters. They became involved with the McArdle brothers, which your uncle's distillery describes as semi-heroic figures. I think you and I would guess the truth is more nuanced. Some of our community are people who moved here later, and their children, and so on. There are not many people who live on Ensay, but there are more now than at any time in the past."

If Connor is not amazed by this story, I am. This is not the history of Ensay. At least not the history that has been taught to me. A moment ago, I was in an unbroken line of Celtic pagans emerging from history. Now I am an incomer, or the great-great-granddaughter of a nun. The table I'm sitting at could be on fire – I wouldn't know about it.

"And do people on the island all know this?" Connor asks.

"Of course," says Mrs. Douglas. "Everyone who's lived here for any time knows our history. Though most tourists come for the birds and the scenery, I'm sure Mister Murdoch tells people fragments of the story."

"Why wouldn't the site be listed anywhere?"

"Ensay is still an autonomous religious enclave. Our rights are medieval, but still in force. We can, and do, choose to operate without the supervision of some Scottish public bodies. We believe the permanent preservation of historic sites is absurd – for religious reasons. I and my predecessors have always blocked any attempts to excavate or list Ensay Abbey. And I imagine we always will."

I want to grab her and shake her. What does she mean, *everyone who's lived here knows our history*? I have never been anywhere else and this is a funhouse mirror held up to the island. But what she says is the sound of a bell. She is not lying. This is not a trick to deceive Connor, or to conceal the details of what we are and what we do. Somehow this history and this rationale are true. I know it in my bones and my guts.

A hush falls across the room. A door has opened.

I turn and see my mum walking in bearing the weight of a cake fit for any occasion. Virgin white. Sides iced smooth as Bakelite. Dusted with golden glitter. Radiant with its own light. Surmounted by sixteen glowing candles.

Our eyes meet.

It starts the way an avalanche must begin. An audible sign – on the alpine mountainside it would be a thud as metric tonnes of snow shift together for the first time, in the tea room it is a gasp from someone to my right. It slips, the way monuments collapse; the edifice fracturing as inertia and gravity tear it to pieces. One perfect whole becoming – in the time taken for one quarter rotation – an aggregate of inseparable icing and crumbs.

The side of the cake hits the floor and it seems it might bounce. It compresses like a rubber ball and there is an instant – a time period so short that there is no everyday name for it – where it is certain to rebound, up, back onto the plate, reforming itself in mid-air, sticking two cake fingers up to entropy. But it splits – the three layers fall open. Into the mess descends the plate it had been on, and it divides the mass with the finesse of a claw hammer; splattering then sliding to an angular stop.

My mum is falling. Her eyes have closed as she tilts backwards, her knees folding. Someone needs to catch her!

She's on the floor. I cannot breathe. The crowd rushes forward.

She vanishes.

14

I sit on the cold step and brace a hand on each wall. Is the world closing in? Or am I frightened of falling the final few inches to the ground? Falling all the way down.

They have taken her. Minutes ago, and days ago, it seems. The roar of the helicopter rotors was so close, so loud that I thought it might shake the building down – though it landed in a field and I doubt it was in range of any stone I could throw.

They carried her on a stretcher. Strapped down. Her head and neck in a brace. Out the front door and up the street. Through a hole in a crumbling drystone wall. She never woke up.

I could not go past the door. I watched from a window as they took her away. Mrs. Douglas went with her in the air ambulance carrying two overnight bags – my mother's was hastily assembled by Mrs. Olafsson, Mrs. Douglas retrieved her own, which she must have on permanent standby.

They flew over the roof in that bright yellow machine; that dragonfly the size of a house, and I saw them turn over the harbour, swerving north, heading towards Stornoway. It was thirty minutes between her fall and her departure. Which is good. It must be a quiet day for emergencies. I think that now, in retrospect; I do not recall a single thought I had in that half an hour. I do not remember anything I did. Perhaps I did nothing.

And then I was here, in the darkest part of the house, at the foot of the back stairs. My breathing is the only sound, and it carries upwards, rebounding on every step, diminishing but never entirely vanishing. I imagine it escaping through the skylight like clouds of steam.

Without sound or light, the world outside might not exist, and that idea has its appeal. To be alone in the cold darkness of this silo would also mean to be at peace, for as long as peace can last, for as long as there can be darkness. Though today there is a faint natural light that bleeds through from the skylight, peering around the corners as if it were curious. Following the sound of life back to its source.

Under my fingers even the walls feel uncertain. They are cracked in places I had never seen and broken in ways that only touch reveals. They tell me things in this physical exchange they would never whisper in my ear, even if walls could talk. Our conversation is a thing that cannot be said with words.

These stones are straight cut and chiselled flat. They were not pulled raw from the ground and mortared into this house. Over every block, a master mason laboured half a day and was proud of his work. The wounds I feel are later injuries. These stones were a part of something that was whole, unbuilt in haste and without the same skill, and repurposed to become part of something else.

Just above where a broom might sweep, well below where an eye might seek anything at all, in a patch of darkness that might be thick any other day but the longest – there is a flower. A tiny blue flower on a fleck of grey plaster, both as faint as dreams on waking. I know that it has always been here, though I have never been conscious of it. I know that I have almost seen it a thousand times. It has been at the edge of view; my head turned just wrong, my eyes averted, my mind elsewhere. And like the ending of a dream, once I realise, I am awake.

The stairway blooms. A moment of pure sorcery where one familiar thing is entirely altered and yet remains the same as it always was.

The stones all have their blossoms – roses and lilacs, such as never grew on this island, and the purple flowers of wild thyme, and constellations of yarrow – dim and bright as exploding galaxies. They are echoes coming from all directions, growing down and sideways as often as upwards. Their faint edges vanish into rock. Their order with each other and with the world is upset so that unless there was that one single flower standing clear and upright, all the others would be invisible.

And I see it.

These fragments of whitewash, or paint or plaster, were not aborted attempts to cover the rough stones. They are the last traces of something which every effort was made to obliterate. Surfaces have been scraped clean: scoured with wire brushes: excoriated and mortified. The stone was revealed from under coloured fields. It would have been easier to paint had the purpose been only to obscure, but the person who painted would always know what lay beneath one layer – or ten layers.

These images were destroyed and their destruction was preserved as its own kind of coarse art.

And some part of me must have known these were here in plain sight all my life, or how would I have realised the truth when Connor told me? How would I have known that we were linked?

Connor discovered our abbey was missing, and I have found it. I have been living in its ruin.

The door opens fast, he takes one step forward and stops sharp. He is a pure black silhouette that in a breath acquires tone and depth and features as I adjust to the light from the kitchen. I rise up and push myself at him. It is easier to fall toward him than to fall down. And he catches me with the care one might show to a bird with a broken wing – gentle but unwavering; enough and only enough. I cannot imagine how he learned this in eighteen years, or how it could be learned in eighty.

Connor says, "I thought you'd be in your room," because *I'm terrified of what's happening right now* would be exactly wrong even though it would be perfectly true. The kitchen door swings closed behind him.

"Are they gone?" I ask his shoulder.

"Jean's still here. She wants to speak to you."

"Who's Jean?"

"Jean," he says with a shrug. "She's Jean. I don't know her second name. She's—" he picks his words with extreme care "—full-figured." The particular adjective he settled for doesn't help me. I serve cake to under-active older ladies – charitably they could all be described as *ample, generous, bosomy, matronly,* and perhaps even *traditionally built from locally-sourced materials. Substantial frontage,* as an estate agent might claim. *Substantial backage* is not a phrase I've heard, but someone would know it when they saw it, and they'd see it from distance. "She's got—" he pauses and already I know this further detail will not be detailed "—hair."

"I don't want to speak to anyone." Absent but implicit is the word *else.* I don't want to speak to anyone else. I don't even know that I want to speak to Connor, though I am certain I don't want him to leave.

He does not speak, but he knows something I haven't realised. There has been a discussion elsewhere, between no-nonsense people about practical matters. I feel understanding settle on me like the collar of a cart horse. I can't lock myself away in the dark; I can't sit here until this building unmakes itself again and emerge out of it years from now with the patience of an acorn. This is a fully booked hotel with guests who have nowhere else to go, and in three hours I need to start prep for dinner.

There is no time and no space for despair.

"Alright."

"You're going to speak to her?"

I nod.

He asks, "Do you want to wait a minute?"

Yes. "No."

He releases me, and this feels more like someone stepping away from a house of cards. In marked contrast to the embrace, the release is cynical and somehow self-interested. I might go from being *a* disaster to *his* disaster. Or is it my own anxiety about touch returning; the disease reasserting itself from remission? Or ordinary exhaustion? Surely, I have reason today to feel any of these.

Unsure who I am justifying my feeling too, I spend a moment smoothing down my dress. Connor manoeuvres in the limited space and holds the door open for me.

The kitchen is bright and clean. Today it has been the source of twenty-two breakfasts and fifteen packed lunches, owing to my birthday closing us for food. An hour ago, a cake was being iced on a stand – the only evidence of that process is the stand itself, which sits in isolation. She carried the cake from there to the tea room. If the dishwasher was still cleaning any of the breakfast plates when she left, it has since finished. The surfaces shine. Utensils, pots, and pans are hidden from view by doors that have all been wiped down and disinfected in the last twenty-four hours. The floor is spotless. And the room is empty. Perhaps another word for the kitchen would be sterile.

I hear the sound in reception. An idle rapping of fingers against the wood of the desk. *Bah-ray king rocks in-the hot sun.* Connor walks two steps behind me and I hold the door open for him. *I-fought the-law and-the law won.*

Jean Olafsson – I never knew. Sixteen years and I never knew.

She is sitting on a high chair behind reception and she shuffles to the edge and hops down when she sees me. My whole body can feel the hug coming from across the room. It hits me like a wave made of plump.

"Oh dear," she says. "There, there," she comforts me. I am not, as far as I can tell, displaying any signs of needing to be comforted in that moment, but I am content to indulge Mrs. Olafsson as always.

"Thank you," I say, in an attempt to bring this incident to a rapid conclusion. But she does not release me.

"That must have been a terrible shock," she tells me.

"It was," I confirm. Still being hugged.

"I'm sure she'll be back on her feet in no time."

"Do you know what's wrong with her?"

"Missus Douglas has gone with her and is going to phone as soon as she's spoken to a doctor."

That is not an answer to my question. I push her away. A little. Gently. "If you don't know what's wrong with her, how can you be sure she'll be back on her feet in no time?" But this is unfair; I feel it as soon as I've said it, and I can see the impact on her face. She is a nice old lady just being nice. This is not her fault.

Yet I have unlocked something in my chest: the red-hot door to a furnace in me swings open. I feel my hands clench at my sides. I don't think I move, and I don't think she does either, but the shadow play of our emotions dance between us. I want to slap her, and she is – for a fleeting moment – afraid

160

that I might; as if she has expected it. As if she has always expected it.

Then I am more bewildered than angry, and it is seconds before she can cover her own reaction. I can see a secret in her eyes like the moon at the bottom of a well. Guilt: by her own judgement, Mrs. Olafsson is guilty. Though I can't guess what she is guilty of, I can feel the truth of it.

"You're right," she says. "And with Missus Alexander gone, you could be on your own for a long time. I don't think there has been any progress finding a replacement."

"I'll cope." Why did I say that? Of course I won't cope. All the guests will leave and be replaced in the next four days – check-in and cleaning rooms will be a full-time job. Everyone can either starve or live in filth – and neither of those look good in a Trip Advisor review. *Everything had mushrooms on it except the breakfast – two stars. Nobody at reception, so I exited stage-left, followed by a bear, who also couldn't get a room – one star. Died – one star.*

"You must be sensible. Your mother needed two other people to help her part time and your mother worked every hour of the day. Someone from the island will be able to help out."

"I'll do it," says Connor. "I'm only here for a couple of months, but that's when you're busy, right? I mean – pay me. But otherwise, I'm available."

Connor is behind me and to my left, so he can't see my face. I worry about the expression I might have made when he volunteered – because I think several things. The number of times he has used a washing machine in his life is still in single figures. He has, to the best of my knowledge, never made a bed. I'd concede this might not come up in conversation – I could have misread him; he may very well have hospital corners as tight as a straightjacket and as sharp as a coffee table edge.

Then there is the not-so-simple issue of power. I think I am Connor's girlfriend. For want of any better way of describing our relationship, girlfriend feels right, and even if we are on the fringes of typical, I don't think he would disagree. If he's working here all day, then I also become his employer – his *boss*. We have standards. I have standards. How do I get someone who is my very-probably boyfriend to meet my standards when I've never had to make anyone who is my definitely-not boyfriend meet them. I feel like even the slave masters in the old biblical epics did more than crack whips and expect pyramids to rise up out of the sand as a result. There must have been some basic pyramid training, an orientation on joining Team Pyramid, with regular catch-ups to discuss performance issues and, where necessary, dispense and receive whippings.

Mrs. Olafsson was not exaggerating about my mum's workload. For four months of the year, my mum works eighteen-hour days. Can I? And if I can, that leaves no time for Connor outside of work. I would be his boss for twelve hours a day, longer than I've ever been his sort-of girlfriend.

Indiana Jones and the Last Crusade. Spoilers. They're about to take the Holy

Grail out of the temple and there's an earthquake. Alison Doody – she's playing Elsa, the Nazi who was Indy's sidekick for the first half the film – falls in a crevasse which reaches to the centre of the planet. Harrison Ford, being basically a good guy, still tries to save her, but she sees the Grail and can't resist grabbing for it. She wants to have her immortality and eat Indiana Jones too – which the laws of films say can't happen – and she, predictably, falls to her death.

If the Indiana Jones franchise has only two lessons for us, they are these: that the premature death of River Phoenix will remain a tragedy until the human species evolves a different face and acquires strange new aesthetics; and that too much of what you want is bad for you, whether that's Arks of the Covenant, Holy Grails, Sankara Stones or Crystal Skulls, and eventually you're going to find yourself on a crumbling rope bridge over crocodile-infested waters while some guy accuses you of betraying Shiva, and the God of Abraham melts your face off for looking at his stuff – plus, somehow, aliens.

"Well," says Mrs. Olafsson, "that's settled then."

What?

"Cool," says Connor.

I was having a fucking internal monologue.

"I'll come back tonight and we'll see where we are," says Mrs. Olafsson. She half-turns, then stops. "I never thought about it until just then. I must have left your mum's bedroom in such a mess packing her bag. I didn't know where anything was."

"It's fine," I say, perhaps a bit sharp, and repeat, "It's fine. Thank you for earlier. I'll deal with it."

She smiles and leaves through the front door. It is, discounting the actual events, a lovely day outside. A day fully justifying a summer dress. I can't imagine when I'll wear it again.

When I finally face him, Connor has his hands in his pockets.

"So," he says, rocking on his heels, "what now?"

* * *

There is no sense crying over spilled milk – a phrase which is almost universally applicable, as long as you aren't tied to any of the words in the phrase. There's no point moping when confronted with cake trodden into your carpet – this is my specific inspiration as I sponge sponge and icing out of the tile. It's hard-wearing carpet tile covering the stone floor, and though I keep it well, it hasn't been this thoroughly cleaned in years.

Connor makes trips up to my room with gifts and when they're relocated, he stands at relaxed attention and waits to be given another task. I am only being asked for his second task and already the burden of leadership is like having a wasp in the room.

Satisfied that there is nothing else to do with the carpet but wait for it to dry out, I hand Connor the bucket and realise I should have changed before I started this. The hem of my dress is damp and iced. Not ruined – it is only sugar and butter and water; a little soap and it'll be fine for me to wear alone, on a cold day in October, which is the next time I won't have a guest to tend to or a floor to clean. Though that is, obviously, mad, and so I hopefully won't.

I go upstairs to slip into something a little more practical. In my bathroom I wash out the fabric of the dress at the hem and, holding it up for detailed scrutiny, I'm sure there won't be any discolouration. I put it on a hanger on the shower curtain rail and leave it to drip dry over the bath.

My mum has mastered doing any task in heels and a black, knee-length skirt that fits her as a second skin. How she manages to kneel down or stand up afterwards is a secret she has not shared with me, though I believe it's calf strength and witchcraft.

I decide to put on black trousers and a white blouse – a simple and classic front-of-house look, serious and adult and responsible and absolutely right and, of course, I don't own a white blouse. In the tea room we keep it chill, yo. And in the kitchen, we keep it easy wipe. Yo. I have never been called to serve my country in a command role before, and I lack the uniform.

I put on a t-shirt and head down to the first floor, because even though I'm only going from my room to my mum's room, I don't want to flash any of the elderly guests.

My husband had a heart attack and nearly died – one star.

I nearly died; best holiday ever – five stars.

I'm halfway along the corridor before I remember Mrs. Olafsson will still have the key – which she recovered from my mum's pocket and hasn't returned – at least to me. By the time I've processed that thought, I'm at the door, and I try the handle just in case, in the rush, she had neglected—

The door swings open. Not only wasn't the door locked, the latch had not quite caught. Her room is much smaller than mine. I don't suppose this matters to her so much, since she is almost never here and when she is, she is unconscious. The hotel has larger rooms, but we can charge more for those. It has one small window on the north side of the building; it's dark and feels colder than it is.

In exchange for this small and constrained life she gets the dark half of the year on the Atlantic coast of Scotland, and me. That's not a fair trade.

Mrs. Olafsson undersold the state of the room with *such a mess*. Everything that opens has been opened and, like the door, none of it has been closed. Her dresser looks the way I would imagine it would if she had put a hand grenade in with her knickers, and the pin in the wardrobe. Approaching, I see the contents have been rifled and some things that have been pulled out have disturbed everything else. The combination of clothes I guess are missing – and in the overnight bag prepared for my mum – include pyjamas, underwear, socks, tights, a scarf, a Fair Isle jumper, and possibly a bobble hat. Mrs. Olafsson expects my mum to come home in a blizzard or not at all.

I refold, reorder, and close. Each of the drawers returns to its acceptable state, which is one of perfect order, and I move to the wardrobe. There has been no less disruption here. The shoe rack at the bottom has been upended so that the shoes lie in a heap underneath it. I pull the rack out first, then the shoes, and refit the rack and begin pairing everything up. The slippers my mum wears all of twice a year are gone.

I check the spaces. My mum has exactly as much room for shoes as she has shoes. When she wears through or breaks a pair, they are replaced. Like most of the people on Ensay, we have become very comfortable with ordering online when we have to, and otherwise giving a roaring trade to Mrs. Obbins – our island's only dedicated cobbler and ship-in-a-bottle maker. (Though this is not to say that other people don't make ships in bottles recreationally, only that Mrs. Obbins is a professional).

There is room for only two pairs of shoes: the slippers which I assume Mrs. Olafsson packed and the shoes my mum was wearing.

So Mrs. Olafsson opened this wardrobe and did what? Upturned the shoe rack by accident? Filled with shoes, it feels heavy, and it fits closely into the wardrobe – it's hard to see how it might be knocked over in any direction. The more closely I look at it, the more certain I am that it couldn't be done accidentally; that the only way the shoe rack ends up on top of the shoes is because it has been lifted up. And the only reason someone would have for lifting the shoe rack is to search underneath it.

I look around the room again and see it with fresh eyes. I came in assuming that someone had been compiling a collection of appropriate clothing in a hurry – but how would the room look any different if it had instead been ransacked by a person seeking something?

I think critically about the space. The hotel has a small safe in reception used for storing guest valuables and where we keep cash and a couple of items of jewellery belonging to my mum. The only desktop computer we have is in reception. My mum has a couple of bottles of perfume on her small vanity – they have not been touched. There are no valuables in this room – at least nothing I know about.

The bedsheets have been disturbed. Like me, my mum would always make her bed in the morning. The mattress has been lifted. Nobody would believe any jewellery or electronics would be stored under a mattress – what does that leave? Cash – but there's no reason this wouldn't be kept in the safe where it would be covered by insurance. Important documents? Our insurance documents are online, our health and safety information is posted in reception, the hotel isn't mortgaged and I would know because our bank statements are electronic and I see all the money going in and out. My mum has a passport in case she needs to fly somewhere – this may have expired, actually – but I'm sure this is in the safe with both of our birth certificates and other sundry proofs of existence: premium bonds nobody has ever checked, papers that seem useless and will almost certainly prove essential if ever discarded.

What else is there?

Something small enough that it could be hidden in any drawer in the room, under clothes, under a mattress. Something flat? Or at least something very small. A disc or memory stick? This is becoming ridiculous – there are any number of small things, why not a matchbox filled with fifty-three unique items including a wasabi pea that looks like Churchill?

I'm coming at this from the wrong direction. I have no idea what the item is. Can I instead tell who was looking for it? I think it must be Mrs. Olafsson. There is, of course, the slim possibility that after Mrs. Olafsson left the room in a mess an unknown third party entered the room and searched it, but that could be anyone, including one of the guests. Hundreds of people had the opportunity because they knew my birthday was today and we wouldn't be paying attention. But unless my mum collapsed, her door would be locked. All the doors in the hotel would be locked. Nobody would know Mrs. Olafsson would be so careless as to leave the door open. I'm not even sure who would know which room was my mum's.

It must be Mrs. Olafsson. As the person with the key, she had the opportunity to lock the door from the inside knowing she could not be disturbed in her search. *If* she thought about it. And she might not have.

So, what would my mum have that Mrs. Olafsson would want? Discounting all of those other valuable things which we would keep in the safe leaves nothing. I need to stop trying to think of the thing!

My mum had an insert-thing-here which Mrs. Olafsson was trying to find. So Mrs. Olafsson knew she had the thing and knew what it was. *And* knew it was in her room and not in the safe. *And* knew it was *hidden* in her room – otherwise why check underneath the shoe rack and the mattress?

The only person who can access the safe other than my mum . . . is me.

Whatever Mrs. Olafsson was looking for, somewhere in this room, is something she knows about, but which my mum is keeping hidden from *me*.

I sit down on the bed.

I feel that I have been circling this for weeks. Whatever it is Mrs. Olafsson was trying to find is the secret Mrs. Alexander knew. A secret my mum actively concealed and that Mrs. Olafsson wanted to keep me from discovering even if she died. And she could be dead now. My mum could be miles away and dead, and some terrible truth would hang between us forever.

But was Mrs. Olafsson trying to steal the insert-thing-here because she wanted it to remain a secret, or because she wanted it for herself?

There is a knock on the bedroom door and it swings open – the latch, it seems, does not work and the door stays closed only when locked. Connor's hand is mid knock.

He takes in the room with a glance and says, "And you thought I was messy."

"Inappropriate."

"Sorry. Is there anything I can do?"

"Yes," I say and stand up. "You can help me search this room."

"Okay," he says, gung-ho. "Search it for what?"

"I've no idea. But we might have to lift the carpet and punch holes in the wall."

"Is this one of those things I'm supposed to talk you out of because you're in shock?"

"No."

"Okay. I had to ask. But this thing that you don't know what we're looking for, do you know what sort of a thing it is?"

"No."

"Is that it?" he asks, pointing at the bed.

"No."

"Maybe I should start in the bathroom?"

"Yes."

Connor edges around the bottom of the bed and into the bathroom. The room is too small for a wardrobe, a dresser, the vanity and chair, *and* a bed. If there was no bed, this bedroom would be an ideal size for single occupancy. If it didn't have doors or windows influencing where furniture could be placed, then two people could comfortably stay here, sleeping on the floor. There might even be room for a cot.

I pull out an ironed white blouse on a hanger from the wardrobe and lay it on the bed. The state of the room is such that Mrs. Olafsson cannot have found what she was looking for – I'm sure. Or rather, I'm confident in the probabilities. The chance is slim that she would have gone through the entire contents of the room and that the very last place there was to search was where the thing was. She needed to pack a bag. There was a limited amount of time – if she'd had more, she would have covered her tracks. Urgency forced her to stop searching.

If what she was looking for is still here, that means it's in a place she wouldn't think to look. My mum hid this from me – where would she be confident that I wouldn't look? Not the dresser, since I might very easily take her clothes from the laundry and put them away. Not the vanity – when I was younger, I was strongly discouraged from putting on her lipstick and eyeshadow, but she's made it clear recently I can borrow whatever I want; I am, in fact, wearing her mascara right now. She gave it to me, but she would have expected I might return it. That would be too careless if there was anything to find.

My mum is a vault when she wants to be, but she's not a spy. What I'm looking for isn't going to be behind a secret panel or taped to the bottom of a drawer. If she kept it in her room, she wanted it to be accessible, not just hidden.

I turn back to the wardrobe. Aside from the row of clothes and the shoe rack, the wardrobe also has a shelf at the top used for storing sheets. I can see from slight disturbances that Mrs. Olafsson has considered the space under the sheets, between the sheets, and even behind them. There are eight bedsheets in two piles of four, all identical, and indistinguishable from the sheets on my bed and those everywhere else in the hotel.

My mum makes her own bed every day, as soon as she wakes up. If the sheets need to be changed, she removes them, and she does it before she unlocks her bedroom door, which she has to lock, otherwise it springs open. It is a process she can be confident will happen in private.

I take the bottommost sheet from the pile on the left out and give it a testing squeeze. There is nothing inside. Nothing solid. I unfold it far enough that I can see there's nothing, then refold it and slot it back underneath the others. I pull out the bottom sheet from the four on the right and it is the same story. I feel nothing in the fabric, see nothing as I unfold it. In frustration I shake the sheet, as if threatening it, but that makes no difference; these sheets have been waterboarded and ironingboarded. The worst we can think of has already been done.

As I refold the sheet, I hear the delicate sound of one smooth surface moving against another. I look down and at my feet is a white envelope the size of a postcard. In the motion of picking up the envelope, I abandon the sheet.

The envelope has no discernible age, but it's not part of the current stationery of the hotel; it is at least four years old. The flap is not sealed but has been tucked inside. There is a flash of colour as it slips open. I have never held one before, though I immediately recognise what it is.

A photograph. The sort printed on thick cardstock by a chemist before everyone had a camera on them all the time and shared things on the internet. A proper photograph. The sort nobody on Ensay has, because we're forbidden to have images of the dead – and eventually everyone falls into that group.

The fact of the photograph is so arresting that I realise I hadn't even considered what the photograph is of. A baby – still amorphously young, without any of the signs of being a boy or a girl. He or she sits in a white crocheted robe – a gift from a godparent, if we had godparents, and used for christenings, if we had those either. A precious gift for a precious child. The baby is smiling at something to the right of the camera, which could be a parent or a shiny thing, or a patch of space.

I feel the photograph move between my fingers. There was not one photograph in the envelope, but two. The second shows a couple seated on a tartan rug on a wide patch of grass. The angle is low, as if the camera were resting on something – a timed shot to get them both in; the preservation of a moment they had not shared with anyone else.

The man is perhaps twenty and no older than twenty-five. He has shed every trace of puppy fat and has a lean, angular face clean-shaven that morning, with a hint of red on his neck where the collar of his shirt has rubbed. His hair is dark brown and he wears it with a casual side parting – something that might be slicked on a work day, but this is a weekend. He looks into the lens of the camera and the smile on his lips is just beginning to vanish; he believes he has messed up the timer on the camera and is a second away from standing up and retrieving it.

I turn the photographs over, looking for a name, a note, or a date marked in light pencil. There is a Kodak watermark and nothing else. But then the only person who would ever see these photographs would know the names and the dates; they would remember the way the grass smelled and could close their eyes and still feel the heat of the sun on their face from that afternoon.

I turn the photograph around again. The woman – the girl – in the second photograph is my mum. Sixteen years old or thereabouts. She sits with one leg folded underneath her and leans against the man. She is pregnant. Her belly is round and highly visible, but not quite impossible to manage – six months gone. Her left hand rests idly on the bump and she looks at the man, her face lit internally. She is mid-laugh. It is a thin slice of what it means to be in love. I can understand why she kept this contraband and why she hid it from everyone – even me.

The man in the photograph is my father.

A clatter from the bathroom startles me. I don't know if I've just found the photographs in my hands or if that happened hours ago.

"You okay?" I call out. He does not respond. "Connor?" Nothing.

I step over the dropped sheet and towards the bathroom door. There is a second clatter the second before I get there and find him unnaturally poised. He has his hand on the mirrored door of the bathroom cabinet, as if to keep it closed from an internal force trying to open it. I must see the trace of it in his expression; my mind makes one of those perceptive leaps which cannot be immediately explained by the information I am conscious of. A switch flips – *click!* – and it is not a bathroom cabinet anymore. It is a different object altogether, with another purpose and another meaning.

His hand is on the mirrored door of the medicine cabinet.

"What did you find?" he asks me.

"What did you find?" I reply. He looks stricken. He would like to be somewhere else at this moment, and possibly someone else. His anxiety escalates my own and I break the silence. "Show me."

He considers not doing it. I watch him search for a way to avoid giving me the answer I've demanded. But there is none. Mute, he opens the door.

On the glass upper shelf of the small cabinet is a line of dispensary bottles – brown plastic with oversize white child safety caps.

He says, "You didn't know." It isn't a question: I didn't.

"She never said." I take half a step forward. "What are they for?"

"Cancer. I think."

"How do you—?" But I know the answer before I finish the question.

"My mum took the same stuff. She had blister packs, the pills you pop out, but this is probably the same thing. Morphine for pain, prochlorperazine for being sick, the morphine makes it difficult to sleep – so there's temazepam – and it also makes you constipated – so there's this, which I think is over-the-counter laxative . . ." He picks up each item in turn and gives it a little shake, pausing only to read the back of the last item, a colourful box, before declaring, "Yeah, it's a laxative, but it's different than what my mum got."

Cancer.

"It's serious?" I ask. I suppose I'm looking for him to dispense me a dose of hope. For him to crack open one of those bottles and discover they're full of mislabelled aspirin. For him to say that this line of exotic and powerful chemicals is what doctors prescribe for mild, early-stage, survivable cancer. A little black lie to get me from this moment to the next.

He puts the box back on the shelf.

He takes my hand.

15

Life fragile, life robust.

Something like one-point-two billion years ago life began on Earth – accounts differ, but it may have been a Tuesday. It is suspected that life may only have started once, in one place, under specific circumstances; though it is equally possible that life can only begin one way, and it did so in precisely this way thousands of times. In either case, once life gets started, it is very difficult to stop. By Wednesday there would have been piles of life all over the place, and it would probably have been slimy.

A quarter of a billion years ago the Permian age was brought to an end by the Permian Extinction – which fans of extinctions sometimes call The Great Extinction. It's not certain what caused it: there are no surviving eyewitnesses, but whatever it was killed nearly all of nearly everything. The meteor that did for the dinosaurs was a day at the beach by comparison.

Was the Permian Extinction caused by another, bigger meteor? – maybe.

Volcanoes? – could have been; a chain of volcanoes erupting continuously for a hundred years would certainly depress property prices north, south, west, and east of Java.

Very thorough interstellar butterfly collectors who were also careless about how many fish and trees they abducted? – I wouldn't dismiss it entirely.

How about a trillion Mentos falling into an ocean of Coke? – no.

The point is – an event can be significant enough to kill nearly everything, everywhere, and still not actually kill everything. Life wears one of those hats that reads *keep on truckin'*.

But individual living things are fragile in the extreme. Mrs. Alexander was taken down by a cream sauce. My mum has cancer. She's being killed by an unfortunate mutated combination of guanine and adenine, or by a gamma ray burst from a supernova. She's being murdered by a genetic clerical error.

Under the circumstances.

It was there in plain sight and I had no idea. How could I not have known? I saw her every day. Mrs. Olafsson and Mrs. Douglas knew weeks ago.

By nine o'clock Mrs. Douglas hasn't called.

I am in the kitchen not really doing anything. Dinner is a lot of work, but it went by in something approaching a dream. Standard menu: no specials. Today has been how I imagine a roller coaster: up, down, spiralling, screaming, and always moving irresistibly forward. Even jumping off is its own kind of forward motion. There is no way to go back.

The last dessert has been served and the dishwasher is loaded and ready for the final few plates. Connor is hovering attentively in the dining room in case someone wants coffee or a drink. It didn't occur to me until just now that neither of us is legally allowed to serve alcohol to the guests since the licensee – the responsible person under Scottish law – is not here. I am sixteen, and Connor probably doesn't qualify as in any way responsible. As we've already sold two bottles and three glasses of wine, and two bottles of beer tonight, I'm happy for this to be tomorrow's problem.

Connor is not as bad at hovering as I had expected he would be – though I'm not sure whether this stretches all the way to being a compliment. He has *are-you-finished-with-that*-ed two people who were not, and ignored a woman seeking butter until she had no more need for it. It's a three-out-of-five performance, but it's where he needs to be, since he cannot, as it turns out, cook anything at all.

When he asked *what is a saucepan?* he was assigned a new posting. Not your fault, lad, but you're not ready for the SAS.

He did, at least, remember to charge everyone and has made twenty-two pounds in tips, which is more than he was getting paid and more than I ever got. He has a young, firm, helplessness about him which the older ladies amongst our guests are responding to with what I'll call enthusiasm, because enthusiasm is not a moral judgement. He relays the facts of these events; the interpretation of their meaning is entirely my own.

I check dates on frozen food, cans, dried things, and notice we have six cans of prunes that will expire next month. Something with prunes. It'll have to be a cake. It'll have to be both a cake and other things – there's no cake that can bear the weight of that many prunes. I pick up a can and pretend to smell it. Well, I actually smell the aluminium top, but I pretend I can smell prunes. *Mmm – prunes*, said nobody.

This does not help. People recognise smell, it is powerfully evocative, but memory doesn't include smell. Dreams are odourless.

In Mrs. Alexander's voice I say aloud, "Eleanor, hand me those prunes, I'm making—" *Kozani chicken*. And all the information I need is there. Kozani: city and region in northern Greece; one-pot dish made with saffron, paprika, and prunes. It would be saffron – now I'm trying to save a couple of pounds in canned prunes by spending a couple of pounds on saffron. I could always substitute . . . more prunes?

This needs additional planning.

The restaurant door swings open and Connor returns with a dramatic burden of three plates. He crosses the floor the way a serious, professional unicyclist would; tongue jutting out of the corner of his mouth; I imagine but do not see a bead of concentration sweat roll down his forehead. He loads all three plates into the dishwasher. Sturdy ceramic sounds. The chitter of unclean cutlery.

"Done?" I ask him.

"Done," he confirms and closes the dishwasher. It clunks and hums into action. "I thought that went okay."

"It did."

It is quarter past nine. There are guests in the lounge, we can hear the murmur of their conversation. The stereo, similarly muffled by distance and walls, plays Bonnie Raitt. *Streetlights* – an old vinyl print, possibly from the original nineteen-seventy-four run – produced by Arif Mardin before he won any of his eleven Grammys. Someone else has put the record on, almost certainly an American.

The song is *Angel from Montgomery*.

I watch him wash his hands in water so hot that they glow pink. He dries them on a kitchen towel. I have become familiar with his movement through hours of observation, with the understanding of an artist: not following a form like ballet positions or proceeding to the count of a metronome, but with an implicit understanding of true and false. Better and worse. Right and other.

He will turn his wrist just so, and the pronator teres, the pronator quadratus, and the flexor carpi radialis in his arm will change shape. They are fine and functional, beautiful and elegant, but my strange favourite of all the flesh that makes him is his brachioradialis, the elongated teardrop that falls towards his upper arm. No more or less physically remarkable than any, I suppose, but a muscle memory causes him to react whenever I touch him there. An incident in childhood, perhaps; or the way he lay in the womb; something forgotten but always present. A fingertip here will focus him as nothing else. He does not know this: I already know his body better than he ever will. And as I know him, I have come to possess him, the way a cartographer may have rights on entire continents and name rivers as they please, though they cannot dictate their flow.

I never intended to know him with this detail: he is just the place where, with increasing frequency, my eyes have come to rest. I could choreograph around his movements, and if I were a dancer, and if he trusted me, I could move perfectly with him. Next to him. Around him.

How well does he know my body? Without the *Grey's Anatomy* of anatomical terms – yes – but instinctively am I as familiar to him? Are there points of pressure he has found unlabelled and made his own?

He turns, with no particular thought in his head, and smiles.

If dreams were thunder, and lightning was desire, this old house would have burned down a long time ago.

You know it, Bonnie.

"What?" he asks.

"What?"

You ridiculous boy, how you make me silly, and how serious my silliness is.

"You're looking at me funny," he says. It may be that I am.

"You're looking at me funnier."

"I suppose."

"I supposier."

I am ever so much smaller than what I feel.

Over the sound of country music's heart breaking, the phone rings in reception. For the moment the spell is broken.

* * *

"She didn't want you to know." Mrs. Douglas says this like *check* in a game of chess. The rules of the game are clear, the actions are what the actions are, the result is check. She herself does not feel anything about this; it is neither just nor unjust, but it is. My mum did not want me to know about her cancer.

"I understand," I tell her. There is no sense in arguing: Mrs. Douglas cannot change the past, even if she were inclined to do so. My voice is raised because although we have an internet connection on Ensay, all of our phone calls take place via a length of string held taut between two tin cans. Her call from a hospital corridor in Stornoway has the texture of an Apollo transmission from the Sea of Tranquility. "What kind of cancer is it?"

"I do not know."

"Did she not tell you?"

She replies, but the answer is lost to a wash of static and echoes, either on her side or somewhere in the space between us. I ask her to repeat.

"She has not woken up. I spoke to her doctor—"

"And they didn't tell you?"

"It does not matter." Her voice is louder. Implicitly I have criticised her.

"It's the only thing that matters."

"She is dying." *Check.* "She has known for some time that she is dying. Her doctor told me she has tumours throughout her body. She cannot be treated, will not recover, and is not expected to regain consciousness."

I will never see her again. She is on the other side of a journey no more complicated than a shopping trip, and it might as well be farther than the moon. I cannot make it. The scale of the distance between us is beyond all my experience. She will die half an hour away by helicopter. She will die in the Western Isles Hospital, opened in nineteen ninety-three by His Royal Highness Prince Charles, who in Scotland is called the Duke of Rothesay and not the Prince of Wales. That information is completely useless. I have stored it like treasure and it is worth nothing.

She will die and I will never see her again.

"I understand."

"I'm staying in Stornoway tonight and will be back in the morning."

"She'll be alone," I say it and I must sound pathetic.

"There is nothing to be done. I spoke to Missus Olafsson; I trust I can rely on you to keep the hotel running for the rest of the season. We will need to discuss what happens afterwards."

The hotel?

She is listening for my response. It is the first time I have ever sensed anxiety from Mrs. Douglas. She has been unfailingly composed. She delivers the news of my mum's imminent death with dispassion, but the hotel, the hotel is important. The mystery falls away from Mrs. Douglas in that moment. I can see the wheels turning as they have always turned, moving in their fixed circular paths.

I am not sure how much it would cost us to close. After we'd repaid all the booking fees and very probably compensated some people for having to go elsewhere, we would certainly be able to survive to next spring. I think *we*, but it would not be we, it would be *me*. I would be able to survive until next year and have my isolation. Submerge myself in mourning and be reborn in the spring in any form I chose.

But I am not Mrs. Douglas's concern. If the hotel closes there would be no walking tours, no tartan nude portraits, no overpriced jam, no semi-Celtic jewellery. At a stroke, half the island's income would be gone. Over the long, cold winter it would wither, everyone who could leave would have to go, and in the spring, whatever remained of the rest of Ensay would never recover. There is no island-sized chrysalis.

Mrs. Douglas sees it all. The Ensay House Hotel makes everything possible. She can no more close its doors than she can cut off her right hand. It had not occurred to me that the person who held this island together was not its symbolic or administrative head – it was my mum. With her and Mrs. Alexander gone, and lacking any other substitute, the person holding this community together is me.

I say, "You can rely on me," though whether I have convinced her I don't know. I haven't convinced myself.

* * *

The night is warm. When the wind blows into the kitchen, it brings a summer smell of dry grass and salt which pushes out all the odours of cooking. The back door of the house is open and Connor has propped it with a round rock taken from the garden.

He stands on the edge of the step, looking out at the magenta night, gazing at the infinite gradations of colour between red and blue. The sky in Scotland cannot be so different to any other sky, I think. That must mean the sky is magical everywhere. I turn out the kitchen light so that in the moment while my eyes adjust, we are in darkness, and I stand behind him, resting my cheek against the flat plate of his shoulder blade. My hand circles his waist and he takes it in his own.

We stand like this as the noise in my head recedes. There are no sea birds this late in the evening. If this were the American plains, there would still be crickets fiddling their songs. In the silence, small sounds become symphonies. A television is on in a house nearby, loud to reach this far, but still quiet for us. Plants move in a light breeze, whispering to each other. His breath is a whale song, and I hear him prepare to speak long before he does.

"There was a woman in hospital next to my mum. She'd been in a car crash. Her nose was broken, and she had this metal frame around her head and neck to keep her still. They needed to operate on her brain, and she was in a coma. I saw her husband every day for a week. He would come in and sit by her bed for a couple of hours – they had kids, so he couldn't be there all the time like I was – and he'd read to her. The nurses told him that sometimes people in comas know you're there. So, he read to her. He was halfway through *Pride and Prejudice* when I first saw him. He finished that and read something else – *sane people do what their neighbours do?*"

"*Middlemarch.*"

"He read that for ages. Didn't finish it before she woke up. It was like one of those things on TV: she didn't remember anything, not who she was, who he was, anything about the crash. The Gardaí turned up to ask her questions and she got so upset the nurses made them leave. After that they put her in a private room and I never saw her again. But her husband was in the hospital cafe the next day. He looked pretty beat. He'd lost his wife twice; she'd been as good as dead, then she was alive but was basically a different person.

"He asked me if I wanted the book so I could finish it myself. I suppose he knew I was listening to him read it. I couldn't not listen. And maybe he was reading it to me as much as he was reading it to her. I took it, because it seemed like the kindest thing to do, but I still haven't finished it. I think I left it in the hospital. I must have.

"Anyway, the nurses tell you to read things. People tell you to talk to someone who can't wake up. But I don't think they can hear you. Not any more than you can listen to music while you're asleep." He gets to his point. "She won't know that you're not there."

I say, "I'll know."

"That won't make any difference."

"What do you mean?"

"You'll feel guilty anyway. Feeling guilty is how people cope with things they can't cope with. Your mum is dying. It's not fair and it's nothing to do with you at all. It's not even happening near you. Everything you do when people you love die is about you. Guilt is selfish, but you'll feel guilty anyway because it's not about what you did or didn't do; it's about believing that somebody else's life belongs to you, and it's being taken away from you, and it's not fair."

I don't believe this. I don't *think* I believe this. I want to jab him for intruding on this moment – on my personal grief. And then it is so obviously true that I distrust it. I love her, therefore some fractional part of her belongs to me, and that means her joy, her pain, and her death – a little piece of her death is my death. But if I had been raised by wolves instead, and my birth mother had died in a distant place without me knowing, I would feel nothing of her pain. If I died instead, she would not know.

Still, what can I do with this? Clinically accurate as it might be. Wise as it might prove. Knowing does not change me. I feel what I feel. This is why psychotherapy takes years, and whole notepads full of thoughts, and all manner of home-office furniture. Knowing is not enough. Somewhere in my head are a million things I know, all pulling against each other, and what I am is the tension between these experiences, between the lived and the taught.

"I still want to be there. I don't want her to be alone." Somewhat more honestly, I confide, "I don't want to be alone."

"Who would look after the hotel?"

"Not forever. Just for an hour. Just to see her and say goodbye. I'd like to be able to do that."

He turns around and embraces me. We sway slightly, as if dancing to the music from earlier in the evening now that we have the time.

"I love you, Eleanor," he whispers to me. Absurd. He is eighteen and I am sixteen and our hormones can be detected from space. He has been orphaned, as I am about to be – shared trauma might make someone a good pen pal, but otherwise this screams co-dependency.

We have known each other for two and a half weeks – less if you don't count the time separated by a door. I have spent less total cumulative time in his company than I have spent in the shower *just this year*. I have seen him on fewer individual days this year than I have seen Mr. Jones – who, on one of those days, I saw naked.

Connor cannot possibly love me and I cannot possibly love him.

Help me, but I do.

"Connor," I say. I feel his arms tighten around me, like he might not let me go unless I reciprocate. I want to. I am conscious of my own heartbeat against him and I can feel blood rushing to every part of my body except my brain. This too, is unfair. In this moment I would make every irrational trade; I would swap every day after today to be with him tonight. I am out of my mind with want and need and grief and if there is any line between these things, I cannot find it. A sense of weightlessness hits me, as if I am no longer touching the floor.

Connor steps backwards and down – *out of the house.*

I scream.

He has my arms pressed to my sides and he holds me up off the ground. The ground, not the floor. I shut my eyes, but I know, I can feel the emptiness around me and the panic passes through me like a vibration. I am aware of my body shaking uncontrollably as I struggle to free myself, and I can feel even this loose purchase on my senses slipping away. I am at the bottom of a well and the world is a tiny, distant speck of inconceivable light.

"It's okay," he says. "It's okay."

I kick out at him and it's luck rather than strength that makes him lose his balance. He releases me and I drop a few inches to the ground, but I fall down like a rag doll, my palms hitting the draft excluder on the back door even as my shins hit the edge of the step. Connor falls backwards onto the grass. I scramble back into the house, noticing the bright colour of blood, assuming it is mine. He is back on his feet in a second.

"Eleanor, wait!"

I lift the stone he had placed at the door and throw it in one motion. It travels in an arc, and he dodges to his left to let it sail through the space where his body had been. I catch the expression on his face – bewilderment – before I kick the door closed.

16

I look in the mirror and judge myself. There are heavy red circles around my eyes – as if I had a gluten allergy and had spent the previous evening doing lines of flour. Just seeing them is painful. I feel more raw than I ever did with hunger. I am more bruised than bruises could make me.

The bathroom is as cold as it is in winter, or it feels that way. It is darker than it was yesterday at the same time, and I have no idea if this is the profundity of melodrama or a passing cloud across the sun.

But hot water is reliable magic. After the shower I regain motion; my muscles unclench, my shoulders un-hunch, my mouth un-un-smiles. It is a change between states of matter: I was a solid, now I am a liquid.

My iPad is on the bed next to me. I brush out my hair and pretend not to look at it, though I'm not sure who this pretence is for since I know I'm doing it and the little electronic device does not know or care. I dry my hair, pausing in motion but not turning off the flow of warm air to press the button on the screen.

The black surface illuminates, telling me the time. There are no alerts, no messages.

Well, if that don't beat all. The idiom arrives and carries the debate. Doesn't that just beat all? He doesn't even have the decency to have already sent me a grovelling apology. Here I am, in pieces – like a schmuck – and there he is, doing something else. He probably slept an unbroken eight hours – like he's the King of England. (Though, as it's five-thirty and it was after ten when I last saw him, eight hours of anything is technically impossible).

There is something cathartic about surrendering one's internal monologue to the parlance of American screwball comedies. I am not, in fact, an emotional wreck. I am not even especially angry – I'm angry, but it's background radiation; my anger will be detectable with a radio telescope until the end of time, but it won't interfere with a mobile phone signal. And there is a mobile phone signal on Ensay – on good days, on high ground, so I'm told – so he doesn't have that as an excuse.

I understand what he was trying to do and I understand why he tried to do it. If he had told me in advance, I would have told him it's not practical to teach people to swim by throwing them in the ocean and shouting encouragement. Or at least any successes an instructor might enjoy would be more than offset by even a couple of drownings – two drownings, because everybody gets one.

I am much smarter than he is – I would have told him that, still might – and if my problem could be solved by keeping calm and carrying on, I would have already solved it thank-you-and-good-day-sir-I-said-good-day. It is not a question of resolution, rather the capacity of any human being to become another specific human being. Change is inevitable, but alchemists spent thousands of years trying to turn lead into gold and, all they got for their trouble was lead poisoning. Even if they had the benefit of the nuclear furnace of a star far older and larger than the sun, they would find that their lead would transform into gold – yes, good job – and plutonium and iron and a smaller amount of lead – so it's tough to sell this gold in a jewellers because it rusts and disintegrates your DNA. It's not even much good as lead.

Profound change is unfocused, and for every dimension in which it is predictable, it is unpredictable in two others. This is not a rallying cry for apathy – after all, who would rally? – but it is to acknowledge a truth I have understood for a long time, and which Connor has only now approached.

I cannot leave the hotel. If someone ever leaves this house, it will not be me.

$* * *$

Breakfast prep, packed lunches, breakfast, check-outs.
"It's such a beautiful island."
"That's why we're here."
"Ah-ha-ha-ha."
"Well, the ferry's due to leave in about ten minutes."
"Goodbye."
"Have a nice trip home."
Three of those, give or take a comment about the weather, or a remark about how nice the food was. Nowadays everything is paid for in advance, so there are no credit cards and no cash changes hands. I print out invoices for tax purposes, in case one of our guests can justify a visit to the Hebrides on business. It does happen – photographers, artists, and writers all come here. None of those people doing it professionally look any different from the ones doing it for fun. I once heard an American accountant tell another

American accountant an accountant joke: *the more you enjoy it, the harder it is to deduct.* He was talking about a time when a Thai girl gave him a rub-and-tug, but I think it's a good general rule.

Everyone who is checking out has checked out by ten, and anyone who had intended to go out, has gone. An English landscape artist, who insisted on being called Joan, has a migraine and retired to her room after breakfast. She is the only other person in the hotel and will be no trouble. I have an hour before the team room opens to strip, clean, and remake three bedrooms, and make the beds and empty the bins in all others (excepting Joan's). This cannot be done.

If one were the sort of person who goes to pieces when presented with an impossible task, one would not last long in either hospitality or a wartime hospital. Whether being faced with a leg that needs to be amputated or a guest who has stolen a hair dryer, the most important thing is to remain calm. Triage is the process of deciding what needs to be done immediately, what needs to be done soon, what can be left on a gurney for a couple of hours, and – shifting to a nautical metaphor – who should be sewn up in their hammock and thrown overboard tomorrow.

I triage.

I do beds, bins, and bath towels in all the occupied guest rooms. I clean one toilet; the rest look fine. Nobody's room gets a hoover – Joan and the dust mites (cool band name) will doubtless rejoice. It is a seven-out-of-ten result, which was all that could be done, and it takes fifty-seven minutes. The three empty rooms must wait. I take all the used bath towels down the back stairs in a large canvas bag and put on a wash. Which brings me to fifty-nine and a half minutes – more than enough time to check myself in a reflective surface, find inner peace, radiate positivity, and turn the sign in the tea room window from closed to open.

But not enough time to have baked any fucking cakes!

The tea room has three identical cake stands, each with their own glass cloche. They have the heavy feel of antique items made for a hundred years of daily use. Underneath each cloche is, normally, a cake in some stage of being eaten slice-by-slice. But the day before the day before yesterday, my mum didn't make any cakes, the day before yesterday she sold the remaining cake cheap, yesterday was my birthday so we didn't need any extra cake, and the cake that we had was destroyed and uninsured. Yesterday afternoon my mum would have made more cake, but she was dying and I – distracted by this and having never been allowed to make a cake before – forgot.

The cloches are empty.

We also don't have any scones. This thought is like realising that the Titanic, already fatally wounded and heading for the icy depths of the North Atlantic, probably had a squeaky floorboard in one of the staterooms which maintenance are never getting around to. It's annoying: it's less than the standard we at the White Star Line hope to deliver to our customers, but it is unlikely to generate any complaints given the broader context of events.

The front door opens. Rubber soles on the hall flooring.

"Hey," Connor says. He stands in the tea room doorway with his hands in his pockets as far as they will go.

"Hello," I say, and then it's his turn to speak. I will be absolutely furious if I have to make the first move towards reconciliation – and coming over and saying *hey* does not count as the first move.

He says, "I didn't mean for that to happen."

"Oh – did your lawyer tell you to say that?"

"You know what I mean."

"*I didn't mean for that to happen* is the same thing as *I'm sorry you were offended.*"

"I'm sorry you were offended."

"I'm not asking you to say *I'm sorry you were offended*; I'm saying what you're saying is bullshit absent contrition or admission of wrongdoing."

"Maybe that's because I don't want to admit that I've done anything wrong."

"If you don't think you've done anything wrong, why are you standing there looking so guilty?"

He pulls his hands out of his pockets and straightens. "*You* threw a rock at *my* head."

"*I* missed." Attempted murder is, while serious, significantly less serious than successful murder. In my defence, your honour, I failed. "*You* actually lifted me outside."

"Hugs and rocks are different."

"If you won't say you're sorry and mean it, how am I supposed to forgive you?"

"Don't forgive me," he shrugs enormously, expansively, like a woman demanding to be called Joan and not Ms. Bellfield. "I didn't ask for you to forgive me. Don't forgive me for trying to get you out of here because . . . because I'd do it again. You're trapped here. You don't want to be here. I thought maybe—"

"Nobody had tried just taking me outside before?"

"Yes," he says, sounding dumb. "I thought it was worth a shot."

"No," I say. "It was a stupid idea and you're stupid."

There is about seven feet of space between us. I move forward six and he comes the rest of the way. Our hands find each other and our fingers intertwine. Either I kiss him or he kisses me – in the final moment I can't tell which of us is moving and which is standing still. With my eyes closed I slightly lose balance, tip back, and our contact is broken. He looks down, smiles, and looks up. I wonder how much my expression reveals me – am I as open to him as he is to me?

I say, "And if you do it again, I'll break your nose."

He gives this long and serious consideration, then says, "Okay."

"Well . . . as long as we understand each other."

"You're hard work."

"I'm the most accommodating, least demanding person I know – by the way, I'm going to need you to work twelve to ten, not two to ten, and I'm going to need you to sign a form that says you voluntarily opt-out of the European Working Time Directive."

"Okay."

"But today you have to start right now."

"What am I doing? Charming old ladies?"

"Less exciting."

"Charming old men?"

"I need you to go to the shop and buy whatever cake they have."

He is fake aghast. "*Bought* cake?"

"We don't have any cake. They'll take what they get. You get back with the cake, I'll make some scones—"

"We don't have any scones either? Oh-em-gee."

"—I'll make some scones and I need you to strip—"

"Cool."

"—three bedrooms—"

"Sad times."

"—and hoover."

* * *

But an hour later, the tea room is empty.

Except for me, of course. And the scones I made. And the stand-in cakes. Under glass sits a tower of Mr. Kipling's individual apple pies, a plastic-looking Battenberg, and a curiously sweaty Madeira cake which I patted dry with some paper towels and iced. All long-life cakes, of course. Bread comes into the shop daily and Mrs. Brown would rather run out than throw out. Even as a person who has made something approaching a career selling cakes, I would have to admit cake is not an everyday item.

While a bag of salad might be packed in a protective atmosphere – the oxygen in the bag having been replaced with nitrogen – durable cake needs to last months rather than a few more days, and that requires baking in preservation. Calcium propionate isn't on any domestic cook's shopping list but if a cake is to stay mould free for longer than a loaf of bread, delicious calcium propionate is a good guy to know. (I don't know if it's delicious actually; were I to guess, I'd guess it tastes like chalk). Xanthan gum sounds like an obscure comic book villain from the planet Gum, who has the ability to stick his enemies fast in Xanthan. Or the reverse – whatever. But Xanthan Gum, as well as being the avowed enemy of The Flash, is what keeps plastic-wrapped cakes disgustingly moist months after baking. (I don't know if Xanthan Gum is delicious either; I imagine he tastes of hate and contempt for the world's most historic pavements).

They make it from a sort of bacterial poop. Xanthan gum. I'm still thinking about it as I peer through the windows into the street, where I expect to see the only two cars on the island have crashed into each other and formed a flaming barricade between me and the people of Ensay. *Throw us the scones and tea and we'll throw you the money* – they shout. *How the eff am I supposed to throw tea?* – I shout back. There is no response: I have stumped them – and they don't exist.

The food industry takes what bacteria secretes – a sticky liquid substance – and they dry it out and put it into food as if it were any other ingredient. And not just cake, not even mostly cake. Fruit juice. Soup. Essentially anything you want to be liquid-but-not-that-liquid or solid-but-not-that-solid.

I press the side of my face against the glass to get the best possible field of vision, but I don't see anything that might prevent people coming for tea, or any people obviously prevented from coming. There is a bench outside Mr. Peters' house. He put the bench there himself, but it is on the sunny side of the street when there is sun, so there's no shortage of casual visitors who have come to regard it as a bench held for the common good. Mr. Peters sits on it today reading yesterday's newspaper.

Or not really reading it? I detect the slightest motion when my eyes fall on him – a moment before, had he been staring into the window of the tea room? He turns the page in his newspaper and flaps it, using the action as an excuse to raise the edge of the paper up so that it is above his eye level. He holds it there for an unnaturally long time, I'm tempted to walk away then turn around suddenly to see if he looks back. I don't do this, because he might actually look and therefore see me doing this, and I would both look and feel ridiculous.

I hear Connor approach down the stairs, across the hall, and pause at the tea room door. "I've hoovered," he says. I imagine he looks very pleased with himself.

"Uh-huh," I say, still watching Mr. Peters' *Glasgow Herald.*

"Quiet today?"

"It *is* quiet." I turn away from the window.

Connor arches an eyebrow and says, "Almost *too* quiet. Some might say suspiciously quiet."

"Well – it's odd."

"The oddest. It's as if all the people who normally come here have been replaced by aliens."

"Is it like that, though?"

"Aliens for whom tea is a deadly poison!"

"You know it's just stuff in water but with the stuff taken out. I don't

184

think you can be poisoned by the concept of tea."

He edges towards me as if wary of observation, or fearful of a sniper's bullet. "You and I could be the only human beings left alive on Earth, protected by the aliens' terror of brown water."

"Sometimes it's other colours."

"That's what they fear the most."

"Because on Xanthan there is no water."

"And all the seas are made of rocks."

"That's just land."

"Oh yeah," he says, smiles, and leans in to kiss me. Which is nice, but I have kept one eye open and trained on the spot so that I can check for movement of the front and back pages of the *Herald*. There is none.

I break off. "Okay. We're closing."

"The hotel?"

"No – just this bit. I'm not standing here all day to serve tea to nobody. Do you like scones?"

"Not especially. I mean they're fine. Though I expect your scones are great and I will definitely love them."

"For lunch I'm giving you scones," I say and I turn the sign from open to closed. "So, grab some scones and follow me."

"Am I not getting any tea?"

"No."

"What about the aliens?"

"Bring Coke," I tell him. I am already at the top of the hall stairs when he emerges from the tea room, the pockets of his jeans overstuffed with cans and his hands full of fruit scones. Why he didn't bring a plate I don't know, but we're not going back now.

On the first floor landing we transfer to the back stair and go up to the top of the house. This room is weather. When it rains, there is no colder, greyer or more depressing space in the house. But when the sun shines and the windows are open, it is an acre of sea grass; a rough meadow by a beach of fine white sand. Today is bright. I hold the door and Connor follows a few steps behind me.

He puts the scones and drinks on my dresser and I go straight to my easel.

"I want to show you something," I say. The sheet makes a whoosh as I sweep it away and she stares out at me. Her expression is different each time I look at her, this mirror-unalike imprint of me. Today she is very pleased with herself indeed.

Connor stands behind me. "Jesus."

"No, try again."

He says nothing.

"It's my first self-portrait," I tell him. "And it's probably the best thing

I've done. I hadn't planned to paint her, but there I was, and there she was – hanging in the air, waiting to be put on canvas. We found each other."

I hear his mouth open and close; the false start of a thought. Then he says, "Did your mum hit you?"

"Sometimes," I say. It is easy to say it. The statement is ordinary. Ask a fish about water and it would say the same.

"My mum never hit me."

"I know." Though I could not say how I knew it.

"I'm sorry."

I shrug and he puts his arms around me. We stand looking at the painting for a long time. In the beginning it feels like I am comforting him, then we are comforting each other, and finally that all the injury is mine. That feels intolerable and I shake him off.

"Do you like it?"

He scoffs, "It's good. It's really good. It's better than everything else. And no – I don't like it."

"You're a tough critic."

"It doesn't feel like you."

"Who else could it be?"

"I dunno. Why did you paint yourself with brown eyes?"

"They're not brown, they're hazel."

"I'm not the artist, and that may be so, but your eyes are green."

"My eyes are hazel," I correct him.

He turns me around and lifts my chin with his finger. He stares into the left, he stares into the right, he shakes his head and affects an expression of grave sadness which fractures as he has a devilish thought.

"You should paint me."

I feel the frown on my forehead. "The usual form is to enquire if the artist would be interested in taking a commission, so as to avoid offence when the artist tells you Old Holland's artisan manufacturing process doesn't produce that shade of ugly."

"You just said a whole lot of other stuff, when what you meant to say was, *I will paint you, thanks for offering to be painted.*"

"You really want me to paint you?"

"Defo," he says.

"It takes a long time to paint someone."

"We've got hours before dinner."

I roll my eyes at how little he understands and how much he assumes, but I don't hate the idea. "Don't get upset if it turns out weird, okay? Because I've only ever painted me before. And don't be surprised if you come out looking like me."

"You don't look weird," he says. "Okay, let's go."

I sigh for effect – I am a secret convert. I retrieve the brushes he gave me from the pile of still-wrapped birthday gifts – they feel *right* in my hand. I move the old canvas to the side and replace it with a fresh one. It slips before it reaches the easel and clatters to the floor.

Connor is half-naked. His shoes, socks, and top are scattered like a breadcrumb trail. With his back to me, he unbuckles his belt and slips out of his jeans. Then he is entirely naked and he leaps onto my bed as he tosses his underpants through the air to land somewhere behind me.

It is an act of brazen confidence from a skinny, pale Irish boy. A level of confidence that seems to require, or at least coincide with, tattoos of guns and dragons and images inspired by prog rock albums of the sixties and seventies. He has none of these: not an armadillo tank or a space prism anywhere on his skin, which is a whiter shade of washing machine.

And I am looking at an actual penis. At *his* actual penis. Because where else is one supposed to look?

Connor reclines and says, "Paint me like one of your French girls."

I pick up the canvas, place it just so – landscape rather than portrait – secure it, put my brushes away, kick off my shoes, and abandon the whole idea of painting.

I'm still mostly clothed by the time I get to the bed, but that's fixed in about eight seconds. My toes touching his shins. Our limbs colliding. His hands on me. I want him and I want to give him what he wants.

Nobody will see or hear. Nobody will ever know. And right now, I don't even know if I care about the consequences. The voice inside me which has urged caution is a whisper, lost to the heartbeat sound of drums.

"Connor. You can't tell anyone."

"Who am I going to tell?"

"It's important. Do you promise?"

How unreasonable. Even as I ask, I know that he would promise anything, giving no thought to how difficult such a promise might be to keep.

"Are you worried that I might sue you? Because I am still on the clock, you know. Is this workplace sexual harassment? Are you harassing me right now? Here? In my workplace?"

"I didn't ask you to take your clothes off. If anything, this is gross misconduct."

"Gross? The cheek. I did a hundred sit-ups this morning. Well, not sit-ups, because they're bad for your back – crunches. And not a hundred, but at least twenty."

"Connor, I'm not like other girls."

"Oh really? Does yours go sideways?"

"Promise me."

"I will never tell a soul until the end of my days, may the Lord strike me deaf, blind, and dumb. May He take all my good looks and leave me bald. May He cause my willy to—"

I kiss him and pull myself as close as skin and bone allow. I have read that girls are often afraid the first time. It may hurt and each pain is like only itself. But I have been beaten and bruised, cut and starved, I have been lonely and ashamed. I am not afraid of this. All my body tells me is *begin. Let it begin.*

He moves on top of me and between my legs. I feel the weight of his body over me and I want to submit to him. This is what is really true about love being the most powerful force in the universe: knowing everything I know; I would still choose this. With all the risks for him, with all the risks for me. I would choose this over both of our futures. He reaches for his jeans and takes out a wallet which is closed with Velcro.

"Connor," I say. My tone arrests him in tearing open the foil packet. "You're leaving, right? You're going to university in September?"

He looks abashed. He loves me; I know he does. But he won't turn his life for me – a girl much like other girls, on an island at the end of the world. I'll have him for the span of a summer and he'll leave long before the equinox and there won't be anything to be done about it.

Maybe they'll kill me instead.

He nods. "Yeah. We don't have to . . . I don't want to lead you on."

I kiss him on the mouth, on the neck – as he rolls down the latex – and I pull him back, so we are lying down again. I kiss him on the shoulder where the clavicle pushes his skin up into a mound. I kiss him on the breastbone. The manubrium first: the last protective bone before the soft, vulnerable throat. Then the gladiolus: the centre of his chest: poetically the bone that covers the human heart (though unlike the bones of the body, the organs are asymmetric; his heart is to the right and beats under the palm of my left hand). I push myself down the bed. He is using his arms to prop himself up, and I can see his whole body: tense and hard; eager and uncertain.

I put my hands in his hair and bring him by gentle increments to rest against me. He asks me for some final consent, his voice so soft I cannot hear the words – or is he only saying something sweet; a sound with meaning but without form?

I wrap my legs around him so that my heels touch. I put my hands on his back so that my outstretched fingers overlap.

Perhaps I am frightened now. But if I'm to die on this island, then first I'll live here.

17

"Nesting birds?" she asks.

"I have never seen them myself, but it's a sufficiently ordinary thing that I don't believe anyone would benefit from making them up. I know someone who fell through a bird hide. I know him very well, in fact. Also, you should watch yourself because I don't think anyone will have fixed that collapsed bird hide."

"So, people sit in these bird hides and watch birds?"

"I can sense your scepticism, but I assure you – people do it. They come from all over the world to look at those birds. Now, you may be a person who thinks that you can get everything you need from birds from TV – or your local supermarket. Quick skwatch at a bird David Attenborough has made friends with, or a few chicken nuggets, you're fine for birds for six months. And for you there might be no thrill to be had in distinguishing a herring gull – the *Larus argentatus*, known for its earthworm dance – from a lesser black-backed gull – the *Larus fuscus*, known for being basically identical to three other species unless you're the sort of odd-flexing super-fussy person who wants to get credit for discovering a gull species. For you, I expect, one gull is much like another, and there are millions of them all over the place, and all of them are a nuisance. Our views may not be widely divergent on this issue, if I can confide that to you as one woman of the world to another. But out there, living amongst us like normal people, there are philatelists. They look like normal people, but instead of being normal people, they collect stamps. King of hobbies, hobby of kings, and about as boring a thing to do as I can imagine. But *people* do it. So, when I handed you this leaflet from the Royal Society for Protection of Birds on *Scottish Seabirds,* I was not trying to trick you. This isn't one of those old Scottish tourist jokes like tartan paint, bottled Scotch mist, shooting wild haggis, bagpipe music, there being a monster in Loch Ness, kilts, and Dundee being a place you should visit. Looking at birds is *a real thing.*"

Her husband says, "I enjoyed learning about the Tay Bridge Disaster."

I take the leaflet away from her and give it to him. "This is something better suited for you. Ma'am – if I can suggest walking on the beach on the other side of the island where the seabirds don't nest. Then perhaps the two of you can meet up tomorrow afternoon for high tea?"

"That does sound nice," he says, because he's a man who knows when to seize time on his own whenever the opportunity presents itself, and if he needs to spend that time looking at gulls, then so be it. He's probably thinking he can just shut his eyes if he doesn't like looking. Pop in some headphones. Crank up the Toto.

She asks, "What time does the dining room open?"

I say, "Another hour. Please make yourself comfortable in the lounge."

Here I am, standing behind this perfectly ordinary wooden counter in the hall of the hotel, with no outward indication of what I was doing only a few hours before. It's like a magic trick. Had I imagined that a scarlet letter would appear over my head in flashing neon? (In my case probably an H for harlot. Harlot. Harlot.)

The couple making their way to the lounge – where Connor is serving aperitifs with measures designed to get people drunk before parents come home and end the party – had no idea. For all I know, that mousy middle-aged couple could have been doing the same thing even more recently. How much of it is happening somewhere on Ensay right now? Almost certainly more than I had expected. The RSPB put a leaflet out about the birds, but for all I know there's a colony of rutting humans to the south, and in nearby hides they are being observed through binoculars by men in raincoats with flasks of tea and supplies of small square sandwiches.

Sex. I have had / done / partaken of /enjoyed? / enjoyed / committed sex.

If I were to compare the *act* to something else, there would be no shortage of useful metaphors or similes. I think if I had ever played sports I would be able to see the physical as the first return of a tennis serve, where observation and theory snap into *feeling.* This is what it feels like to do the thing I've imagined, and I had better get over my surprise because that ball is coming right back at me. But the emotional experience is — if someone were in a terrible accident and had one of those full-body casts that only exist in movies, when the cast came off, that's how it feels. Liberated and vulnerable. Also, trepidatious and slightly gross. Pink and shiny, like scrubbed skin – the way a lobster is when it sheds its shell. But inside.

What I'm doing right now is using things I've never experienced, to explain a thing I have experience of, to myself.

Then afterwards, in a moment of quiet, the guilt arises. One wrong word from Connor to the wrong person and they would know. He'll put his hand on the small of my back, or he'll move to kiss me, or I'll remove a stray hair of mine from his clothes without thinking. A secret this obvious can't be kept for long. He's walking around with a bomb strapped to him. I was the radical cleric who clipped him into the fastenings of a suicide vest. That's a lot of guilt. I'm not saying Nathaniel Hawthorne's protagonist had it easy, but the average New England pilgrim thought everyone (else) was going to hell anyway. Hester Prynne was probably quite the unifying figure in seventeenth century Boston: trading pleasantries and being shunned by an entire community – *morning goodwife adulteress* – *morning Reverend* – *just off to hell, are you?* – *and to buy some fish, sir* – then she'd walk into the market and everyone would yell *adulteress!* and a recently docked sailor would play a sea shanty interpretation of the theme from *Cheers* on a scrimshaw fife.

"Knock, knock," says Mrs. Olafsson. We had already seen each other through the open door when she *knock-knock*ed and came in without being invited, rendering the *knock-knock*ing pointless. She smiles at me – a smile which is burdened with the usual patronising sympathy. She knew about my mum's illness some time ago and said nothing. A day before she was rummaging in my mum's underwear trying to find those old photos – she'll say nothing about them as she didn't find them, and would certainly have destroyed them if she had. It is hard to reconcile her matronly warmth with the way she must think about me – as child, as an idiot, as someone who should be lied to and deceived for their own good.

"Oh, my dear," she says and hurls me into her bosom. "Mrs. Douglas told me the terrible news about your mother."

It must say something about me that I have not spent the last several hours thinking about my terminally ill mum lying unconscious in a hospital, waiting to die. What it says can't be good, either. But the feeling I have is not more guilt – it's anger. This cheerful middle-aged woman knew about the cancer and said nothing. Perhaps she doesn't know that I know. Perhaps Mrs. Olafsson believes as Mrs. Douglas does – *she didn't want you to know* – and that is enough.

She releases me, takes a half step back and I say, "It's been a great shock to all of us." Zing, bitch.

"I need to talk to you about Connor."

If I had eaten more than half a scone for lunch it would be all over the floor in that instant. She knows. And she can't possibly know. My stomach is a collapsing star sucking in the rest of my body to a point of pressure and nothingness past explanation by physical laws.

"What about him?" I ask, and try to ignore the fact that my voice broke during the question.

Mrs. Olafsson rubs my arm and says, "I think I might have put you in a difficult position. It was very good of him to put himself forward to help. I can't fault him. But with everything happening, I never gave a moment's thought to the fact that you'd be working all day with your boyfriend."

The words rush to get out of my mouth, "Connor isn't—"

"Tsh," she interrupts me with an expression of knowing humour. "Of course he is. A blind woman could see it on a dark night. And your first boyfriend too. It all feels new and exciting, but it's going to be very stressful even if your mum was here."

"But he isn't my boyfriend."

"I mean I didn't want to intrude, but it is rather obvious. He's a good-looking boy, he's the only boy your age on the island, you spend a lot of time—"

"He was staying at the hotel. We didn't *spend time* together."

"That's how these things happen, dear. People around the same age *spend time* together and later but usually sooner they will have feelings for each other. That boy is most certainly your boyfriend, and he knows it even if you don't."

"But he isn't Missus Olafsson, I promise. He's just a friend."

"You *promise*?" She isn't looking for affirmation, she's questioning the word itself. "Why would you promise me he wasn't?"

"I promise. He's not . . . I don't even like him."

"Eleanor, you are a terrible liar. And I've never seen you get yourself so upset about anything."

"I'm not upset. I just don't want you saying—" I'm crying. Fuck. I *heard* a tear hit the floor; a tiny, soft thud and splatter of hysteria. "—I don't want anyone saying that he's my boyfriend when it's not true."

"Eleanor. What is the matter?" I can see the thought turn in her head like the gears of a machine. "Has he hurt you?"

"*No.*" Oh! the opposite. I have hurt him. I've killed him. The denial comes out as a plaintive sound. "Please don't tell Missus Douglas. *Please*. He's going to leave the island after the summer. I'll never see him again. Nobody needs to know."

"Missus Douglas?"

"I love him. I tried not to, I didn't want to, but I do. I love him. And I can't. I can't. I can't burn him. I can't. There has to be another way. Anybody else. I'll choose someone else and nobody will know. Please. Not him."

Another mechanical shift happens inside Mrs. Olafsson. Her eyes become hard and her lips purse. It occurs to me that I have never seen this woman angry until today. She verifies her suspicions with the expression on my face, and I look down, not to avoid the inquisition, but so I am at least a passive victim of it rather than a participant.

"Eleanor. Will you go and wait in the private dining room please."

"Why?"

Mrs. Olafsson reaches over the counter and picks up the telephone. "I am going to call Missus Douglas. She will want to speak to you about this herself."

* * *

Yesterday I was not allowed to be in this room at all, and now I am in it alone with the doors closed. On the back of those doors, the ones which always felt and indeed are older than the house, is a quite beautiful geometric relief like the structure of a honeycomb; rounded hexagons fill the space, each a handspan across. The recesses of each chamber are dark and heavy with a century of wax, and as I wait for the doors to open, I stare into the illusory depths, each concealing numberless swarms.

I was led here mutely. I unlocked the door – I have the key – and I sit here awaiting judgement. I accept the authority of Mrs. Douglas and I am subject to it. I could not leave this room if it were on fire. My world has shrunk by another factor – the island, the house, and now this one room is the limit of where I can go.

But if I could warn Connor, he might be able to get away before anyone knows. It has been five minutes, not more than ten, since Mrs. Olafsson called Mrs. Douglas. The news could not have spread that fast. He could make it to the boat and a few tourists might be on it; enough so that nobody would dare stop him leaving.

Would he believe me? If I told him to run and never look back, would he trust me enough to go?

I am on my feet.

I have to try.

I reach for the handle.

But the doors swing open towards me.

Mrs. Douglas' countenance is a stone wall. I step back, the chair I had been sitting on hits the back of my knees and I fall onto it. Mrs. Olafsson stands behind her, her face is beetroot and her fists are clenched tight enough to turn her knuckles white.

Mrs. Douglas says, "I think it would be best if you told me everything Missus Carlyle has said to you."

* * *

How would anyone know if everything they had been told was a lie?

At six I was told that my religion believed Ensay's rites would end the world. Superstition, of course. Even at six I understood that to conduct oneself with regard to faith was different than believing in magic. Catholics do not literally believe in transubstantiation; they do not consume the flesh and blood of Christ. Flesh and blood do not taste like wafers and red wine, the act of consuming them is metaphorical and symbolic. Our blood sacrifice is treated with equal seriousness – yet nobody believed the burning of the wicker man would end the world.

But what if that six-year-old child were told that it would one day be their job to cut the flesh from the body of the living Christ and to drain his blood. Would it be so obvious that this was not exactly what was expected? The lie is inseparable from the truth; logic cannot divide one superstition from another.

My mum told me that I was chosen to be the acolyte because I was the only girl who would turn sixteen this year. True. She told me that I must pick a man to be sacrificed. True. She said that I must have sex with him and that this sin would mark him for death. Then he would be burned alive.

Mrs. Douglas, in a steady voice, careful of every nuance, explained it quite differently.

"The acolyte chooses the sacrifice; he has usually been her actual boyfriend or is a prospective boyfriend. The sacrifice is placed into the wicker man and at the appointed time makes a show of trying to escape. Then it is the job of the high priestess to distract the crowd by lighting a torch and at the same time the sacrifice slips out the open back of the rowan cage and is replaced by a scarecrow – a man-shaped figure of clothes stuffed with dry grass. The younger children make it in the days before the equinox, though Missus Carlyle never allowed you to participate.

"This is what gets burned."

She went on to say that although the acolyte and the sacrifice are often romantically involved, *requiring* the acolyte to give her virginity to the sacrifice is unheard of. According to Mrs. Douglas, a similar shortage of suitable young men on Ensay has meant that three of the last forty acolytes have chosen their own brothers. One picked her father.

And the reason for the shortage of men on the island? There is no simple answer. Mrs. Olafsson recalled that when they found oil in the North Sea twelve men left in one month to go to Aberdeen, settled there, never came back. The idea caught hold and fifty had gone by the end of that year.

But Mrs. Douglas, with her superior knowledge of the island's records, said there was probably something genetic. Families descended from the McArdle brothers produced only daughters for three generations. Even today, boys are rare, but Mrs. Harper is pregnant and expecting a son. There is no expectation that she will have him adopted or throw him into the sea.

Mrs. Douglas wasn't sure whether this was the brothers themselves or the nuns or a combination, but an acute shortage led to conventional marriage falling out of fashion and convention meant they never went back. Since then, women took to calling themselves *missus* and taking the name of their partner, who would usually be the father of their first child. The sacrifices make a similar symbolic change – they give up their old name and select a new one.

Mr. Urquhart was, in his youth, a strapping young man with a full head of hair and a winning smile. And his name was John Douglas. Mrs. Douglas, like Mrs. Alexander, was drawn away to do bigger and better things with her life. Mr. Urquhart stayed and withered.

Mr. Jones visited the island on a short-lived exchange programme between Scotland and its Scandinavian neighbours while still at school. He fell in love with a girl during his two weeks in the Western Isles and, after a long and decorous correspondence during which time his English improved significantly, he came back and married her. While he took a strange delight in perfecting a faux-Welsh accent, his Icelandic heritage was always clear in his pale blue eyes. His original name was Olafsson.

Yes, we burn our dead. As do hundreds of millions of other people in a diversity of cultures around the world. We do not move the dead except to be cremated. We do not keep photographs of the dead – officially. Unofficially Mrs. Douglas does not believe anyone, including herself, fully complies with that. Photographs used to be rare and this meant it was easier to be compliant. She has never enforced disposal.

We do not burn the living, though the other islanders keep such rumours in wide circulation. There is a monster in Loch Ness. There are wild haggis in the glens. Kelpies take men unawares from the waterside. And woe betide those who fall for the charms of an island woman, for the daughters of Ensay burn the sons of Adam in their Wicker Man.

It is not *a real thing*. It is only a thing people say.

Mrs. Olafsson, on the point of tears – as if the injury were hers – said, "This should never have been allowed."

Mrs. Douglas said, "Missus Carlyle has not been well for a long time."

To which I replied, "You'll have to excuse me, ladies. The restaurant is opening for dinner and I am very busy."

* * *

The presents from yesterday's party are unopened, with the exception of the brushes – though these are unused. I wonder if there is a great significance to this, if they represent fragments of truth which have always been there waiting to be unwrapped. If each person's gift were a secret, what would unwrapping them teach me about this island and about myself? Would I weigh them and guess their contents? Would I even tear a corner of their paper? Or would I throw every one in the fire of our entirely symbolic wicker man?

I am still the acolyte, but what that means is different than I expected. Perhaps it means nothing at all. I am – in that archaic Judeo-Christian sense – a woman, and this is an equally false transition. I am entirely the person I was. A little pummelled by the speed and magnitude of events, but I woke up this morning in the same bed I will sleep in tonight, and Connor will sleep beside me. I watch him on his back, idling on his phone, a relative innocent in all of this.

I cannot tell him what might have happened. I have heard a thousand stories where the keeping and revealing of a secret, tears apart a life – my own story is one of these – but Connor is also unchanged from today. In a few weeks he will be gone forever. I choose not to deceive myself with a notion that he will change his mind, or that when he has completed his years at university, he will come back to me. This is absurd. I'm sure there is enough heartbreak waiting for me that I don't need to manufacture more.

I was willing to risk his life for what I feel for him; for this flash of summer romance. This choice was reprehensible. I judge myself to be flawed and weak, and things worse than this which I can't precisely name or describe. By any reasonable standard I am a bad person. And as a bad person, I am more than willing to lie about being a bad person if the only consequence of honesty is to let him know I'm a monster, so he never speaks to me again.

I have heard a thousand stories where people are undone by the guilt of keeping a secret about their own wrongdoing. I am not one of those people. I felt guilty about the act, the risk, the consequences. If anything, I now feel less guilty than I have in weeks. Maybe years. The idea of seducing and sacrificing Mr. Maxwell had been weighing on me too, and that feeling has evaporated leaving nothing at all.

I think.

"It's a shame you aren't staying until the equinox," I say.

"Huh?" Conner replies but is only half-listening.

"I was thinking that you'd be my choice as the sacrifice we burn in the wicker man."

"Yeah?" He scrolls down a screen with his thumb.

"I think I would definitely pick you as the annual sacrifice."

"Sorry I'll miss it."

"You know about the wicker man, do you?"

"Yeah, my uncle said something about it. Edith said you would probably pick me because I'm a *big handsome lad*."

Oh, did she now? And who the fuck is Edith? I say nothing.

"And I've got *lovely blue eyes* and a *wicked smile just like Bill had*."

Of course, he knew. Of course, he did. Wander around Loch Ness and try to avoid hearing stories about the last living dinosaur. I'm this year's monster. Angus and Duncan knew it, and maybe even believed it a bit while they were drunk, but the islanders must talk about me more as a tourist attraction than a loaded gun. They watched me all these years; their own little monster.

"She said if she was fifty years younger, she'd fight you for me."

Edith *Crevinge?*

I say, "Missus Crevinge needs to step off. She's got a bad knee and a glass jaw and if she was fifty years younger, she'd only be fourteen and her mother would turn you into bait for the lobster pots."

"Well, if she's got a bad knee, I guess that's that. I'll have to stick with you."

"So, would you do it? If you could, I mean?"

"The wicker man thing? Sure, why not? Sounds like a laugh."

"Before you got here, I'd been thinking about burning your uncle."

"Well, you didn't have much to choose from before I showed up with my *Bill*-ish smile. He'll probably still do it – but don't tell him I was your first choice . . . Let me tell him."

All possible guilt is assuaged. I have told him all of the relevant facts. We have a wicker man. I was thinking about burning his uncle in it. I considered burning him instead. All the facts are out there in the open. Now whether he has fully understood the import of what I have said – am I the thought police? I can't know what is inside his head. Frankly it's insulting of me to suggest that he doesn't understand. For the sake of his dignity, I should assume we've reached an understanding.

"Are you going to open any of those presents or are you going to stand there rustling the paper all night?"

"I'm not rustling—" I am *worrying* the paper. My hand playing across the edges where tape has not fully sealed the unknown item, my fingers teasing corners that can never be flush with the object underneath – that behaviour is called *worrying*. If I were *rustling*, I would just be scrunching the paper purposelessly instead of teasing it the way a wily sheepdog would control a flock, or a lioness would drive her prey. So, if you're going to be picky, please be correct, and sorry about very nearly getting you murdered, thanks, bye. "—and yes, I am."

Connor assists by ordering the opening of the gifts in a way that pleases him. I guess his system somehow alternates interesting and uninteresting, large and small, square and unsquare, but it could just as easily be random. I sit on the bed and he brings them to me one at a time – he enjoys this game and has almost no interest in the gifts themselves.

The contents of the packages are eclectic, which is to be expected, as they are from so many different people. There are a number of small items of jewellery, some of which I recognise as being of local manufacture. Both Mrs. Douglas and Mrs. Olafsson have bought me earrings, though the two sets could not be any more different. One set is an understated pair of studs with a dark green stone – I would guess they are jade. Small, and of impeccable taste, a mugger would not think to ask for them, but the Chinese Ambassador would be most impressed. The others are triple drop zirconia – holding them up against the light I cannot imagine a smaller space holding more sparkle. Neither item has been purchased carelessly and I can imagine both women giving long, serious, and private consideration to the choice.

I tear open the Christmas wrapping on the gift from Mr. Jones and laugh.

"What's funny?" Connor asks.

"It's a guest book."

"For the hotel?"

"A brand new, blank, leather-bound, watermarked ledger to replace the one we currently have."

"That's a bit shit for a birthday present."

"No, that's perfect. It's the most practical thing he could think I would want."

"If you're ever buying me a present," Connor says, gravely serious, "I do not want a big blank book."

"Noted."

"Or any other kind of book."

"When am I buying you a present? For what?"

"Men have birthdays."

"Oh, *men* do. I see. You'll get socks."

"I have socks."

"You'll get socks I like."

"How is that a present for me?"

"I might take them off."

"Is this our sexy talk?"

I kiss him and he pulls away.

"Wait," he says, "two more."

"Leave them. I'll do them tomorrow."

"This one's from your mum," he says, holding up a bag.

That's a mood killer. She must have placed it on the table with the others, because she never gave it to me herself. But here is the last gift I'll ever get from my mum, who has lied to me my entire life because – why? – because she's non-specifically nuts? Here's the sixteenth birthday present from the woman who locked me up, starved me, and beat me for years for no sane reason. Something to help me remember the one-woman cult who gave birth to me. There can't be anything good in that bag.

There are only three options. The gift will be special and touching, I will swell with love and joy, and in that same moment discover a new way that I am the bad one. Or the gift will be entirely irrelevant to me; it'll be a summer hat or a t-shirt from a Travis tour – remember Travis? They existed. Or, option three, the gift will be totally fucking mad. It will crack open the door to her madness a little wider and all I'll worry about is falling through after her, because let's face it – I'm not normal.

So here are three doors. Behind two of these doors are goats, but behind one of these doors is a brand new *another goat*. Nobody wants goat, Monty!

Connor drops the bag in my lap. Decision made.

The bag itself is a gift bag; a container as generic as wrapping paper, it has nothing to do with the contents other than both were picked by the same person. The bag is matte grey with silver *happy birthdays* patterned across it. A matching tag bears the message *love mum*. The handles are black. The top is sealed with a single fastener of transparent adhesive plastic.

I split the seal with my thumbnail. Inside the bag is black fabric. I reach in and pull out an item which seems to keep going forever like a magic trick. It is a black hooded cloak – wool outer, with a lining of satin. It has been made by hand and, given how closely it resembles hers, it must have been made by her.

Connor says, "Is that a cloak?"

"It is."

"It's—" he reaches for a safe descriptor "—very nice."

"It's one of the best I've seen."

"Well . . . I guess you're a wizard, Harry?"

"What's the last one?"

"So, your mum gave you a cloak and that's just what it is?"

"I suppose so."

"All right." He brings the final present over. Wrapped in brown paper and tied with string, the knots cut flush to be as tamper-proof as any high-tech solution or wax seal. It is Mrs. Alexander's gift that she entrusted to Mrs. Olafsson, because she believed *I'll be dead soon* and she was eventually proven to be correct.

I take the box from him. It's the first time I have held it and I get the immediate sense of a solid, heavy core, but it weighs only a few pounds. I need scissors to cut the string, and under the brown paper there is a cardboard box, and in the box is bubble wrap, which has been carefully taped – and again, I am sure this is the original handiwork of Mrs. Alexander.

The bubble wrap peels off to reveal a silver picture frame and a photograph. The photograph is of the front of the hotel. Mrs. Alexander is there, on the left of the main subjects – my mum, the man from the photograph in my mum's wardrobe, who I must assume is my dad . . . and me. A chubby little girl of two or three years standing between them, on the step – *outside* – and seeming mostly uninterested in the whole business of being photographed.

How could I not have thought to ask?

My father – Mr. Carlyle – wasn't burned in the wicker man before I was born. So, what happened to him? Why isn't there a man living in my house calling himself Mr. Smith to honour our tradition of weird renaming?

Where is my dad?

And why don't I remember any of this? Don't children have memories before the age of three? I was outside, and I was fine, and I don't remember it.

My mind has been so clouded with thinking about my mum and Connor and then my mum being crazy that I forgot what I started looking for in the first place.

"She didn't know."

"What?" Connor asks.

"She didn't know," I say. Everything my mum had told me about Ensay, about our beliefs, and about my role as the acolyte. She had no idea my mum had lied to me for years because she would have told me the truth, just as happened today. "Missus Alexander didn't know." Mrs. Douglas didn't know either. As soon as Mrs. Olafsson suspected what had happened, the structure came crashing down. But it is still falling, *we* are still falling, and I have no idea where the bottom is.

Connor asks, "Missus Alexander didn't know what?"

The secret they all shared – my mum, Mrs. Douglas, Mrs. Olafsson, Mrs. Alexander – the secret they have kept from me – is something else.

18

Why keep a photo in a frame?

One of the reasons must be that empty photo frames look stupid. Go into any shop that sells photo frames and – I certainly assume – those frames will have photos in them. Families, children, dogs adoring athletic young American men, moments that are – for all their falseness – emotionally real. A photograph of emotions elicits those emotions in people who see it. Photos sell photo frames the way photos of attractive, smiling students sell universities.

An empty photo frame is an emotionally complex object that makes us think of absence, loneliness, and isolation: things that are terrifying during life, as well as the eventual void of death. Boo – empty frames – boo! If Mrs. Alexander had an empty frame, she would have put something in it, or put it away.

The frame she gave me is solid silver – hallmarked with the castle of Edinburgh (where it was assayed) and the thistle (indicating it is sterling silver of at least nine hundred and twenty-five parts silver in every thousand). The date mark is illegible to me; rubbed flat with a hundred polishes, but the maker's mark (which took about five minutes to google) is Alexander Taylor Reid from St Andrews. I can't find a current listing for the maker, so I assume he's dead, which would make sense since his maker's mark was registered in nineteen twenty-nine. Mrs. Alexander lived in London after she left Ensay, so the chances of her buying a silver frame from an obscure St Andrews-based maker while she was there are slim. And if she had bought the frame when she was in London, she would have used it for her almost-husband or for her son, or maybe for her mother or her sister. Sure, whatever, she could have done *any* of those things. But she would *never* have taken one of those photos out of the frame to make room for a photo of a woman she did not like (my mum).

So Mrs. Alexander acquired the frame when she came back to Scotland. If it was a family possession or a bequest from a friend who died, it seems likely it would have contained a photo of significance to the previous owner. Mrs. Alexander might well have known the people in the photo, and so to replace that photo with the new one, the new photo must have been more significant to her. *Or* she could just have bought an antique-ish frame – but having bought the antique-ish frame she then had to decide to put *this* photo into it. In both cases she chose this photo over all the other photos she must own, because Mrs. Douglas said nobody observes the rule about destroying photos.

I unclasp the back of the frame to study the photo in more detail. The words *Summer 2004* have been written in pencil on the back in the bottom left corner. There is no other note on the back or the front. Would it have killed her sooner to write me a note saying what she wanted to say?

The image is printed on Kodak paper – which tells me nothing whatsoever. The film was posted away for development, and not done by a generic developer such as a local chemist on Lewis and Harris. I think this was probably done for convenience; I can't infer that a pharmacist in Stornoway is a co-conspirator because they didn't develop the photos any more than I can assume French pen manufacturer Bic were involved in keeping the secret because Mrs. Alexander wrote the date with a pencil. What is interesting about the photo paper is a line of discolouration around the image. Being an older frame, it does not perfectly match the size of a modern photograph. Sunlight has slightly bleached the middle, while the few millimetres of the periphery that has been covered by the frame has been protected. I have no idea how long a photo takes to bleach, but I would expect it is years. I google this and there's a whole lot of *it depends*, but years seems right: it's reasonable to assume she had the photo on display a long time, perhaps since it was developed.

Mrs. Alexander did not put this photo into this frame to give it to me. She put this photo into this frame years ago and kept it out on display, and because silver tarnishes she also regularly cleaned it and therefore had many opportunities to change the photo or put the frame away.

This was not a neglected item; it was a prized thing which she cared for.

Mrs. Alexander loved someone in this picture and wanted to be reminded of them. Not my mum, certainly. And not herself – she was proud of her skills, but not vain about her appearance. That only leaves my dad and me. Mrs. Alexander saw me every day and never struck me as being enormously sentimental. She had a son and she had three grandchildren from him – they would be in pride of place before me, surely?

Is it my dad? If Mrs. Alexander had another son before she left Ensay, could he have received her – air quotes – maiden name? Was Mrs.

Alexander's born name Carlyle? That would make her my grandmother and me her granddaughter and . . . why wouldn't she tell me that? None of the women on Ensay are actually married (except Mr. and Mrs. Murdoch, who moved here in retirement). Why keep a – air quotes – bastard son a secret for all these years?

Besides, Mrs. Alexander said *I'd left to study catering at a college . . . This was sixty-two, or thereabouts.* If she'd had my dad on Ensay, he'd be about forty-two in the photo and he isn't. It would be a big push to think he was thirty-two. They would have had him on Oprah talking about his skincare routine. On the other hand, he's clearly too old to be another grandson – the son of her so-far imaginary and presumptively illegitimate son. Did her sister have children? I have no idea. She moved to Canada years before I was born – and for all the details I have about her, she might as well have gone to the politest region of an unnamed planet in the goldilocks zone of Proxima Centauri. There is almost certainly some kind of tangential familial relationship between Mrs. Alexander and me, she'll be both my distant cousin and my great aunt, and my dad and my mum and everybody else will be similarly closely related. That's island life. So that's not it.

She is *happy* in that picture. Not the feigned happiness of someone being forced to stand in a group photo of co-workers they dislike. This is a family photo in the sense that Mrs. Alexander worked with them every day, and probably looked after me sometimes, and knew what my parents' hopes and ambitions were. They *liked* each other. Then something happened that made Mrs. Alexander keep this photo on display on her house, come to work every day in this hotel, and hate my mum.

At some point after this photo was taken my mum did something – or maybe Mrs. Alexander *found out* she did something – that destroyed this relationship. At some point after this photo was taken my dad was gone. Did she kill him? Did she build her own wicker man and actually burn him?

I am struck by the strangest certainty – she would have been capable of it. There is no part of burning someone alive that my mum couldn't have done if she had her strength and her wits. She has that unshakeable determination that one associates with wartime leaders and all the more prolific serial killers.

My alarm goes off and I jump, then fumble for the stop button. Connor does not stir.

I didn't sleep very well – two nights in a row; today's going to be a treat. I think sleeping in the same bed as someone requires practice. My usual sleeping position – spread-eagle directly in the middle of the bed – was occupied. And though Connor doesn't really snore, he is *there*. He's in my bed occupying space that (not to get all Israel-Palestine about it) rightfully belongs to me. My person has occupied that space for generation. I didn't think my identity was inextricable from where I slept, but here I am, complaining about it to myself at six in the morning.

He does look nice though. To see him sleeping in my bed, on my pillows, gives me a sense of ownership. My bed, my pillows, my boyfriend. This little shit is going to break my heart when he goes to Maynooth. I'm being left for collection of buildings. And *Maynooth* of all places – it's like going to university in a field. I can say that because I've checked the university rankings and it's behind several well-respected tertiary education institutions with a focus on agriculture and I don't want him to go. Yeah, top ten in Ireland, blah, blah. Alumni include Eimear Quinn who won the Eurovision Song Contest twenty years ago – but how many Eurovisions have its graduates won lately? None. Twenty years, not even close. And all the Nobel prizes its staff have won have been *shared*.

I will cut you, Maynooth.

"Why are you staring at me?" Connor speaks into the pillow.

"I'm planning an elaborate, pre-emptive revenge that involves burning down the John Paul the Second Library."

". . . Okay."

"Don't tell anyone."

". . . Okay."

"I probably won't do it. It's just one of those things people like to think about."

". . . Do they?"

"Yes?"

"Where's the John Paul the Second Library?"

"It's not important." It's the main library at Maynooth University, built in eighty-four and extended five years ago, jammed full of all the essential biomedical science books one would need to study biomedical science. Connor doesn't know the name of his university library building because he's normal, and I do because I'm not. My brain goes sideways. Even now I know that I could keep him; it would be safe to keep him, I want him to get as far away from this mad girl as he can and never look back. At least, not for longer than an occasional daydream. "Go back to sleep."

I reassemble the photo frame, being not much wiser than I was. Shower. Dress. Breakfasts. My own breakfast. Dishwasher on. Reception. There's only one check-out today and I'm ready before they are.

I could *ask*.

The reason I haven't asked was because I lived in a religious community with a strict hierarchy. But I actually live in a slightly-but-not-very-religious community with a social structure full of nuance, where I might suddenly be quite near the top.

Do you expect the high priestess to explain such things to you? The answer to that question was so obvious as to be rhetorical. Though now that I've had a good, long think about it – yes. I do expect her to explain. Though I don't expect her to *want* to explain.

I pick up the phone from the reception desk. Mrs. Douglas was the last number called from this phone (unless one of the guests has been making long-distance calls in the middle of the night – which did happen once) so I hit redial.

Mrs. Douglas answers with a *hello*. I say that *I just had Mrs. Crevinge on asking about whether you had booked the private dining room for this evening.* I profess my ignorance but say it's *not impossible you spoke to Connor* and that I would check. Mrs. Douglas wonders *why would I have booked the private dining room* when no meeting is scheduled? I have *no idea* and I say I'll confirm with Mrs. Crevinge. I call Mrs. Crevinge and we exchange *good morning*s and sympathies and I tell her that *Mrs. Douglas is emphatic that there will not be any meeting tonight.* She *oh-indeed-is-that-so*s my news and I have already looked up Mrs. Brown's number while we talk and immediately dial it when I hang up from her. Mrs. Brown *good-morning*s me and I ask if – *given your central location and connections –* she's heard anything about a rumour of the private dining room at the hotel being booked tonight.

"I just spoke to Mrs. Crevinge on the phone and told her the private dining room wasn't booked."

Mrs. Brown says, "Missus Crevinge wanted to know if the private dining room was booked for this evening?"

I reply, in perfect honesty, "She seemed very interested."

"And is the dining room booked for tonight?"

I smile, then stop smiling, because people can hear smiles. "Missus Douglas told me to tell Missus Crevinge the dining room was not booked for this evening."

"Missus Douglas told you to tell her that?"

"Yes," I say. "I thought you might want to know."

"What? Oh, yes. Yes, I do. You're a good girl, Eleanor. Sorry about your mother. I need to go." And she hangs up abruptly.

Mrs. Olafsson trills and coos at me when I call and I fight my way through the pleasantries to say that I've had *several strange calls this morning* talking to people about whether the private dining room is booked for this evening.

"Which people?" she asks.

"I'm just off the phone with Mrs. Brown and before that Mrs. Crevinge."

"Missus Brown? Why did she think there would be a meeting tonight?"

"I'm sure I don't know."

"Is there a meeting tonight?"

"Missus Douglas has told me tell people there isn't."

"Missus Douglas *told you* to *tell people* there is *no meeting*?" The line crackles loudly – it's going to be a bad phone day on the island. We're always going to get our own mobile phone and satellite connection *next year*. The cable fails entirely twice a year and we're entirely disconnected from the mainland while someone somewhere fixes something (*technical details I don't have go here*). I mumble my response which gets lost in interference. "What was that?"

"Yes. She told me to say there is no meeting."

"Oh, did she? Well. We'll see about that. Thank you very much Eleanor."

She hangs up. I dial Mrs. MacArthur, whose phone is especially bad, and we shout at each other for thirty seconds with no real consequences before I apologise and hang up. Mrs. MacArthur is not invited to meetings, but she will pass any information back to Mrs. Brown.

It takes about three minutes for my phone to ring.

"Eleanor, we will need the private dining room for this evening," Mrs. Douglas says.

"Of course," I reply, and smile and give the guests checking out the one-minute signal. "That won't be a problem at all."

* * *

They do not trust one another and so it is easy to trick them. The remaining senior sisters call or drop by and attempt to pump me for information but '*I don't know anything other than there will be a meeting tonight.*' My ignorance only encourages their speculation.

Mrs. Douglas is going to step down early.

Mrs. Douglas is ill.

Mrs. Douglas is dying.

Mrs. Brown is planning a coup.

Mrs. Olafsson has the numbers.

In the hours between now and then, the island will catch fire. When they show up tonight, I'll confront them as a battered, wearied, and bedraggled group who have exhausted themselves with in-fighting and imaginary plots.

Mrs. Douglas met a man in Glasgow and they're running away together.

Some plots requiring more imagination than others.

I notice that the last guest has filled the last section of the guest book and I read their message.

It was the best hotel we've stayed at in all our years of coming to the west of Scotland. I only wish we'd come here before and we'll definitely be back.

I thumb idly through the pages. A few entries in recent years stand out, but most of the guests blur together even for me.

And I *curse* myself for not realising sooner – this hotel is full of witnesses. We have a record of bookings going back to when the hotel opened. I know who was staying in each room on every night. I have their email addresses and I have their phone numbers. I know who was staying on Ensay in the summer when the photograph was taken.

What was his name? *I've dealt with Mister Melville. Who's Mister Melville? The gentleman who helped Connor back to the house* – Alan Melville. *There's three of them that were built by the RSPB in two-thousand-and-four. I used to work for them.* Alan Melville was here around the time that photo was taken and my mum – did she stop me from speaking to him? She removed all the reasons I had for speaking to him, and I never thought about him after that. But he looked at me so strangely.

I slide the keyboard out from under the little shelf the monitor sits on and hit the shortcuts that bring up booking history. There is one booking for Alan Melville – the recent one. Maybe he never stayed at the hotel? He could have camped on the island or stayed with someone. It's possible he doesn't know anything. But his number is right there in front of me, I'm overconfident with phone-based scheming, and it's ringing before I've any idea how I'm going to approach this.

"Hello," says a man's voice.

"Hello, is that Alan Melville?"

"Yes."

"This is Eleanor Carlyle from the Ensay House Hotel."

"Oh, hello," he says, sounding relieved that I am not someone calling to try and sell him a trip-or-fall-at-work-that-wasn't-his-fault. "How's Connor's leg?"

"What? Oh – fine. He was up and around in a couple of days. All of him is fine. Look – this is going to sound strange, but that night when you brought Connor back and I told you my name, you looked surprised."

"I suppose I must have."

"Why?"

"Something I misheard a long time ago."

"What?"

The line crackles in silence while he considers his response. "I don't think it would be appropriate. I am at work just now." If it's inappropriate I have to hear it.

"I'm sure it'll only take a minute."

"But I obviously only heard half the story."

"Then tell me the half you heard and it'll only take half a minute." Wocka wocka, just *tell me*.

He shifts, I imagine him in an office somewhere turning to face a wall or walking away from his desk. "I was getting onto the boat when it happened. That's the only reason I knew about it at all. The owner of the boat wasn't sure whether to wait for people going to the mainland or get to the mainland quicker to bring people back to Ensay. In the end I sat on the dock for two hours, but I only heard rumours. And nothing you'd want to hear, I'm sure."

"Please. Don't think about my feelings and just tell me what you heard."

"Well, look, all I know for sure was there was an accident. A group of people were walking out on the cliffs at the west of the island, and there was a landslide. I actually heard it, if you can believe that, sounded like thunder, though, and I didn't think any more about it. What people told me later was three adults and a little girl fell when the rocks gave way, and that they all died. I was told that two of the people were guests at the hotel, and the other two were Eleanor Carlyle and her father.

"Now, obviously, I heard it wrong, because you're calling me right now."

"When was this?"

"Two-thousand-and-four. August, if I remember correctly."

"I don't have you listed as staying in August."

"Maybe under the name of the company I was working for? JTC? J. T. Construction?"

A few more keystrokes and there it is. "Yes. Your booking finished on Wednesday, the sixth of August."

"I don't remember one way or another, but that could be right. Look, can I ask what all of this is about?"

"Just checking if you were happy with your stay."

"My stay thirteen years ago? Or the last one?"

"Oh, either, really."

"Well, I—"

"Can I encourage you to rate us on Trip Advisor? We read all the reviews. Thank you for your time."

I end the call and stare at the screen.

Two hotel guests, my dad, and I died in a landslide. This cannot be true, since I am still alive. Unless I'm a ghost? I feel like this would have come up before. I would be able to pass through walls or someone would have turned up to exorcise and/or bust me. I wouldn't need food. I wouldn't have grown into an adult if I'd died as a child – that's the clincher: child ghosts don't grow up, and everybody who knows things about ghosts knows that.

So, I'm not dead – that part of the story is wrong. What about the rest?

I search for other bookings on the same day. Mr. Melville's was the only one that ended on Wednesday, and all the other rooms were booked. If two guests died, even my mum wasn't hard-boiled enough to think to change their room booking. But which guests?

It's pretty easy to find out if someone famous is alive or dead, but ordinary people need more detective work. I think any deaths in Scotland would be registered in Scotland even if the people dying were elsewhere. A few searches take me to ScotlandsPeople – the open register of births, marriages, and deaths – and while it seems to be organised around finding named people, I can also search for all deaths in a given year at a specific location – Ensay, Eileanan Siar.

Six deaths. The name that stands out from the list is the last one: *Winthrop, Mary*; age at death seventy-six. The Mrs. Winthrop who made our guest book and died of pneumonia (those two events presumably unrelated).

The website doesn't record how she died, only that she died.

McDonald, Archie, twenty-three. That's him. The man in the photograph with my mum on the grass, and the photograph outside of the hotel with Mrs. Alexander. I mean I assume it's him – he's the only one whose age makes sense. I don't want to get ahead of myself here; this page only gives me the year of death and it could easily be that all the details of Mr. Melville's story are wrong. I need two dead guests.

I scan the guest list of the hotel and see a matching name immediately. *Edwards.* I check the register. *Edwards, Catherine, twenty-nine. Edwards, Jack, thirty-two.*

Edwards, Sarah, three.

I open the room booking – they booked and paid for a family room; one containing both a double bed and a rollaway single. Jack and Catherine Edwards and their daughter Sarah stayed in this hotel and died in an accident with my dad. He was probably taking them for a walk around the island.

And then what? My mum went mad with grief and never let me outside again? Made me terrified of the outside? Is that what they have been keeping from me? I was a perfectly ordinary girl until she terrorised me into being trapped inside.

It seems like a reasonable answer to the question. It makes its own kind of sense. It is troubled enough to be an abiding secret that would isolate and shame a woman on an island of mothers and grandmothers. It is awful.

But why would Mr. Melville think I was dead? The hours afterwards must have been confused. But he said *I was told that two of the people were guests at the hotel, and the other two were Eleanor Carlyle and her father.* My name specifically. He wouldn't have known my name unless someone had told him. Jack and Catherine Edwards would have taken their daughter Sarah on their walk – that seems reasonable. Would Archie McDonald have taken Eleanor? He might have. Probably would have, to get her out of the hotel and give his wife a break.

Then there is Mrs. Alexander, at the hotel, in the photograph, *during the day.* She wasn't doing the minimum she could.

Would Mrs. Carlyle and Mr. McDonald take their daughter Eleanor for a walk with the Edwards family while Mrs. Alexander minded the hotel? Two couples not vastly unalike in age with the shared experience of having a three-year-old.

What if there were not four people on the cliffside, but six? And what if four of them died? A wife, two husbands, and a daughter.

I feel my heart could crack like an eggshell, and I have no idea what might fall, or stumble, or fly out.

I find myself taking the stairs two at a time. I turn hard on the first-floor landing, change to the back stairs, and circle up to my room. I knock the blank canvas onto the floor – I think it breaks, I heard a sound but don't check – and put the self-portrait back on the easel.

She stares at me and I know. I can barely see the bruises. Her hair is different: mine as it was at the time of painting.

But this was never a self-portrait. It is a painting from memory. And because memories are caricatures, my own face was the cypher that let me reveal hers. Those are her eyes, which I could only see when my face was old enough to hold them. Her face is without any hint of childhood's softness and untouched by the slightest sliver of age. Now that I see her, it is as if a mask has been lifted from the canvas.

With daddy and mommy, mommy standing by.

The BBC's sleeping commentator Jim Moir stands beside me. He doesn't speak. I don't remember the real sound of his voice, but I know he was my father. There is sadness and happiness in his eyes. Worry and pride. And so much kindness it hurts to look back at him. If he were a phantom, he might reach out for a second, touch me, chill my blood by his nature if not his intent – but he is a trick of light and shadow; when I blink, he returns to nothing.

One of these mornings—

I have kept them somewhere in my mind for thirteen years, alongside song lyrics and the names of muscles and bones, and the way people drink their tea. Submerged in an ocean of facts, they have lain quiet as shipwrecks, waiting for me to rediscover them.

One of these mornings—

Without knowing, I have conjured them, given them form and strange purpose. But we three ghosts have existed together in this attic space since the beginning.

One of these mornings you're gonna rise up—

I am the ghost of Eleanor Carlyle, a girl who died on the sixth of August, two-thousand-and-four.

One of these mornings you're gonna rise up— screaming.

19

It is a strange sensation: the ground going. The ground has always been there and has always been trusted. Everything else is doubted before the ground. *I tripped over my feet. I lost my balance. I didn't see. I didn't notice.* I am the one to blame.

But some days the sun comes up like it's supposed to, the clocks tick anyway, dogs bark, and the ground . . . goes.

I remember it as a cold, sunny day with the wind whipping my hair into my eyes. This was our first holiday, and in my developing vocabulary *holiday* had become another word for *beach*. There were no beaches in London as far as I had experience – which was the most overbuilt part of the city between the triple stone arches of Chiswick Bridge and the twin gothic pylons of Tower Bridge. Where the water touched the land, it left a brown-grey mark that smelled of rot. But in Scotland everywhere was beach – a line of sand or rocks or shale brokered a dispute between the mountains and the waves; the underside of each rock was alive; every limpet pool was a remote kingdom.

I remember the sky: huge to a horizon made entirely of water. And I remember being scared of the edge, even though we were not that close, and my dad's arm stretched out to take my hand and bring me a few steps nearer.

Then he was gone.

They were all gone, save for the stranger standing next to me. Her screams were the wind that drove the waves.

* * *

I have left open the door that is older than the house. I have waited for them to gather. I have waited for them to turn on each other with recriminations and recollections of sleights real and imagined. When I finally enter, they don't even see me. I stand at the end of the table while they hurl accusations the way cobras spit venom.

"Eleanor, this is a private meeting," says Mrs. Douglas. And then they notice me. I feel the stages of their recognition. I am a shape. I am a girl. I am Eleanor. I am something else.

When I give no indication of moving – or explaining, or even apologising for interrupting them – they exchange glances with each other, like a game of pass the parcel, until all eyes are on Mrs. Douglas at the far end of the table.

She sits silent, sober, and stony. She must realise in this moment that tonight was my doing, if she did not know already.

I recite the date as accusation: "The sixth of August, two-thousand-and-four."

She knows the date. She has collected this island's history and ordered it. Mrs. Douglas lowers her eyes, as if somewhere on the table there is a carving of these past events where she can lose herself or collect her thoughts. She looks up at me again and says, "It was done."

The others flutter but no one speaks.

Mrs. Douglas says, "By the time anyone knew—"

I interrupt: "People knew the instant it happened. The story changed hours later."

"Yes," she says after a pause. She nods and corrects her own memory. "That was how it happened. I found you together and I knew what had happened, but I did not appreciate what Missus Carlyle already believed. By the time I got to her, she *believed* that you were her daughter. She was inconsolable and she held onto you so tightly I thought she would hurt you. We could not separate you."

"She had just lost her husband," says Mrs. Brown, urgently reasonable.

Mrs. Douglas continues, "She took you back to the hotel, and I thought it better to keep you both out of the way for a couple of hours until the police arrived. But the police were investigating an assault on North Uist. They couldn't come right away. A sailing boat capsized in the Minch, and an hour later a storm blew up and grounded all the helicopters.

"All the while, Missus Carlyle would not let you go. Not even into another room, not to the other side of the room. I thought nothing of it until she said *at least Eleanor is safe. I've lost him,* she said, *but at least Eleanor is safe.*

"It was the next morning before anyone from the mainland arrived. The tide had risen and fallen, took the bodies, smashed them on the rocks until they weren't recognisable. When the police asked me who had died, I told them it was all three of the family staying at the hotel. Missus Carlyle kept you away, saying you were far too upset to talk to police, and that was it. Two little girls without anything more than a passing resemblance. One substituted for the other. And that was it."

"I imagined that the next day or the day after someone would find out, someone would ask questions. But when a little girl and her parents die in a random accident, nobody asks questions. Not even their family – if they had any. Then I supposed that one morning she would wake up and realise you weren't her daughter; that she would . . . get *better*. For a while I think we all believed that she would come to her senses.

"I gave up hope of that six weeks later when I realised, all of a sudden, that she hadn't let you outside. When I demanded to see you, I knew what was happening. I knew what she was doing to you even if she didn't."

"What were you to do?" Mrs. Olafsson says. "What could she have done? We loved her. What were we to do? Rip away another child? To do what? Send her off to some family who didn't know her well enough to recognise her hair or her clothes? We all believed we could care for you better than anyone else because you were our responsibility."

"We believed," says Mrs. Douglas, "and we were wrong. By the time we all understood that, it was too late. You called yourself Eleanor and you called Missus Carlyle mother."

Mrs. Alexander had the same reason. *I made my peace with that a long time ago.*

I see it like a light through fog. The burning body of a wooden man atop a cliff. A cinder that shreds the darkness and removes every trace of uncertainty.

"You did love her," I say. "But not now."

I can hear the sound of their breathing.

"You all hate her. Not just Missus Alexander; you *all* hate her."

Mrs. Douglas says, "I made the decision I thought was best for the both of you."

Mrs. Brown says, "We all made that decision."

I shake my head. "You didn't do it because you *loved* her – you did it to save this place. You could have changed your mind at any point, any one of hundreds of you could have called the police but you didn't, and it wasn't *love* for her or *care* for me.

"You let a woman steal a child to save a hotel. A *hotel*. This nothing place at the end of the world. You sat and watched while she . . ." The words escape me. There are so many acts which they could not know, and the cruelty is interwoven with kindness so that no one could understand it without living it.

"I have been in prison my whole life! She beat me!" It is the easiest way to express it. It is not the whole of the experience. Fear and violence are universal, but this is a unique betrayal, one which involved everyone I have ever known. "You all knew, and you did nothing."

Mrs. Olafsson says, "We tried to—"

"How is my condition, Missus Olafsson? You *tried*? You *helped*. You were

213

an *accomplice. We'll have no witnesses.* How is my condition, Missus Brown? All you had to do was speak up once and it would have been over. Once in thirteen years, if one of you had said anything it would have been over."

Mrs. Douglas puts her hand to her mouth. She struggles to suppress her emotion though it breaks through anyway, and her shoulders lurch as tears roll into the lines of her hand.

I am surprised by how unmoved I am.

"How is my condition, Missus Douglas? *I think it would be best if you told me everything* Missus Carlyle *has said to you.* Not *your mother,* but *Missus Carlyle.* You couldn't even bring yourself to say it. Govern *the* child. Not *your* child. And not *Eleanor,* either. Because that's not my name, is it, Missus Douglas? You kept that lie at arm's reach because I think it's the worst thing you ever did. But. You. *All.* Did. It."

I am not Eleanor Carlyle, the girl who died with her father. I am not Sarah Edwards: she was a girl who never grew up, whose life ended the same day as Eleanor's. Instead, I am a jumble of knotted threads that was pulled from that disaster, some tied to one history, some tied to another, and now inseparable from each other.

"What is my name?" I ask them. "What do I call myself now?"

The question goes unanswered. They are, after all, just ordinary people, and people who barely know me at all.

"Please leave," I say.

The instruction moves them, as if they had been waiting for it; for any reason to not be here anymore.

They shuffle past me, their eyes noticing only the carpet, then the tiles.

Mrs. Olafsson puts a hand on my arm for an instant, then withdraws it as she might from a hot stove top. It occurs to me that there are no pure lies or pure truths, that the one blends with the other. A pure lie is as recognisable as an orange on an iceberg. I could not have been deceived by lies alone; what has fooled me all these years is the truth. This woman, who for the first time fears to touch me, has loved me like a daughter. Her affection has never been dishonest.

Mrs. Douglas has dried her eyes, but those were no crocodile tears. She is the most respected member of this community because her character is a rock. She did not put what she had allowed to happen out of her mind; she must have thought about it every day and her concern for me was a wedge between her and . . . Mrs. Carlyle.

I understand their choice as well as they do. I have respected, admired, and even loved these women, and perhaps I always will. But I also hate them: I feel anger I have no means of releasing. In a week will I feel differently? In a year will I have softened against them or hardened? I cannot imagine forgiveness, so I will not try.

Mrs. Douglas is the last to leave and I feel her pause beside me, searching for a few words of wisdom to give me comfort, to justify her actions, to seek absolution. Whatever she wants she cannot find any way to ask for it. I hear her shoes clack across the tiled floor and I feel the emptiness of the hall at my back.

I would like to go to bed now. If I could sleep for a week, I think I might wake up as a different creature entirely. I would shed my skin and liquify my bones, turn my heart into a soup of cells and pour all my parts into a new mould. I should rise up and spread wings and set them under a new sun.

I move to answer the phone automatically. A single ring activated my subconscious mind and I was three steps across the hall before my brain remembered that I could not possibly care about who was calling or what they had to say. I am standing still when it rings for a second time.

But I can't just let it ring. The phone has a built-in answering machine. If I don't pick it up either: the answering machine will kick in, and then I'll have to call someone back, I'll miss them, they'll call here again, and then we're both stuck in a very English play about etiquette and embarrassment; or Connor will come in and pick up the phone, then will try to do things, fail because he doesn't know how to do things, and I'll have to intervene.

It rings again and I finish my epic journey to the reception desk.

I am tempted to raise the receiver, tell whoever it is to fuck off, then hang up. That would make me feel good for about a second, and then I would feel guilty because at this time of night, the person calling can only be an elderly American who does not trust the internet and doesn't know about time zones and has been given this telephone number by another elderly American who once stayed here – a drinking buddy of Mr. Wolanski and/or a mortal enemy of Mrs. Wolanski. If I suddenly insult someone Mrs. Wolanski hates and they suffer a heart attack, that would please her no end.

I interrupt the fourth ring by picking up.

"Hello?"

All I hear is crackle, then a voice speaks up – evidently repeating themselves – asking, "Can I speak to Eleanor Carlyle?"

A burst of laughter escapes me like a hiccup. Can you speak to Eleanor? Not unless you've got Madame Arcati or Tangina Barrons standing by.

"This is Eleanor."

The voice says its name, but the sound is completely obscured. My best guess: it's a woman.

"You're going to have to speak up," I say. The connection is worse than it was this morning. The something, somewhere, is approaching a critical thingy and someone will need to something it soon – I'm basically an engineer.

She replies, and in the confusion of sounds I hear the phrase *Western Isles Hospital*.

"I can barely hear you. You're calling from the hospital?"

"We— contact Missus Douglas— next— mother—." A group of words which could be just about anything. *We think aliens have been trying to contact Mrs. Douglas about the next steps to build a star gate and we are sick of these motherfucking snakes on this motherfucking plane.* Probably not that. Probably she said they had been unable to contact Mrs. Douglas – because she was here – and that I was the next contact.

"I really can't understand you at all," I say, knowing very well she will probably have heard me ask her a question about the weather and her favourite member of the Beatles (George, obviously; the correct answer is George).

"—your mother is gone—"

"What?"

The line goes dead.

It does not even emit the delicate electric hum of power. It is as if the phone changed in my hand and became a replica of itself; a wax copy with no working parts; merely an appearance, absent all function.

I stare at nothing in particular. The lightless tea room. The empty lounge. The paintings that follow the stairs. There is no sound in the world. A deafening dullness has fallen and all objects and places are photographs, their meaning collapsed into two dimensions as their substance vanished.

I put the receiver back into its cradle. It clicks.

I hear the familiar thrum of the dishwasher beginning its cycle, and a moment later, Connor emerges from the kitchen. I left him to deal with the last of the dinner and the guests. His eyes widen and he rushes to me – what must I look like? One of the soldiers of the First World War who stagger out of mustard gas blind, half-dead, certain of dying?

He says, "What's happened?" But that could not be a larger question or more difficult to answer. I shake my head and he pulls me against him, wrapping his arms around me, assuming as much as he could.

I'm not sure when I made the decision, but I find the execution comes to me easily, and in such detail, that I must have thought about a hundred times.

I ask him, "How far do you think you can carry me?"

"What?"

I lift my head off his chest and repeat my question.

"Why?"

"Could you carry me as far as the boat?"

"Maybe," he says. "I think so."

"Tomorrow morning, after breakfast, I want you to take a bag of my things to Stornoway. Get a room at a hotel. Then come back and get me. We'll take the last boat out."

20

Due to unforeseen circumstances, the hotel will close today. Please check-out by ten to make sure you catch the boat. I apologise for any inconvenience.

She brandishes the note at me unnecessarily. I typed it up, I printed it out, I placed it into an envelope, and I slid the envelope under her bedroom door. I know what the note says.

She demands to know: "What is the meaning of this?" Classic dialogue, though a bit clichéd; if we workshopped this scene I think we could find something better. Maybe *what do you think you're playing at?* or *this is outrageous!* If she was in the mood, she could have slammed the reception desk and demanded to speak to the management – because a woman in her mid-fifties would naturally assume that a girl in her mid-teens was not the management, but I'd have her there; I'd say *Madam, I am the management.* Curtain, applause, bow, applause, roses, dinner at Sardi's.

"Well," I say, "due to unforeseen circumstances, the hotel will close today."

"What does that *mean?*"

"It means that you need to check out now, and get on the boat, and go somewhere else, otherwise you'll have nowhere to sleep tonight."

"But I paid for my room in advance." This seems like one of those arguments they teach to defuse volatile situations. If a madman comes at you with a broken bottle, say something entirely random to engage him. *I don't know where the bus stop is and my father visited Greece only the once.* Unfortunately for her, I am well aware of the technique and it has no effect on me.

"All charges have already been refunded." I have not actually slept yet, but since the phone and the internet came back on at three in the morning, what I have done is cancel every future booking, repay everyone who has paid in advance, settle with all our suppliers, cancel all future orders, take down the booking system, learned what an electronic wallet is, and packed. "The hotel is closed."

"This has never happened to me before." She says this and I believe her, because it's never happened to me either, but here we both are in this brave new world of hotels closing and people being told to sling their hook. Is this what Dr. Martin Luther King Jr. dreamed of? I certainly think so. "The least you could do is organise alternative accommodation."

I find the phrase *the least you could do* very interesting, because its meaning is clear – *I beseech thee to act responsibly, dost thou know that we art living in an society?* – while the literal expression is always wrong. I'm not even sure what the least I could do is. How would one run the numbers on lowest possible effort without effort? The least I could do can therefore only be done by chance, by making no conscious choice and allowing oneself to be subject entirely to circumstances. Perhaps the philosopher, astrophysicist and mathematician Christopher Cross was closest when he wrote *when you get caught between the Moon and New York City, the* least *that you can do, the* least *that you can do is fall in love.*

I suggest, "Perhaps you'd like to leave us feedback on Trip Advisor."

"Feedback? I'll sue!"

"Well, you know where we are."

The guests express varying levels of disappointment, disaffection, anger, and one man says he's *going to call the police.* Good for him. Rage against the closing of the hotel. But rage or not, the hotel is closing. In six hours, I'm going to leave Ensay House, then I'm going to leave the island, and I'm never coming back.

It is a plan as audacious as a moon landing and, from my perspective, almost as unprecedented. I have not experienced a moment of perfect recall where all the details of my former life have come back to me. Two or three memories of childhood are all that I have; uncertain, partial, confused, and mixed with other lived experiences, thoughts and imaginings. I am going into a different world.

Connor does not know the reasons for my requests. He has not asked, which is good because I don't know what I would tell him. My plan is sixty miles long and ends in Stornoway. Should I contact the police? Should I try to find out if I have any surviving family? In a few weeks I'll get my exam results – if I can leave this house I could apply for a place through clearing and go to university.

I could even go to Maynooth. Nice enough place, I suppose. It has its attractions. And I already know the layout of the library.

This seems too bold. Absurdly unsafe. I'm sitting in a rocket-powered tin can at Cape Canaveral picking the curtains for my Martian dream home. But I could do it. I know that all it would require is for me to reach out and take it. If my life has been any kind of lesson at all it is that determination can overcome anything – even death, in its own way.

Connor opens the kitchen door wheeling a suitcase. We always keep a few suitcases for sale – the most common cause of luggage destruction (after going through an airport) is going on a little boat across the sea.

Into that bag I have packed almost everything I own, with the notable exception of coat hangers, oil paints, solvent, and some mostly-empty bottles of hair products. It is not a large suitcase. I have a matching backpack which I'll carry myself, though it will only need to hold my iPad, some makeup and the last of the cash we have on hand. I don't even own a purse.

Connor says, "Is this everything?"

"Everything I'm taking."

"What about your paintings?"

I shrug. I lie to him to cover the gap between what I'm planning and what he believes he's helping me with. "I can come back for them later, when I'm settled somewhere else."

"You're sure about this?"

"This was basically your idea."

"Yeah, but it didn't go so well last time."

I wonder how much responsibility he feels. Not for the events of today – today will be an adventure; today will be a story to tell – but about what happens next. When the prince rescues the maiden, the story does not usually end with high-fives and them both going their separate ways. Indeed, the whole purpose of princes roaming the countryside would appear to be seeking fair maidens to rescue and then marry. It's unclear if medieval peasantry would even accept a future queen who hadn't at one time been imperilled by an evil witch. Tradition is tradition.

What does he think I want from him? If I haven't planned beyond my escape, has he? I have no idea how I might compare against other girls he's known, or others he might like to know. It's possible I'm boring. There's a thought. *Weird girl* he called me. A few weeks with a weird girl might be all he can stand.

He says, "What's the matter?"

"Am I boring?"

"Are you boring?"

"Me. Yes. Am I boring? And not boring, just, look, if you thought about yourself being with a girl, do you— Not *if*, obviously it's *when*. *When* you think— When you imagine yourself being with a girl, do you imagine . . . me? Someone like me?" Nice job; that's going in the Oxford Dictionary of Quotations.

"No," he says and shakes his head.

I suppose it's better that I know. Honesty. Certainty. He could have lied to me or avoided answering. Also, *ow*.

"I never imagined anyone like you."

Oh?

"You're the most unexpected person I've ever met."

Is this good? He hasn't said anything about my personality – which is good – but he did call me a *person*. I don't care what the feminists say, not being identified by your sex by someone you've had sex with is unsettling. Am I reading too much into this?

Is he going to kiss me? He is. This was his attempt at a romantic statement and he feels like he's done well and should have a prize. It was a bit non-committal, but then I didn't ask him to commit to anything. I want him to be an option. I want to be able to choose him. I also want him to want me to choose him. Instead, what I got was a tap on the chin and a *here's lookin' at you kid*.

When he kisses me, I don't entirely forget this, though it is a compensation, and it is a reminder. What I really want is to be unworried about a chain of a thousand tomorrows and to live from breath to breath with him. For a while, at least. For what is left of the summer.

I break away, saying, "You need to go. You'll miss the boat."

"I could get the next boat," he eyes me friskily and I'm not indifferent to being eyed.

"The next boat doesn't leave you enough time to get the bus to Stornoway, come back here and get me – are you going to carry me and the suitcase?" I watch him try to form a clever answer for all of one second. "Go!"

"Okay, okay."

"And if anyone asks you about the suitcase, tell them you're helping one of the guests."

"What if one of the guests asks?"

"You're helping a different guest."

"What if, as a group, they all ask me together?"

"Break down, admit you're running away to join the circus."

"What if some or all of the guests are professional circus recruiters?"

"What if *all* of the guests are professional circus recruiters?"

"Yeah."

"Well then you're fucked, aren't you? This must have been their global conference. You'll have to join one of their circuses and we'll never see each other again."

"I could learn the trapeze – or lion taming."

"You need to learn both of those quickly, and you just got suckered into joining a circus because you were carrying a suitcase."

"Or maybe that thing with the goldfish bowls and the ping pong ball?"

"Just let me know which circus and I'll come find you."

"I can't believe you'd run away with a carny."

"I'm a wild spirit. I feel like there's gypsy blood in my veins. I like Stevie

Nicks. I own a bangle. I could roam the roads selling clothes pegs by day and stealing children by night. Also, like, help out with the circus in some way, probably admin . . . payroll . . . VAT."

"And these children that you've stolen – what would you do with them?"

"I dunno – turn them into clothes pegs? Not on a one-to-one ratio, you'd never make any money out of that."

"That's what makes the idea crazy."

"Because where's the money in clothes pegs anyway, right?"

"Sure."

"Boat."

"What?"

"You need to get on the boat."

"Oh, the *boat*. I thought you meant a *different* boat."

I shove him out the door. I'm not sure how much danger he's in of missing the boat – but neither is he – we've both never left this island by boat before. He needs to be on this boat and off the island, or later he might get into trouble.

I hear the clatter of wheels on the cobbles and he is gone.

The hotel is empty. It feels different than in the past when all the guests were out – because I was still here. But I don't live here anymore, and because nobody lives here this is not a house. As a business, it is closed. What the Ensay House Hotel is now is a thing without purpose.

The space held between the walls and under the roof is subdivided into smaller areas, but without people, these demarcations are a product of alien geometry: shapes fitted together in accordance with a ratio that obeys the natural law in a place where nature is entirely other; where a sun of a different colour grows trees stranger than Joshuas.

I can wander from room to room and experience detachment from function – the way I might attempt to see things if I were painting shapes and colours: what is actually there rather than what I imagine. The cake stands in the tea room bear waxy constructions that seem more artificial than before, though they have not changed and will not in a month or a year. In the kitchen are a hundred eggs that will never hatch, each tray resembling an antiquarian counting machine; a way of doing things which has fallen out of use. A bed that will never be slept on again takes on the qualities of a desert obelisk.

Perhaps later, when they know I am gone, the islanders will break down this building into individual parts and reorganise them in accordance with a new, great purpose. I will not see it. I cannot imagine any trace of me will remain here; I have not painted summer flowers onto its stones and they will forget me as I hope to forget them.

I pace out the attic floorboards, and through a window I fancy that I can see the boat ploughing the sea, though it is only a speck of white, and I have walked through these empty rooms for hours. Connor will be in Stornoway by now. The passengers will have transferred to a bus and its cargo of old people and luggage and complaints, dirty washing, souvenirs and travel documents will certainly have disappointed anyone at the stop waiting for a quinquireme loaded with ivory and apes and peacocks.

If it is a boat, Connor is not on it. I try not to imagine a summer squall and the vessel overturning, but that is exactly the kind of reversal of fortune I expect. The more time passes, the more I fear an unexpected, tragic upset – a disaster. The root of the word *disaster* is *astrum*, meaning *star*: a disaster is literally an ill-starred event. I feel that I have reason to believe the stars I was born under were the illest of all, and not in the way the old-school rappers meant.

I have no idea when my birthday is.

I celebrated Eleanor's birthday two days ago; the odds of both of us both being born on the same day are, what? – a hundred thousand to one? A hundred and thirty thousand to one? One hundred and thirty-three thousand-ish to one? Pretty unlikely. Am I even sixteen? Wait – if Eleanor died in August and Sarah Edwards was three at the time, it's much more likely Sarah's third birthday (*my* birthday) was before mid-July than between mid-July and early August. But what if her birthday (*my damn birthday*) was later in August? She could have been almost four – so, I could be almost seventeen. I might not have been skipped forward two years, but one. Am I even smart? I don't even know my own star sign – how can I possibly be smart? Deep breaths.

Birth records are searchable just like death records. I can work back to find the right Sarah Edwards, probably born in London, and prove that I'm not stupid and my boyfriend isn't an accidental nonce. Easy. Phew!

I put it out of my mind because I don't have time to check right now, and there's a lot still to do. I have some old woollen jumpers that I'm not taking with me. I take them down to the kitchen and cut them up, then combine them with jam jars and vodka. I'm actually quite impressed with my ingenuity.

When everything is ready, I still have time for a shower. If I'm going to be carried screaming down the street, I will not be screaming in jogging bottoms and an old t-shirt, so I change into my summer dress, which has a one in one hundred and thirty-three thousand chance of being my birthday dress— what am I even thinking? Eleanor's birthday isn't a variable – it's a fixed date. The odds of Sarah's birthday being on that day are only three hundred and sixty-five to one, as our birthdays couldn't be on a twenty-ninth of February. Now that is still fairly unlikely, but it's three hundred and sixty-four times more likely than I thought it was earlier.

And without me noticing when it happened, Connor is late. My head has been too full to track the minutes, but now it is an hour gone. The boat is never an hour late. Could he have missed the bus coming back? It's not impossible. I check my iPad and I've had no messages. I send him a casual hey-how-are-you-please-be-alive and watch as the message status updates – sent . . . But not received? His phone could be turned off, or damaged – or he might simply be moving through one of those huge swathes of island that have no coverage. It means nothing.

Or it means he's dead. The boat has foundered in the thin stretch of water that shears Ensay from the big island. All lives lost.

Why were there so many American tourists on that little boat, Sam?

Well, it turns out some crazy bitch threw them all out of her hotel on the same day, Diane.

I think you mean, some crazy murderous *bitch, Sam.*

Right you are, Diane. A-ha-ha-ha.

A-ha-ha-ha.

Now here's Woody with the weather.

Why the American news network in my head is run by characters from the eighties sitcom *Cheers*, I don't know. It just is. That was some surreal banter, and it probably gets great ratings.

There is also that nagging doubt that he is fine and that he has decided not to help me. He's in Stornoway, nestled into a pub, chatting up the island's only goth, who has a pierced labia and nine tattoos of Marilyn Manson from back when people knew who that was. She's thirty-five, Connor! She's got active herpes and three kids with names that all sound like bad metal bands. In my mind's eye I see him run off to join the circus of intercourse-with-a-sexually-confident-older-woman-and-being-a-step-dad-to-a-man-two-years-older-than-him-who-has-had-five-step-dads-already.

But before I can get too invested in the relationship between Connor and Isaac Fury, I hear the bell on the front desk and race down stairs. He dropped his phone in the sea. Mid-selfie, a dolphin leapt out of the water and knocked it out of his hand. Would he ring the bell? He wouldn't know where I was in the hotel – he might. I push the kitchen door open a little too hard, rush through into the hall and there, standing at the reception desk, is Mr. Jones with the regular order of jam jars tucked under his arm.

"Afternoon," he says, his smile contouring his beard.

"Oh," I say, which is very rude, but it was the thought first in the queue when I opened my mouth. I follow up with, "Good afternoon" and walk the rest of the way over to him.

Mr. Jones wrinkles his nose and says, "There's a very funny smell in here."

"I'm doing some deep cleaning, it's fine. Mister Jones, where's Connor?"

"Your boyfriend? I haven't seen him. I've got your jars—"

"He didn't come back on the last trip?"

He looks confused. "Come back?"

"On the boat?"

"I haven't seen him all day – how did he get to Harris?"

"On your boat, this morning. With you."

"The only people I took out this morning were a lot of angry tourists. Does Missus Douglas know you've closed the hotel?"

I ignore his question; she'll find out soon if she doesn't know. "Connor didn't leave the island this morning?"

"Not unless he flew," he laughs. "Look, does your mum know you've put everyone out? I can't imagine she'll be happy about that."

Of course, Mr. Jones is early-to-bed, early-to-rise and on the water for most of the day. He's missing a lot of information about recent events, and about my awareness of past events. But with the phone line cutting out for hours last night, it's possible I'm the only one on Ensay who knows.

"She died," I say. "Last night."

Mr. Jones puts the jam jars down on the reception desk and says, "Who died?"

"Missus Carlyle died last night."

"Missus Carlyle?"

It sticks in my throat and takes two attempts. "My mum died last night in hospital."

Mr. Jones continues to look confused, then smiles broadly, his white teeth visible through his grey whiskers. "Well, that's just not so. I brought her back first thing this morning."

Your mother is gone. Not dead. Of course, she's not *dead*; she worked eighteen-hour days with terminal cancer. A day in hospital is the most rest she's had in years; she's pulled herself out of that bed and come back to this island for—

"She didn't look well, though, and I told her. She said she was planning to spend her last days gardening. She told me she was going to borrow Missus Gough's wheelbarrow. I didn't even know she was interested in gardening."

I pick up the package of jam jars and hand them back to Mr. Jones.

"We won't be needing these, I'm afraid. Thank you for all your help. And thank you for the book, it's been very useful."

"Aren't you going to make jam anymore?"

"No, Mister Jones. I am not going to make jam. I am not going to make beds. I am not going to cook or clean or brew tea unless it is for myself. The hotel is closed." I hold out my hand towards the door.

As he moves away, I can see the pieces fall into place for him; his thoughts are somewhere else. This was all a game for him. When he began this, it was a young man's make-believe, a story of passion and requited love. He was a fictional character – a voice and a name he put on like an actor in a play. And at some point, the mask doesn't come off, does it Mr. Jones?

At the door he stops.

Without turning around Mr. Jones says, "I'm sorry."

When he is gone, I close the door, lock it, bolt it, and leave the key on the desk. I'm not going out that way. I place the iPad into the backpack, slip it on, and tighten the straps at my shoulders. Perhaps a little too tight; I have no experience with backpacks.

Between one door and the other there are as many steps as I take. I could spend an hour going from the hall to the laundry room, but there is no more time to consider, no more time to pause. I stop in the kitchen and finish my last task, then close the door of the laundry room behind me.

In this small space filled by the washer and the dryer, the back door seems enormous. I imagine that under other circumstances I might have been paralysed on this spot for days. But we have removed that possibility – all three of us – Connor, Mrs. Carlyle, and I have conspired to force me out of the house at this moment. Stay in this spot for a minute and I'll die here.

I open the lock and remove the key, then open the door and in the same breath step outside, down onto the stone step whose paper-thin indentation is evidence of ten thousand journeys taken by other people.

The sun is shining only for me – a spotlight on the moment; a lighthouse for the ship lost at sea. Above me I feel nothing, not a ceiling or a roof, not even the sky; above me is infinite. It exists like the future: certain and uncertain, known and unseen.

I feel the door swing closed at my back.

And I am not afraid.

I turn, lock the door, and throw the key to the bottom of the garden where it lands soundlessly and invisibly in bare earth.

We are done now, house.

We are done now, Eleanor.

Beyond the garden gate and between two whitewashed walls, a shard of ocean flashes foam. A white edge to an arc of shadow, crashing blue. It is still apart from me, but it is the leopard glimpsed in the wild wood, not the cat caged in glass. It speaks – not at me, not to me, and not in any language I understand. But I know the words as the rhythm of a childhood lullaby, and my ignorance of their meaning would not prevent me singing along.

I unlatch the gate. It is the first material thing I have touched outside of the hotel. My hand lingers on the black, cold iron until it warms. Then I am through and on a path between the hunched and collapsing houses, the waves saluting my progress.

I can still feel the shape of the gate latch in my right hand, fading as quickly as the iron heated, but for the moment it is a pressure on my skin, against my muscles and bones.

On my left, another sea rises from the pale shore; tufted grass the colour of straw and brass, of honey and weathered lead. It is shaped like the body of a sheepdog – undulating, low, but with a quality of movement even in its stillness. Punctuated by patches of blackening growth already dying back after an early summer flowering. I stand on a path worn into the earth by footsteps so that the ground is flat and hard beyond the insistence of any weed, past the determination of any root. A dead track runs across the island and I cannot imagine that one year or five years of being unwalked will bring it back to life.

This is a landscape I have seen every day, but I have never been here, and though it is beautiful in all the ways that desolate places are, it is not my home.

I have gone from seeing the world through a window to seeing it as it is. The meaning of each object changes subject to my perspective. The sea and the sky are things so much larger than the words that describe them. All things I have known by name are slipping their pages and picture frames.

How much of my world was assumption?

The island of Ensay is home to four hundred and six people – and I don't know any of them, not really. I recognise their masks, but I have only glimpsed the faces underneath, and though these people have withheld my history, they do not know me either. This is an island of strangers.

I was a child who was stolen. I was a child who was held prisoner. But I have grown to maturity in the dark. What I am now is a secret I could not tell.

I turn at a sound that I identify as a cry of alarm. A man – so far away that I cannot guess which one of the few he is – has thrown up his arms; a gesture of surprise that has frozen him in place. He is staring up at the hotel as black curls of smoke rise from its open windows.

Good ventilation is necessary for building heat in a fire. Almost anything can burn, but to burn something quickly and completely, so there is no possibility of extinguishing it and no chance that anything will remain afterward; what's needed is a continuous flow of air.

I locked the ground-floor doors, so no one could get in to attempt a heroic rescue, I opened all the windows on opposite sides of the building, and I set individual flash points in each of the rooms. Crunched up pages from a guest book that will never record a single name. Firelighters. Cooking alcohol. Paint thinner. Jars full of vodka with tapers made of old clothes. Modern fabrics are fire resistant, but real wooden furniture will burn forever once it gets started.

There is a trail of flammable liquid that leads from my bedroom in the attic, down the stairs, along the first-floor landing, down the main stairs and back into the kitchen, where I draped sheets soaked in cooking oil over the burners. It was a busy morning and a busy afternoon.

By now all the paintings are burning. The piper at the foot of the stairs. The girl and the sea. The hedgehog that was painted by the other girl, by the real Eleanor. *The Gull.* I can imagine my mother's face staring out of her own flames. I don't need the painting to remember her.

I see a few licks of fire at a first-floor window and I realise I don't remember seeing the house from the outside before this. It will also be the last. I cannot burn this island into the sea, but I can kill it. I know Ensay will struggle on for years, but this is the fatal wound. I feel no shame for what I have done, nor remorse.

I resume my walk up the hill. The golden light of summer evening is colouring the water so it seems the world is on fire all the way to the horizon.

I crest the rise and see to the edge of the cliff, an abrupt line against the deep water; a trick of perspective. The wind is up and whips my hair, my dress. It presses against me, pushing me back, and in the time between footsteps I am flying. I cannot stop. She is here.

The work is half-finished and badly done even considering this. There is no giant man – no god of wood and straw whose body is a cage for sacrifice. It is a funeral pyre still being stacked, its mundane kindling reaching no higher than my knee. On the far side a body lies in a wheelbarrow, its limbs unmoving, its head the rusted colour of blood.

She kneels with her back to me, building her fire. She wears stolen clothes – a man's blue shirt and cream-coloured trousers which are too large for her and are constrained at the waist by a brown leather belt.

I watch her push branches and broken timbers in no sensible pattern. Her hands have lost their cunning. Her movements are uncertain, as she searches for a structure she cannot remember in the fragments of what was once living wood.

I continue towards her and whether my shoes make sound on the grass or I sound in the wind like a chime, I am only a few steps closer when she sees me. I know that she also sees my cage burning. The old house belching smoke and flame. Everything she has given her life to, I have torched. Her precious photos are gone. Her daughter is dead.

Her face is ashen without her makeup, and I understand that it had been this way for some time. She is hollowed out by the cancer and by this war which she has waged against her community, and against her friends, until she had neither.

One brilliant, bright morning, everything she loved was destroyed. I think I know something about how that feels.

On that day she was subject to a complete madness; one which caused her to get up in the morning, which numbered the hours of her day, which marked the progress of thirteen years to bring her to this point. She will complete the sacrifice. She will end the world.

She is the strongest person I can even imagine, and the worst.

I do not know what I expected her to do upon seeing me. I should have been prepared for her to return to the woodpile, to her purposeless adjustments, but it strikes me as hard as any physical blow she ever laid on me. I am nothing to her now. Daughter or no – I have completed my Purpose and she has no further need of me.

My fists clench. My nails are in my palms. My feet are moving. I charge, shoulder into her, knock us both tumbling and sprawling away from the pyre.

In the same instant I am on my feet and I pull a thick branch from the others.

But I am prepared for a different fight. Her power has gone. She lies on her back, her eyes swivelling in her head. She does not understand what has happened and like some hard-shelled beetle she is for a moment unable to turn over.

I feel the weight of the weapon in my hands. To hold it is to understand what it would mean to use it. It is righteous: I know that this branch grew to be justice; that each year it became stronger only so it might be a hammer today. I could crack her skull and I would know it was the right thing to do, and nobody who knew her would say differently.

But my fingers slacken. My anger cools. What is left is not so dramatic as disgust or pity. Perhaps I feel nothing at all for her. The branch drops to the ground and I go to Connor.

A single blow to the head just at the hairline. A round rock, something that could be held in one hand and swung. He would not have expected it and must have gone down immediately. The blood from the wound coats his face on one side, thick and tacky and dripping in different directions as his body has moved on the course of their journey from wherever she ambushed him to here.

The blood flowed in different directions.

I lift his chin and push my hand against his neck. Once. Twice. A pulse!

Behind me I hear a sound and I twist, rise up, find myself again ready to fight. But she is not near me. She has righted herself, stood, and walked all the way to the edge of the cliff. The wind makes her overlarge clothes billow like a sail. Her hair blows back, unrestrained, and thinner now than I remembered. Mrs. Carlyle's spirit wears her body the way her body wears stolen clothes.

"It has to stop," she says. "I just want it to stop."

I do nothing.

The cliff is steep before it becomes sheer. She takes a step off the edge, and she seems to hang in the air for a moment, then drops out of sight. If she makes any noise, the wind takes it, smothers it, forgets it.

I watch the empty space where she had been, and I feel everything.

21

It is uncomfortably warm – everywhere. There is no room in this building which isn't working hard to kill the planet.

"Two pounds, seventy."

Apparently, people drink coffee. First thing in the morning, eleven, lunchtime, afternoon, after dinner, trying to stay up at night – the world is full of coffee. It's not the most surprising thing I've learned about Scotland in the last three days, but it's also not the least unsettling. I had assumed we were a tea country; one of those misconceptions that result from living in an Escher drawing.

I pay in cash, nod, smile, leave. The cardboard sleeve on the cup is not quite thick enough and the coffee is too hot to drink. I swap it between hands as I walk along the uniform corridors, following signs.

I have learned that the police treat you very differently depending on whether they believe you are a criminal, a victim, or a family member, and when you are all three of those things simultaneously, they have no idea what to do with you.

I am, and they were very clear about this, an arsonist. This is a very serious offence. However, it is not, in the hierarchy of crimes, equally as serious as kidnapping and imprisonment. Does one cancel out the other? They aren't sure; it isn't their job to decide.

The scale of what has been done to me is overwhelming, even for the specialist police from G-Division (greater Glasgow; I am not on the islands anymore). The scale of what I have done is something only an islander would understand; in their mainland thinking it was only natural justice in desperate form. I know the truth.

So, I'm not under arrest. I have been told not to go anywhere, though I have nowhere to stay, so they are actually okay if I go *somewhere* as long as I tell them. *Her*, actually. The officer handling my case is Inspector Rachel Macleod – just Rachel, not inspector, not Ms. Macleod. People find my practice of calling people by their second name to be unnerving.

They call me *Miss*. That is all they ever call me, even the female police officers who have certainly been trained to call me by my first name; to establish rapport; to build trust. I don't know what they have written on their official forms. Person A. Jane Doe, perhaps. Grand Duchess Anastasia. I am not Eleanor: I refuse to be identified as Eleanor. I suspect that there has been a serious meeting involving dedicated professionals where everyone was told not to call me anything until I decided what to be called. I have had other things on my mind and I put less stock in names than I used to.

I take the lift. It's more out of novelty than need. This is my fifth ride in an elevator and I try not to look too much like a tourist in front of the patients or their families.

Rachel has told me that I am sixteen. My birthday is on the twenty-first of April: I am a Taurus; I am the most stubborn of the made-up personalities. Being sixteen I am technically a ward of the state until events with my birth family are resolved. Rachel's team has only been looking since yesterday and (what they won't say to me is) any living relatives will also be in shock once they find out I'm alive.

I believe Rachel is trying to do what is right and trying to do what is best for me, but our relationship is not entirely honest. I have told her about the abuse. I have told her all I know about how I came to be on Ensay. I have not told her that even after I refunded all bookings, there was a little more than fifty thousand pounds in the hotel's and Mrs. Carlyle's bank accounts, and that I used it to put cryptocurrency into an anonymous wallet – which sounds like the work of a criminal mastermind but actually took about twenty minutes. I have moved the money around a few times since and split it into different wallets, just to be sure. Will I be able to hold onto it? Maybe. I would rather it was difficult for them to find. If it comes to it, I think I can probably give back half and have it look like I was giving back everything and just lost the rest. (Though I feel like this *is* the work of a mastermind – I'm basically the Napoleon of crime).

When Rachel first met me, she used the word *crazy*. It was an offhand remark, of the sort someone would make deliberately when trying to emphasise how they were a human part of a faceless bureaucracy, to elicit someone to lower their guard.

This whole thing is crazy.

I shrugged. I'm not sure that I understand the difference between crazy and sane – though I don't go around saying that. Yes, I was brainwashed into believing I lived on an island of doomsday cultists who practiced human sacrifice. I feel partially responsible for this. There is a grey area between victim and participant. If I had not believed I was chosen, that I was special, might I have viewed the process differently? I heard what I wanted to hear, and I believed what I wanted to believe as much as I did what I was told. A day of detachment is all that I need to see myself as a character on television.

But how is this reality any saner? I flew into Glasgow on a helicopter – a metal engine modelled on a sycamore seed. I'm the subject of a high-profile police enquiry. This coffee was almost three pounds. This part of my life feels more unrealistic than the false narrative I have escaped.

Rachel told me there would be interest from newspapers and television whenever I was interested in talking about my experiences. She said this positively – it is an opportunity, and one she expects me to take. I don't know that I will ever be ready to talk about it. The story is simple to tell, but not understandable in only one way: it is a proverb, or a meditation.

My relationship with Mrs. Carlyle was founded on a belief and on evidence – what relationship is not? The daily rituals of our lives were evidence. When I woke in the morning and when I lay down at night, she was my mother. There is no superior science that can disprove this; the details of my birth and the code in my blood are also facts, but everyone knows the sun when it rises, and to call it only a yellow dwarf star and define its mass in estimable kilograms would be to forget that description ever reaches out to meaning.

I turn onto the ward and sharp again into the first room. Four bed spaces, three beds, two occupied, both occupants unconscious, one nurse. She is checking Harry's drip. Look at me with all the informality in the world – *Harold* Feher is a hillwalker who fell off some part of a mountain. A slippery bit would be my guess. He's cracked several lumbar vertebrae (likely he fell onto a hard and lumpy bit of mountain), he has blunt force trauma to the back, neck, and head, and lacerations and abrasions on his hands – the total pattern indicates he probably tumbled and had several collisions, rather than one long fall. There's no sign of intracranial bleeding and his pressure is only slightly elevated. Harry's had the equivalent of a damn good kicking, but if he wakes up today, he'll probably be able to move his arms and might very well be able to walk out of here eventually. The longer he is unconscious, the worse it will go for him. This is my prognosis – having read his chart yesterday after he was brought in.

The nurse looks over at me and I smile and put down my coffee on the bedside table. I have several items in my backpack. A notepad and pencil, my iPad, three bags of sweets, and a soft-bound copy of *Middlemarch* which I bought from a bookshop in the city. The bookshop was also selling coffee – this appears to be what all businesses do. I dump all of these items on the bed and pull the big chair over from the opposite corner of the room.

As it scrapes along the floor, the nurse tuts. A very loud tut for a stranger to make. The kind of tut that surely indicates she wants these hands. But I let it go. Nurses are probably under a lot of stress. Not kidnapped-for-thirteen-years-and-brainwashed-and-possibly-facing-criminal-charges stress, but I'm sure there's long hours and an abundance of both literal and metaphorical assholes.

I settle myself into the chair and use my teeth to open a packet of fruit pastilles. I offer one to Connor – he does not respond.

"Are you, his girlfriend?" the nurse asks. She is standing at the foot of his bed with her hands on her hips. Clearly, she has no idea she's addressing the country's most famous arsonist and up-and-coming nemesis for an up-and-coming Sherlock Holmes. It's *Miss* McCavity the Mystery Cat, thank you very much.

I say, "I honestly don't know. It's complicated. At some point after he wakes up, I'll ask him."

She frowns. "You're not supposed to be in here unless you're family."

"Well, I guess I must be family." I pop a purple fruit pastille in my mouth. "I did say it was complicated."

She has no answer to that. She has evidently taken Connor's blood pressure and pulse and changed the fluids going in through the drip and the fluids coming out through the catheter. She soundlessly *harrumphs* then leaves. She has better things to do and she's not the bouncer.

Connor lies the way people do in films: straight with his arms at his sides. Nobody sleeps like that in real life outside of hospitals – I, for example, am a starfish.

He has a very large bandage on his head which makes him look stupid.

"You look stupid," I tell him. "I bet they've shaved off half your hair under that. Kids are going to point at you and laugh. It's not right, but you can't beat them; they're only kids." He does not rise to the bait.

"If we have to, I think we can make you a bandana out of a pillowcase. I've never made a bandana because I'm not too old to be in a band anymore, but it seems easy enough. Will people know it's a pillowcase? Probably. But will they say they think it's a pillowcase? Probably not. You might have cancer. Are you sure I can't tempt you with a Revel?"

He gives no indication that he wants a Revel.

"I don't blame you. They're a bit risky in your current state. You think you're getting one thing; you plan for one thing; you do everything to prepare for one thing and then boom – you don't know where you are. Happens every day. I'm just saying that if you wanted to wake up, now would be a really good time. I think everything would be, you know, much better if right at this moment you opened your eyes.

"Or now . . . Now is also good."

Connor continues to breathe – which is great; I'm not *un*happy about that – but he does nothing else.

So, I crack open the book, I clear my throat, and I start at the beginning.

ACKNOWLEDGEMENTS

I do not understand how to write a book, but every not-so-often a book appears and when I show it to people, they tell me to show it to others. Perhaps it's all a joke.

I am grateful, in no particular order, to the following people for their support and indulgence. To the first readers of this book – Chris Adams, Eleanor Cunningham and Verdi Wilson – who are canaries in the coal mine and must surely share a portion of any blame.

Chris urged me from the beginning to pick a different title, and to actually stay in a hotel in the Western Isles before setting a story there. While not taken, this advice is obviously wise.

Eleanor leant me her name for this book, and in return I have kept any and all flannel to a necessary minimum.

As well as being one my youngest friends, Verdi is my number one fan both chronologically and in terms of books given as gifts, or otherwise thrust upon the unwary.

David Craig leant me some of Connor's story involving James Mahoney. All the names were changed to protect the innocent.

Raygan Earl has picked through this book with a fine-tooth comb to produce the final manuscript. I am immensely grateful for her efforts. Any eccentricities that remain in the text result from irresolvable problems in, and with, the author himself.

ABOUT THE AUTHOR

David F Porteous was born in Edinburgh, Scotland on the day Peter Sellers died in London, England. And though these facts are unrelated, it was certainly a bad day for comedy.

As a genius polymath, he's been known to turn his hand to all manner of things. As a feckless idler, he actually does all of these things slowly and infrequently. He has written four books and will not stop until his demands are met, or he stops.

Singular

The Death of Jack Nylund

Good Witch

The Wicker Man Preservation Society

Printed in Great Britain
by Amazon

38307977R00138